The QUEEN'S CHOICE

ANNE O'BRIEN

HARLEQUIN®MIRA®

First Published in Great Britain 2016
By Harlequin Mira, an imprint of HarperCollins*Publishers*
1 London Bridge Street, London, SE1 9GF

The Queen's Choice © 2016 Anne O'Brien

ISBN HB: 978-1-848-45407-1
     C: 978-1-848-45434-7

58-0116

Also by
ANNE O'BRIEN

VIRGIN WIDOW
DEVIL'S CONSORT
THE KING'S CONCUBINE
THE FORBIDDEN QUEEN
THE SCANDALOUS DUCHESS
THE KING'S SISTER

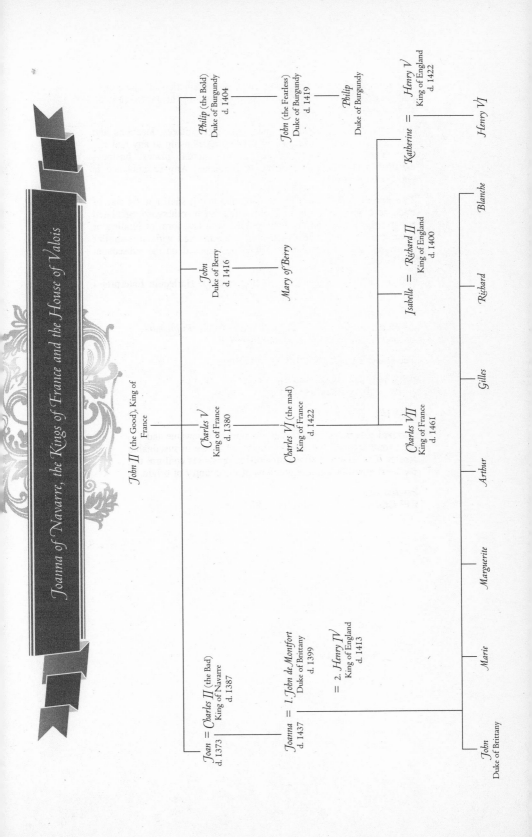

Joanna of Navarre, the Kings of France and the House of Valois

John II (the Good), King of France

Joan = Charles II (the Bad) King of Navarre
d. 1373   d. 1387

Joanna = 1. John de Montfort Duke of Brittany
d. 1437   d. 1399

= 2. Henry IV King of England
d. 1413

Charles V King of France d. 1380

John Duke of Berry d. 1416

Mary of Berry

Philip (the Bold) Duke of Burgundy d. 1404

John (the Fearless) Duke of Burgundy d. 1419

Philip Duke of Burgundy

Charles VI (the mad) King of France d. 1422

Charles VII King of France d. 1461

Isabelle = Richard II King of England d. 1400

Katherine = Henry V King of England d. 1422

Henry VI

John Duke of Brittany   Marie   Marguerite   Arthur   Gilles   Richard   Blanche

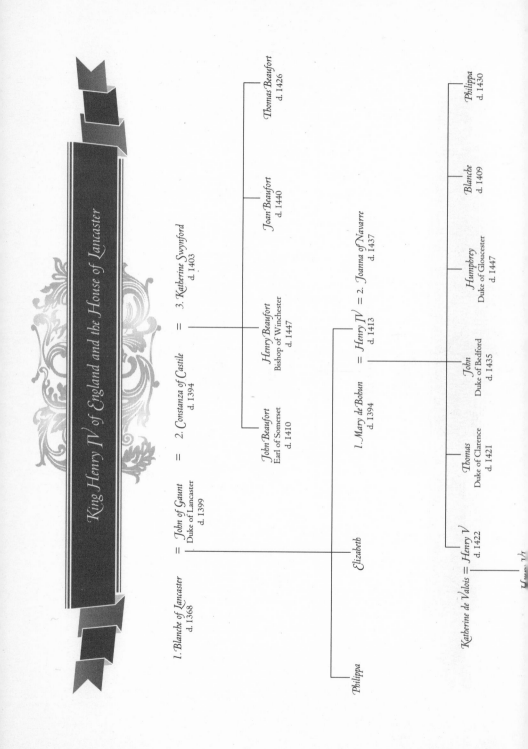

King Henry IV of England and the House of Lancaster

1. Blanche of Lancaster = John of Gaunt = 2. Constanza of Castile = 3. Katherine Swynford
d. 1368   Duke of Lancaster   d. 1394   d. 1403
              d. 1399

                                              John Beaufort   Henry Beaufort   Joan Beaufort   Thomas Beaufort
                                              Earl of Somerset   Bishop of Winchester d. 1440   d. 1426
                                              d. 1410   d. 1447

1. Mary de Bohun = Henry IV = 2. Joanna of Navarre
   d. 1394   d. 1413   d. 1437

Elizabeth

Philippa

Henry V   Thomas   John   Humphrey   Blanche   Philippa
d. 1422   Duke of Clarence Duke of Bedford Duke of Gloucester d. 1409   d. 1430
               d. 1421   d. 1435   d. 1447

Katherine de Valois = Henry V
                      d. 1422

Henry VI

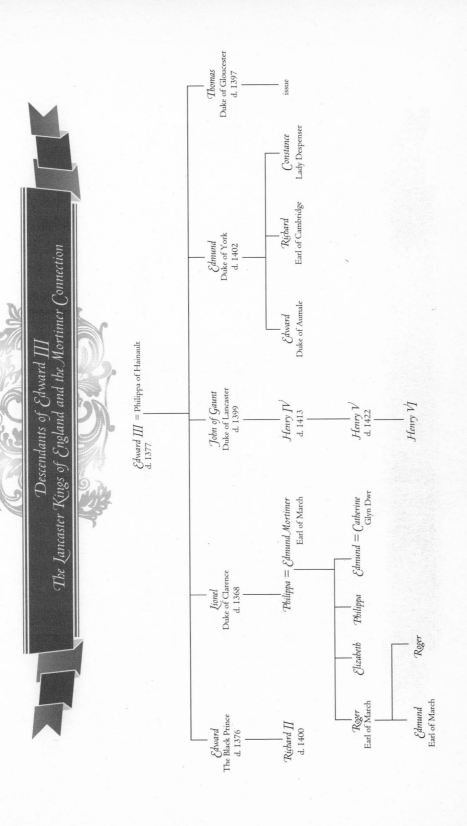

Descendants of Edward III
The Lancaster Kings of England and the Mortimer Connection

Edward III = Philippa of Hainault
d. 1377

Edward
The Black Prince
d. 1376

Richard II
d. 1400

Lionel
Duke of Clarence
d. 1368

Philippa = *Edmund Mortimer*
Earl of March

Roger
Earl of March

Elizabeth   *Philippa*   *Edmund* = *Catherine*
Glyn Dŵr

Roger

Edmund
Earl of March

John of Gaunt
Duke of Lancaster
d. 1399

Henry IV
d. 1413

Henry V
d. 1422

Henry VI

Edmund
Duke of York
d. 1402

Edward
Duke of Aumale

Richard
Earl of Cambridge

Constance
Lady Despenser

Thomas
Duke of Gloucester
d. 1397

issue

To George, as always with my love, and thanks for allowing me to fill the house with music and songs of courtly love from the medieval troubadours. As Joanna might have sung to Henry:

'To you, sweet good-natured one, have I give my heart. Never shall it be taken from you.'

Jehan de Lescurel d.1304

Who ever lov'd, that lov'd not at first sight?

Christopher Marlowe 1564–1593:
Hero and Leander

Forasmuch as I am eager to hear of your good estate...I pray you, my most dear and most honoured lord and cousin, that you would tell me often of the certainty of it, for the great comfort and gladness of my heart. For whenever I am able to hear a good account of you, my heart rejoices exceedingly.

Written at Vannes 15th February 1400:
the duchess of Brittany to King Henry IV

(The wives of powerful noblemen) must be highly knowledgeable about government, and wise...

Christine de Pizan: *The Book of the City of Ladies* c. 1405

Thou shalt not suffer a witch to live.

Exodus 22.18

Chapter 1

October 1396: the town of Ardres, near Calais

It was to be the day, although I did not know it when my women confined my hair to a jewelled caul and coronet, my feet to gilded-toed shoes, and all in between to layers of fine linen, silk damask and fur.

It was to be the day that my life tilted on its even keel; the day that my ordered existence warped, as a tapestry, ill-formed in the hands of a careless Arras weaver, would stretch immoderately in the damp of winter. I had one such in my audience chamber at the Château of Vannes, until I dispatched it, ruined, to some distant storeroom. On this day it was as if some power had disturbed an exact balance that throughout my life had been secure and unquestioned.

It was the day that I met Henry, Earl of Derby.

Not that I had any presentiment of such meddling in what fate, my father and my husband had decreed for me.

Nor did I look for such turbulence in my life, for I lived in placid luxury, always predictable, sometimes dull, but never less than harmonious. My life demanded no emotional response from me, rather a practical acceptance of my role as wife, mother, ducal consort. Indeed my whole life had been one of acceptance. I was particularly good at it. I was nobly born, twenty-eight years old, and had been Duchess of Brittany for ten of them. But on that bright morning, my thoughts occupied far from any intrusive dabbling, all was overset.

'What do you think?'

A soft voice in my ear managed to pierce the snap and flap of canvas of the dozens of pavilions, a huge encampment constructed for the occasion. The voice of John de Montfort, my husband, the fifth Duke of Brittany.

'Poor mite. It's no age to be wed,' I whispered back. I would not wish for one of my daughters to be wed at so tender an age, but dynastic marriages demanded sacrifice. My mother, undoubtedly a sacrifice in her union with my father, had been wed at eight years.

'He'll only get her allegiance.' John frowned at the charming scene where the bridegroom kissed the cheek of his child-bride. 'Not her body.'

'So I should hope.'

I smiled.

I liked weddings. Such an opportunity to reunite with family and friends, and erstwhile enemies too, without the prospect of drawn swords or blows traded in the aftermath of too many toasts to the happy couple. Although, I considered as the two puissant kings, one of England, the other of France, drew close to exchange the desired kiss of peace, that could not always be guaranteed. I remembered occasions when good manners had drowned in a pot of ale almost before the marriage vows had been taken.

But not today. Today, we had been assured, would be a day of good omen. We all knelt in a gleaming shiver of silk and satin as Richard of England and Charles of France clasped hands and beamed their goodwill.

I particularly like French weddings, with the wealth of aunts and uncles and a fistful of cousins here for me to enjoy, for through my mother's blood I was a Valois princess. And now that the greatest blot on the political landscape, my father, no longer defiled this earth with his presence, there was no need for me to hold my breath as I had as a young girl. My father was dead, and had been for almost ten years. He and his vile temper and even viler habits would not be missed.

My father, of atrocious repute, had been King of Navarre, that prestigious little kingdom which bordered with France and English possessions to the south, and so was much desired in alliance. But it was my mother, daughter of the Valois King John the Good, who gave me my true rank. King Charles the Sixth of France was my first cousin, the Dukes of Berry and Burgundy my uncles. I could claim cousinship with every man or woman at the Valois Court of France. Every man or woman who mattered in the politics of Europe. I had been raised to know my worth.

'I see that Charles is in his right mind,' I observed, my eyes lowered in deepest respect for this royal cousin who was acknowledged as mad and could become violent in the blink of an eye. 'I expect the whole Court has been offering up novenas to St Jude.'

'Ha! It would take more than a petition to lost causes. I wager it would take a full Requiem Mass to guarantee Charles's sanity for more than a day at a time,' my husband replied.

We were here for a momentous alliance that might bring some vestige of peace to our troubled lands. And there he was, the bridegroom, tall and resplendent in red, smiling and gracious, luminous with satisfaction. We had heard that it was not altogether a popular move across the sea, a French woman to be crowned Queen of England, but the English King would have his way. King Richard the Second, a widower, was in need of a wife and an heir. A country was precarious without heirs, and here I could admit to my own smugness. I came from fertile stock, with six stalwart children of my own, four of them sons to safeguard the inheritance of Brittany. I had every reason to enjoy my own achievements. Was family not everything?

We rose to our feet, my husband's hand beneath my arm, allowing me the time to cast an eye over the bride, this child Isabelle who was still four weeks from her seventh birthday. I did not fear for her. She would be given all the time she needed to grow up before she must become a wife.

'He will care for her.'

I turned to the owner of the voice who had echoed my thoughts, John, solid in dark velvet, as handily at ease in silk and fur and jewelled rings as he was in armour. My lord was given to opulence when the occasion demanded it.

'He looks at her as if she were a present wrapped in gold,'

I said. The bride giggled as Richard bent again to kiss her cheek. 'Do you think it will bring an end to the conflict?'

'King Richard does not have a name for warfare,' John said, and in truth the rancorous relations between England and France had settled a little since Richard had taken the throne. 'He's not of a mind to pursue English claims in France, lost by Edward, the old King.'

And there the discussion of rights and wrongs, of who should wear the Crown of France ended, as the royal families moved towards the dais. The crowds milled. The musicians and minstrels puffed and blew with enthusiastic disharmony. Platters of food and vessels of wine were produced. I sighed a little.

'Do you wish to go? I can arrange for you to retire.'

John's hand was again solicitously on my arm, for I was carrying another child. No one would notice—there was no need yet for my sempstresses to loosen the stitching of my bodice—but John had a protective care for me and I covered his hand with mine.

'Certainly not.'

John, wisely, did not waste his breath in argument. 'Then if you are feeling robust, my love, come and meet a family for whom I have the greatest affection.'

John set about forcing a path, the bejewelled crowd parting before his impressive figure like the Red Sea before Moses. We were heading, I realised, towards the English contingent that had accompanied their King, now standing in an elegant little group to one side of the dais. Superbly dressed, superbly self-aware as they viewed the proceedings, they were here to honour the event and be gracious. I did not know them.

'John of Lancaster. The King's uncle.' My husband, coming to my rescue, shepherded me between two gesticulating parties, Burgundian by their accent. 'An interesting family and a powerful one. They make good friends and bad enemies. They're not without a little pride and their blood is more royal than most.' He looked back at me over his shoulder with a speculative gleam. 'Much like you. I think you will like them.'

Which allowed me in the few seconds left to me to claw through my knowledge of this illustrious grouping. For this was an important family: a family of the highest rank, a family worthy of my own status. Duke John of Lancaster, royal uncle to the King of England. His new wife Katherine, a woman of some scandals before marriage made her respectable. And with them a cluster of young men and women of their family and household, wearing conspicuous livery collars that bore the emblem of the white hart, the showiness of the enamelled gold at odds with the understated costliness of their robes. Clearly a gift from King Richard on this momentous day that they were unable to refuse.

Lancaster's face lit with pleasure when his eye fell on my husband, and rather than a formal handclasp, they embraced, two men who wielded power with utmost confidence in their right to do so, two men of an age although it seemed to me that my husband was carrying his years more easily than Lancaster. There was no reticence in the welcome.

'I hoped I would see you,' Lancaster said after some male shoulder-smacking.

'My wife would not allow me to stay away,' John replied, drawing me forward.

The introductions were made and I was drawn into the Lancaster circle, to talk with Duchess Katherine while Lancaster and my husband relived their youth, their boyhood rivalry and their military exploits when fighting together in France.

'I first recall your husband at Court when King Edward made him a Knight of the Garter,' the Duchess said. 'He enjoyed every minute of the pomp and pageantry.'

'Now, why am I not surprised?'

I turned my head to watch him with a certain pride, admiring his present flamboyance in managing the folds of a Court houppelande that swept the floor with hem and dagged sleeve. Many, who did not know us, would think him to be my father. There were twenty-eight years between us, all well lived by John through war and diplomacy.

'We are being summoned,' the Duchess remarked as Richard raised an imperious hand. 'We are to formally meet the bride.' And as the Lancaster family regrouped and approached the dais with suitable obeisance, I was left with John to watch the little ceremony develop.

'They were the strongest friends I ever had in England,' he said, 'when I was sorely in need of friends. I wonder where Lancaster's son is…?' As he turned his head, a man garbed in blue and white emerged from the crowd. 'Ah. There you are. I thought you'd made a bolt for it,' John observed with friendly cynicism.

'You're not far short of it. The temptation is strong. But, as you see, I am royally imprinted for the occasion, making me noticeable in any crowd.'

The voice was light-timbred, pleasant on the ear, with

a hint of humour beneath an impatience as he slapped his palm onto the arresting white hart on his breast. Then as he clasped hands with John, the man's gaze rested on me. 'And this must be your incomparable Duchess, of whom I have heard much but whom I have yet to meet. I am honoured.'

A tall man with a swordsman's shoulders and the mark of his father in his dark hair, uncovered now, kissed with autumn in the bright sunshine. His eyes were dark, direct and agate-bright.

I began to smile my appreciation of his flattery as I felt the weight of that gaze. I felt the authority of his soldierly presence. I felt a sense of him deep within me, a sense that continued to reverberate like the solemn tone of the passing bell in the Cathedral at Nantes. Unaccountably, for I was not inexperienced in the demands of polite conversation, I was at a loss for a response.

'This is Joanna,' John was saying whilst I grasped at good manners. 'Who rules my household with a rod of iron but a velvet glove and sleeve. Don't be fooled for one minute by this frivolity.' He lifted the gold-stitched fullness of one of my over-sleeves in wry acknowledgement. 'And this, my love, is Henry Bolingbroke, Earl of Derby. Lancaster's heir.'

I extended my hand as if this introduction was nothing more than a commonplace between members of one high-bred family and another, as I ignored the fact that my heart had given a little leap, as if it had recognised the imminence of something long yearned for. This was so far beyond my experience that I resented it. No man, however puissant his family, had the right to disturb me beyond my habitual poise.

'My lord Henry,' I murmured.

'Lady Joanna.'

His fingers, heavy with rings, were light around mine, the salute against my cheek such as might be exchanged between a man and woman meeting for the first time, but that formal embrace stiffened the planes of my face, seizing my pulses to set them alive. And as I sought for some comment suitable to the occasion, John's attention was claimed by my uncle of Burgundy, leaving me to take up the reins of prudent conversation.

I inhaled steadily, confidence restored. I had been conversing through the courts of Europe since before I had reached my twentieth year. Any strange imaginings were a product of the heat of the day, the weight of the fur at hem and neck and insufficient sleep in the closet that was called a chamber. I smiled with regal grace as the Earl restored my hand to me.

'My husband was pleased to meet with your father again,' I said.

But instead of responding in kind, he asked abruptly, 'Are you enjoying this?' He gestured with his arm to the royal party, as if it were a question that needed to be asked.

'Yes. Certainly I am.' It could be tedious with much posturing, certainly overlong, but what was there not to like?

'I can't imagine why.' The Earl's reply could have been presumed sour.

'Because I have enough relatives here to fill, and indeed overflow, one of these vulgarly glittering pavilions,' I said. 'I enjoy gossip.'

'You'll not be disappointed then. There's plenty to gossip about.' A frown was directed towards his royal cousin who was still addressing King Charles with expansive animation. 'They say it has cost our illustrious King not far short of two hundred thousand pounds to stage this spectacle.'

I could not understand why the cost should trouble him. Given the quality of his raiment, a Court houppelande brilliant with spangles, sweeping down to his soft boots, and the size of the jewels in his rings, the House of Lancaster was not without wealth.

'Is the bride not worth the expenditure?' I asked.

'Is any bride worth it?' Earl Henry responded smartly. 'The English Exchequer will barely stand the cost. Besides, it's not the bride Richard seeks to honour. He'll make such a spectacle that no one will ever forget His Gracious Majesty King Richard the Second, condescending to take a French bride. No one is ever at the forefront of Richard's mind except Richard.'

No one could mistake the sardonic overtones, and not spoken softly. I thought it not wise, given the company, and risked a glance over my shoulder to guard against eavesdroppers. A quick movement that Earl Henry noted, with a frown, as if I had accused him of a wilful indiscretion. Which, of course, it was.

'There's no one to hear, or I wouldn't have said it.'

'There's me.' His observation had amused me. Shocked me.

A glimmer of a smile lightened the severe features, smoothing the indented corners of his mouth. 'You will think me too harsh. But you seem to me a woman of great common sense. Extravagance is a sin when a state lacks gold in its coffers. Do you not agree?'

'Certainly. As we know in Brittany.' I paused, then because

we seemed to have dived headlong into a stream of personal comment: 'But you are very judgemental, sir, against a man who is not only your King but also your cousin.'

'Forgive me.' He grimaced slightly, before allowing another more expansive smile. 'This is supposed to be a day of celebration. There's no reason to inflict my particular brand of disillusion on you, Madam Joanna. Will you forgive what must seem to you to be a nasty case of envy?'

'Yes.'

I said it without hesitation.

'Well that's got the introductions over with. What—or should I say whom, since you have a mind for gossip—shall we discuss now?'

I liked him. I liked his candour. As I allowed myself to acknowledge this, we found our attention once more drawn towards the royal tableau on the dais.

'Shouldn't you be with your family?' I asked.

'Richard won't miss me.' There again, the edge had crept back into his voice; the cynicism darkening his eye. 'Look at him, wringing every drop of glamour from this alliance. That's not to say that he will not do well by his bride. He will dress her in silk, laden her with jewels and treat her as she treats her dolls. She will be his little sister.' His mouth twisted. 'Perhaps he'll not allow her to keep all the jewels in her dowry. He'll wear most of them himself. Richard likes to glitter when in company.'

The bride had a collar of rubies that almost out-weighed her.

Aware of the sudden silence beside me, I turned to look, to see that Earl Henry was regarding the King of England,

and in the muscles of his jaw and the brilliance of his eye, I thought I read not so much displeasure at Richard's unwise open-handedness but a very personal dislike.

'You don't like him, do you?' I said before I could think of the wisdom of such an observation.

'Liking is too facile an emotion for my relationship with Richard. He is my King and my cousin. I am duty-bound to be loyal.' My companion's spine stiffened a little, words and expression immediately shuttered like a storm candle, obscuring the light. And I was sorry. I liked his honesty rather than the discreet presence bred in him by his father. I liked his smile, rather than the present grim demeanour. Perhaps I could entice him back into this intriguing view of the English King.

'You can admit to not liking him,' I said softly. 'Certainly in my company. I didn't like my father at all.'

Earl Henry's eyes gleamed with appreciation until suave diplomacy once more invested his features. 'I dare to surmise, Madam, that no one liked your august father.'

'It would be beyond the powers of any normal human to view my father with anything but disgust. My father was accused of every sin from poisoning to sorcery with a deal of blood-letting in between. And I expect he was guilty of all of it.' What point in being circumspect? 'Hence Charles the Bad. Charles the *very* Bad!' And when my companion's brows arched expressively, I continued: 'I say only what everyone here knows. There was much rejoicing at his death even if not for the manner of it, although many expressed the opinion that it was a well-deserved foretaste of the fires of Hell.' My father had been consumed in a conflagration in his bed when the bandages he wore, soaked in brandy against some sweating disease, had been set alight by a careless servant with a candle. 'Why don't you like your cousin?'

Earl Henry slid a speculative glance but his response was smooth and I felt that he was restoring us to the realms of polite discourse. 'A mere memory of youthful frictions. Richard and I were raised together, and not always amicably, I suppose because our tastes and interests are vastly different. Richard is the most inept wielder of a sword that I know. There you are. Nothing more and nothing less than child-hood conflicts. You might say that I should have grown beyond such trivial grievances.'

'I would not be so indiscreet as to say any such thing, sir.'

I did not believe him. There was a stern brooding involved here, but our acquaintance was so transient that I must allow his diversion, however much I might like to discover more.

'No. I don't suppose you would,' he replied, lightly now. 'Not only a lady of common sense but one of great discern-ment, I think. And of considerable presence. Duke John is a fortunate man to have a wife who is as handsome in character as she is in person.'

I wondered if he was guilty of a soft mockery at my expense, for I had never been considered a great beauty, even when touched with the kind hand of youth, and so I challenged him, my brows a little raised, but he met my provocation directly and held it. Once again I experienced that uncomfortable little jump of my heartbeat; a warmth spreading beneath my bodice as if a flame had been lit.

And I was intrigued. There was no mockery in his steady regard. Instead there was a curious arrest, almost a bafflement as if some unexpected emotion had intruded on our innocuous exchange of opinion. Even the air felt heavy with portent. His lips parted as if he would express what was occupying his thoughts.

Then it was gone, the moment broken, the tension that held us falling away, so that the air settled quietly around us again, as my husband, abandoned by Burgundy, rested a hand on Earl Henry's shoulder, and I was left to wonder if I had imagined the whole episode as John observed: 'You were a child when I saw you last. And here you are, Earl of Derby, with a reputation as an expert jouster.' His eye twinkled. 'How old were you? Ten?'

'About that. And I remember, sir.' Earl Henry was at ease again, and whatever he had been about to say was lost for ever. 'You gave me a hunting knife when we rode out at Windsor and I had lost mine. I still have your gift. It has a fine engraved blade. If I recall, I didn't let it out of my sight for months.'

John laughed. 'You'll do your father proud. It's good to have an heir. Richard will have a long time to wait for his bride to grow up and bear him a son.'

Once again we inspected the group on the dais where Richard spoke gravely to King Charles, who looked mildly interested, and Isabelle threaded her fingers through the gems on her girdle.

'Do you stay for the whole of the celebrations?' Earl Henry asked.

'Unfortunately, yes. My wife will not allow it to be otherwise.'

With promises to meet again, we prepared to follow the

royal party, Earl Henry saluting my fingers with a chivalric grace worthy of the most famous of troubadours.

'Thank you for your discretion, my lady.'

'It is my pleasure, my lord.'

'And what was that about?' John asked as Earl Henry threaded his way to his father's side.

'I have promised to keep secret the fact that Earl Henry detests his royal cousin,' I replied, following his progress, struck again by the unconscious grace.

'I expect King Richard knows it full well,' John growled. 'We'll do well to keep out of English politics, for our own health. And particularly out of the sphere of that young man. As your uncle of Burgundy was kind enough to advise, although why he should think that I cannot judge the matter for myself I have no idea. Who knows more about treachery than I? Burgundy says to steer clear.'

'Did he?' I was surprised.

'He considers the Earl of Derby to be a dangerous fire-brand. There is already the taint of treason about him. He raised arms against Richard ten years ago.' John eased his shoulders beneath the weight of bullion. 'I see no danger but we will keep our friendship warm but appropriately circumspect.'

It was a warning but softly given and not one I needed. I had no intention of becoming involved. As for Henry, Earl of Derby, ours was a mere passing acquaintance. A friendship. An opportunity to give open and honest exchange of opinion, where neither of us needed to be circumspect. That was trust. Was that not the essence of friendship?

But then I recalled that first brilliant moment of

awareness. Something, some close link, like those in the Earl's glittering livery chain, had scattered my thoughts like the stars in the heavens, nudging into life a longing I could not recognise. It disquieted me, unnerved me. How could it be that I could trust a man within a handful of minutes of my setting eyes on him? I was certainly not given to immoderate confidences.

And he stayed in my mind as I retired to our cramped chamber to rest my ankles that, in these early days of my pregnancy, had a tendency to swell in the heat. With soothing cloths soaked in a tincture of red wine and cinquefoil, my hair loosed from its confines, I lay back against the pillows and had no difficulty at all in summoning the Lancaster heir into my presence. The fan of lines at the corner of his eyes that had smiled so readily, when not shadowed and sombre. The flare of passion when he had admitted his dislike of his King, even if one born out of childhood antipathy. The austere nose, a mark of all the Lancasters, that spoke of command. The agile carriage, albeit swathed in fragile cloth, of a man of action. Instinctively I knew that the extravagantly ringed hands could wield a sword and manage reins with force and skill. And as for the pride, it infiltrated his every movement, every turn of his head. He too knew his own value as a scion of the Plantagenets, raised into it by a powerful father, the most influential of the sons of old King Edward.

'This is inappropriate, for a married women who is content with her situation,' I announced aloud, dismayed by the detail of my recollection. 'And one who is carrying a child. He is nothing to you.'

Yet the sense of distress would not leave me. And the little punch of guilt. Engaged in a marriage not of my choosing to a man certainly of advanced age, I had discovered through this marriage, and to my delight, an unexpected blessing. John had given me his friendship and a deep respect that proved to be mutual, as was the firm affection that under-pinned our life together as the years passed and our children were conceived. I could not have hoped for a better mate when, through necessity as a child of a royal family intent on building powerful alliances, I had been placed in this marriage with the Duke of Brittany.

Did I know love in my marriage? No. Not if love was the emotion of which our minstrels sang, extolling the heating of blood and heart so that the loved one was essential to the drawing of breath. For John I experienced a warm acceptance of all he was to me, but I was not dependent on him for every moment of happiness. Nor was I a necessity for him. We were content together but distance, when John travelled to the far reaches of his domains, did not destroy us.

Henry of Derby, in the space of that brief meeting, had forced me to consider an entirely new landscape.

'What is it, my lady?' Marie de Parency, the most intimate of my Breton ladies-in-waiting, was instantly at hand, always watchful for my needs.

I shook my head, sighing as I stretched on my bed, trying for comfort as my ankles throbbed. 'Hand me my rosary, Marie. I have need of a self-inflicted penance.'

A small flame that had been lit in some far recess still flickered, but of course it had not been lit for him. Earl Henry had been blessed with true love with his wife, now sadly departed this life. I closed my eyes as I spread my hands on my belly where the child grew, confident in the knowledge that my own strange discomforts would soon vanish.

Early pregnancy made a woman overly imaginative.

★

A grand hunt brought to conclusion the wedding of Richard and Isabelle. We made a combined party, it becoming evident that the Lancaster family was as fiercely keen on hunting as we were in Brittany. An occasion of much laughter and chatter, of reminiscence and proposals for future meetings. My pregnancy offering no hindrance to my participation, when we halted in a clearing in the woodland to draw breath, I found myself in the close company of Earl Henry.

I had been aware of him, riding in the forefront, from the moment the royal huntsman had given us the office to start, and I had seen enough of him to know that he was a peerless proponent of the sport. Not that I had watched him, of course. Riding at a more sedate pace, not always of my own choosing, beside Duchess Katherine, I had made the most of the opportunity to darn the holes in my knowledge of this family.

Now it was Earl Henry who manoeuvred his horse to my side while I determined to keep him at an amicable distance. I noticed that he had dispensed with the white hart on his gold livery collar.

'I see you number horsemanship amongst your many talents, Madam Joanna.'

'As you have a silken tongue amongst yours, sir,' I replied smartly. 'This wretched animal, lent to me by my uncle of Burgundy, has barely extended herself out of a slow trot.'

He smiled at me. And I smiled back.

And there was that same intensity that had unsettled me on the previous day. A sense of closeness, of keen understanding. More than that. Like the click of a key turning in the lock of a jewel coffer so that all the intricate parts slid smoothly together as if our acquaintance was of long-standing. Why should I resist? Why should I not take him as my friend? I had few outside my immediate family. The household in which I had been raised in Navarre, redolent with suspicion and vicious deeds, had not encouraged friendship. I would enjoy what this man had to offer me, and it would be no sin.

This thought in your mind is not friendship, a whisper in my mind. *Don't pretend that it is. This is entirely different. Have a care.*

Wary now, even dismayed, I hid it behind a light smile and even lighter remark.

'That is a fine falcon you have, my lord.'

The Earl reached across to take the bird from his falconer, removing her hood, then one of his gauntlets so that he could run his hand affectionately over her head and wings. The finely marked bird bobbed her head and shook out her pinions.

'She is beautiful,' he agreed, indulgently possessive. 'She was bred from my own birds at Hertford. She is inordinately partial to chicken, when she can get it.'

'Extravagant!'

'If she is worth her value to me, then it behoves me to feed her well.'

I stroked the feathers of her neck, admiring the fervour of this man in his appreciation for his hunting hawk. 'What will you do after this gathering, my lord? I hear you have been on Crusade.' Having discovered as much from Duchess Katherine.

'And I might again,' the Earl was replying as, with dexterous fingers, one-handed, he re-hooded the falcon. 'I have a desire to return to Jerusalem. To stand before the Holy Sepulchre and experience God's infinite grace. But I'm more like to go back to England. To see my own children, to take over some of the administration of the Lancaster estates. I have two young daughters as well as four sons to raise. The boys are as strong and active as a small herd of hill ponies. I think you have sons. You'll know what I mean.'

His enthusiasm was compulsive. 'Indeed I do.'

'And then…'

Gravity descended, like an obscuring shadow. I considered it to be born of a concern long held, some bone of contention long debated. I saw it in John when he broached some intricate matter of business, most often Breton trade disputes with our mercantile neighbours.

'Is there a problem for you at home, sir?'

Handing the falcon to John who, approaching, was eyeing the bird with some envy, Earl Henry considered for a moment, then replied with striking frankness:

'I have a need to return. Sometimes it seems to me that my position in England is under a subtle duress. I am being pushed to the margins of political life. Positions and dignities are given elsewhere. My cousin Edward of York is preferred before me, even though as heir to Lancaster my supremacy is unquestionable.'

So here was pride again. And rightly so. With the death of two of King Edward's sons, Edward of Woodstock and

Lionel, Duke of Clarence, the Lancaster heirs with their true male line were foremost in the land after the King Richard. As I had suspected, the hostility between Earl Henry and King Richard, first cousins though they might be, was not merely a remnant of childhood tussles in the mud.

'Richard fears me,' the Earl said, the line between his brows dug deep. 'I dare not be absent from England any longer. It might give our King the opportunity to find some means of casting a pall of disgrace over my family. That must not be. My father is ageing. The duty is mine to protect and hold fast to what we have, and fight for what we should have.'

'Why would he fear you?' I asked bluntly. 'Do you threaten him?'

'It has to be said that I did,' the Earl admitted. 'In my youth I was one of the five Lords Appellant who forced Richard to rule more circumspectly after we removed his favourite de Vere from the scene. A decade ago now, but it will rankle still. Richard hadn't the strength to oppose us then, but he has never forgiven us.'

Which explained a lot. 'Hardly the basis for a sound friendship.'

'As you say. Although why I am burdening you with this, on a fine hunting day, I have no clear idea.'

'Because I can be a good listener,' I said.

He looked at me, eyes as incisively watchful as those of the hawk on John's fist, but there was a smile there too.

'So that's why I've been lured into this eddy of self-pity. Would you tell me that all is lost, between Lancaster and the King?'

I thought about it as my mare tossed her head, deceptively

eager to be on the move. 'I think you could well redeem yourself. I think you should…' I stopped. I was in no position to give him advice. He would find me intrusive at best, unjustified at worst.

Earl Henry tilted his head. 'Do you advise your husband in matters of government?'

'Most certainly I do.'

'Does he accept it?'

I thought about this. 'Sometimes.' And paused under John's sudden acerbic scrutiny. 'Often.'

'Almost always,' John added from behind my shoulder. 'I would not dare do otherwise. She has a rare talent for seeing the smoothest road between two irreconcilable parties. I'd take her advice if I were you.'

He rode off, still in possession of the hawk, leaving me to collect my composure.

'Then tell me, Madam Joanna. What should I do?'

'You should go home. Be gracious and charming on all occasions. Never criticise Richard's choice of counsellors. Make friends with your cousin of York…'

I hesitated, seeing a glint of speculation in his eye.

'Don't stop now. I stand corrected and ashamed for all past behaviour.'

How could I not continue? The rich wine of European government and intrigue ran in my blood. 'Then this is what I think. Set your jaw and tolerate Richard's behaviour towards you. It may be nothing more than jealousy and spite. He cannot harm you. You have your own authority over your Lancaster lands. How can he destroy your illustrious name? Give him gifts on every possible occasion and make yourself pleasant to Isabelle. You have daughters. You know how to do it. She likes dolls.'

'What excellent advice.' And then, smoothing the leather of his reins between his fingers as he considered: 'There is some pressure on me to marry again. It has been two years since Mary's death. I have resisted taking a new wife so soon, but it would be wise, even if I have no need of an heir. A strong alliance with one of our English families would be good policy. It behoves me to do it, whatever my personal inclination.'

A coldly sobering thought that took me aback, when it should not have. Were we not surrounded by death; by marriage and remarriage to tie powerful families with bonds of blood and allegiance? Would John feel a reluctance to remarry if I were to die within a few months in childbirth? Or would he wed again within the year? I was his third wife. He might happily take a fourth, and why should he not? Marriage for us was a matter of politics, not of passion, and Brittany must look to the security of her borders. My husband would be looking for another bride, and perhaps another Valois princess, within the week of my death. Which made me observe, with an intimacy I could not claim:

'You were fortunate indeed, sir.'

'In what manner?'

'To find such love with your wife. That you would consider not marrying again after her loss.'

He looked at me, his brows raised in query.

'It does not come to everyone of our rank,' I reminded him, not that he would need the reminding. 'Some would say it is a rarity.'

He looked as if he might have replied with some polite usage. Instead: 'Are you happy in your marriage?'

Since no one had ever asked such an intrusive question, I did not readily reply. I had never had to consider it in quite such terms. Content yes. Happy? What constituted happiness? And for a moment I resented the question. But since mine to the Earl had been very particular, I could hardly take issue with him. But I was aware of the chill in my voice.

'Why do you ask that? Do I appear discontented?'

'No. But your husband is more my father's age than mine. How old are you?'

'Twenty-eight years.'

'As I thought. We are much of an age. I warrant the Breton Duke is at least in his fiftieth year.'

'And a better man I do not know.' I was sharp. I would not be pitied, or made to feel uneasy by what could be counted an impertinence. 'It could have been worse.' Never had I spoken so openly, so plainly. 'My father was not known for altruistic gestures. I could have been married to a monster such as he. I thank God daily for an amenable husband who speaks to me as an equal, considers my wellbeing before his own and does not berate me when I am undoubtedly extravagant in the purchase of a gown or a new hound. No, I have never experienced the love that came to you and your wife, sir, if that is the overblown passion of which my troubadours and minstrels sing, but I have experienced much affection, and for that I am grateful.'

Earl Henry inclined his head in acceptance of what was undoubtedly a reprimand. 'Then I too will thank God for his blessings on you. It was not my intention to discomfit you. If I have offended, I ask pardon.'

'You have not.'

Off to our left, a horn blew, as if to call a halt to such an exchange. We gathered up our reins and turned our mounts to follow the massed ranks.

'And will you?' I asked, importunate to the last.

'Will I what? Return to England?' He was thoughtful. 'Yes. I think I would be wise to act on your advice.'

But that is not what I had meant. I should have let it lie. I did not. 'Will you wed again?'

He turned his head to look at me, foursquare, bringing his animal to a halt again so that others perforce must jostle round us. His eyes skimmed my face.

'I have no plans. I have not yet met the woman whom I would choose to marry,' he said simply.

His gaze as bright as the dark jewels on his breast, Earl Henry lifted his hand, so that I thought that it was his intention to touch my arm. Instead he raised it to his cap, to touch the feather secured by a jewelled pin in a smart salute. Then, using his heels, making the high-bred animal he rode jump, he urged his horse on. Another raucous blast prevented any reply from me as we once more followed the hunt, the hounds picking up the scent of our quarry, leaving me to follow slowly, unnervingly wistful, in his wake.

Not that there was anything of merit to say.

'You have only met him twice.' I took myself to task.

Sadly twice was enough. For joy. For dismay.

Next morning I turned my back on the pavilions, urging my horse to keep up with John's mount as we began our long journey to the west, to Vannes. As the miles unfolded, I considered with some grim amusement what I had learned about myself at Isabelle's wedding; that the state of unrequited love, however mild a form it might take, did not suit me. Too much superfluous emotion to disturb the even tenor of my days. Too much uncertainty. Too much undignified craving. I had too much self-esteem to allow myself to succumb to an emotion that could never have a future. It would be no better than suffering a permanent stone in a shoe: an aggravation, an annoyance, with no resolution until the stone was removed. I did not want such uncertainty in my life. I would accept a simple steady platform of equanimity without the highs and lows of blazing desire.

But there it had been: a touch of minds, a brush of yearning, which I would never forget. A thing of wonder, an awakening. A response to a man that was neither friendship nor affection but something far stronger and beyond my control. Indeed it was a hunger. A taste, a sip, of what had never been part of my life's banquet, and never would.

Chapter 2

October 1398: Hotel de St Pol in Paris

There was an unexpected tension in the air. Not of hostility or incipient warfare, nor of some blood-soaked treachery, but of a nose-twitching, ear-straining, prurient interest. Such as when there might be a scandal, dripping with innuendo, to be enjoyed. It was present in the sparkle of every eye, in the whisperings, with no attempt at discretion. It might be considered beneath my dignity as Duchess of Brittany to be lured by such hints of someone's depravity, but my senses came alive, like a mouse scenting cheese.

John and I were engaged in one of our frequent visits to Paris, to reassure the Valois that the loyalty of the Duke of Brittany to their interests was beyond question. Our family was left comfortably behind in Nantes with governors and nursemaids, including the recent addition to the family. I had been safely delivered of a child, another daughter Blanche, over a year ago now. I had not met my end in childbed. There had been no need for my husband to consider a precipitate remarriage after all.

We had expected to occupy rooms in the royal residence, the Hotel de St Pol, as was our wont, with its rabbit-warren of chambers and antechambers, but it seemed an unlikely prospect, for here was a bustle of royal dukes, prelates and barons. Of the royal dukes I recognised my uncles of Berry and Burgundy and my cousin of Orleans. It all had a strangely festive air about it as we found ourselves ushered into the most opulent of King Charles's audience chambers, as if we were part of the invited gathering.

Charles was sitting upright, enthroned on a dais, his servants having reminded him to don robes that added to his authority. So this must be some important foreign deputation come to request an alliance or impress with gifts. I could see no crowd of foreign dignitaries, yet someone was speaking. Charles was nodding.

I touched John's arm, which was all that was needed. Using his bulk and a degree of charm, he pushed between the audience, while I flattened the fullness of my skirts and followed, until we came to the front ranks. The delegate was still speaking, a flat measured delivery, in perfect, uninflected French. Some puissant lord then. Perhaps an ambassador from the east, but ambassadors rarely attracted so much commotion. The petitioner was still hid from my view but he was flanked by the Dukes of Orleans and Burgundy. Such personal condescension on their arrogant part indicated a visitor of some merit.

Charles was in the process of rising to his feet, smiling

vaguely in our direction as if he might eventually recall who we were, before returning his limpid gaze to the man who stood before him. Smile deepening, Charles raised both hands, palms up, in acceptance of what had been offered.

'We are pleased that you decided to come to us in your extremity, sir.'

'I am honoured by your invitation to find refuge here, Sire.'

'You were at Calais?'

'I was, Sire, but briefly. His Majesty King Richard pronounced that I might spend only a week there, with a mere twelve of my men. I had, perforce, to leave.'

The direction of this conversation had little meaning for me; but the visitor had, and my heart registered a slow roll of recognition. Henry, Earl of Derby, returned to France. No, Henry, Duke of Hereford now, I reminded myself. Henry, heir of Lancaster. Duke Henry who had once, many months ago now, stirred some novel emotion to life in my heart, when I wished he had not. I had wished that persistent longing a quick death. It was inappropriate, disloyal.

Had it died?

I thought it had. Absence could deal a death blow to the most rabid of passions, or so I believed. Standing to the side as I was, my regard was fixed on his flat shoulders, the hawk-like outline of his profile, simply because he was an acquaintance and this was an event that spiked the air with danger. I was a mere onlooker, with more interest than good manners.

'We welcome you, my lord of Hereford.' Charles beckoned to one of his many minions, who approached with a cushion bearing a livery collar. 'I would present you with this note of our esteem.'

Duke Henry knelt at Charles's feet and the chain was cast over his bowed head to lie, glinting opulently.

'I am honoured, Sire.'

'Good. Good. That's how it should be. We give you use of the Hotel de Clisson during your residence in Paris. It is close to us, here at the Hotel de St Pol. I wish you to feel at home as you take your place at my Court.' Charles beamed.

Henry, standing again, said, 'I would return to England soon, Sire.'

'As I know. Your family ties are strong. But I think it will not be possible. Make yourself at ease with us, until you see in which direction the English wind will blow.'

'My thanks, Sire. And my gratitude for this haven in a time of storms.'

Everything about him was familiar, yet I acknowledged the difference from the man who had asked my advice and, I presumed, had acted on it and bought Isabelle a doll, only two years ago. Now there was a rigidity about him that I did not recall, his shoulders tense under the livery chain. Magnificently groomed, clad as befitted an English prince, his voice was smooth and cultured yet lacking any emotion. There was none of the vibrancy of the Earl who had ridden to hounds with such panache, or who had shone in gilded Italian armour at the tournament. It was as if he was applying the demands of courtesy because it was inherent in a man of his breeding, but it seemed to be a bleak response, with little pleasure in it. How could that be when Charles had offered him a house for his own particular use in Paris? But what was this extremity? Why would Duke Henry need to test the English wind? My curiosity was roused, even more when I realised that Charles was continuing his extravagant welcome, that did not match the troubled frown on his brow.

'My brother Orleans will see to your comfort, my lord. And here is the Duke of Brittany and his fair wife, well known to you.' Charles gestured, with a hint of desperation, for us to step forward. 'You will not lack for friends here, however long or short your stay. We will make it our priority that you pass the time agreeably with us.'

'My thanks, Sire. I do not have the words to express my gratitude.'

The royal frown might mean nothing of course. Charles was not always in command of his reactions. And there was Duke Henry coming to clasp hands with my husband and salute my proffered fingers. The expression on his face could only be described as engraved in flint.

I smiled, murmured suitable words of welcome to cover my alarm. Now that I could inspect his face I could see that the passage of time, not of any great length, had for some reason taken its toll. There was a new level of gravity beneath the perfect manners, a tightening of the muscles of his jaw. He might smile in return but there was strain too in the deepening of the lines beside eye and mouth. They were not created by laughter or joy. Here was a man with trouble on his brow.

'Come and dine with us when we are settled,' John invited, offsetting a similar attempt by the Duke of Orleans to commandeer Duke Henry's company. Which was interesting in itself, for Orleans was never without self-interest. 'And then you may tell us why you are to stay as an honoured guest in France. My wife is, I believe, bursting with curiosity.'

'I was too polite to mention it,' I said, supremely matter-of-fact. 'I endorse my husband's invitation, but I promise we will not hound you if you do not wish to speak of it.'

Henry's smile was sardonic. 'I will, and with thanks. You deserve to know the truth. But you may not like the hearing. And I will not enjoy the telling.'

And I would discover what it was that had drawn the line between Henry's brows, deep as a trench, and invited his mouth to shut like a trap, as if to speak again would allow the truth to pour out and scald us all. Whatever it was that had driven Duke Henry to take refuge at the Valois Court had hurt him deeply.

And no, the attraction was not dead at all. Merely dormant. Now it was shaken most thoroughly back into life.

*

The following day the Duke came to dine with us, a roil of temper all but visible beneath the Valois livery that he still wore out of deference to his host. In the meagre chambers found for us in the Hotel de St Pol, while our servants supplied us with platters of meats and good wine, we spoke of inconsequential matters, of family, of friends, even though Duke Henry's mind was occupied elsewhere, and not pleasantly. I prompted him to talk of his sons and daughters. He asked after our own.

It was a good pretence. Some might have been led to believe that the Duke was troubled by nothing more than the discovery of some high-bred prince whom he considered a suitable match for his daughters. Some might have thought that I had no more than a desire to know of the health of Duchess Katherine.

Such ill-informed persons would have been wrong on both counts.

Servants dismissed, the door barely closing on their heels, the Duke cast his knife onto the table with a clatter. 'You will have heard by now. I warrant the Court is talking of nothing else.'

So we had, and the Court was rife with it. The astonishing behaviour of the English King; the slight to his cousin who sat at our board with little appetite. We knew exactly why the Lancaster heir had found need to throw himself on the mercy of King Charles, and was detesting every minute of it. The heir to Lancaster had no wish to beg for sanctuary, here or at any other Court of Europe. I felt his shame, while John launched into the heart of the matter.

'So you have been banished from England?'

Any relaxation engendered by the meat and wine vanished in the blink of the Duke's eye, which became full of ire. Duke Henry placed his hands flat on the table with a flare of baleful fire from his rings and took a breath.

'I have, by God, and for no good reason.'

'Then tell us. What's in your royal cousin's mind?'

'A false accusation of treason against me, which Richard chooses to believe for his own purposes.'

'How long?' John asked, the one pertinent question.

'Ten years. God's Blood! The Duke of Norfolk and I played magnificently into Richard's hands, without realising what vicious calumny he had in mind. We fell into his trap as neatly as wolves into a hunter's pit.' Duke Henry's explanation was clipped, almost expressionless in its delivery, but it was not difficult to read the underlying abhorrence. It positively simmered over the folds of his fashionable thigh-length tunic. 'There was no reasoning with Richard. He would not even consider what might be owed to Lancaster, for our support and loyalty from the day he took the Crown as a boy of ten years. He owes my father so much, but there was no compassion in him.' Now Duke Henry smoothed the fair cloth beneath his hands with short angry sweeps. 'He banished Norfolk, who made the accusation of treason against me, for life. There was no leniency at all for him in Richard's black heart.'

'It will soon pass.' I tried to be encouraging, but could see no encouragement in the vast expanse of ten years. 'Could he not be persuaded to reconsider? Richard's anger might grow cold as the weeks pass.'

'I don't anticipate it.' Duke Henry's regard was fierce as it rested momentarily on my face. 'Do you see what he has achieved in this neat little strategy? Richard has rid himself of the last of the two Lords Appellant with one blow. Norfolk and I were two of the five who stood against him, and forced him to accept the advice of his counsellors. Three of the five are dead. Norfolk and I are the only two left, and so Richard struck, hard and sure. Richard will not go back on it. It's not Richard's way. There was no treason, simply an opportunity for Richard to take his revenge. I imagine he's rubbing his hands with royal glee.'

'What of your children?' I asked, because I knew it would be a concern.

'I don't fear for them, if that's what you mean. Hal, my heir, has been taken into the royal household, a hostage for my good behaviour. I despise Richard for that, but I don't believe Hal's in any danger except for being bored out of his mind by the never-ending ceremony of Richard's Court. Besides, there's nothing I can do about it other than have my brothers—my Beaufort half-brothers—keep a watchful eye.' A pause grew, lengthening out as Duke Henry took up his cup and contemplated the wine in it, and I exchanged a hopeless glance with John. 'I think it does not need saying—my real fear is for my father. Lancaster's health is not good. My banishment aged him ten years overnight, so my fear is that he'll not see out the length of my banishment before death claims him. It is in my mind that we will not meet again this side of the grave.'

It was a desperate cry that echoed beneath the formidable control. All I could do was leave John to make the only possible response: 'We must hope you are wrong. We will assuredly pray for a swift resolution and a speedy return for you.'

Duke Henry drained his cup. 'It is in my mind to return to England, with or without royal permission.' And seeing some reaction from John's raised hand—a brusque denial of such a plan, of what the consequences might be—he looked towards me, with something approaching a scowl. 'Will you offer advice again, Madam Joanna, to remedy this parlous state in which I find myself?'

Yet something in his request, polite as it was, suggested that Duke Henry did not want advice from me. Or from anyone. I raised my chin a little, detecting an underlying aggression. If he was humouring me, there was no need. I barely recognised this brittle individual from whom all the joy and the laughter had been stripped clean.

Understandable of course, but I would be the target of no man's ill-humour.

'I will if you wish it,' I said. 'Although it had no good effect last time. As I recall, I advised the building of bridges and pleasing Isabelle. Which either failed—or you ignored.'

The heavy brows twitched together. Perhaps the dart had been unkind in the circumstances.

'I worked hard to mend any quarrel with Richard. It failed, but that doesn't mean your advice was flawed. What do you say now?'

I thought for a moment, weighing what I might say. Here was a man whose self-esteem had been damaged. How much he must resent having to bend the knee before Charles of Valois to beg for protection, to accept the condescending invitations of Orleans and Burgundy. To accept that he no longer wielded authority over his own lands and his own people. Even worse, to have the taint of treason hanging over him.

'I would say…' I began.

Before I could expand Duke Henry placed his cup, which he had been turning and turning in his hands, quietly onto the table, and quite deliberately let his gaze drop away from me.

'No,' he said, silencing me with a shake of his head. 'No. There is no need. I know what I must do. My heart might pull me to return to England where I should cast myself on Richard's mercy and hope for restoration so that my father will not be alone in his final years. Who's to say that the climate in England might not change, so that I can return with the promise of a pardon?' He grimaced, pushing the cup beyond his reach. 'A pardon for something I had no hand in. Before God, it would stick in my gullet like week-old bread to have to beg for Richard's forgiveness.

'But we all know it would be to no avail. So, rejecting what my heart tells me, I know in my mind that it would be a fatal step to put myself in Richard's hands. All my instincts tell me that I must stay clear of the shores of England until I have the chance of returning with more than a hope of redemption. As it is, I am declared traitor. If I went home, my life would be forfeit.'

'It is what I would have advised,' I said briskly, not a little ruffled, 'if you had allowed it.' Thinking that I might add: 'Why ask, if you did not want to listen?'

But out of propriety I did not, and Duke Henry did not look at me but studied his hands, now loosely clasped.

'And you have the right of it. I must not return. As long as my father continues in good health, I remain here in banishment.'

'And I would say—stay in Paris,' John added. 'If things change in England, it's not far for you to hear and take action. If you have to return fast, it can be arranged.'

'I have no choice, do I?'

'No. I don't think you do.'

With no lightening of his countenance Duke Henry made his departure to his new residence, but not before a forthright explosion of his disillusionment.

'How long will it be before King Charles decides that having a traitor in his midst is not good policy? Traitors are too dangerous to entertain, even visiting ones. I doubt I can rely on the friendship of Berry and Burgundy.' He settled the velvet folds of his chaperon into an elegant sweep and pulled on his gloves with savage exactness. 'I will be turned out of the Hotel Clisson and forced to make my living at the tournament.'

'If such comes to pass,' John remarked calmly, 'you will come to us, of course.'

Which generated, at last, the semblance of a smile. 'Only after I have apologised for my crude manners here today. Forgive me, Madam Joanna.'

His bow was as courtly as I could have expected, his salute on my hand the briefest brush of his lips. His final glance at me barely touched my face.

Alone, John wrapped his arm companionably around my waist as we walked through to the space that masqueraded as a bedchamber.

'Although where we should put him I have no idea,' he said as I sank onto the bed so that John could reach the coffer at the foot. 'Do we support him, Joanna? It is a hard road for a young man with so many expectations. How fortunate that he did not remarry, in the circumstances.' He sat back on his haunches, elbows resting on knees. 'Treason leaves a bitter taste in my mouth. Many here—your uncle of Burgundy for one—will take the line that there's no smoke without a real conflagration. Officially he is accused of treason to the King of England, judged and banished. Many would question his right to be here at all. It's a dangerous policy to support a traitor against a rightful king. Do we hold out the hand of friendship, or do we turn a cold shoulder?'

'I suppose it all depends on if we consider him to be guilty,' I said. 'Do we?'

John did not take any time to consider. 'No. I cannot

think that. His sense of duty was engrained since birth. But what I do think is that we have to protect him from himself. He'll not accept this lightly, and might be driven to some intemperate action.'

'He'll make his own decision.' And found myself announcing, when I had sworn that I would not, because it sounded petulant even to my ears: 'He did not want my opinion, did he?'

'Not every man is as foresighted as I.' John smiled at my displeasure and, as he rose, patted me, neatly, on my head, forcing me to laugh. 'I see your worth. One day Henry might too.' He turned a book in his hand. 'Now, what do you wish to do before the next interminable royal audience?'

'Walk in the gardens. This place has no air.'

★

We fell into a pattern. Duke Henry came to us, formality abandoned. And when he did, John and Henry discussed politics: the uneasy stalemate between England and France, the dire situation of English and Breton piracy. They played chess, rode out to hunt, sampled some of John's best wines, talked about Henry's extensive travels in the east.

With me Henry also played chess but with less harmonious results.

'You let me win.' Indignantly I snatched up my knight that had cornered his king after a clumsy move by one of his pawns, a move a man gifted in the art of warfare, even if only on a chessboard, should never have contemplated.

'I did no such thing.' His regard was disconcertingly innocent.

'You will never win a battle,' I pronounced. 'Your strategy is atrocious.'

'Then I must learn, before I take to the battlefield,' he pronounced gravely.

'You walk a narrow path between truth and dissimulation, sir.'

Henry smiled.

'And frequently fall off the edge,' I added.

Indeed there had been no need for him to sacrifice his pawn. I was a match on the chessboard for any man. But he was chivalrous, impressive in his good manners, his mouth was generous when he smiled, and he was gifted in more than warfare. I discovered in him a love of the written word as he leafed through the pages of our books. Music moved him, and poetry. He tuned a discordant lute of mine to perfection.

So Henry and John took pleasure in each other's company. But did I?

It was a bittersweet experience, driving me to my knees in repentance. Henry of Hereford took up residence in my thoughts once more and I could not dislodge him. He was there, like the annoyance of a bramble thorn beneath the skin. There were too many times when his entrance into a room where I sat or stood caused my heart to jump like one of our golden carp in our fishponds at Nantes. Or my blood to surge with the heat of mulled wine. Well, I would have to tolerate this discomfort until it passed me by, like the annoyance of a bad cold in winter. I could achieve that with equanimity. I would achieve it. I never held my breath when a man walked into the room.

I held it when Duke Henry visited and bowed over my

hand. I held it when, his sleeve brushing against mine as we set up the chessmen once again, his proximity destroyed all my assurance. I held it when he took my lute, making it sing with bright joy or heart-wrenching grief, drawing his battle-hardened fingers across the strings. Duke Henry could sing too, effortlessly, without reticence, quick to be charmed into a rendition of Dante Alighieri's song that could enflame any woman's heart.

'Love reigns serenely in my lady's eyes,
Ennobling everything she looks upon;
Towards her, when she passes, all men turn,
And he whom she salutes feels his heart fail...'

Uninvited I joined my voice to his in counterpoint, so that he smiled:

'All sweetness, all humility of thought
Stir in the heart of him who hears her speak;
And he who sees her first is blest indeed.'

It was sung with commitment, with delight in the words and music, but with no wilful treachery. We were not lovers exclaiming over our enchantment. Henry was not moved by the same yearning as I, that undermined with desire every lightly offered melody, and nor was I capable of such deceit. John, an indulgent audience, was tolerant but music moved him less than his gardens and the tales of travellers. He retreated into plans for planting aromatic shrubs at Nantes, leaving me awash with the seduction of music and shared passions. More breathless than ever, and not from the singing.

I stowed away the chess pieces in their box, placed my lute in my travelling coffer. It seemed to me to be a wise move.

And then my royal cousin King Charles, in his innocence, intervened.

'So what is Charles doing to entertain you this week?' John asked with more slyness than necessary as we finished off the crumbs and sweetmeats of a desultory supper. 'Any more theological arguments to exercise your mind when you have nothing else to think about?'

'This week it's marriage,' Henry announced, his expression carefully austere.

'Whose?'

'Mine.'

'You are to be wed?' John was obviously amused.

'King Charles, in a fit of sanity, sees a means of chaining me to his side, whatever the future might hold. He seeks a bride for me. A French lady of some distinction.'

John might be amused, but did I find amusement in this clever strategic manoeuvring? I could understand it well enough. Whatever the outcome of this temporary isolation for Duke Henry, since one day he would assuredly regain his inheritance it might be good policy to make him a friend of France through a desirable marriage. Good policy indeed. And yet my hands stilled on my lap, my knuckles as white as the sun-bleached linen that covered the table. A new bride. Was that not what we had all expected? I should wish him well.

'And who is the fortunate lady?' I sounded to have a genuine interest.

'A cousin of yours. The Duke of Berry's daughter.'

I allowed my brows to rise gently. 'A powerful match. An important bride. King Charles values you highly.'

'Even though I am banished, my reputation tarnished beyond repair.'

'You will not always be.' His cynicism was difficult to bear, particularly when he spoke nought but the truth.

'It seems a lifetime.' Henry promptly adopted a bleak stoicism. 'So the Valois would condescend to me, and I must accept. Tell me about her. Should I seek it? After all, I have nothing to lose.'

'And much to gain.' John waved his hand in my direction. 'Joanna will tell you all you need to know about the lady. She has the convoluted relationships of the Valois family at her fingertips.'

'Yes, indeed,' I replied immediately. 'You should snatch at it.'

I would have dragged him away from such a marriage. From any marriage.

How can you be so selfish? His future is not yours to direct.

I forced an astonishing depth of approval into my voice. She would make him an exemplary wife. And as I did so, became aware of John beaming at me. My lord and husband. My dear friend. He did not deserve my disloyalty, not to any degree. Morality decreed that I turn my thoughts to him, not to Duke Henry. Was I not a woman of high principle?

Never had I known such inner conflict. When a woman knew nothing of love-lorn longings, she did not yearn for them. Now my heart was sore with them, wretched with jealousy.

'She is a widow, I understand,' Henry was observing.

'Twice over,' determined, in atonement, to paint Cousin
Mary in the best of lights, 'but she married very young and
was widowed within five years. She has four children by her
second husband. She administers the land for her son with
considerable aplomb.' I took another breath and began to dig
a grave for my own sharp desire as my fingers picked apart
the tough skin of a late fig. 'Mary would make an excellent
wife for a man of rank.'

'She is younger than I.'

'By a good few years,' I admitted with praiseworthy warmth.
'Mary is held to be elegant and attractive. If my uncle of Berry
considers you a suitable match for his daughter, you should be
honoured. His pride is a thing of wonder, as is his wealth. Take
her.' I paused, reading the set of his mouth very well. 'I don't
believe you need my advice,' I chided. 'I think you knew what
you intended to do, without any eulogies from me.'

'Perhaps. But I wanted to know what you would say.' His
eyes were lightly appreciative on mine. 'If you vouch for her
abilities and affections, I would be a fool to refuse.'

Aware of the uncomfortable warmth at my temples, I
forced a smile. 'So now you know that I can say nothing but
good about her. Tell Charles that you will take a French bride.'

Henry's shoulder lifted, a touch of grace. 'If I must wed,
this elegant and attractive lady would seem the perfect choice.
It will not harm me to have the Duke of Berry on my side.
Or King Charles if he is willing to entrust his niece to my
care. And since you are so eloquent in her cause…'

'Have you not met her?' John asked, forestalling me.

'No. It is arranged that I will do so next week. She is

invited to attend one of the assemblies at the Hotel de St Pol. I am invited too.'

'Give her my love,' I said dryly. 'And my felicitations for a fruitful union.'

Wishing my elegant and attractive cousin Mary, quite frankly, to the devil.

★

The meeting was duly arranged to introduce the bridal pair, and because it was a family occasion, John and I were invited too. As on all such prestigious occasions, my charming cousin Mary was paraded before Henry as an exemplary wife, tricked out in courtly style with a fortune of fine gems in the collar that enhanced her not insignificant bosom. The Court watched indulgently. I watched less indulgently, and then I did not watch indulgently at all.

Henry saluted Mary's fingers, then her cheek, with rare grace.

They talked seriously, with much to say between them.

They laughed.

They danced.

It would be an exceptional marriage for both of them.

Mary was young, younger than I, and beautiful.

Earl Henry smiled with true enjoyment as he led his partner in the procession, tilting his head so that he could hear her flattering address and reply.

I could watch no more.

I was ashamed.

★

'Will you dance, Madam Joanna?'

I considered refusing, but that would be too particular. Of course he would invite me, because Duke Henry was courteous to the tips of his finely curled hair. And I would accept. It was inappropriate to draw attention to one's emotions when surrounded by a keen-eyed, gossip-ridden, manipulative Court. In my own family, in Navarre, I had learned early that it was dangerous to show either pain or pleasure; it threw you into the clutches of those who would use their knowledge to their own advantage. Such as my father. My father's children developed a disinterestedness worthy of the purest saint facing his martyrdom.

I was intent on moving out of the shadow of King Charles the Bad, to prove myself to be a woman of integrity and honesty and strong principle. Charles the Bad might have trampled over the talents of his daughters, unaware that they even existed, but I would show the world that Joanna of Navarre was worthy of note.

'It will be my pleasure, sir,' I consented, magnificently mild in my accord.

Taking my hand, Duke Henry led me into yet another formal procession which did not allow for conversation or privacy, except for:

'Did you enjoy Mary's company?' I asked, curious despite my antipathy.

'Lady Mary is a woman of great charm.' Our palms kissed, parted, rejoined. 'She dances with a formidable lightness of foot.'

Oh, it hurt.

'An exemplary woman,' I agreed as we came together

again, his fingers a quick intimacy, a most impersonal one, as he led me through a trio of light dancing steps, in which I apparently was no match for my superlative cousin.

'She converses well too.'

'Which will be an advantage, I believe, at Richard's Court when you return home.'

'Indeed. Richard will admire her and take her to his heart.'

With a decided gleam, Duke Henry's eyes touched on mine. Then held there, considering. I thought he would have spoken, but the interweaving of the procession led us apart again so the moment was lost when I found myself partnered with my cousin of Orleans, my concentration taken up in avoiding his large and inept feet. Until, restored to Duke Henry at the completing of the procession, the minstrels falling silent, our companion dancers drifted away to find refreshment and new partners. Duke Henry remained holding my hand, our arms raised aloft in an elegant arch, as if we still had the final steps to complete, his face set in surprisingly solemn lines.

'I have you to thank. Your judgement of your cousin was correct in all aspects.' He lowered our arms, but did not completely break the contact. 'She is lovely, in face and in mind. She is intelligent, well read, devout. A woman who has more in her thoughts than the cloth of her gown and the cut of her bodice.' He paused. His soft voice was in no manner sardonic. 'A woman who I consider to be capable of great loyalty, and affection. She would be a perfect bride for a Lancaster.'

Whereas he had described me as merely handsome. Jealousy, sour as unripe pippins, nibbled at the edges of my smile so that my reply was more barbed than I would have wished. 'And all this discovered within the time and space of one dance.'

'Of course. We had much to talk about. If we are to be wed, we must make up for lost opportunities.'

I turned to look at him. There was nothing in his face but discreet admiration for my spritely cousin, now dancing with another Valois lord.

'You forgot her ability to ride to the hunt and play the lute,' I added.

'No. I did not forget. It did not need mentioning. She will be acceptable in every way, my lady.'

'Then I wish you every happiness.'

Why should the Duke not wed her? Why should he not find happiness with this charming cousin? Her connections were impeccable. She would be of inestimable value. Yet such a declaration of admiration on so short an acquaintance shook me, even as I knew that I was too old and too wise for such unwarranted sentiments. Sadly, my envy knew no bounds. With the briefest of curtseys I turned on my heel and left him. I did not want him to marry my decidedly attractive cousin. I wanted…but I did not know what I wanted. Nor could I have it, even if I did.

I prayed hard that night. For composure. For a return of the stillness in my mind and heart. For a return of the acceptance of my life as it was. Inflicting my own penance, I prayed for the success of this marriage to Mary of Berry. It would be suitable reparation and the pain for me would be immeasurable. Which I undoubtedly deserved.

★

The next week we all attended one of the regular Court audiences. King Charles, shuffling his feet, encased in an unfortunate shade of vermilion, let his gaze slide to one side, then slide back again. The sudden sharp tension, that came to hang in the air like a noisome odour, increased when he stared at Henry, his mouth twisting in disapprobation.

Henry, straight-backed, was absorbing the tension too.

And then I saw, as Mary turned her head to look at her betrothed. What I read there made my belly lurch. When I would have expected her to show her approval, her pleasure, her mouth was as sharp set as if she had been dosed against worms with bitter purge of hyssop. Present with her family, she bent her head to hear some whispered comment from her father.

And in that moment, touched by a presentiment of danger, if I could have stopped the whole proceedings by some deep magic I would have done so. Instead all I could do was to stand, perfectly still and let events take their course.

Blinking furiously, Charles beckoned the Duke of Burgundy who, horribly prepared, stepped forward from his place beside the royal throne. He cleared his throat loudly, before announcing in the clearest of accents, staring at Henry as he did so:

'King Charles wishes it to be known. This proposed marriage between the Lady Mary of Berry and the Duke of Hereford is anathema. We cannot think of marrying our cousin the Lady Mary to a traitor.'

Traitor. The fatal word dropped into a sudden silence.

What a masterpiece of insensitivity. Of cold discourtesy. Of humiliation directed at a son of so noble and royal a family.

It was beyond belief that such a rebuttal should have been made, when Duke Henry had been received and feted for so many weeks at the royal court. And announced by the Duke of Burgundy no less, and so publically. A wall of held breath seemed to hem us in.

'So now we know what this was all about,' John murmured at my side.

'Yes.'

My throat was as dry as the dust motes glinting in the stale air. My heart bled for the Duke. Every inch of him was governed, his voice evenly controlled, now addressing the King rather than Burgundy.

'I am no traitor, Sire. If any man here charges me with treason I will answer him in combat. Now, or at whatever time the King may appoint.'

'No, cousin.' It was Charles who replied. 'I do not believe you will find a man in all of France who will challenge your honour. The expression my uncle saw fit to use comes from England, not from us.'

'From England?'

And there, in the two words, was the anger in him, the sheer fury, burning hot beneath his denial.

'We have had an embassy. From your cousin, King Richard.' Charles's gaze once again slid away, his words as slippery as his expression. 'He advised that no marriage should be contemplated with a man under the burden of treachery against his King.' He paused. 'But rest assured. We will stand as your friend—until better times. We will not cast you off entirely. We hope that you will one day prove your innocence.'

But you will question his integrity before the whole court,

I thought. It could not have been plainer. All eyes were on Henry. Deny it, I willed him. Argue the rightness of your cause. But of what value would that have been?

Henry knew it too. With stark elegance he sank to his knees before the King, head bent in submission. 'Then may God preserve my friends and confound my enemies!' He could not hide the bitterness, but Charles chose to ignore it, waving to him to rise.

'We will talk of marriage again. But first you must obtain your inheritance, for it will be necessary for you to make provision for your wife before we can move forward.' Charles beamed as if he had hit on the perfect way to rid himself of this uncomfortable situation. 'You will understand, my lord. When your inheritance is secure, return to our Court, and we will listen to you again.'

Which left Duke Henry no path to take but one of acceptance. Turning, his gaze swept over the ranks of avid courtiers who slavered over his every word, like a pack of hunting dogs scenting its prey; lingered on the Duke of Berry and his lovely daughter who looked anywhere but at Henry; touched on the frowning figure of the Duke of Burgundy. And then they rested on me, but momentarily, with what message I could not read, while I tried to wish him courage.

'My thanks, Sire,' was all he said. 'I am grateful for your forbearance. And for that of your tolerant Court.'

Without a further acknowledgement of those present, Henry did what I knew he would do. He bowed with grace and walked from the room. And as if this ultimate degradation of one of its number had never occurred, the Valois

Court again broke into conversation and laughter; hard and callous and unfeeling.

Anger drove out all other thoughts from my mind. 'Could it have been done no other way?' I demanded of John, sotto voce.

'It was not tactful. Burgundy is never tactful.' He took my arm. 'I think we had better rescue our protégé from the depths of despair.'

I had seen anger. But despair? 'But the King absolved him of treason. Didn't he?'

John's flat brows said it all. There had been no absolution here, only a cowardly sidestepping of the issue. But first things first.

'I have need of a moment with my cousin,' I said.

I could not leave it like this. Calmly smiling, answering greetings as I went, I was at Mary's side, wasting no time in fine words.

'You knew, didn't you? You knew what was planned here. You knew it would strip his pride from him. How could you not warn him of this little conspiracy to humiliate him and damage his reputation for honesty and integrity beyond repair.'

'What is it to you?' There was undoubtedly guilt from the set of Mary's fine jaw to the clench of her hands into inelegant fists. 'What could I have done?'

'Could you not have warned him?'

'I was told not to discuss it.'

'So you let him go into that bear pit unprotected. To be torn apart by the dogs.'

Mary tilted her chin. 'Duke Henry needed no protection from me.'

'He deserved to know that he would be proclaimed traitor before the whole Court!'

There was high colour in her cheeks. 'It's a marriage I'm well out of. If a man feels threatened, his judgement can be impaired.' Her eyes flitted over my face. 'What I don't understand is why you should take me to task. What is he to you?'

'He is a friend.' I would not be discomfited. 'Friends should be treated with honour.'

Her mouth twisted. 'You are very hot in his defence, Joanna.'

'And you are cold for a woman who, yesterday, was not averse to marriage.'

'Such heat, my dear Joanna, is unbecoming and could be misconstrued.'

Here was danger. 'I know the value of friendship,' I replied, smooth as the silk of my girdle. Yet gratitude was strong as John appeared at my side to rescue me, saying: 'My wife is supportive of Duke Henry, for my sake. The family is very much in my heart. We take it ill when his good name is blackened for no reason.'

Mary, a little flushed at the mild chastisement, bit her lip, while I withdrew into icy civility. Perhaps I had been intemperate but injustice could not be tolerated. If I had known as she did, I would have done all in my power to protect him.

'Forgive me, Mary, but it was not well done. Not at all.'

'Would you have disobeyed your father? I doubt it.'

'I might well if I thought it honourable. You are no longer a child. You have a right to your own thoughts on these matters.'

Mary turned away, leaving me to explain my intemperance to John, who was regarding me with some irony.

'Well, that put Mary firmly in her place, didn't it?'

'It had to be said.'

'But perhaps not so furiously.'

'I thought I was very restrained.'

'Then God help us when you are not.'

★

In the aftermath, Henry bore the affront to his dignity with a fortitude stronger than any I had ever witnessed, even knowing that it was King Richard who, in the name of his little Valois wife, had dispatched an ambassador, the Earl of Salisbury, festooned with seals and letters of credence, demanding that Charles rescind his offer of marriage and sanctuary. Duke Henry accepted the judgement with nerve-chilling control.

'My father's loyalty to the English Crown, and mine, is beyond debate. This is how Richard repays me, making me *persona non grata* in every Court of Europe. A political liability.' He was pale, as if he had suffered a blow from a mailed fist, but his delivery was eloquent. 'I have been conspicuously loyal to him for ten years, since the Lords Appellant set his feet on the path to fair government. I have done everything in my power to support my cousin. Now he destroys my good name, hounding me when I could have made a temporary life for myself here in France. My every motive, my principles, every tenet of my life—all now suspect. So Charles will think again of the marriage, when I have come into my inheritance? Before God, he will not!'

Which summed it up succinctly, as cold and crisp as winter ice beneath the tumult in his eyes. Duke Henry glowered like a thunder cloud about to break and deluge us all.

'Richard considers me a traitor, worthy of banishment. How can the courts of Europe cast that aside, as an accusation of no merit? I know that Charles has tolerated me because of my Lancaster blood, and you too because of past friendships, but unless I can clear my name there will always be rank suspicion hanging over me. And how can I clear my name? Until I can return to England and take my place again as heir to Lancaster with Richard's blessing, there is no hope for my restitution. And I think I will never have Richard's blessing. He has covered it well over the years with smiles and gestures of friendship, but he despises the air I breathe.'

Henry had understood from the beginning the insecurity of his position. He might have been lured into believing he could make a home here and wait out the empty years with French support and a French wife, but I thought he had never truly believed that. He had always envisaged this ending. Now his masterly summing up left neither John nor I with anything to say. As he faced the uncertain future, I admired him more than I dared admit. A proud man driven to his knees. A man of honour forced to accept the charge, and bear it, because there was no evidence that he was not a traitor. What would his denial weigh against the conviction of King Richard?

'What can we do to help him?' I asked John, hollow with regret when he had gone.

'Not a thing.'

As bleak a reply as I could envisage.

★

Couriers brought the news. Surely there should have been storms and fiery comets lighting the heavens, signs of great portent? There were none. The stars continued to pursue their habitual path. The sun rose and set without interruption, when John, Duke of Lancaster, the greatest of the Plantagenet princes, passed from this life. It was rumoured that King Richard heard of his uncle's demise with a sort of joy, but no one spoke of it in Duke Henry's hearing. There would have been no rejoicing at Leicester where Lancaster breathed his last, alone except for his wife Katherine, without the comfort of his son and heir, over whose unprotected head the clouds grew blacker yet.

In Paris a High Mass was ordered by King Charles, to pray for Lancaster's soul.

But Henry was Lancaster now. A man of title, of land and pre-eminent rank, yet a man destined to kick his heels in whichever court of Europe would accept him for the next hand-span of years, the charge of treason dogging his every step.

The Mass, honoured by the entire Valois household, was a dour occasion despite the glitter of jewels on every shoulder, every breast. Incense clogged every sense, flattening the responses, while Henry was immaculately calm under the pressure of so much official compassion. But beneath the composure the degradation and fury continued to seethe, for his pride had been stripped from him along with his freedom to order his life as he wished. I could sense it in the manner in which he held his head, his gaze fixed on the glitter of gold and candles on the high altar, his lips barely moving as we prayed for his father's soul. Lancaster might be at peace but his son was not. I prayed for him too.

Holy Virgin. Grant him succour when he despairs of the future.

'Have courage,' John said, when Henry had extricated himself from the Valois embrace, and we returned to our chambers where we could take our leave in private. We were going home to Brittany. 'Is that not what your father would have advised? Hold to what you know is right. We cannot see the future.'

'That's what I fear.'

His expression was as aloof as the one he had maintained throughout the Mass.

'It may be better than you envisage. Where will you go?'

'There's nothing to stop me crusading again now. A crusade is being planned,' Duke Henry announced. 'To rescue the King of Hungary from the Bayezid. What better way to earn my redemption than in the service of God? I have nine years to fill.' He rolled his shoulders, as if to do so could dislodge the guilt that sat there like some malevolent imp. 'I am Duke of Lancaster. I have a duty to that title. My lands need me. My people need me.'

'We have talked of this, Henry. To return now could be to sign your death warrant.' John clasped his hand. 'We have good hunting in Brittany. Come and enjoy it and let your mind rest a little.' John smiled at me, placed a hand on my shoulder with a light pressure. 'I have a courier awaiting my pleasure. I'll leave you to persuade him, Joanna, or send him on his way…'

We were alone. Folding my hands flat over the crucifix on its heavy chain, pressing its wrought silver outline hard against my heart, I ordered my words to those of emotionless leave taking.

'Farewell, Henry. I wish you well, whatever life holds for you. I will pray for you.'

For a moment he did not reply, head bent. Then, looking up, startling me:

'Tell me what is in your heart, Joanna.'

It was a shock, to be invited to speak of what had lived with me for so long. My eyes searched his face, trying to detect the pattern of his thoughts, but could read nothing there except the familiar intensity when emotion rode him hard, as it had been since Burgundy's so very public denunciation.

'I cannot. You know that I cannot,' I said.

The curve of his lips was wry, before disappearing completely beneath a stern line. 'No. For it would simply compound the issue between us, would it not? It was wrong of me to ask it of you. I will not press you.'

The cross made indentation into the embroidered funeral damask of my bodice. And into my palm. My heart thudded beneath both. I watched his breathing beneath the black silk of his tunic pause as, slowly, he raised and held out his hand, in his offered palm a request. For the length of a breath I did not move, until compelled by some unseen force I released the crucifix. I placed my hand in his. But when I expected him to kiss my fingertips, as he might in farewell, he turned it palm up, and traced the imprint of the cross there with his thumb.

'Even here we are reminded of solemn vows, of lines of duty and honour and conviction that we must not cross,' he said. 'It is not an easy choice, is it?'

Henry pressed his mouth to my palm where the indentation was beginning to disappear, leaving an even more burning imprint, rendering me breathless, my skin aware of the sudden brilliance in the air around me.

I looked at him, every nerve stretched tight. Henry looked at me, every thought governed. The walls of the room seemed to close in around us, suffocatingly, the flatly stitched faces on Charles's expensive tapestries agog, the figures almost leaning to hear more.

There was no more to hear. With a bow Duke Henry was gone, leaving the chamber, and me, echoing in emptiness. The tapestried figures retreated to their seats in the flowery glade. I could do nothing but stand and regard the closed door, my fingers tight-closed over my palm where I would swear the imprint still remained.

How guarded we had been. How vigilant in our use of words. Not once had we spoken of what might be in our hearts. But then, I did not know what was in his, for he had never said.

Chapter 3

June 1399: Château of Nantes, Brittany

I lifted my head, interrupted from the conversation with my eldest daughter. Visitors. The clamour of a distant arrival: voices, orders given, the clatter of hooves. A small party, I assumed, coming to visit us at Nantes where we had settled for the summer months, fending off the heat and lethargy as best we might with breezes from the coast. It was a good time, with a visit from my eldest daughter Marie, who was chattering beside me like a small blue-clad bird. We were shade-seeking, in the garden overlooking the placid estuary waters of the River Loire.

'Are you enjoying your new home?' I asked her.

'Yes, *maman*. Although I miss you and my sisters. Not my brothers so much. But Jean is kind to me. And Madam his mother.'

Seated on a low stool, she crossed her ankles and linked

her fingers. How unsettlingly adult she was. Eight years old. It was a year since we had celebrated her marriage to Jean, the fourteen-year-old heir to the Count of Alençon, and now Marie was living in the Alençon household in the Château de l'Hermine. I recalled being adamant, on the occasion of Isabelle's wedding to the English king, that no daughter of mine would be dispatched to so early a union, but alliances were necessary, marriages made. The Alençons were cousins and kind. I had no complaint in their care of her as she grew up to become a wife in more than name. It amused me when, abandoning her dignity, she took possession of a bat and ball, hitching her sophisticated skirts.

I left them to the care of their multitude of maids and servants, making my way without urgency, considering where the visitors might be with mild interest. In an audience chamber if official, more comfortably in one of our private rooms if family or friend. John had not sent to tell me. If it was my sister, she would have come out to me immediately. Perhaps the Duke of Burgundy over some matter of high politics that did not require my presence.

And then I heard the raised voice through the door which led into one of our private rooms, a voice, usually beautifully modulated, but now with an edge that would hack through steel. I recognised it immediately, stepping from the tranquillity of the garden to this hotbed of fury. Pausing for only one moment to guard my features, I entered quietly to see the one man I did not expect, who was draining a cup of wine as if he had been lost for days in a desert. Any reaction of my senses in meeting Henry of Lancaster again was subsumed in a blast of anger that pulsed from the walls.

'Would you believe what he has done?' Henry, in a sheen of dust and leather and the distinct aroma of horse, wiped his mouth with the back of his hand, holding out the cup for a refill as his voice acquired a resonant growl. 'Well, of course you would. You know as well as I just what he is capable of. God rot his foul soul in hell!'

Such lack of restraint. I had never seen this in Henry. Anger yes, frustration certainly, a deep melancholy on occasion, but never this fury, threatening to run wild like a forest fire in summer, consuming all before it. There was no control here. And although there had been no name so far uttered, I knew without doubt it must be King Richard who had lit the conflagration.

Henry had not even noticed my entrance.

'He will destroy me. God's Wounds! I should have expected it. But even if I had, how could I have pre-empted such a mendacious act? He has me spitted on the point of his fancy dagger!'

John was in the act of pouring more wine. Henry was continuing, each word bitten off at the root as he dug forceful fingers into his skull, dishevelling further his sweat-flattened hair. 'I am come here because you are the only friend I have in whom I trust. I know I can be honest with you. By the Body of Christ! I trust no one at the Valois Court where it has been made plain as a scoured bread-pan that I am an embarrassment.'

The cup, emptied again, was returned to the surface of the coffer with dangerous force.

'I can't argue against any of that.' John took his arm. 'Come and sit. Ah, Joanna. We have a guest…'

Henry turned his head, so that now I could see the passion that had him in its grip. There was a pallor to his face, below the summer bronze from wind and weather.

'Forgive me, my lady.' He bowed brusquely. 'I was not aware.'

'So I see. And hear… Welcome, Henry.'

I smiled to put him at his ease, walking to join them, taking a stool beside them and a cup of wine. It was all Henry could do to sit, his hands on his thighs, fisting and flexing with hard-leashed energy.

'My cousin has disinherited me.'

He could sit no longer but strode to the window as if he could see across the water to England where events developed without him. I looked at John who shrugged in ignorance.

'The King of England has used his fair judgement against me,' Henry stated, knuckles white where he gripped the carved stonework, lip curling. 'My banishment is no longer one of a mere ten years. It is for life. As for the Lancaster inheritance—my rightful inheritance as my father's heir—it now rests in Richard's hands. Every castle, every acre, every coffer of coin. Richard has enriched himself at my expense. He has no right. Not even the King of England has that right.' He paused, as if this one terrible fact still would not be absorbed. 'But that's not all. In lack of a son, Richard has chosen his heir. It is to be my uncle of York, and so, in the order of things, my cousin of Aumale, York's eldest son, is now regarded as Richard's brother. I am disinherited from my own inheritance. But by God he has destroyed my claim to the English throne as well. Perpetual banishment and forfeiture for Lancaster. And my son Hal still a hostage to my good behaviour at Richard's Court.'

'It is a despicable act,' I agreed in the face of this wanton destruction.

'He has robbed me of everything. I'll not accept it. Everything within me demands vengeance and restitution.'

'Of course you will not bow before such injustice. What man of honour would?' John rose to stand with him, his eye too on the tidal river, busy with traffic. 'How many ships do you need to borrow? Four? Five? I have them at your disposal.'

If I had been astounded at Richard's perfidy, now I was horrified. John offering ships. Was this John encouraging Henry to plot invasion? I looked from one to the other. This was dangerous work. This was rebellion. However gross the humiliation for Henry, this was insurrection.

'John!'

My husband swung round to look across at me. 'It's what he's thinking. Isn't it?'

'It is exactly what I am thinking,' Henry confirmed, the light of battle in his eye.

A suspicion of anger heated my blood. I too rose, to grip my husband's arm. 'It's too dangerous. You should be persuading him to wait. To negotiate. To return would be to compound the charge of treason.'

Which Henry ignored, focusing on John. 'Why would you lend me ships?'

'It's to my advantage,' John replied promptly. 'If you come out of this with any influence in England, I would demand a trade treaty in recompense. An advantageous position for my Bretons with English merchants.'

A hovering stillness took possession. A presumption that dried the mouth and set the heart beating. All three of us saw the implication here.

'I could only promise that,' Henry said steadily, 'if I became King of England.'

'Is that not what you are thinking? At this juncture, can you reclaim your inheritance any other way?' John closed his hand over mine, where it still creased his expensive velvet. 'I think you are wrong, Joanna. I don't see Richard being open to negotiation. Not now, not ever. If you want your inheritance, Henry, you will have to take it by force. Yes, it could be construed as treason, but what choice do you have? Go for the land and the Crown, I'd say. If negotiation becomes possible, then…'

I interrupted, dismay deepening with every word. 'Is that what you are planning?'

'Of course.' There was no irresolution in Henry. 'To return to England and take back what is mine. If I don't, I remain a penniless exile for life. To accept this would be to betray my father and all he had created.'

'It's too hazardous.'

'What would you have me do? There is not one man in England who will support what Richard has done. And I will have justice.'

'But you will be returning as an invader. How many men in England will rise to support an invading force against the true King?'

'There is no other way.'

I let my hand fall from John's arm and took a step back. 'I cannot like it.'

'I don't like it either.' Henry was unmoved by my distress. 'But to accept it is beyond tolerance. Would you in your heart advise me to sit tight and wait for better things?'

'I would say that to invade puts you in the wrong. And might threaten your life. But I suppose you would say that such is soft advice.' I could not quite mask the bitterness. 'A woman's advice.'

'Yes,' said John.

'Yes,' echoed Henry.

'Does that make it of less value?'

'On this occasion, I think it does,' said Henry, but with less ire as if he would smooth my ruffled feathers, as he had smoothed his falcon, so long ago when Henry's future was still reconcilable without resort to arms. 'I cannot wait. I was banished as Hereford. I will return as Lancaster as soon as I can arrange a ship to take me there.'

But my feathers would not be smoothed and I walked from the room, unable to stay in that heated atmosphere where the plans were all of blood and conquest, with the high risk of death. I could hear the two men begin to talk tactics even before I closed the door. Of course I understood. Who would not want justice for so vicious an act? In truth I knew that Richard would never soften with time: there would never be negotiation. Richard wanted the Lancaster inheritance; he had seized it and would not give it up, for it seemed to me that Richard did indeed both hate and fear his cousin. The death of Duke John of Lancaster had provided the English King with the perfect opportunity to rid himself of what he saw as a perennial threat.

But for Henry to invade—was that not too great a risk? If

he was innocent of treason before, to return with an invading force, to take up arms against a King anointed with God's holy oil, would cast him fully into the arms of unspeakable treachery. There was no argument to justify such an act.

So how could I wish him well in this chancy venture? All I saw were the dangers. Even if he accepted John's offer, of men and ships, how many men would stand with him in England, where he might well find himself facing an army led by Richard himself? What then? I imagined the possibilities with a cold dread. Death on the battlefield. Capture, imprisonment and execution, hanged as a traitor. In that bright, empty antechamber where the shimmer of light from the river touched every surface, Henry's death had a terrible inevitability about it.

Unless Henry could command more support than Richard…

But even then the future would be fraught with untold dangers. If it became a struggle for the Crown of England, France for one would oppose him at every step. France would be a dangerous enemy if Queen Isabelle's position was threatened. That I could not wish on him. Would he find a friend anywhere in Europe? I thought not. A usurper, an invader who threatened to overthrow the God-chosen King would have a name poisoned by the worst of betrayals. Henry would be friendless.

I came to a halt in the centre of the antechamber, eyes tight-shut against the images of death and dishonour, to the unease of a passing servant, until I forced my mind into the pragmatic steps that any ruler must consider. Invasion might be the only way for Henry to take back what was his, and knowing him as I did, would he respond in any other way? Even now he was plotting routes and advantageous landings. He would challenge the dragon and fight it to the death. There would be as little compassion in him when facing Richard as St George had dispensed to his scaly adversary.

As for my thoughts in this matter, that Henry should tread with utmost care, they had been swept aside as nothing better than women's thoughts by both those opinionated men. But why should a woman not have an opinion on affairs of government, as valid as that of any man? Was I, Duchess of Brittany, alone in my belief that a woman should have much to say in the ruling of a state, and considerable skill in the saying of it?

Certainly I was not, for there were ideas coming from France, from the pen of the redoubtable Madam Christine, a widow of Italian birth in Pizzano, that would give credence to any stand that I might make. A woman after my own heart: erudite, educated, cultured, a lady of letters with a growing reputation for her forthright approach, she too believed that a woman's body might be more fragile than a man's, but her understanding was far deeper. A woman, Madam Christine pronounced, should concern herself with the promotion of peace because men by nature were foolhardy and headstrong. Their desire for vengeance blinded them to the resulting dangers and terrors of war.

Which was all very well, I considered, riven with frustrations. But of course the man in question must be persuaded to actually listen to this capable woman. I doubted that Madam Christine had ever had to deal with masculine self-will as strong as that of John of Brittany and Henry of Lancaster.

And I sighed. My fears for Henry, still very lively, did not excuse my ill-mannered flight. My fears would not persuade Henry to take a different path. An apology was demanded from me, unless he had departed precipitately with his offer of ships, his mind full of strategy, without his taking his leave of me. I almost wished he had. Until, in my mind's eye, I saw Richard, smiling and victorious and Henry dead at his feet.

'Well, Madam Christine,' I announced to the empty room. 'I suppose I must apply the wit and wisdom God has given me and try to bring peace to bear on the discussion. But I'd not wager on my success.'

So I retraced my steps and re-entered, taking my seat silently, to John's announcement, somewhat dryly: 'And here is Joanna again, repentant of her discourtesy.'

I managed a smile of reparation and a little open-handed gesture of apology towards Henry. 'My abhorrence of this plan still stands, but I am guilty as charged.'

'I know why you advise me not to go. I see the dangers, and I like the role of invader as little as you do. But what choice do I have?' Henry too managed a smile of sorts. 'You would not wish to see me begging at your cousin Charles's table for the rest of my life, living in a house that was not my own.'

No, I would not wish it. Nor would I argue further against the inevitable, but I could not summon a blessing on such a venture. I heard my voice, cool and even. 'Do you take John's help?'

'No, lady, I do not.' He acknowledged my chill with a brisk response. 'To land a force in Breton ships might seem like strength, but it also smacks too highly of a foreign invasion. I need to win support when I get to England, not antagonise the English lords who might throw in their lot with me. I'll go alone, with a handful of men who will follow me, and hope it will persuade my fellow Englishmen that I have come to put myself in their hands. The power will be theirs, to win justice for me. I hope they will see the right of my cause.'

'And Richard?' I asked, anticipating a reply I would not like.

And how simple it was, spoken without any rancour. 'I cannot trust Richard to keep any promise he decides to make. I must not allow myself to forget that.'

Which confirmed all I feared. My thoughts were once again drenched with blood as Henry clasped hands with John, saying: 'I'm for the coast and a ship to take me to England. We talk easily of destiny. This is mine. It is not easy at all, but by God I will take it and hold it fast.'

After which his leaving was short and formal, a warm God Speed from John. A cool farewell from me. Madam Christine's maxims had been notable only in their failure.

'You should not have encouraged him.' As soon as Henry was beyond the door I rounded on my husband. 'It is treason, John. I see no good outcome.'

But John was unperturbed. 'He would have done it anyway. With or without my support. If you think there was even the faintest chance that we could turn him from it, you don't know him.'

But I did know him. I knew he would fight for his rights. Henry had begun a venture of great danger and, many would say, no certain outcome. Richard's army was in battle-readiness for a campaign in Ireland. Henry had no army at all, merely the anticipation of goodwill from those whom Richard's heavy-handed foolishnesses had pushed into enmity.

'I am afraid for him.'

'He knows what he is doing. He'll not take unnecessary risks.' John took my hand, rubbing it as if to warm my flesh on a cold day, even though the heat in the room was great. 'It is his destiny. Victory or death. We cannot help him now.'

It gave me no satisfaction. He had gone. The echo of his retreating footsteps had fallen silent, leaving nothing but a memory of sharp dissension and clash of will. How disturbing it had all been.

And yet I knew the outcome as if I were a practised soothsayer peering into a scrying glass. He would win his own again, driven by justice and honour to retrieve what was undoubtedly his by birth and blood and true inheritance. Would this ambition carry him through this campaign to seize the Crown of England? It might indeed. And then France, faced with a new king de facto might just come begging, with Mary of Berry as a simpering offering, a new bride who would be Queen of England.

'Joanna?'

'Yes?' I blinked. I had been standing with my ever-circling, troubled thoughts, a huge sense of loss bearing down on me, my hand still lightly held by John.

'I'm sorry.' I smiled in apology. 'I was just thinking how hard it will be for him.' And feeling the weight of John's strangely speculative gaze: 'I must return to the children...'

'Not yet.' John rubbed his thumb along the edge of my chin, then walked slowly to the coffer beneath the window, the one that stored the most precious of his books and documents. Raising its lid, he delved inside to extract a book, which he held out to me.

'That's a family possession,' I said, not moving to take it, not understanding.

'Yes it is.' His eyes were clear, his voice matter-of-fact. 'I want you to take it down to Henry before he leaves. I meant to give it to him. I forgot. It will strengthen him when his courage is at its lowest ebb, surrounded by enemies, as he will be. When he needs to feel God's presence and guidance, this will help.'

It was a Book of Hours, belonging to some long-dead Duchess of Brittany, illuminated with jewel-like pictures of angels and saints.

'Are you sure?' I frowned, very unsure. 'You could send a servant.'

'I could, of course. I think you should take it.' He was still holding it out to me, his voice suddenly gruff. 'If you don't hurry, he'll be gone.'

I took it, smoothing my hands over the old vellum and gilding. I did not need to open it to know the beauty of the inks, the fine clerical script with its decorative letters. It had great value.

'Tell him that the Duke and Duchess of Brittany will keep him in their thoughts and their prayers,' John was saying. 'And you can give him your own personal good wishes. Which you failed to do when he left. It may be hotter than the fires of Hell in here but I swear there was ice under your feet.'

Which I deserved.

'Yes,' I said. 'Yes I will.'

John's eyes were bright on mine, his face stern and then he smiled. I still did not understand.

'Run, Joanna.'

★

I ran, my skirts hitched, as uncaring of appearances as my daughter in her spirited game, the book clasped tight as I navigated the turn in the stair and out onto the shallow flight of steps. The stables. That is where he would be. His escort was already mounted in the courtyard but there was no sign of Henry. I slowed to a walk more suitable to my rank, entering the dusty dimness, blinded by the bright rays slanting in bars through the small apertures. There was his horse, saddled and bridled but still waiting, a squire at its head.

'Where is he?' I asked.

'Gone to the chapel, my lady.'

I should have known. I turned and, manoeuvring my way through the handful of mounted men who made up his escort, I walked, more slowly now, to the carved arch that led into the tower where our private chapel was housed, pushing open the door, reluctant to disturb Henry in this final moment of prayer.

But there he was, already striding out into the little ante-chamber between apse and outer door, sword, gloves and hood in one hand as he tucked a crucifix into the neck of his tunic with the other. It was plain, I noticed, such as any soldier might use, and there was about him a serenity that had been absent before.

I stopped.

So did he.

I could thrust the book into his hand with the briefest of explanations and apologies for my previous lack, and make my escape before stepping into dangerous waters. I did no such thing. With a rare commitment to what I felt rather than what I was thinking, I closed the door behind me.

The sun which had made prison bars in the stable, here, in this octagonal space with its joyously painted floor-tiles, bathed us in iridescence through a trio of little stained-glass windows depicting brave saints and martyrs, John's pride and joy. It was like a holy blessing over us, as for one of the few times in my life, no words came to me. It was as if the whole essence of me was held in suspension, like fragrant dust in the liquid of some herbal potion.

Words did not escape Henry.

'You came to me.' The sudden light in Henry's face was so bright that I was transfixed. 'I could not hope that you would. Knowing that you had no liking for my venture.' Then the light faded. Henry's brows flattened. 'You should not be here. I should send you away.'

'I will not go yet.' I proffered the book. 'I am here to give you this. In honour of our friendship. To give you strength in times of need. It was John's idea, but you should know that I am in agreement.'

Slowly he walked the few steps towards me, taking the book from me, placing it unopened on the stone window embrasure at his side along with gloves and hood. His sword was propped against the wall. Not once in the disposal of his property did his gaze move from mine, and my breath was compromised as he drew me towards him until his hands released mine and framed my face. Then I was even more breathless when his mouth found mine and he kissed me.

It was no affectionate kiss exchanged between close cousins, no formal salute between family, or even between friends. Or not in my limited experience. Beginning softly with a brush of lip against lip, it gained an intensity. An assurance. A depth. In the end a knowledge that it would be reciprocated. And as he kissed me a new horizon spread before me. A new geography beneath my feet. I drank from him, as from a bottomless well to slake a thirst I had never known I had. I clung to him. I buried my guilt in his embrace as I buried my nails in the thick stuff of his gambeson.

It was an intoxication such I had never known, even from spiced wine. Even more, it was an astonishment that he should have a need to kiss me in this manner. I could never have anticipated it, not in all the months I had known him.

Slowly Henry lifted his head and let me go.

'Do you know how much I love you?'

His expression was grave. He continued to speak while I simply stood and absorbed the enormity of what he was saying:

'I would not kiss you in Paris because you were wed and it would not be honourable for me to do so. Neither would I speak to you of what was in my heart from the first moment that our paths crossed at Richard's marriage. Did you realise? I thought that you must. I could repeat every part of that conversation when you told me that you had never known love in life. My soul cried out to tell you that you were loved. That I loved and desired you. I almost abandoned honour. I almost held you and kissed you, but I knew I must not with the imprint of the cross on your palm. All I could do was seal that precious image with my lips. And now I have done both—kissed you and declared my love—in your own husband's castle, in his chapel where I have just sought God's blessing. How much honour have I? And yet I have not one regret.' His fingertips moved gently over my cheeks. 'I promised myself that I would never say this. But some promises are made to be broken. I love you, Joanna.'

The words stroked over my mind with such sweetness.

'I don't understand how this can be,' I said.

'Nor do I.'

'I thought you admired my cousin.' I was still struggling to quiet my breathing, baffled at the suddenness of it all.

'Admiration is not love.'

'Your description of her was that of a man bent on love.'

'My description was of you. Did you not recognise yourself, most handsome of women?' There was his smile that melted my bones. 'As you so wisely remarked, how would I know Lady Mary to such a degree after one dance?'

And I laughed, a little in relief, in wordless delight, as Henry continued to pour his words of love over me.

'How can I deny something that has become a part of me? I have not seen you for six months, I have not heard your voice, but you are fixed in my memory as brightly as an illuminated initial in that magnificent gift you have bestowed on me. I cannot deny it. I will not, even though there is no future for us together. If it is honour to let you go, then I will. But I will say this first, so that, in the rest of our lives apart, you will never forget it and you will always know it. You are loved, Joanna. You are my most treasured delight.'

The words shivered over me, through me, and I replied as I wished to, as he would want me to. As, now I realised in those moments of blinding revelation, John had given me permission to reply. Flattening all my pride, my lips burning as I spoke, my tongue forming the words I had never said before to any man, and with such ease: 'I love you, Henry of Lancaster.'

'There, it is done. Our love acknowledged in God's presence.' He smiled at me, all his beauty restored, all the harsh anger of the last hour stripped away. Yet he took a step away from me. 'I will not kiss you again.'

But it was not enough. Not at all enough.

'Then I will kiss you.'

And with a step I did so, abandoning my habitual reserve, as with grave courtesy, mouth against mouth, reawakening the same sensations so that my heart beat hard beneath my bodice, my blood raced beneath skin that suddenly felt fragile.

The kiss ending, I pursued what I desired without permission, tracing the contours of Henry's face with my fingertips, as he had traced mine. The straight nose, the uncompromising brows, the line of his lips, the springing texture of his hair, the contour of his jaw, as if I might absorb a memory that would remain with me for the rest of my life. And this from a woman who guarded her emotions, shielding herself from any power to hurt or destroy. I was shaken with amazement at my courage as I allowed Henry to read my thoughts, my utter longing.

At last I let my hand fall away.

'Will you remember me?' Henry asked.

'Yes. I will remember.'

It seemed to me that an abyss was suddenly yawning between us.

'You will be careful,' I said.

'Yes.'

A tense little silence fell, tight-held with unspoken emotion, as once more he gathered my hands into his. The warmth was enough. It would have to be enough.

'I will use the Book of Hours, every day.' It was Henry who broke the silence. 'Will you pray for me? Even though…' He shrugged, his smile a little twisted.

Even though I stir up insurrection against my cousin. 'Yes. I will pray for you.'

'There is so much I would say. But we both know it would be wrong.'

'A betrayal of trust and much kindness.' I sought for the words amidst my grief that we might never speak again. 'It is in my heart that you succeed. And that you find a wife who will bring you strength and comfort.'

'She will always be second best. A pale shadow. I must not let her know my heart is given elsewhere.' He raised his head, listening, becoming aware of the outside world and all it demanded from him. 'I must go, Joanna. It will be best if you remain here…'

One of the little windows beside us had been opened by the priest to allow a breath of air to enter. Seeing it, inspired by some quirk of his imagination, Henry drew me with him as he placed the palm of his hand flat against the dusty glass, fingers spread across the deep blue and red and gold of the craftsman's art in depicting an angelic throng. And without a word passing between us, I placed mine on the opposite side of the pane, so that my palm matched his perfectly, spreading my fingers so that they covered his as much as I was able. The glass was sun-warmed, the colours deep and rich, heavy with gilding.

It was not a kiss. No it was not, but it was as if the colours bound us together.

'I will never forget you,' he said softly.

'Will you write and tell us?' I asked. 'To tell us how you fare?' And then I wished I had not asked. Better to let our lives diverge as they must without keeping the useless skeins intact. 'No. I think you should not,' I added.

I knew he understood, for he nodded. 'I will when I can. It will be all about armies and finance and inheritance. Farewell, Joanna. Farewell, my love.'

'Adieu. God go with you, Henry.'

He was the first to remove his hand. The colours around me seemed less bright.

When Henry collected his accoutrements and the book, despite his express wishes, I followed him out into the courtyard to keep a last, final image of him, and as I did so, a thought touched me.

'Why did you come here today? If you would refuse John's proffered aid, why travel so far? You could have told us of your intent by courier.'

Henry turned.

'You know the answer, Joanna.' Never had my name sounded so like a caress. 'It was to see you, even if we could not be alone, to say goodbye. I was not so soaked in passion at Richard's injustice that I could leave you without your knowing.'

So he feared death. He feared for the future. But he loved me enough to put his fears aside and come to me.

Henry bowed, to any onlooker the bow of the most respectful of courtiers to the Duchess of Brittany.

'I may die in battle. I may succeed in taking back what is mine. I may wed again. Whatever the future holds for me, I swear I will never forget you, in this world or the next.'

★

'He has gone.'

Could any phrase be more empty, more lacking in hope?

I had returned to our chamber with its rounded walls and fair aspect. I could have gone back to the garden, where the shouts and laughter of the children carried to us, a shrill squawk of impatience cutting through the rest. But I could not laugh with them. I could have returned to the chapel antechamber, to sit on the tiles in the dust and allow the sun-warmed colours to heal my loss. But the Duchess of Brittany did not sit on the floor and mourn. Besides, it would have been a coward's way out. I had to face my husband. The generosity of what he had done shivered over my skin, like the brush of a goose-quill. For now I understood the quality of the gift that John had bestowed on me, a gift of vast proportions, worthy of a man with a truly great soul.

Where was my loyalty now? Treachery was not only committed by men who took up arms against their liege lord, for had I not snatched at the gift John had given me?

Head lifted, spine straight, I walked in, to stand before

the table where John had taken up his occupation with pen in hand, a map under his elbow. At his side, Henry's empty chair and discarded wine cup. My eyes were on my husband's when they lifted to my face.

'He has gone,' I said. 'I gave him the Book of Hours.'

'Yes.' His voice was very gentle. 'I knew you would. And you said farewell.'

'Yes.'

'You have an attraction towards him. Or I might even say that you love him.'

A statement. Two statements, not questions. And so simply expressed. Not wrapped around in troubadour's words or in the accusation of a furious husband. It was as if John had struck me, but not a hard blow and there was indeed no accusation in his face. Only an acceptance.

'Yes, I do,' I admitted simply. I would not deny his generosity with a lie. 'I love him without reason. Without cause. Without any encouragement from him. Or from me.'

Hands folded, breathing held in check, I could say no other. Nor could I apologise for what had been not of my seeking. All I could do was hope he would understand. And forgive.

'I can see it in you.'

'You sent me with the book,' I said, as all had become plain, like an outline etched on glass. 'So that we could say adieu alone.'

'And anything else that needed to be said between you— without an audience.'

So he had. It had been deliberate, as I now realised. An offering of such impossible indulgence, so that Henry and I might speak of this emotion that held us so strongly. For John had given me—had given both of us—his permission to say farewell. He had offered me his permission to acknowledge the love that had so wantonly undermined the vows made in my marriage to him. He had allowed me his permission to admit, without treachery, that I loved Henry of Lancaster, and then draw a line of finality beneath it, for the Duke's future was far distant from mine.

In that one astonishingly clever and compassionate move, John had demolished the pride in me that had refused to allow me to acknowledge, or certainly act on, so flighty an emotion as love. What manner of man did that make my husband? One of such honour and magnanimity beyond my imagining. Or beyond my deserts.

'I cannot believe your indulgence towards me,' I said with difficulty. 'And I am ashamed. I am sorry. I have betrayed you.'

John shook his head. 'You have never done that.' Then: 'Will you go with him? To England?'

If John's knowledge of my feelings had rocked the foundations of my self-control, this set my belly to roil. Go with Henry? Abandon my marriage and family? How could he think it of me?

'No, John! Never! How could I do that?'

As he swept the feather of the pen across the carefully drawn coastline, his expression was benign.

'You could if you wished it enough. There would be scandal, but men and women have parted throughout the ages, when the horror of living apart from the one they loved became stronger than the fear of the world's condemnation.' He placed the pen on the table and linked his fingers quite calmly as if discussing some matter of business. 'It is not given to everyone to love with fervour.' And when I would have denied any emotion so extreme, John raised his hand. 'Your love for him is immeasurable. I see it in your face when you look at him. It astonishes you.' His mouth took on the faintest of smiles although I thought there was no humour in him. 'You never looked at me like that. Nor did I expect it. Ours was never that sort of marriage. Will you go with him?'

'He has not asked it of me.'

'No. He would not, of course. He is a man of honour. But would he wish it?'

'I don't know. We did not speak of such things.'

'Both too honourable.'

'But I am not honourable.' Confession was difficult but must be made. 'I would never betray you in body, but my mind knows only disobedience. I cannot govern it.'

'Nor do you have to.' John stood, walking round the table to stand before me. 'Our marriage was one of political alignment. We both knew that. It was not one of love.'

'But it should have been one of loyalty. I hope I have been a good wife to you.'

He took my hands in his, his thumbs stroking over my wrists where the blood beat, heavy with guilt. And loss.

'I can think of none better. Three times I took a new wife to bed, making the best alliances I could for Brittany. Mary Plantagenet. Joan Holland. Both English, they were good wives. But you have been the best. Do we not talk? Do we not share interests and laugh together? Do you not share my duties in this land which is not yours by birth? No man could ask for a better woman at his side in affairs of business. You have given me the gift of your intellect and the finest brood of children any man could ask for.' Leaning, he placed a kiss between my brows. 'I'll not upbraid you for discovering an attraction for another man. I am nearing my sixtieth year and can never give you the passion that Henry of Lancaster could give you. You are still so young...'

He touched my lips with one finger when I would have remonstrated.

'No. Listen. I give you permission to think of Henry without guilt. It was never my intention to replace the tyranny of a deranged father with that of an old and importunate husband.'

I would not be silenced. His nobility was a marvel that tore at my heart. So much emotion, all in one afternoon.

'Ah, John. That is not how I see you. You are no tyrant. Nor will I ever leave you. My duty lies here with you and our children. More than duty. My affection is bound up in all we have here together. Can you question my loyalty?'

'No, never. And I accept your word. I think you are my friend as well as my wife. You always have been, since that first day when as a young girl you took your vows.'

'And so I shall remain. I have said my farewells. Henry will go to England, he will become King if fortune smiles on him, and perhaps my cousin Mary will be offered to him once he is respectable again with a crown on his head.'

'Perhaps so.'

And John folded me into his arms, his hand gently on my head so that my face was pressed against his shoulder. Tears were heavy in my chest, for Henry's danger, for John's nobility, for my guilt, but I would not weep for another man in John's arms. That would indeed be a betrayal. How generous. How caring. I had not thought that John loved me, but then, there were so many degrees of love. My gratitude for his understanding was overwhelming but I would not thank him again for it. It would be a denial of his own grace and compassion in making the sacrifice.

It would be another layer of betrayal, if I accepted the right to think of Henry.

Thus, all decided however hard it might be, I would continue to be the best wife that I could. I would banish Henry. And if I could not, then he must exist on the very edges of my thoughts. That was what I promised with my forehead pressed tight against the sumptuous weave of John's tunic, his arms a haven around me. I would put Henry in his proper place. I was Duchess of Brittany. I would dedicate my life to that.

John was the first to move, raising his head, looking towards the window.

'That sounded like tears. Perhaps we should intervene...'

'I think so. Our daughter still has not the patience worthy of the future Countess of Alençon.'

'She will learn. She will learn well from her mother.'

We went down to the riverside in accord. No one would ever guess that my thoughts struggled to fly elsewhere, rather than remain here in this sun-washed garden where my daughters clamoured for attention and my husband dropped a kiss on my cheek as he placed Blanche on my lap. I hugged her close, as I held tight to the marvellous gift that John had just given to me, the freedom to admit, at last, freely and without restraint, my love for Henry of Lancaster.

★

'He has done it! He has actually done it, by God!'

'Who has done what?' I barely looked up from yet another damaged lute-string. Marguerite had been practising, ineptly.

John patted me on the head as if I were Marguerite, an endearing habit. 'Henry, of course. Our Duke of Lancaster has achieved the impossible, and, in retrospect, I'm not sure what I think about it. And the fact that I actually encouraged him. Write to him!'

Thus John's announcement in the autumn of that year. And so I wrote.

> *To my honoured lord and cousin, Henry, King of England,*
> *I write from myself and my lord the Duke to express our*
> *pleasure at your achievements. We heard the news with relief*
> *and know that you will uphold justice in your new realm.*
> *We hope that you continue in good health and that your*
> *children do likewise. We will continue to pray for you, that*
> *the Holy Ghost will keep you safe in His keeping.*

Henry had regained his inheritance, but more than that. Henry had taken the Crown of England for his own. With Richard leading a campaign to Ireland and Henry landing on the coast far to the north east, supporters had come to the exiled Duke of Lancaster, men of power, men of influence. Friendless no longer Henry had taken Richard captive and now, crowned and anointed, it was Henry who occupied the throne of England. I imagined the whole consort of European rulers shivering in their respective shoes at the success of such an enterprise. The rightful King of England was overthrown, another sat in his place. A dangerous precedent indeed. No wonder John's thoughts were ambivalent.

I wrote again, precise and formal as required:

We would ask that you keep us informed of your good fortune. It is in the mind of my lord to remind you of a promise to consider a trading agreement to calm the increasingly acrimonious situation between our fishermen.

I did not think I had ever written so unfeeling or so valueless a letter.

We assure you of our future goodwill.

I signed it Joanna of Brittany, with a flourish, and used John's seal. Then I sat back, imagining what I would have added to the end if I were free to do so.

I have agonised over your safety, and can now rejoice with you in the restoration of all you had hoped for, and more. I am well and my good wishes towards you as fervent as they ever were. There is no place for me in your life, but I hold you close in my heart today and every day.

But I did not express one word of that, rather gave the document into the hands of our chamberlain for it to be dispatched to the English Court by courier. It would be a good thing all round if Henry did not reply. My moment of passion, joyous as it had been, was at an end. Henry's destiny was assured.

Chapter 4

November 1399: Château of Nantes, Brittany

'Do you suppose we'll be ready some time before our Christmas festivities begin?'

It was an excellent day for hunting, bright and cool with fitful sun and a breeze to shiver the reeds by the river, but John was unusually impatient. We were taking out the hawks, a brace of brache hounds and our eldest children.

We had not heard from the new English King. How would he have time to write personal letters when his days were dominated by settling England into good government after surviving the throes of insurrection? With Richard imprisoned in Pontefract Castle, Henry would be faced with a delicate handling of affairs. Writing to Brittany would be the last thing on his mind. Deliberately I had thrust him into the shadows of my life at the same time as I continued to include him and his family in my prayers. I would be happy for him, reunited with his sons and daughters, the injustices of the past laid to rest, but I refused to let any further memories encroach. There was no place for memories in my life.

'Are we perhaps ready at last?' John surveyed the party.

And in that moment, in the splash of sunlight across his face, I thought he looked weary. He had not slept well, that I knew, nor, unusually, had much enthusiasm for breaking his fast.

'Do you really want to do this?' I asked quietly.

John had been from home until the previous day, travelling to the far outreaches of his jurisdiction, renewing friendships over wine and hunting, sitting in judgement where necessary, while I had held audience with diplomats and merchants here at Nantes, discussing new tolls and minting rights, employing new minstrels to enhance John's dignity when he entertained visiting magnates. Essential but minor matters compared with John's constant burden. I knew that it was no easy task for him to preserve his hold on this volatile duchy whose past history had swooped acrimoniously between the territorial claims of both England and France. How hard he had worked to keep the Breton lords firmly behind him, not least in creating his new chivalric Order of the Ermine to enhance loyalty to his dynasty. With four thriving sons, of which John was inordinately proud, our dynasty was under no threat.

'Hunting can wait until you are more rested,' I suggested, concerned by the imprint of strain around his eyes, the unexpected shadows.

'And what would our offspring say if I called it all off now?'

'They would be polite, as they have been raised.'

'Their disappointment would be palpable. Not to mention tears from Marguerite.' Who had a tendency to play on her father's soft heart. 'We go. Don't worry, Joanna. I am too tough an old bird to be brought low by a se'enight of touchy vassals demanding my time. Just too many hard roads, too many fast meals between one meeting and the next and too much inferior wine. It rots the gut faster than being on campaign. Now—let's show the children how to fly a hawk.' He already had one, hooded and leashed, on his fist. But as we rode out I saw him hand it back to his huntsman and rub the heel of his hand against his breastbone.

'John...'

'Don't fuss, woman. Keep an eye on Arthur.'

He kicked his mount into a smart canter, not waiting to see if we followed to cross the water meadows towards the river. At fifty-nine years he was as hale as the young huntsman who kept pace with him, as energetic as the children who could all ride well. We pulled up in good form amongst the sedges where there was a quantity of duck and heron to give us sport.

'Look.' Marguerite pointed at the geese that dabbled in the shallows further along the river.

John pushed his horse on again. Then stopped, pulling clumsily on the reins. He coughed harshly. In an instant I was beside him.

'John...'

He waved me aside, gripping his reins more firmly as if he would canter on, then dropped them, grinding a fist hard against the centre of his chest.

'We don't need to do this.' I dug my fingers into his sleeve, trying to recover his reins at the same time, touched by a sudden dread. I had never before seen John drop his reins.

'I need a moment. Just a moment…' And then a harsh rattling breath in his chest, and I felt his weight press against my grip. I tightened it but I knew I could not hold him.

'I need help…' I raised my voice.

The servants were beside me in an instant, but help did not come fast enough and indeed I could not hold him. John toppled from saddle to ground with a groan. I followed, abandoning both horses, sinking to the chill grass to take his head and shoulders across my lap. His face was ashen, lips pulled back in a rictus.

'Wine…' His throat could barely form the word, but I found a wine container thrust into my hand by our falconer and I held it to his lips. He could not drink. It splashed from his mouth onto his tunic, onto the grass.

'John! Listen to me.' I strove for calm. 'We will get you home where you can rest.'

He could not speak, his breathing becoming more laboured. And then, with a cry of sheer agony, I felt the muscles in his body stiffen against the pain.

'What can we do?' I looked up, in momentary panic, at the huntsman who had come to kneel at my side. 'He cannot ride. You must return to the castle and fetch a wagon…'

His hand closed over my shoulder.

'Not now, my lady.'

'But we must. He cannot lie here…'

'Not now.'

And, at last hearing the words he would not speak, I looked down at John's face where I saw the inexorable shadows gathered there, the grey pall of death. I knew it as I smoothed my hand over his forehead, down his cheek. I knew that death stalked him, here in his own meadows, as well as I knew that I would still be alive on the morrow.

'Joanna…' he whispered on a long exhalation.

'I'm here. I'm here with you.'

And that was the end. No more, no less, his eyes empty and sightless, every muscle in his face still after that final breath. How could a man leave this life so fast, with so little tremor in the movement of the world around us? I could not accept what my mind told me. How could it be that this man, who had laughed with his children, who had ridden across his own land with such energy not moments ago, was no more than the lifeless clay to which we would all one day return? Yet here was the truth. The heart beneath my hand no longer beat.

John was dead. My dear John, with all his care and compassion, was dead. Of all my knowledge of tinctures and potions and salves, of the powerful value of herbs and plants, nothing would restore life to John's inert body. His bright sprit was gone.

I looked up at the faces around, all looking down at us with various qualities of curiosity or horror. Our servants who saw the truth. My children who still could not grasp the magnitude of what had happened. I found myself staring at my eldest son, at John's heir, who, at ten years old, was observing his father with some species of shock that had drained his young face of all its colour.

He was now Duke of Brittany, with all the nobility and authority dependent on that great inheritance. So young, so inexperienced, so lacking in knowledge of the world. He would never prove to his father that he could read and write. He would never win the promised goshawk. I saw the instinctive swallow in his thin neck. Perhaps it was being driven home for him at last as I stood and began to issue detailed instructions, dispatching two servants to fetch a carriage, for I was determined: John would not travel on that final journey home across the saddle of his horse. He would return home to his castle with grace.

So under my guidance John was lifted onto the bed of a wagon made seemly with a woollen coverlet, while I brushed the rime from his sleeves, combed my fingers through his hair and replaced his hat so that the jewels glimmered bravely. I closed his eyes with a gentle hand. Finally I ordered the placing of a cloth embroidered with even squares of gold and blue across his body; he would return with all the gravity of his heraldic symbols on his breast.

Remounting to follow in sad procession, seeing the residue of terror still imprinted on every line of my eldest son's face: 'Wait.'

And I took the hawk from the falconer onto my own wrist and held it out to John, my son.

'The goshawk is yours now. You will carry him home. Your father would want it. He would have given him to you.'

My son gulped but the tears dried and raising his arm he carried the hawk with great pride. It was well done.

Thus began the saddest journey of my life as I rode beside my husband's body. Such were my regrets: no final words to recall, no deathbed speech, no struggle to defeat the hand of death. No opportunity for me to tell him of my regard.

It had come so fast and without warning. He had lived for fifty-nine years, many of them difficult ones when he could not call his inheritance his own, then left this life as fast as a soft breath when falling asleep, just when his hold on Brittany was stronger than it had ever been and he should have been able to anticipate years of good government.

'It was his heart, my lady. I have seen such before. It can strike when least expected. He was a great man. It was a blessing that you were there with him.' Father Clement who had been advised and had ridden out with the wagon, pulled his mount to ride alongside. 'He loved you greatly, my lady.'

'Thank you. I know it.'

What more to say? I had lost the one person I considered to be my friend, who had given my life stability. Not a lover, although we had shared a bed with pleasure and obvious results, but a friend in whom I could trust. John had been courteous and affectionate. He had respect for me, the third of his wives. Never burdening me with the heady concept of love, he had treated me with a warmth and closeness that I could never have imagined. He had acknowledged my inexplicable feelings for Henry, without castigating me for disloyalty.

Could any husband deal with his wife with such sensitivity as John had dealt with me?

We had been wed for thirteen years and now it was over. I should have expected it perhaps, for he was no longer a young man, but I had not. His energies had not once waned, nor had his mind grown lax. I had, foolishly, thought my comfortable life would last for ever. Who would I talk with now, about the ambitions of the Duke of Orleans or the consequences of King Charles's fragile mind?

We made a sorry party as we rode through the arched gateway into the courtyard where news had gone out and the servants and household were gathering. Many wept openly. I did not. It behoved me to take command and set in motion the needs of the day. Accepting that it was my role to be strong where others were weak, my thoughts were crammed with detail that must be addressed until I forced them into ordered ranks. All attention was focused on me. I must thrust aside all distractions and concentrate on what must happen now.

My son was Duke of Brittany. But who would rule in his stead, until he was of an age to take on the mantle? Had John made provision? Surely there was a will that would make all clear. Maybe John had chosen the Duke of Burgundy, an obvious choice for many, a man of wide experience and reputation, yet I felt my lips tighten in distaste. I would not like his interference in Breton affairs and in the life of my son. Nor, I thought, would John. As for myself, I could not envisage my future, my role, in this state that had become mine through marriage, but no longer. Now it was under the authority of my son, however incongruous it seemed.

Mindful of this slide of power into such small and inexperienced hands, I took my son's shoulders in my grasp as he slid down from his horse. First steps. Small ones, but as a pattern for the future, entirely necessary.

'Go to our steward,' I ordered gently, taking the goshawk from him at last, seeing the panic leap into my son's eye.

'Where will he be, *maman*?'

'In the muniment room. If not, one of the servants will take you to him. Tell him that we need to meet with him in my solar, in an hour. We have couriers to send out. Can you do that?'

'Yes, *maman*.' He drew himself up another few inches. I would not dishonour his new dignity by straightening his hair or wiping the stain of tears from his cheeks. But as he turned away:

'You must not run. Not today. It is a stark and solemn day. You may run again tomorrow.'

He went. His first task as Duke of Brittany. And Arthur walked with him with such brotherly care it near broke my heart. It would take his mind from the horror of seeing his father drop from his saddle into death.

What of me?

I accompanied John's body to the chapel to ensure that all was seemly. Then stood in the antechamber where the iridescent light through the little windows gave the brilliance of jewels to every surface, patterning on my skirts. I must remember to order black mourning garb for the household. I was alone. For the first time in my life I was alone, under the jurisdiction of no one.

There was a freedom attached to that aloneness. Just as there was memory present in that room where so much and so little had been said. It would have been rank dishonesty in me to say that that there was not.

★

First things first. I sought out the Duke's man of law.

'Did my lord the Duke leave a will?'

'Indeed he did, my lady.' The clerk laid his hand, in his busy fashion, on a scroll he had already extricated from a coffer. 'I thought you would have need of it.'

'To whom has he give authority, during my son's minority?' Better to know sooner than later. 'Is it the Duke of Burgundy?'

'No, my lady.'

'The Duke of Berry?' I was surprised, and prayed that it was not my cousin of Orleans. I did not like his ambitions.

The lawyer was shaking his head. 'No, my lady. You misunderstand. My lord the Duke has left the power to yourself.' He smoothed the document, turning it so that I might read. 'You are named Regent during the young lord's minority.'

I stared at the words and the ducal seals, heavily impressed in the wax, that confirmed all, and as I did so, all thoughts of freedom drained away and a chill hand closed over my nape. I was Regent. The authority to govern in Brittany was my own, with no interference from Burgundy or Berry or Orleans. It was mine. A blessing? At least my role was now clear, sanctified by the law and the Duke's final wishes.

'Some might be astounded, my lady. That the Duke—the late Duke, I should say—should choose a woman...'

'They might.' I was brusque. 'I am not.'

For would not John see me as the best choice, the obvious choice to guide and guard his son?

It was in that moment that my decisions were made; my promise, to myself and to my son, as I shrugged off the cold sense of imprisonment. I would rule Brittany well. I would allow nothing that John had achieved to be destroyed by this death. Brittany would remain strong and secure under my hand. Had I not enough influential connections, in France, in Navarre, in Burgundy, to stand by me if I found myself in need? I would shoulder the burden myself, for that was my duty, my chosen path for the future, until my son was old enough to take his father's sword and armour as his own. Since John had seen the ability in me in naming me Regent, I would never denigrate his choice. I would stand at my son's side as he grew, to give advice, support, to instil courage. I would do it for John who was dead. For my son John who was alive. For my adoptive country that had taken me into its care and give me much happiness. As well as for my own pride.

Despite my female state, I would be a most effective Regent.

And the price that I must pay?

Here was no freedom.

The price was a heavy one, demanding that I brace my spine to take the weight, for I was no longer alone, under no man's jurisdiction. My life was now bound with invisible chains of duty and service, of honour and a true dedication to the role that John had assigned to me. I was not free. I would never be free until my son no longer needed me, taking his place amongst the rulers of Europe with confidence and authority. I walked to my solar, aware of the figure that strode beside me in the making of those decisions. The figure who had leapt into vivid, vital life in the many-hued light of the chapel's antechamber.

With no more than one thought of regret, I banished him. I drove him away. As well as the duty and service, my shoulders would bear the pain of that entirely necessary rejection too.

We sent off couriers that day, with letters written by our clerks, to France, to Navarre, to Burgundy. And because it was the diplomatic thing to do, I sent one to England too. It was not a personal letter.

Then I ordered black for my household.

★

The letter from England arrived on my table in my chamber of business. It took no longer than a dozen heartbeats to absorb the gist of it.

> To my most honoured and respected cousin,
> We can imagine your pain. Our thoughts are with you at this difficult time, and our prayers. We were remiss in our lack of communication in recent months, but we assure you of our compassion. We pray daily for your comfort and healing in your grief, as we know you have prayed for us in the past. We know that the future of Brittany is in good hands. We know that you will stand as our good friend, as you have in the past.
> Your cousin,
> Henry, King of England.
> Written at Eltham, on this date in March, in the year 1400.

And that was that. There was no need for me to read it again.

Disappointment welled up in me. I recalled Henry saying that when he wrote it would be of armies and finance and inheritance, but this was so impersonal it might have been written by a palace clerk. In fact, studying the hand that was tight and even, I thought that it was. It was not Henry's doing. It was the manner of condolence that might have been written as a diplomatic gesture to any ruler experiencing loss; or to an acquaintance, when a proposal to buy a high-blooded warhorse had fallen through, I thought savagely. This bleak notion of sympathy was not what my wayward heart had hoped for. I doubted that the signature scrawled at the bottom was his own, but then, I had never witnessed it.

I cast the letter aside.

No doubt one of my clerks could write a suitable reply, at some point in the coming days, from the exceedingly busy Duchess Joanna, Regent of Brittany. There was no urgency. No urgency at all.

Chapter 5

Spring 1400: Château at Vannes, Brittany

The heraldic device, gracing the inner court of my castle, was gold and red and silver, hanging limply on pennon and banner in the warm air. I did not know it.

'Who is it?' I asked my steward, viewing it at an angle from the window of the muniment chamber.

'A courier, come from England, my lady, so I am informed.'

'But a courier from whom?'

An occurrence unusual enough that I arranged to meet with this English visitor in the audience chamber. It would be a matter of trade, a mercantile dispute over some commodity or toll or shoal of herring. Anticipating an hour of tedious exchange of views on cloth and fish, I was already seated, clad in a cote-hardie, embroidered and jewelled and suitable to the occasion, my furred sleeves sweeping the floor to either side, when the man was announced. A member of the merchant elite perhaps, as he strode through the door, for he was not lacking in poise. Or perhaps a notary attached to one of their trading interests, although his garments and the livery of his escort suggested he was a man of some wealth. I would give him the time commensurate with the problem. It did not do to neglect matters of trade where the Bretons were concerned. So with two of my women and my steward to give the occasion the importance it deserved, I settled on the high-backed chair on the dais, arranging my skirts, folding my hands in my lap. At my side sat my son, the sixth Duke John of Brittany. It would be good experience for him.

The visitor approached to bow with a spare courtliness, awakening me to the fact that here was neither merchant nor notary. Tall, lean, long past the first bloom of youth certainly, but there was evidence of an active life in his upright stance, the firm flesh beneath his houppelande that fell in stately fashion to his calves. A soldier, I decided on closer inspection, now become a courtier, nearing perhaps his fiftieth year. When he swept off the velvet folds of his hat it was to show a mass of dark hair, well silvered.

'My Lord Thomas, Baron de Camoys,' my steward announced.

Lord Thomas de Camoys bowed again, not lacking some flamboyance, to me and to my son.

'I am grateful that you consent to receive me, my lady, my lord. I am come from my lord Henry, King of England.'

My folded hands tightened against each other. For as Lord Thomas de Camoys smiled his thanks, his eyes confidently on mine, I knew that this was no ordinary courier, but a very personal envoy from Henry. An ambassador, forsooth.

'Lord Thomas. We make you welcome.' I found myself returning the smile, for he was a very personable man, his air distinguished. So what had Henry to say to me? I felt a little beat of blood at my wrist.

'My lady,' Lord Thomas confirmed. 'I am here as envoy from my King. I am empowered to give you this, with his warmest regards.'

Stepping forward he handed over the folded square of a document, the royal seal vivid and untouched by travel. Lord Thomas had cared for it well. Perhaps I should have been more circumspect, waiting until I was alone to read it, but I could not wait, sliding my nail beneath the seal, but not before placing a warning hand on the shoulder of my son who had begun to shuffle. Then I began to read.

My first impression was that, once again, it was disappointingly brief. Preserving a magisterial expression, I read rapidly to the end, the beat in my blood subsiding into the dullness of dismay.

My dear and most honoured lady and cousin.

That was good of course. And at least this time I believed it to be in Henry's own hand. The uneven, hastily written letters were not those of a clerk.

My eye ran on, absorbing the comments, the requests, the hopes. My state of health. That of my children. Assurances that he would respond to any call for aid should I find myself in need. He was keeping me in his prayers. He was assured that the Holy Ghost would protect me in my hour of need.

All very good and proper. So why did despondency wash

over me in a cool wave, so that I was heavy with it? As a king newly come into his kingdom, to which his claim was not altogether clear, Henry would have serious matters on his mind. Writing to the Duchess of Brittany would not be a priority since our merchants, hampered by winter storms, were enjoying a period of truce. It was a foolish woman who dreamed of more from a man struggling to retain the throne he had just snatched from his royal cousin. A sensible woman would be grateful that he had found the time and the thought to write to her at all.

It did not assuage my regret that there was not more.

Rubbing my thumb over the signature, I folded the page with precision. I would read it again at my leisure, but I knew there was no hidden message to give substance to the first leap of hope when I had seen Lord Thomas holding out a letter. I stood with a brief smile, and gestured to my steward.

'My thanks, Lord Thomas. I will write my reply. We will of course make you comfortable meanwhile. My steward will accompany you to your accommodation. You will dine with us, I hope. Will you perhaps hunt later in the day with me and my children?'

I could not imagine why Henry would send so impressive a personage to deliver so unimpressive a message, but so he had and Lord Thomas deserved that I see to his comfort and entertainment before his departing. Lifting my heavy skirts, I stepped down from the dais and began to walk towards the door, my hand once more lightly on my son's shoulder.

'My lady.' Lord Thomas, straight as an arrow, neither acknowledged his dismissal nor moved one foot. 'I will be honoured to dine and hunt with you. But I have a private message to deliver to you, from my King.'

I paused, looked back over my shoulder, a little impatient. 'Indeed. I have read it, sir. And I will respond in due course.'

'It is not written, my lady. It was delivered by my King to me in person, and I must repeat it to you, if you will allow me the liberty of a private audience.'

His eye moved over my little son, and back to me.

A personal message. A private audience. The little throb began again, as well as the puzzlement.

'It is most delicate, my lady. A matter of greatest discretion,' he added as I continued to hesitate. 'For all of us.'

How persuasive. And how could I resist such an intriguing request? But it seemed that I too must be discreet, and so rose to the occasion, as any Regent would.

'A matter of alliances perhaps, Lord Thomas?'

'It is, my lady. To be negotiated with utmost secrecy, for the wellbeing of all concerned.'

'Then I must not disappoint your King.' I dismissed my women, my steward. And to Duke John: 'If you would instruct our chamberlain that we have a guest at our table tonight.' And as John departed, enthusiastic in his freedom: 'Come with me, if you please, Lord Thomas.'

I led the way to a private parlour where I arranged for wine and a platter of sweetmeats, and so we talked of his journey and the state of the roads, the length of his crossing, inconsequential affairs while the wine was poured into my favourite silver cups and my mind ran ahead to what he might say. What Henry might say. Meanwhile I watched Thomas de Camoys. Dignified and familiar with court affairs, there was no frivolity or flippancy in his manner. Certainly a soldier rather than a courtier. An interesting choice of envoy for Henry to make. Here might be a friend or a loyal comrade in arms despite the difference in years, rather than a royal official.

The beat in my blood quickened.

'Do you have a family, Lord Camoys?' I asked as the servant fussed with the fire that had burned low.

'I have a son, Richard,' he replied with obvious pride. 'And a newborn child, I expect, when I have returned. My wife Elizabeth was near her time.'

'You must have been sorry to leave her.'

'It was necessary, my lady.'

'I think you have been a soldier, sir.'

'I have been so, in my youth. I have served in France.'

At last, at last, the servant closed the door and we were alone.

'So, Lord Thomas.' I raised my cup in a little toast, that he returned. 'Now that we are private and supremely discreet, tell me what it is that your King will not commit to a written document.'

I saw him take a breath as if he were marshalling a text that he had committed to memory. He stood. Then he began, fluently, confidently.

'This is what I am to tell you, my lady. These are the words of my King. He would exchange opinions with you, my lady, on affairs of the utmost privacy. What cannot be read, cannot be discovered by others beyond this room. I am to tell you, my lady, that my King puts every confidence in my discretion. You are, he suggests, to treat my ears like the ears of King Henry himself.'

'Indeed, Lord Thomas.'

I admitted to being taken aback. This surely was no formal alliance between our two countries. Not that it would ever be possible as things stood, without considerable negotiation to hammer out the piracy menace in our respective ports. But was such a level of secrecy really necessary? I thought not. I frowned a little.

'I confess to some surprise. This is not, then, an exchange of views to engender an alliance of mutual satisfaction between England and Brittany,' I said.

'But yes, my lady, it most certainly is.' I suspected a gleam in the stern eye of Lord Thomas. 'My King has one particular alliance in mind.'

I waited.

'My King asks that you will consider the benefits of a marriage alliance.'

It should not have been a surprise. Henry had sons and daughters of marriageable age. As did I. He might consider looking across the sea to find a valuable connection for his heir. Who better than a child of Brittany, bringing with her the blood of France and Navarre. But I could not understand why such a proposition could not be addressed formally through a royal herald complete with trumpet blast, marriage documents and seals.

'Between our children?' I remarked. 'It would not be impossible, with careful negotiation to please the Breton merchants…'

'You misunderstand, my lady. The marriage would be between yourself and my King. Now that you are free to consider remarriage. After the sad death of Duke John.'

Placing my cup gently on the table at my side, I refused to allow my fingers to clasp hard into the damask of my skirts, even though my heart tripped like the tuck of a military drum. Through years of long practice I knew that my composure remained unaltered to any interested eye. No one would guess at the inner turmoil. I resisted the urge to recover the cup and take a long, slow mouthful of wine.

'Indeed?' I observed with exemplary restraint.

'Indeed, my lady.' Lord Thomas was unperturbed by what could well be interpreted as a lack of enthusiasm. 'My King recalls your meetings with him in the past, the pleasure you took in each other's company. He is of the opinion that you would not be averse to such a suggestion. And now that you are widowed, and the initial period of mourning over, he sends a formal request. My King has dispatched me to offer you his hand in marriage.'

Marriage. Marriage to the man I could not forget. The word hung in the air, with a weight all its own.

And how politely worded. I wondered if Henry had been so polite. When driven by ambition or injustice, as I knew, he could be as trenchant as a swordsman fighting to the death. Would desire for marriage so move him? I could imagine him issuing his orders to Lord Thomas; I want the Duchess for my wife. Tell her that she must wed me. I will arrange time and place. Leave her in no doubt of my sentiments. No circling round with flowery phrases or troubadour sentiments of honeyed nothings. Yet I smiled, enjoying my image of Henry striding through his antechambers, as sleek and powerful as the golden-crowned antelope on his heraldic achievements as he issued his orders, at the same time as I appreciated Lord

Thomas's diplomatic rendering. And seeing it, Lord Thomas, visibly relaxing, returned it.

'I can see that the offer is not an unpleasant one, my lady.'

'No, Lord Thomas. It is not.' But that was my heart speaking, and my mind was fast taking control, rearranging thoughts and impressions. The results were not good.

'Do I tell my King that you will consider his offer?'

The smile was gone.

'These are heavy matters, sir.' Abruptly I stood to walk to the window to look out over the river and meadows of my country by marriage, seeing it greening on hedge and tree, keeping my face turned from him so that he would not read my disappointment: 'Why did your King not come himself, with so important a consideration?'

There was no hesitation. 'My King is beleaguered, my lady.'

'So strongly beleaguered that he must embark on a proxy wooing?'

I turned to look at my proxy suitor, the light falling fully on his dignified figure, his eyes dark with some difficult level of understanding. I did not like what I thought might be pity in them. I did not appreciate pity.

'There has been insurrection, my lady. And with the recent unfortunate death of the late King Richard while incarcerated in Pontefract Castle, it is no time for my King to be absent from his realm, even for so crucial a visit as this.' And when I might have interrupted, 'I speak personally now, as I read the situation in England, my lady. It is the priority of my King to settle the realm into peace and firm rule. Yet still he thinks of you with such affection and respect that he would woo you, even from afar.'

It was a better reply than many. I directed my thoughts determinedly away from how King Richard might have died. It would merely cloud an already murky issue. So I nodded briskly. 'I will consider it carefully, Lord Thomas.'

'As must every woman in the land, my lady.'

I stared at him, unsure of his meaning, disturbed by the glint of what might have been humour in his face.

'My lady wife—Elizabeth—must always consider deeply every action she takes,' he explained. 'I meant no disrespect. This is an important decision for you to make. For you and for Brittany. I know that you will be aware of the difficulties such a marriage must face. As is my King.'

It unnerved me that he had read me so well.

'I think the difficulties, as you word it, Lord Thomas, might be insurmountable. We will speak again.'

★

How accurate his assessment. Once I came to terms with the fact that Henry had not come himself, no doubt with good enough reason, the difficulties began to multiply, much like the quantity of books in John's library.

Marriage. A second marriage. To King Henry the fourth of that name of England. Was there any reason why I should not? There was every reason in the world. They tumbled over me, to lie in a discouraging heap of impossibilities at my feet as soon as I was alone to consider. Surely Henry must be aware of how unfeasible it would be, for himself and for me.

Seated at my table where I read and signed documents every morning, I took a pen and wrote a reply to Henry, full of nothing but family and affection and prayers for his safety, as he had written to me. As blandly unexciting as a Lenten meal of salt fish and dried beans, expressing nothing of the terrible mix of longing and dismay that his offer had awoken. When there had been no possibility of such a union between us, I had tucked the notion away, as if with John's old legal texts, to be forgotten and gather dust. Now it was dragged into the open, shaken out, where it proceeded to run amok through my thoughts.

To cure myself of this nonsense, my polite little reply being complete and signed, I set myself to write a list of all the traps that opened up before me. And I suspected there were many more that I had not yet appreciated. I wrote them in a rapidly growing list, watching as all the obstacles fell into place, my hand strong and sure, even as my belly chilled, for as a denial of this marriage proposal, they were bone-crushingly brutal.

The Valois will never support such a union. They will oppose it tooth and nail. The Duke of Burgundy will use every means at his disposal to stop it.

I am Regent of Brittany. Who will rule in my stead?

Do I wish to renounce my authority in Brittany?

I have a duty to my son, to Brittany, imposed on me by John and willingly undertaken.

There is long-standing antipathy between English and Breton.

Would I be despised as an enemy Queen?

If I leave Brittany, what will happen…

My hand faltered at the last. There was one final cataclysmic consequence that I foresaw and that I could not write. That I did not have the capacity to even contemplate. It was far too distressing. Instead I read through each dismal objection to this marriage, each one more intimidating than the last, until, screwing up the page in my hands I tossed it into the fire where the costly parchment was consumed in a bright flame. Commit nothing to the written word, Henry had said, not even my fears. It was good advice, and fire would scour the longing from my mind.

Oh, but I wanted it. I wanted this marriage. If only this desire could be obliterated as consummately as the fire had reduced my concerns to formless ash. I wanted to know once again the physical enjoyment of Henry's nearness. I wanted to enjoy his quick mind, the skill of his hands on the lute. I wanted to play chess again with him, and capture his king on my own merits. I wanted the time to talk with him, for there was so much to this man I had yet to discover. More than anything, to my mortification, I wanted to enjoy the experience of his lips against mine.

I simply wanted to be with him.

But my mind continued to lurch from one insurmountable hurdle to the next, until I gave up on them and went to discover my children whose chatter would soon distract me. And we would go hunting with my surrogate wooer, Lord Thomas de Camoys.

★

We hunted, at a sedate pace, for all my children accompanied us except for Blanche at three years, but which proved to be no obstacle to Lord Thomas's enjoyment. What an equable temperament he had. Our ambling disturbed him not at all as he conversed companionably with my children.

'This is my land.' Duke John, with regrettable self-importance.

'And well governed, as I see.'

'I have a new pony.' Marguerite, eight years old, and shy but intent on drawing attention from her brothers.

'And you ride the pretty creature with grace, my lady.'

'I will be a knight when I am grown.' Richard, sturdy and ambitious.

'Perhaps you will come to me in England, to be a page in my household.'

At last turning for home, the children streaming ahead, with all the exuberance of unleashed hounds with servants and huntsmen in attendance, I was presented with an opportunity to uncover more.

'Does King Henry find time to hunt?'

'No, my lady. Unless it is the Scots.' Lord Thomas grunted a laugh. 'It colours his language frequently.'

I raised a brow in query.

And Lord Thomas complied. 'There is the prospect of war against the Scots if they will not come to terms. When I left England my King was at York. As he says, he has little time for anything but war and insurrection.'

'Is there much unrest?'

'There has been a threat against his life, and that of his sons.' He must have caught my expression, adding quickly, 'It was at Epiphany, but has since been diffused, my lady.'

Henry, in his brief note, had not told me of any dangers he might be facing. But then, why would he? Would I tell him all my concerns for Brittany and my family? We were both entirely self-sufficient and capable of managing our own affairs without interference from interested onlookers.

'Apart from bringing the Scots to heel, my King is also negotiating marriages for his two daughters.' Lord Thomas proceeded to enlighten me. 'Blanche it is hoped will wed the heir of the Holy Roman Emperor, a most advantageous match, and Philippa to the future King of Sweden. My King is aware of the importance of such dynastic alliances. Given the circumstances in which he acquired the Crown, he knows that he cannot afford to be complacent. It is imperative that he ties his family securely into a European entente.'

Such inconsequentially offered discourse. With such blighting consequences for me.

'I imagine it would be of great importance,' I managed. 'As is the marriage of my own children.' My mouth was dry, my lips stiff as I formed the words.

'The princesses are still very young, of course,' Lord Thomas continued, unaware that he was applying a second coat of pitch to my spirits. 'But daughters are very valuable. As you yourself know. And for my King, since the assassination attempts against him, the need for these alliances has become critical.'

'And has he wives in mind for his sons?' My voice was as smooth as my pleated hair beneath my veil, but my senses turbulent.

Lord Thomas waxed suitably eloquent. 'My King has hopes that Isabelle, Richard's widow, might make an acceptable bride for his heir, Prince Hal. She has a considerable dowry.' He noted my startled reaction. 'You may not have heard, Madam. Richard has died in Pontefract Castle.'

No, I had not heard, until Lord Thomas had so carelessly announced the bleak fact on the previous day. I noticed that my English companion made no explanation of Richard's sudden death, but my mind was preoccupied with our original conversation.

'Such a marriage between Isabelle and the Prince would bring him money and an enviable Valois connection.'

'So it would. A connection of far too great an importance to be overlooked. My King would be ill-advised to send Isabelle and her dowry back to her father.'

'Indeed. Now I understand why it should be so imperative for your King to seek a bride of his own.'

I marvelled at how level I could keep my observation, as flat as the marsh-grass through which our horses strode. And just as unemotional.

'Indeed.' Baron Camoys nodded in agreement. 'An obvious step to take, to seek a wife of rank and reputation. King Henry's appreciation of such affairs is second to none. I swear that he will achieve his desired goal, against all the odds.'

So innocently observed. The final nail in the coffin of my resurrected hopes and dreams. Did Baron de Camoys not realise what it was that he had imparted to me? I should have realised, as would any woman of intellect and experience. Thus does physical desire undermine political experience. In self-disgust, I used my heel against my mare's side.

'Let us ride on, Lord Thomas.'

I resisted his quizzical look. No, he had no inkling of what he had done. And I needed to think, long and hard, even though it did not make for comfortable thinking as the wind took my veil, pulling at it in spritely mood while

I snatched at its fullness to anchor it against my neck, all the time regretting that I had allowed my hopes to rise because of something so foolishly charming as a distant wooing. All was not as it seemed. How could I have ever thought that it was?

I had thought that Henry wanted me for his wife because he loved me for myself. Because he remembered the knitting of that strange bond between us. Because he believed there was a place for me in his life that no other woman could fill. Because he would play chess with me again and capture my king fair and square.

How wrong I had been. I had become simply a priceless piece in the mosaic of King Henry's strategy to place his new dynasty on the map of Europe, beyond assault. I had become the desirable Queen on the chessboard of King Henry's new political strategies.

★

'Good morning, Lord Thomas.'

Returned once more to the audience chamber, but this time alone, I stood on the dais in regal splendour and prepared to be gracious. It was not the dignified Baron de Camoys's fault. He would have no idea of the death blow he had dealt to my hopes. Now he was garbed in the wool and leather appropriate for travel, with no suspicion of what I would say. I handed over my innocuous and thoroughly dull reply to Henry's letter, which he took and stowed in the purse at his belt.

'Have you a response that I might take to my King, my lady?'

'I have, sir.' I did not even bring to mind the list I had compiled and destroyed. 'If you will be so good as to tell this to your King. I find that I cannot accept his offer. I am honoured, but I will not be his wife.'

A shadow of surprise crossed the weathered face, before being fast smoothed-over in the manner of an experienced diplomat.

'Do I say no more, my lady?'

'That is all that needs to be said,' I replied with hauteur.

Baron de Camoys undoubtedly deserved more, but how could I give my private doubts into the keeping of a man I had not known until a matter of hours ago? I would have told Henry. I would have been more than forthright with Henry. But he had found more pressing demands on his time.

Unfair, my conscience whispered.

But true, I replied. *I, in my own right, am not a priority in King Henry's schemes. He will find a new bride with more impressive credentials than mine.*

In response to my silence, Lord Thomas was regarding me with what I could only interpret as disapprobation. 'I have been given leave to answer your concerns, my lady, or carry them to England for my King to give his consideration. If that is what you would prefer.'

'It is not an alliance I wish to make, my lord. It is my personal decision, based on my own inclination. It is not a matter of high politics. You must thank your King and explain my regrets.'

Such was my dismissal of a once most desired proposal of marriage. Cool, calm, unmoved. Rejected out of hand, with no concessions to the baron's kindness.

'I regret that, my lady. Why can it not be done?' Lord Thomas asked the question as a friend would ask it. And reading I knew not what in my face he ignored my ducal trappings, took my hand in his and led me to step down from the dais before asking: 'Was it something I said? Have I said something to turn you against my King?'

'No.'

'But I think I must have been at fault. I understood that you were not averse to this match when first broached.'

I found myself sitting on the cushions of a window seat. With Lord Thomas sitting beside me, my hand still in his. And against all my intentions in how to conduct this brief little audience, I found myself replying as if he were indeed a friend.

'King Henry is intent on building a powerful dynasty. You indicated as much yesterday. I understand why it must be. A usurper can do no less.' I recalled the humiliation at the Valois Court, when Mary's hand was denied him because he had been declared traitor. Henry would remember it too, and be determined to do all in his power to rebuild his pride and his acceptability to the courts of Europe. Even little Isabelle, widowed but still in England, was to play a role in the scheme.

'Marriages are the surest way to consolidate connections and build a block of alliances to give a ruler strength and standing in diplomacy and discussion,' I continued as if instructing my own son in the role of European negotiation. Who would know better than I? Valois princesses had married into every royal family in Europe over the years. And acknowledging it, a cold hand closed even more firmly around my heart. If I asked outright, would this man tell me the truth? Yet I did not think I even needed him to do so. I knew it for myself. 'I accept that I would be the perfect consort for a man in King Henry's position. It would make absolute sense. With my son as Duke of Brittany and my brother as King of Navarre—and my first cousin as King of France of course—I would give him the connections he seeks.'

A narrow bar of colour appeared along Lord Thomas's cheekbones as I extricated my hand from his.

'I hope, my lady, I did not give the impression that King Henry is more interested in your blood line than your person.'

'Yes, Lord Thomas. You did. I appear to be part of a well-constructed plan. I do not wish to be part of a dynastic scheme for King Henry's aggrandisement.'

The colour darkened. Baron de Camoys's hands flexed where they rested on his thighs.

'I regret it. It is true that my King is aware of your value as a royal bride. As a princess of Navarre he knows that he could look no higher. As for your vast array of family connections to those who hold power…'

'As I have said,' I interrupted, as stern as my audience, standing briskly, any softness within me at an end. 'It seems I am to be part of a dynastic bulwark to give the King of England recognition.'

'But I would not say so. The King has considered no other European bride but you. Nor any who is English-born from one of our noble families. It was you he wanted.' Lord Thomas paused, also on his feet, considering how to add weight to his argument. 'My King gave you time to mourn Duke John.'

'A bare three months?'

'He thought it would be enough.'

'How do you know?'

'He has told me. Only then did he venture to ask for your hand. You must not pre-judge him, my lady. From my knowledge of King Henry, he sees you as far more value than a bride to bring him enhanced rank and acceptance.'

It was not flattering to see myself in a step on the road to European greatness, even though it was not new to me. As a wealthy, well-connected, powerful widow, I would be much sought after. Did I wish to remarry? I might with the right incentives. I had hoped Henry might have deeper motives, but I must accept that his purpose as King was very different from the day in my chapel when he spoke to me of love. You are loved, he had said. You are my most treasured delight.

Discarding those words, I walked to the door, my robes falling in heavy and expensive lines to the floor. Face calmly disposed, voice coldly authoritative, I knew exactly the impression I wished to give, and did so as I turned to give my final reply.

'You must tell your King that I am not able to gratify him with my acceptance. It is not in my power to do so. Nor in his to persuade me.'

There was no hint of the anger that all but consumed me as Baron de Camoys bowed his way from my presence.

I lingered at the window of my chamber, watching the English courier depart.

'Leave me.'

My women left, warned by my voice, obviously surprised by the raw tone that had crept in. As was I. Surprised and astonished at the anger of which I was capable. I who had rarely experienced anger in my life. Where was this heat born? Out of disappointment and regret, my newly sprouting hopes being shredded to destruction, like a flourishing bed of nettles beneath the peasant's scythe over in the meadows. My hands clenched into fists on the stone window-coping, and I hammered them against the chiselled decoration until my flesh complained. But it did not hurt as much as my hopes that had been dealt their death-blow. I would not be haggled over, like a prime salmon in a fishmonger's basket. Joanna of Navarre would be haggled over by no man. If Joanna of Navarre was to invite a second husband into her bed, he would be of her own choosing and for her own pleasure.

Which thought shocked me a little, until I considered the logic of it. Did I need a husband to enhance my status? To protect my country? To fill my coffers with gold and jewels? I needed none of these. With Brittany's alliances intact, I had no need of a royal husband to ride to my rescue, and I would not be a decorative element in the pattern of Henry's planning, to give pre-eminence to the new English monarchy.

My anger continued to hop and spit, fuelled further by an entirely superficial and unwarrantable irritation. As a prospective bride, was I not worthy of a fanfare, an embassy, an ambassador and a Lancaster herald? Was I not worthy of a finest kid document with seals and illuminated letters? If Henry was serious about marriage, I expected more. I expected more than Baron Thomas de Camoys, a baron of some status perhaps, but not one of the great magnates of England. He had come with no embassy, no fine-clad entourage to give Henry's offer weight. I, Duchess and Regent of Brittany, was worthy of more, and Henry of England must know it. Why must I consent to some secretive arrangement, whispered behind closed doors? My marriage should not be a matter of some conspiratorial negotiating, as if it had some nefarious purpose rather than the alliance between two rulers of esteem.

Pride. Beware the sin of pride, Joanna. Nothing good will come of it. You will regret what you have done today.

I would not regret it. I had wanted, in a selfish corner of my heart, to be desired for myself. Could I not wish for that, for the first, for the only time in my life, rather than for the value of my breeding and the vast spider's web of connection of my family?

It seemed that I could not.

★

'Baron de Camoys,' I said. Not exactly welcoming, some few weeks later. And with some surprise.

'Madam.'

I had not expected a return visit. Had my refusal not be sufficiently plain? I could well imagine Henry's displeasure at my rejection, but he was a pragmatic man and must accept it. I would be my own woman; I might have burnt my list of objections but the content remained true and fair in my mind.

Yet I admitted to my curiosity being engaged. What would my English courier have to say to me now? His return was very rapid. I doubted he had time to do more than repeat my refusal to his King before turning about and retracing his watery steps back to Brittany.

'I bid you good day, my lord.' I achieved a diplomatic smile.

I had just ridden in from the town to discover this English delegation, red and gold pennons once again aflutter.

Already dismounted, my courier approached to take hold of my bridle. But as he looked up into my face, although I read the grave courtesy with which I was familiar, a courtesy that not even my previous blunt refusal could shake, I thought he looked strained. More than strained. Perhaps the crossing had been stormy enough to dig the line between his brows. He deserved a welcome from me, even if I was wary.

'I see that you are in good health. Did you have time to visit your wife and new child?'

'I did, Madam.' He did not return my smile.

'I doubt she was pleased to lose you again so soon. I surmise that King Henry's desires were paramount.'

I slid from the mare to stand beside him. The lines engraved between nose and mouth seemed even heavier now that we were face to face. He opened his mouth as if to reply, then shut it and merely gave a curt bow of the head. My desire to know Henry's desires was pushed aside. There was sadness here, and this was far too public a place for me to encourage him to tell me.

'Come with me, Lord Thomas.'

Silently he followed me, through entrance hall and a succession of chambers and corridors, where I stopped only long enough to redirect a skipping Blanche towards her nursemaid, until we came to a small parlour, a favourite and private place that collected the spring sunshine and overlooked one of John's well-planted gardens. It always seemed to me a place where it was possible to find comfort. It seemed to me that Lord Thomas needed comfort.

Lord Thomas stood, waited, as servants came to divest us of outer garments, to leave wine. Shoulders braced, there was none of the warmth I recalled. Grief was written into every line of his body. Was this Henry's doing? Had he given a difficult message to be delivered?

Then the servants were gone.

'I see trouble in your face, sir.'

'A personal matter, my lady,' he rallied. 'I have a reply from my King.'

Rejecting my overture, he produced a written missive from the breast of his tunic and a small package wrapped in leather. The letter he gave to me, and I took it, tucking it into my sleeve. It could wait. And so could whatever it was that Henry had directed this man to say to me.

'Sit, Lord Thomas,' I commanded. 'Tell me what douses the fire in your eye. Is it the King?'

He remained standing, placing the package on a low coffer. 'No, Madam.'

An inkling came to me. 'Is it perhaps your wife?'

'Yes, Madam.'

'Was she not safely delivered of the child?'

'No, Madam. she was not. Elizabeth is dead. The child lives but my wife is dead.'

It was chilling, as was the unemotional delivery. 'I am sorry.'

Not knowing him well enough to commiserate—for what would I say to him, not knowing the terms of his marriage?—all I could do was offer a cup of wine. Pouring it myself, I urged him to sit, closing my hand over his shoulder where all the muscles were taut.

'Did you love her greatly, sir?'

If it was a true love match I might regret opening wounds, but I could not ignore the silently borne pain.

'It was not a love match, Madam, but we had an affection. It is a grief that stays with me.'

It touched my heart. I knew of such grief for John. Not lover but friend whom I missed more than I would have thought possible.

'Did you laugh together?' I asked.

He looked up, surprised perhaps at what might appear an inconsequential thought.

'Yes,' he replied.

'Then I do indeed understand.' He may not have loved her but he would miss her presence. 'But the child is strong?'

'Yes, Madam. A daughter. She is called Alice.' At last the glimmer of a smile touched the gaunt cheeks. So much sadness.

'And yet you came here to me?'

'King Henry's demands were urgent, my lady. I am his servant.'

And there was the return of the ambassadorial demeanour. And perhaps a glint of something else that caused a familiar jolt of concern. I had refused Henry's offer, giving no hope that I would ever reconsider. Now, it seemed I was to discover how he had reacted to being so summarily dismissed.

'Then tell me,' I said, taking a low stool opposite. 'Will I like what he has to say?'

'I doubt it. Plain speaking, Madam?'

'Plain speaking, Lord Thomas.'

'I think I must stand for this.' He rose, finished the wine in his cup and stood in the centre of the room, facing me.

'Are you quite comfortable, Lord Thomas?' He did not look it.

'I think it would be for the best. I am the messenger but the words and the tone are those of my King.' And he began.

The words were short, the delivery astonishingly abrupt. It was not Henry's usual manner, but it certainly was when his temper was roused. I listened, absorbing the words, the cadence of Lord Thomas's voice as he repeated what was unquestionably a furious complaint from the English King.

His ire, delivered by Lord Thomas, was superb.

'My lord the King bids me inform you that he did not receive your reply kindly. God's Blood! That you should consider him so lacking in grace and sensitivity, by offering marriage so soon after your own sad loss, wounds him deeply. He gave you time to grieve. If a mere four months seems too perfunctory, my lord gave you as much time as he dared. He considered that you might look higher for another husband if you thought him without interest in the matter. Your powerful Valois uncles and cousins might promote another more suitable match if he did not act precipitately.'

Lord Thomas took a breath. I doubted that Henry had. 'My lord the King considered it a case of now or never. If he gave you too little time to mourn, he apologises. Nor did he ever consider your value in a marriage because of the quality of your blood. He was d...' Lord Thomas drew in his breath and began again. 'My King was disturbed that you would consider him capable of this. My lord the King was very graphic on this point, Madam. He spoke at length. I was to tell you he is still desirous of a marriage with yourself, even if you are a prideful woman.'

Lord Thomas paused with a quizzical appraisal of me. 'Do I continue, Madam?'

By now I was on my feet.

'Certainly. I am agog.' Astonished at this tirade at my expense, I waved him to continue. Nothing loath, Lord Thomas picked up where he left off.

'Furthermore, Madam, my lord the King says that he is well aware of all the arguments you will probably produce to offset this union. He will voice every damned one of them. And give you an irrefutable answer for every damned one, that no woman of sense could ignore.'

'And did the lord your King use those exact sentiments?'

'He did indeed, my lady. And others.'

I did not know whether to be amused or affronted.

'I think you, and I, might need more wine, Lord Thomas.'

'I think I might. But I'll finish first, my lady, if it's all the same to you.'

I nodded.

'My lord the King knows that many would consider your two nations of England and Brittany to be enemies. War between France and England also hovers on the cusp. He understands the likelihood of French pressures on you to refuse any offer made from England. Such diplomatic pressures should not be allowed to persuade you. An alliance would be of vast benefit to both England and Brittany. You should put aside your pride and consider that.'

'Very true,' I managed as he drew breath. 'My Valois relatives would oppose such a match without a second thought. I imagine I would be deluged with advice and threats.'

'And your personal opinion, my lady?' He saw the surprise in my eye. 'My lord the King would wish to know.'

'Then you may tell him. For the Duchess of Brittany to jump into a marital bed with the King of England would be anathema.'

'The Duchess of Brittany might not so jump. But is it not the choice of yourself, Madam Joanna, to jump into a marital bed with whomsoever you wish?'

I stiffened, certainly affronted at such impertinence. 'Is that your King's observation, or your own, Lord Thomas?'

Lord Thomas's face was awash with bright colour. 'I would not so presume, my lady.' Henry, through his eloquent courier, continued to assault my ears. 'You are not a woman to give in to threats or persuasion against your better judgement. And particularly from France. So my lord the King would say.'

Affront returned threefold. 'Has Henry had the temerity to discuss this with you?'

'Yes, my lady. Henry said to tell you: Don't let them undermine your own wishes.'

And I noticed that formality had dropped away from Lord Thomas's delivery.

'How can I prevent them undermining my own wishes?'

'Henry says: It's a simple matter. Don't tell them.'

'Don't tell them? How could I not tell them?'

'As he will not tell the English parliament that he has in mind the Duchess of Brittany as his wife.'

Now I was astonished at how fast we had dropped into this political issue.

'What of your parliament?' I asked 'What would your parliament say when my ambassadors arrive in London to discuss the terms of my marriage?' I was shocked at how my thoughts were leaping ahead. 'What would Henry say to them?'

'He would say nothing to the point. He would welcome your ambassadors publically, discuss in private. He is under no compulsion to inform parliament of such private matters. He will say only as much as needs to be said.'

'Is then our proposed marriage as unpopular in England as it would be in Brittany?'

'There are some in England who will not support such a match.' For the first time Lord Thomas's eyes slid from mine to study the tiles at his feet. 'The trading interests are keen on both sides of the channel as you are aware. Henry urges that this should not be seen as a hindrance. Any opposition can be overcome. Your marriage could be a stepping stone to improving relationships between English and Bretons. All obstacles can be set aside. Does the Duchess of Brittany bow to the demands of anyone but herself?' The Baron de Camoys was regarding me again from under level brows.

'She might well bow to the demands of the Duke of Burgundy,' I said honestly.

'Your uncle.'

'And a powerful man.' I imagined him on my doorstep with hard words for me to hear. Had this exact point not been the first in my list of reasons why this alliance could never come to fruition? 'I might wilt like a rose under a hard frost.'

'Henry is of the opinion that you are made of sterner stuff. A hawk, he said. I assure you he does not see you as a frost-smitten rose. He is of the opinion that you will not allow the Duke of Burgundy to dictate to you in the name of your cousin of France.'

I thought about this. Unexpectedly I laughed. It sounded so simple. And it was not. The laughter died abruptly.

'And I will tell Henry,' Lord Thomas said, 'that his advice made you laugh. And laughter made you quite beautiful.'

My eyes flew to his.

'You were pale, my lady. Laughter becomes you.' It was no apology.

'I wish it were a matter to laugh about.'

For there were deep policies to be considered. I would not discuss them. I dare not discuss them. To do so would prove to me that I was actually considering this alteration in my state, when I knew I must not.

'Do you have a reply for my King, my lady?' We had reverted to formality again.

'Yes. Tell your King that I accept his apology. I will consider his forcefully worded views.'

How weak I sounded. But I could not leap into this. I would not be hounded.

'I should warn you that the King will not be satisfied.'

'I need no warning.' I felt my hackles rise. 'I am not a young girl to be swept off her feet by powerful argument other than her own.'

'My King ventured that such would be your reply. That any decision you took would be grave and well-considered. That is what he expects of you, my lady. And he has sent you this, to keep him in your mind. He says to tell you that it was once a gift to him from his father, the Duke of

Lancaster.' Lord Thomas retrieved and held out the strangely shaped package. 'King Henry treasures it and knows it will be in good hands in your keeping. He knows that you will use it well.'

Unable to resist, I unwrapped the gift from its thin leather covering, to discover there an engraved case that would hold a pen, and an inkhorn, silver gilt, created by a master craftsman who had smothered it with a riot of leaves and tendrils. Holding the ink horn to the light, I read the inscription. *God make us goode men.* It was as fine a piece of work as I had ever owned. It was certainly a measure of Henry's regard for me.

'It is beautiful. Will you tell your King? I too will treasure it.'

'And your reply, my lady?'

What did I want? I could not vacillate for ever. It was not in my temperament to do so. Smoothing the fine engraving with my fingers, I decided to open a door into my own heart.

'Give King Henry my thanks, Lord Thomas. And tell him…'

It was not easy at all. I was not given to exchanging confidences.

'My lady?'

'Tell the lord your King this. I will consider marrying again. But that all the arguments in the world are of no weight unless the heart is engaged.'

'They are rarely so between families of power, my lady.'

'As I know. But I am in the position of having a choice. I am under no compulsion, either from friends or family. As your King exhorts me, I will come to my own decision, and in its deciding I will take into the reckoning the state of my heart.'

I shivered at the depth of my honesty.

'King Henry says that it would be regretful if a woman of your quality lived alone for the rest of her life,' came back the reply, and I felt my brows rise at the scope of discussion of my person between these two men. 'But I will tell him of your sentiments.'

'What will he say?' I was suddenly more than curious.

'He'll say be damned to that, I expect. I will tell him. If you will accept my assertion, my King's heart is indeed engaged. He thinks you are a woman of immense courage.'

'But what of duty and service? What of loyalty?'

'They are for you to bear. Forgive my plain-speaking, my lady, and that of my King.'

'I forgive yours, Lord Thomas.'

If he noticed my omission of Henry's lack of grace, he made no comment. We moved, by common consent towards the door. Had we not said all there was to say?

'Will you stay and eat with us?' I invited.

'I am instructed to return with all speed. With your consent, my lady.'

I bowed my consent. 'But I fear that your King is destined to disappointment.' Lord Thomas's speech had presented Henry in full regal indignation, stunningly blasphemous and intemperate flow. The thought came to me that the King had never before been rejected by a woman in his enormously privileged life.

Until now.

Lord Thomas kissed my fingertips with punctilious courtesy. There was a gleam of appreciation in his sad eye.

'My King is well used to disappointment in his life, my lady. Disappointments and reverses, however, have never prevented him from achieving his ultimate desire.'

'Then perhaps this will be his first experience of it,' I replied, unsure whether to be hopeful or even more unsettled.

★

I was left alone to read the letter, Blanche discovering me and climbing into my lap, Marguerite also appearing to lean against my arm. Nothing here that I did not expect. Nothing committed to writing that could be considered dangerous. Was our union the subject of so much English hostility? I did not know. My eye travelled rapidly over Henry's commending me and my children to God's care. If this note fell into the wrong hands no one would possibly consider it to be a letter written by a man with more than familial concern in his heart or on his mind. Warm, affectionate, but no passion.

I dropped a kiss onto the linen coif of Marguerite and then of Blanche.

I would have liked a little passion.

Allowing the letter to fall onto my lap, it was snatched up by my youngest daughter, her interest caught by the ribboned seal, while I found myself speculating on the spot where Thomas de Camoys had stood to deliver his peroration.

It was as if Henry had peeked into my mind. He knew exactly which obstacles would cause me to stumble. In small part it was comforting that he should understand me so well: in major part it was infuriating, as if he had been overlooking my shoulder as I had listed my doubts. Delving into my sleeve, I extracted and examined the beautifully wrought pen case, a costly gift, suitable for one ruler to another, yet more intimate than a livery collar or jewelled hanap. This was a practical gift that I might use, every day. And so think of its giver, every day.

I frowned at the inkhorn, for Henry had discussed all my problems with his envoy, whereas I was not given to confidences. I was never one for gossip in my solar. Who knew where that would end?

And yet I knew that I could trust Thomas de Camoys with every word I had spoken, even touching on my thoughts of love. Perhaps he would return with some chivalric offering from Henry rather than a diatribe against my pride.

Perhaps I should return this costly gift, since I would not accept its giver.

But why will you not accept him, I asked in my silent ruffling of my daughter's unruly hair, escaping from her little coif? Why will you not accept what is offered, welcoming it, appreciating it as a true statement of Henry's love? I had had no doubt of his sincerity in the heated atmosphere of the jewel-bright chapel. But now I balked against that tantalising invitation, like a horse held on a tight rein, my thoughts running free and honestly, for time had passed me by and Henry absent from it. There was nothing like a distant perspective to give a woman a true evaluation of her position.

I rubbed my cheek against my daughter's, laughing as she shrugged me off, then quickly becoming sober as Henry intruded in my vision. For Henry was a man both provocative and seductive, attributes that could so easily hide his power. If I wed him I would, as in the manner of all wives, be putting myself under his dominion. Did I want that? For the first time in my life as the widowed Duchess I had a measure of independence to order my life as I wished, and to my satisfaction. I enjoyed the minutiae of day to day affairs, as well as the great moments of diplomacy. I enjoyed the authority that was mine and could be questioned by no one. Of course it was a finite responsibility; when my son came of age he would take the power himself, as it should be, but until then I ruled Brittany in my own name.

And there was the dilemma that surprised me by its strength. To marry Henry I must relinquish as least some of my powers in Brittany if not all. Would I have the same autonomy as Queen of England? I did not think so. It might be that I must accept a more ceremonial role, or at least must struggle for elements of my new life where I did more than wear a crown and ermine, a voiceless presence at my new husband's side. I realised that this was not an eventuality that I could relish.

Rescuing the inkhorn from Blanche's grasp when she showed signs of gnawing the intricate cap, I dislodged my children, shooing them from the room. Then it pleased me to fill the inkhorn and find a pen that would fit perfectly into the penholder. On a sheet of fine parchment, I began to write.

To my dear lord and cousin…

He had thought of all the worries I had, and swept them away with a forthright ease. Don't tell anyone. Do what you want. Make your own decision. But there were more personal considerations that could not be swept away. I doubted that they had crossed his mind.

I sighed and put the pen down, propping my chin on my fists. So Henry thought I had the courage to sweep everything before me. I wished he were here with me so that I might see him in the flesh. Hear him. Be encouraged by him. Thomas de Camoys was a worthy suitor, but he was not Henry. For a moment I let myself return to the day in the chapel at Nantes, where our hands were encompassed by the jewel-colours from the window. A hopeless love, we had admitted, then. To my mind it still was.

I considered the true dangers here, for it was without doubt an admission of Breton weakness that had dogged John all his days. Brittany had long been at the mercy of English and French ambitions, both competing powers perfectly willing to overrun and annexe this small state given any opportunity. After difficult early years in exile, John had steered a superbly diplomatic path between the two, achieving for Brittany a careful autonomy, but one that could so easily be compromised during a Regency. Was this not John's legacy to me? That I should hold Brittany in safety for our son? It would be the ultimate betrayal if I, through despicable self-interest, abandoning my charge here for the sake of trivial emotion, were to give France grounds for even the slightest interference. I would not sleep easily in my bed, and rightly so. This was the duty so firmly placed on my shoulder as Regent of Brittany. Heavy it might be, but I had the knowledge and the skill to carry it until my son had the years and experience to take it from me. My heart might quail at the height and breadth of the burden but I could not be deflected from lifting it by a personal yearning that I must have the pride to deny.

As I must deny it, even if my heart was wrung with pain.

Chapter 6

January 1402: Château of Vannes, Brittany

'I am come here, Joanna, to see your son, the Duke.'

A visitor. A visitor that was not Baron de Camoys.

The gold and blue of the banners and pennons, every inch of them heartily scattered with fleur-de-lys and recognisable from one end of Europe to the other, had heralded this arrival and my heart sank for I could read his demeanour by the set of his jaw as he strode into my home as if he owned it. The curve of his mouth was not one of goodwill. This was not destined to be an amenable meeting.

I braced myself.

'You are welcome, sir.' I awaited him in my own chamber, on my own territory, hastily donning a furred surcoat, a jewelled chain, an embroidered chaplet and a flowing veil. I had considered the suitability of my ducal coronet, holding it aloft to allow the winter sun to warm the old gold into fire, but then replaced it in its travelling coffer. I did not need such overt magnificence to face my uncle. I might be braced against his displeasure, but I was not of a mind to greet this powerful magnate with anything that might be interpreted as either an apology or a show of power.

'It is good of you to find time in your busy commitments to visit us.' My smile was insouciant, my manner deeply courteous. 'How kind. I am in good health, as you see.'

I extended my hand for him to salute.

Duke Philip of Burgundy, my mother's august and most powerful brother.

'Good, good.' He flushed a little as he restored my hand to me. 'I heard the children as I entered. I presume they are the same.'

I might have reminded him of the need for good manners, but not, I thought, for long. His grunt of refusal when, with impressive grace I offered wine, was not encouraging. Soldier, diplomat, strategist, a man of valour and opinion, earning the title Philip the Bold, he could be smiling and urbane. He could be outspoken to a fault. He could be as foul-mouthed as one of his ostlers.

Which would he be today? The years were beginning to take their toll, and not kindly as the bony Valois nose jutted, the chin lifted and he used his gloves to beat the dust from his sleeves.

'We will go to the practice ground.' I tucked my hand into his arm, an intimacy he reluctantly accepted. 'The Duke will be taking lessons in swordplay at this time of day.'

We descended to watch my sons exhibit the extent of their education to make them knights of renown. Duke

John, now growing strongly at twelve years, was developing a swagger more pronounced than his skill. I remained silent while Burgundy appraised with a stern eye. Burgundy must make his own moves here. There would be no help from me.

'John handles a sword well.'

'Indeed. Do you wish to see the girls? They will be at their lessons within.' I knew full well he did not. It pleased me to see at least a flicker of discomfiture in his staring eyes. 'It is a long journey merely to cast an avuncular eye over my son.'

'It's not my only reason.'

He turned to face me.

'So I thought.' I waited while Burgundy chewed his lower lip. I was not used to seeing him so hesitant. 'A matter of Court diplomacy, perhaps?'

Which unleashed the torrent.

'I am led to understand, Joanna, that there is a path well-worn between here and London. By the feet of English couriers. Is it true?'

'Indubitably.' I smiled thinly. 'My husband was always close to the Lancaster family, as you know. I have kept the connection. They have proved to be good friends.'

His dark-eyed glance skewered me unkindly. 'You would not be considering an inappropriate move, Joanna?'

'What would I possibly consider that was inappropriate?'

'Any connection with England would be denounced as folly by France.'

'Folly? My interest in the wellbeing of the new King of England will have no bearing on the strategies of France. Did you know, sir, that King Henry's children are similar in age to mine? We have much to discuss. I will show you the letters if you wish. I think the content highly appropriate from one ruler to another.'

He eyed me askance, mouth taut. So I had made him uncomfortable.

'Yes, Joanna. I think I do wish to read them. In the interests of European diplomacy.'

A little whisper of fear crept through my blood. I had not expected him to rise to my challenge. Affairs were more serious than I had thought.

'Do you not trust me, uncle?' I asked.

And not waiting for a reply, I walked before him, back into the castle, the whisper becoming a ripple of anger to heat my blood. Once there I made my way calmly up the staircase in the West Tower to my chamber of business where I took Henry's letters from a coffer and offered them without a word. By the time Burgundy had read through them, taking his time to discover any hidden nuances, I could not speak for fury that he should question my actions, demand to see my private correspondence. And I, Regent of Brittany.

Burgundy's glance became more and more perfunctory as he finished reading.

'Hmn. Friendly.'

'What did you expect?' I had my temper under control. When he handed the folded sheets back to me, and I returned them to the coffer, my hands were perfectly steady, but I knew that I had not yet won this battle. Burgundy was not used to being out-manoeuvred. 'You should know that I have replied to them, in similar tone. Do you wish to inspect anything else, sir? My records of rents and outgoings, perhaps?'

Oh, he knew I was angry.

'I am a man of experience,' he observed. 'I'll speak plain. You and the English King are both widowed. You have an acquaintance. Perhaps you found some level of pleasure in each other's company. What would be more natural than that you look for a marriage alliance?'

I raised my brows infinitesimally.

'And I have to tell you,' Burgundy continued, into the silence, 'it will not do.'

'I hope that you are not accusing me of indelicate behaviour during John's lifetime, sir.' I did not wait for a reply. 'I have not seen Henry of Lancaster since he returned to England, more than two years ago. This is the tone of the letters we exchange. Is this indelicate? If there is any policy between us, it is to negotiate an end to the disputes between our merchants. That is not indelicate. That is good policy and John would have approved.'

'If you were considering, my dear Joanna, a more personal arrangement...'

Now I raised my brows with less subtlety. 'If I receive a proposal of marriage, one which I intend to accept, I will of course inform you of it.'

Burgundy glowered. 'You are an attractive woman still. Your connections are worth their weight in gold to any man of high blood and ambition. I am not against your remarriage, Joanna.' And how condescending that was. 'But not with the English King. If you receive an offer from that quarter, you will decline it.'

'I will make my own decision.'

'So you have received a proposal.'

'I did not say that.'

'You don't have to. What are you thinking? How can you give even a minute's thought to an alliance more politically inept? If you must take a husband, take some well-connected man of rank who can come and live in Brittany while you fulfil your obligations. You are Regent of Brittany until your son is of age. How can you even consider a marriage with England?'

'So I remain a widow until my son is of an age to rule? How many years do you suppose will pass? Six? Ten?' My composure held firm. My blood seethed. 'Which man of rank will consider me a good prospect as a wife in ten years? When I will be past the age of his getting me with child.'

Rich colour rose to the roots of Burgundy's hair. 'Your language is surprisingly crude. It is your duty, Joanna, to remain here. To govern Brittany. To support the Bretons and France against English incursions. This is not the marriage for you. You do not leap into bed with the enemy.'

Which reminded me uncomfortably of my exchange of views with Thomas de Camoys. 'Leap into bed?' I observed. 'How salacious you make it sound.'

'You are flippant. Hear me, Joanna.' He leaned his hands on the desk before him, his whole posture threatening. 'If you go ahead with this, there will be repercussions you have not even considered.'

'Do you threaten me, uncle?'

'I do not threaten. But here's the truth of it. Are you willing to give up your position as Regent of Brittany? You are a woman who enjoys power. Then consider well. You will have little practical power as Queen of England other than the pre-eminence of the title. Marry Henry of England and your days as Regent here will be over.'

I could barely master a reply before he was continuing, his face raw with passion.

'Nor will you be a wealthy woman. Your income as Duchess of Brittany will be forfeit. Does your English husband realise this? That he would be taking on a penniless wife, with no dowry?'

'My dowry is within my own authority. It is not in your power to dispose of it.'

'Is it not?' Burgundy would not be distracted. 'If what we hear is true, the English King is deep in debt. He'll want a woman with a sizable portion to her name.'

I was lured into saying, 'If he wanted me as his wife, I think a dowry would not be important.'

'Then he would be a fool.' Pushing himself erect, Burgundy seized his gloves, slapping them hard against his hand as he strode to the door. 'If you try to undertake such a policy, I'll do all in my power to stop you.'

Could he? Could he stand in the way of my marriage to Henry, if that is what I decided to do? The anger within me remained, but was now interlaced with more complex emotions. Did I not know the form of retribution that Burgundy would take towards me? Still I remained obdurate in my challenge.

'I think there is nothing that you could do to stop me.'

Burgundy spun round, and smiled, a cold hard smile. 'If you go to England, you go alone.' The smile became wider, like the gape of a snake. 'If you go to Henry of England as his wife, I'll not let you take the children with you.'

There it was. Spoken aloud to give it a cruel reality. The one weapon that could be used against me that I had feared more than all the rest. That I had been unable to write when I acknowledged all the rest in that trite little list. It was a stone in my belly, a cold hand against my throat. A wrenching tear in my heart.

'You would not be so heartless.'

Could any man be so ruthless, so uncaring of the bond between me and my children? And yet I knew that Burgundy would do exactly as he threatened.

'I'll not have the Duke of Brittany raised in England at the English Court.'

'You cannot take them from me.'

'They stay here. They are Breton. They will not be raised in England. If you go ahead with this, say goodbye to your children, Joanna.'

I lifted my chin, silently defiant.

My uncle walked back, managing a softer tone. 'It is not my intention to be unfeeling. All I do is show you the reality of the future. You are an effective Regent, I'll give you that. And you have raised your children well. But this is the truth of what you must accept if you give in to this foolishness, this unacceptable lust. France forbids such a union. To stop you I'll strip you of your power and your children.'

'I will not accept such a judgement.' Here was desperation. 'I will appeal to King Charles against such monstrous dealings.'

And Burgundy had the temerity to sneer. 'King Charles will do exactly as I say.'

He waited for my reply. My denial or my anger. Which would have gained me nothing, for we both knew it to be true. The Duke of Burgundy held the reins of power in France, in my cousin's imbecility.

His hand was on the latch, his final words crisp and dry, stripped of all emotion. 'I have said all I wish to say. I had thought better of you. The Lancaster heir is not the rightful King. France considered him unsuitable as a husband for Mary of Berry; he is not suitable for you. You will put a stop to this nonsense.'

I remained anchored to the spot, hearing the rattle of horses' hooves as Burgundy and his escort left.

Was it foolishness? Was it lust?

All based on exchanged kisses and the light shining through our joined hands. All based on a longing that might be no more than my imagination. It might well be lust. After so long a separation I was no longer certain of anything. As for this interview, it had shaken me, even though I had always foreseen this particular outcome. I did not need Burgundy to tell me. And yet it drove it home like the point of a sword in the hands of a master of the craft. If I wed Henry I must accept the loss of my authority. And worse, far worse, I would lose my children.

Was that too high a price to pay?

I was afraid that it was. My heart and my mind were at war. Never had I felt so vulnerable as the foundations of my life shook.

Oh, Henry. What a cauldron of broth you have tipped me into.

At that moment I needed to be with my children.

★

Collecting Marguerite and Blanche, to their delight at being released from their lessons, I set them running before me, well wrapped in wool and furs against the cold, back to the practice yard. My sons had finished their sword-practice and were seated in a row on the floor, their breath white in the frosty air, enduring a lecture from their tutor.

'And you must not give up when you think you are tired, Master Richard! On the battlefield you are never tired. And you, Master Gilles, will never be a knight if you don't stand your ground when under attack.'

Gilles hung his head while John and Arthur smirked.

At my side my daughters chattered and giggled over a doll they had brought with them, until Marguerite snatched it for herself and Blanche wailed. Straight-backed, I watched and listened, the minutiae of family life going on around me as I settled my daughters with a reprimand for one and a mopping of tears for the other.

'I'm cold, *maman*,' Marguerite said, bottom lip thrust out.

'We will not stay long.'

Could I live without them? Could I allow them to become adult without seeing the effect of the passage of years? If I allowed the desire of my heart to speak out and be heard, what terrible cost it would be. Blanche still had to reach her fifth year, Richard only a year older. John might be growing fast towards manhood but Arthur and Gilles were still children. My uncle of Burgundy had laid it out for me like the map of a foreign campaign: if I crossed the sea to England, my children would not cross with me. I pulled my furs around my throat as my sons scrambled to their feet and ran to select bows and a handful of arrows. I could no longer procrastinate. Here was truth. Here before me was my present and future life.

A servant appeared at my shoulder. 'There is a delegation come from the town, my lady. They would speak with you about market tolls.'

'Later,' I said, summoning a smile of thanks. 'Give them food and wine in the small audience chamber. Tell them I will be with them in a half hour.'

And I would, however distracted I might be. For this was my duty. To Brittany. To John's people. I dug my fingers into the sable lining of my cloak, yet finding no comfort in its seductive warmth. Was love, love for a man I had not seen for so many passing seasons, and so ephemeral an emotion at best, suitable territory on which to base a marriage that would destroy all I held dear?

I forced my thoughts into calmer channels. I had not heard from Henry for some months now after my last rejection. The Baron de Camoys had found no further need to beat his path to my door. Perhaps after all Henry had seen the advantage of taking some aristocratic English woman as his wife, drawing some noble family into a strong alliance. His image of me as a desirable wife had doubtless faded. I could only assume that Henry had accepted my dismissal of his suit.

The passage of time could be a great healer. Two years could quickly become four and then ten. I would forget him, as he had forgotten me.

It was a bleak acceptance.

'*Maman!*' At my side, Marguerite pulled at my sleeve.

'One minute more,' I said, watching my sons as, with cries

of victory or derision, they loosed their arrows at the butts. It was as if they were aiming them at my heart.

'If you please, my lady.' Now it was Mistress Alicia, once my own nurse, now the guiding hand and stern mentor of my own children despite her advancing hers. Her tone was uncompromising. 'Marguerite has something to say to you. Your daughter has an admission to make.'

Which took my attention fast enough. I studied Marguerite on whose face guilt was suddenly writ large, and Mistress Alicia, who nodded in grim disapproval of her charge.

'What have you done?'

Marguerite studied the toes of her shoes as if she had never seen them before. Mistress Alicia nudged her, though gently. Whereupon my daughter drew from her sleeve an item that had been secreted there all along, and, without a word or a glance, held it out.

I took it, more intrigued than angry, for how important could it be? It was a little silken packet, roughly and inexpertly wrapped in its original leather cover. Some petty keepsake or fairing, fallen into her inquisitive hands.

But no, it was not.

'Delivered by courier last week, my lady,' Mistress Alicia announced so that my heart leapt at the unexpectedness of it. 'As Mistress Marguerite here has now admitted. When you were busy with the lengthy deputation from your brother the King of Navarre. She kept it. For which there will be dire retribution.'

'Come with me,' I said urgently, ushering daughters and Mistress Alicia inside, where I retired to my chamber with the silken packet that Marguerite had kept for her own enjoyment, teasing open a corner to examine the contents. I could not scold her, although Mistress Alicia undoubtedly would. The blue silk was too enticing.

It was from England. It was from Henry.

Alone, throat so dry that I could barely swallow, I released the little packet from its cover, the contents sliding flatly, seductively, beneath my fingers, until, opening the already frayed edge of the silk, a shower of gold fell onto my bed-covering. And I laughed with sheer delight as I scooped it up, allowing it to sift down again through my fingers. Of course Marguerite had been unable to resist.

A shower of golden forget-me-nots from Henry, spangles for a costly gown.

They were beautiful. They were magical in their significance.

I knew all about forget-me-nots, described with loving appreciation in one of my herbal records. I sought in my locked coffer, amongst my vast array of books on herbal lore, on cures and nostrums, on plants benign and dangerous in the hands of those without skill. Books that it was wise to keep locked away from prurient eyes. There I discovered what I wanted, searching through the pages as if they held the secret of my future happiness. Running my fingers once more through the glittering hoard of flowery sequins, I found and read the inscription.

There is a little flower called forget me not which will recommend itself to her who would be in joyous mood. It is worn by her who at no time wants to forget her love.

Was that not a perfect gift for a woman afflicted by inde-cisions too great to contemplate? When I had accepted that Henry had forgotten me, given up on me, he had not. This was a gift with much percipience in its giving. How it pleased me that he knew that I would understand the weight of this particular flower as an offering from a lover to a beloved. It was as precious a gift to me as any jewel-set collar, and I knew immediately what I must do. A length of silk damask in the richest shade of azure, a pair of shears and a needle and thread were soon discovered and the sequins stitched into a shining length, a girdle fit for a lover or a queen. Every stitch a lover's knot, anchoring me to Henry. Every snip of the shears severing me from my past.

And then, after I had dealt with the final gleaming flower, saving that last one for Marguerite for her own, within the silk packet I discovered the tiny note that had been tucked amongst the spangles. No larger than my palm. So small that no one would ever read it but myself.

Come, Joanna. I can wait no longer.

There it was, Henry's declaration, as clear as my reflection in my mirror. Neither, I decided, could I wait.

I sent for my uncle of Burgundy. I had an urgent nego-tiation to undertake.

*

'Blessed Virgin. If in your divine mercy you can see your way to bring me safe to dry land, I vow I will never again follow my own selfish desires. Holy Mother forgive me. It was probably a great sin.' I took a breath. 'But don't let me die now.'

The storm-winds shrieked in the rigging above my head like a soul in torment. When a gust stronger than the one before lashed my skirts tight against my body, my fingers of one hand, the one not clinging to the ship's bulwark, wound tight into the rosary at my waist. The carved beads dug into my palm, offering a different pain from the sharp grief in my heart.

'Holy Virgin protect me. Let my hopes not founder at this eleventh hour. Grant me courage, for I am in sore need.'

I breathed out the plea, silently I thought, except that the ghost of an amen from the man at my side caught my ear before the next blast and buffet whipped it away. Beneath my feet the planks heaved and bucked, forcing me now to hang on to the side with both hands, my nails sliding, tearing, catching in the wood. A deluge of seawater drenched me from head to foot. I shivered and chided myself for a fool in embarking on this voyage.

I had done it. For the first time in all the thirty years of my life I had followed the dictates of my heart. I had disobeyed my uncle of Burgundy, I had disobeyed the power of France. And at what cost? At what terrible cost?

'Holy Virgin forgive my abandoning my children.'

'Amen.'

The response gave me no comfort, for I had lost the battle with Burgundy. It had been a bleak little interlude that inscribed indelibly the consequences of my actions.

'Do you have no compassion?' I asked when Burgundy bent his frown upon me.

'None.'

'*I* have the maternal right to oversee the education of my children. *You* do not have the right to deny me. Even if John remains here in Brittany,' I was willing to compromise, 'the younger ones must accompany me.'

'It is not fitting, Joanna, that the sons of Brittany be raised in a potentially hostile state.' I forbore to point out that my husband had lived all his young life in England. 'In the name of King Charles of France, I will not relent. They do not go with you.'

No, there was no compassion in Burgundy. I admitted defeat, so that when I set sail for England, my sons, even Richard, so young and impressionable as he was, remained behind in Nantes. The memory of our leave-taking threatened to sweep over me, as bitter as the salt spray to my lips. They were stoical, not realising that my farewell was not a temporary one, for they had experience enough of my comings and goings. It was I who mourned their loss, that was sealed in Burgundy's fury.

I kissed them, bade them be obedient sons in memory of their brave father. I advised John to be a good Duke of Brittany. And throughout it all, I displayed no emotion, so that they were not unmanned. But my heart was wrung within me.

I would not think about it. Not now. Not yet.

My skirts wrapped their sodden length around my legs, yet could not quite dampen what I still considered to be a minor triumph. I had lost my sons, but for my daughters I had fought bitterly, using every armament I had against Burgundy, even tears, for which I was ashamed, And so he had relented, since I was as entrenched as he in the final outcome. Burgundy would stand guardian for my sons, but Marguerite and Blanche would come with me.

Here we were, being tossed like pebbles in a bucket in December, a month not known for easy travel. What a day to choose, with one of the worst storms of the winter looming. But I had been determined to sail. The new course of my future was set and I could postpone it no longer.

'You should not be out here, my lady.'

It took a shout for it to reach me, although my companion, the ever-stalwart Lord Thomas de Camoys, sent by Henry as escort, was barely an arm's length away.

'I know I shouldn't,' I mouthed back with a spike of irritation.

In a sudden moment of calm between one squall and the next, catching my breath I struggled to look back over my shoulder, pushing aside the hood from a borrowed cloak. As the ship wallowed and dipped, I could make out no outline, not even a smudge on the horizon. The die was cast, the shore of Brittany already hid in cloud and an oncoming torrent of rain. There was no going back for me now. But neither could I make out any fair haven before us. It was as if we were suspended in some grey miasma, without colour or form, without beginning or end.

'We are helpless,' I said.

It went unheard, or perhaps my companion had nothing to add. The oncoming squall hit us, drenching us, and I pulled the hood back over my hair and cowl, staggering as I did so, grateful for the hand that gripped my elbow through the folds.

'Hold firm, my lady.'

At least he did not chivvy me below again. Not like the young man now lurching across the deck towards me would do, displeasure clear on his face. He would assuredly take me to task with priestly authority, even though his clerical clothing had been packed away from the ravages of salt and water.

'You should be below, my lady. It is not fitting for you to be here.'

As I had thought. Thick set, confident, this young priest considered himself to be closer to God than I. Did he feel God's presence, even in this inferno of sound and motion?

'No, sir. Not yet...' I did not explain why I wished to prolong my discomfort. I did not have to explain.

'As you wish, my lady. I am at your service if you have need.' Henry Beaufort, Bishop of Lincoln, a man already climbing the ladder to political power, made a creditable attempt at a bow and abandoned me to my choice.

Was this deliberate policy by Henry? To ensure that I did not fall into doubt at the eleventh hour and step back from my venture, by sending his two Beaufort half-brothers, sons of Duchess Katherine, as well as Thomas Percy, Earl of Worcester, to bring me across the channel. If I need conviction that Henry was giving me an escort of impeccable lineage, this was it. John Beaufort, Duke of Somerset, who was suffering in his cabin, Bishop Henry who was impervious to discomfort, and the Earl of Worcester who was sheltering in sour mood in the shadow of the mast.

These Beauforts would be my new family, for me to come to know. And what would they think of me? I looked up at my companion through so many negotiations.

'The Bishop is always very proper. How old is he?'

The wind had eased again to make conversation possible.

'Twenty-seven years, give or take a day. But a more astute man I have yet to meet.'

'Does he approve of me? I can't tell.'

'Neither can I.' I caught the glimmer of a grin in the murk. Lord Thomas was unperturbed by our ambitious young cleric. 'And he's not saying. He's a skilled dissembler.'

I fixed Thomas de Camoys with a direct regard, which he returned, as I dropped into informality fitting for the occasion when we were both drenched and windblown.

'Have I made a terrible mistake, Thomas?'

'How can I say, my lady? It is made, and you are on your way. For better or worse.'

'I need reassurance, sir. Not a jaundiced view of the choices made by women.'

Seeing the grin spread again across the lines of experience, I was forced into my own smile, and then he replied, the words I had wanted to hear.

'My King thinks you have made the best possible choice. He will be waiting for you. For him you cannot come soon enough.'

Of course I had made the right decision, and with the making could look ahead to see my chosen path. As long as this vessel was not dragged beneath the waves, or driven onto the rocks of the English coast.

'Holy Virgin. Get me to dry land,' was all I could say, but I gripped Lord Thomas's wet hand in thanks. He had proved a better friend than my lengthy procrastination had sometimes deserved.

'The Virgin will not abandon you, my lady. My King will be praying too.'

In the end, stomach rebelling against the swell, I went below to Marguerite and Blanche, to take refuge in a cup of wine. The coastline of England had not come into view at all, the waves continued to batter at us, driving us in the direction of the wind's choosing, and the King might be praying for me but it was three years and more since I had last seen him. Three years and more since I had been married and widowed. Three years during which I had rejected the possibility of this union.

Yet now I stood on the threshold of a new life.

And here, with me, was the ultimate source of my assurance. Passing my empty cup to Marie de Parency, I struggled to kneel beside a small casket, and lifted the lid. The document, wrapped in leather against the damp, crackled under my hand, the edges of the Burgundian seals snapping. Carefully I returned it. I did not need to see the content to know the ultimate freedom it gave me. I had no need to re-read the agreement I had demanded from my uncle of Brittany who was now Regent for my son. The Duke might govern in my son's name, but never in the name of France or of Burgundy. My son's autonomy was guaranteed by my uncle's sworn oath, as here witnessed. I had done all I could to honour John's faith in my holding Brittany together, ensuring that there would be no French or Burgundian troops in the streets of Nantes, other than my uncle's ceremonial guard.

Enough of politics. Kneeling on the boards of this storm-tossed vessel I lifted from the coffer the cloth-protected girdle I had so painstakingly sewn with the forget-me-nots. What an eye Henry had for a gift for a woman who was far away and whose mood was unfathomable. The spangles gleamed softly against the rich blue of the silk in a shining skein, a gilded waterfall in the candles' flicker. It was beautiful, a true symbol of Henry's love, and his faith that I would have the strength to weather all storms, even this terrifying lashing of wind and rain, to be with him.

I replaced the girdle in its protection. It was done. No regrets. No turning back. I would wear it for my wedding, emblazoned with Henry's heraldic flower. For my second wedding. Was I not already wed in the eye of the church and the law? I had been wedded by proxy since April at a place called Eltham, where my representative Anthony Rhys stood beside Henry, taking the bridal role with all the aplomb of an experienced ducal ambassador. In the eyes of the law I was already a married woman, as witnessed by Rhys, the Beauforts and the powerful Percy aristocracy who had helped Henry to take the English throne.

Now, somewhere on the coast of England, Henry would be waiting for me.

Chapter 7

January 1403: Falmouth

'Where is the King?' I asked.

I had landed, but there was no embassy to greet me. There was no King either. No one even knew where the King was. There was nothing to welcome me but a little sea-washed village, a smattering of fishing boats—probably those that caused my Bretons so much damage—and a chorus of raucous gulls.

Our landfall had been precipitate, product of the whim of wind and storm-waves. This, I was told, was Falmouth, far to the west in the country called Cornwall and as Queen of England, although as yet uncrowned, I must learn that these pungent fishermen who doffed their caps in some astonishment at a woman who probably looked no better than a drowned rat, were now my concern. I must no longer think of the Bretons as my own. No longer Duchess of Brittany, I was Queen of England.

In the rustic inn that gave us temporary shelter, exhausted as we all were, I saw the girls put to bed with broth for their bellies, hot bricks for their feet and a good dose of tincture of pennyroyal, excellent for the lingering effects of *mal de mer*. While they fell into exhausted sleep as the very young can do, sleep was far from me. My restless body demanded action, my anticipation was stretched thin as the sole of a beggar's shoe, so although as hungry and cold as my daughters, I went in search of those who held my immediate future in their hands.

They did not take much finding, in the one room, redolent of smoke and sweat and the all-pervading stench of fish, that housed visitors of whatever rank. There, seated on rough stools around a much used wooden table, cups of ale and wine before them, garments steaming in the heat, was what appeared to be a Council of War. Thus the puissant nobles from Henry's Court in deep discussion. Their heads turned as one as I entered, inclined politely, before returning to the matter in hand, which I suspected was not primarily our progress towards London, but something of greater import. They would shut me out, merely informing me on the morrow of their decision, which was not a circumstance of which I had experience. Did they expect me to leave them to their deliberations and return to my own chamber, a self-effacing woman? If this was my immediate future under discussion, I would be part of it.

I took a stool beside the fire, disposed my wet skirts with a grimace, and listened.

'What do we do now?' Somerset asked, abandoning the previous discussion, deferring to Worcester.

'We could wait here.' The Earl of Worcester, Admiral and Steward of Henry's Household, emerged from his brooding to scowl. 'Until the King comes.' He was in no good mood.

'No point in that.' Bishop Henry forewent the deference to Worcester whatever his age and position. 'Henry was to meet Madam Joanna at Southampton.'

'So do we go there?' Worcester scowled harder. 'I say we should wait.'

By this time I was on my feet.

'How long will it take the King to meet up with us?' I interrupted.

Bishop Henry turned to look at me. Somerset studied the ale-rings on the table. Worcester, in his surprise, forgot to scowl. Lord Thomas did not quite hide a smile.

'It all depends on where he is now, Madam,' Worcester announced. 'He was intending to spend New Year at Windsor.'

My geographical knowledge of where exactly I was at that moment was vague, but what use in sitting here at Falmouth? And so I announced, 'Then we travel east, my lords. Surely the closer to London we are, the more likely the welcoming party is to trip over us somewhere on our route.'

They had not expected me to voice an opinion. Did English queens have no role in decision making, in royal counsels? Perhaps they were merely wary of me, not knowing me. When I was crowned and anointed Queen I would assume the role I expected. Indeed I would make my desires clear now to this dour steward I had inherited through marriage.

'I'm not sure that we should, my lady.' Worcester, scowl returned, rubbed his chin with his hand.

'But I am very certain of it, my lord.'

I allowed my gaze to rest on each one, returning ultimately to my lord of Worcester. Who, gracelessly, did not comply.

It was Bishop Henry who did. 'We go east tomorrow,' he agreed. 'We'll make contact somewhere.'

Which pleased me. And yet a blast of sheer panic, like the shower of hail that was beating against the windows, shook me with its force, making me turn to Lord Thomas as the impromptu council appeared to be preparing to depart to its bed.

'What is it, my lady?'

'I think I have forgotten what he looks like. Is that possible?'

How foolish it sounded. How immature. But I was losing my vision of him, so that it was becoming harder to call his features to mind. All I could see was an outline, a particular stance, a turn of his head. Even though I remembered tracing his features so that they would remain implanted in my imagination, time had robbed me of my certainty. Not all the golden spangles in the world could assuage this fear that he had become a stranger to me.

All I wanted, I acknowledged with a terrible honesty, was to get this meeting over and done with. To be reassured that I had not been mistaken. To be confident that I had directed my feet towards a future that would bring the happiness I had dreamed of. But as the days passed and we plodded east through cold and ice, my fear deepened with every step. I had given up all the safety and security of my existence, all the warmth of family and acknowledged status. And for what? A husband whose claim to the Crown he wore was still suspect. A King who would never be recognised as King by the Valois. A King who was hated by the Bretons simply for being English.

For a husband who was not present.

'What do I say to him?' I heard myself asking.

'You will see him soon. It has been a long journey for you.' And I knew Lord Thomas did not only mean the crossing of the sea. It had been an interminable journey, full of demons and dangers to be overcome. 'As for words—say what is in your heart. That's what he will want to hear, after all this time.'

Still hunched by the fire, Somerset and Worcester together with the Bishop were again in a deep conversation, so essentially furtive that it drew my attention.

'Is there a difficulty?' I asked.

'No, my lady.'

'I feel I am being cushioned from reality.'

'All will be resolved, my lady. Not long now, but you must exercise patience.'

'Why?' I almost asked. Lord Thomas too was keeping me in the dark.

'My King will be just as anxious to meet up with you, as you are with him.'

I looked at him, at the kind eyes, the nose once as straight as a blade, now bent by some past blow in battle, that for some reason reassured me.

'Thank you,' I said, sighing.

I was here in England at last where all would indeed be resolved. I would come to know that emotion that had surprised me by its power. It would still be there in Henry's heart, as it was in mine. I would experience the joy of it. When, that is, I had the fortune to cross Henry's path again.

★

Henry and I met on the side of the road in the environs of Exeter, in the midst of our joint escorts, with much milling and noise and the royal banners, bright and gilded against the grey. Not what I had envisaged, but they had been dreams, without substance. This was reality. Practicality. This was no lovers' tryst. How ridiculous the troubadours' songs of fervent meetings after long partings, of a passionate gaze and the heated caress as if the years of parting did not exist, and the lovers could pick up a conversation from where they had left off, so long ago. This, on the road to Exeter, was what happened when two persons of rank met in the depths of a late freezing January. We were both muffled in furs and wool from head to toe and my erstwhile lover was much occupied in conversation with his envoys. It surprised me that nerves shivered over my skin.

Greetings were exchanged. Handclasps between Henry and his brothers. With Worcester. With Lord Thomas.

'And not before time, my lord.'

I was too caught up in the moment to take note of Worcester's sour welcome, but I was to recall it later. Henry, I noticed, swept it aside, before indulging in some lengthy exchange of information that appeared to be crucial to Henry's late arrival, while his expression reflected nothing but a stern resolve over some matter of policy to which I was not privy. While I, throughout it all, sat on my weary mount and waited.

How long would I have to wait?

Until this vastly important affair of business, assuredly more important than I, was complete. It was a salutary lesson. Here was no lover to fling himself at my feet in a passion of long-envisaged rapprochement. Was that not what any woman would expect from her professed admirer? Yes, I did. I was unused to being reduced to waiting on the convenience of any man, even if he was King of England.

At last, at last, Henry manoeuvred his horse alongside mine. We faced each other. King of England meeting Duchess of Brittany. Husband and wife.

If I expected a cataclysmic thunderclap at the fulfilment of my destiny, I was mistaken. The world went on around us, the escorts eager to move on, a flock of some small finches flying up from the hedgerow with busy twitterings. I was cold and damp. Henry's face was ruddy beneath the dense velvet folds of his chaperon, his outer garments mired from hard travel. No blaze of sunshine thrust through the heavy cloud to highlight our meeting. No gentling of the stiff wind. This was as ordinary as any meeting could be.

'My lady.'

Henry took and raised my gloved fingers to his mouth.

'My lord.'

I inclined my head with due respect. Henry leaned to kiss my cheeks, lips cold, a brief and formal salute between distant royal cousins, inconvenienced by being on horseback. Our smiles were evident, but close-lipped, possibly frozen. Was there the same impact as I recalled when our eyes last acknowledged what we had, incontinently, dared to call love? The same sparkle in my blood, all the way to my fingertips? There was not, even though Henry kept my hand hard-clasped in his for longer than was strictly proper. The layers of leather made it entirely impersonal. The air dank around us, my cloak clammy against my throat, Henry swathed in cloak and hood and a fair amount of mud, we were observed by an audience of well-nigh thirty people.

No meat for my minstrels here.

I felt nothing. This man, this King, might have been a stranger to me, caught up in far more urgent affairs. Which I could understand, of course, for did not kings have heavy duties on their shoulders? But I was a bride, long in journeying. A most desirable one. And I experienced a sharp dismay, which deepened when Henry cast an eye over my entourage.

'By the Rood! Is this an invasion from Brittany? And a popinjay, by God!'

Was this a caustic observation on the impressive extent of my Breton household, male and female as well as the popinjay, that had travelled with me? I could get no sense of him, of the direction of his thoughts.

'I presumed that I had come to stay,' I heard myself reply with what I considered to be excusable acidity, born of weariness and frozen feet. And with a distinct lack of grace.

'I had presumed so too.'

Tilting his head at the chill in my voice, Henry released my hand before nudging his mount over to the travelling litter. 'And who have we here?' He twitched back the curtains, that had already been parted by curious occupants, to survey the girls and their nurse. 'You'll be pleased to see the end of this, mistress,' Henry acknowledged Mistress Alicia.

'Indeed we shall, my lord.' She was far more accommodating than I. 'All of us.'

Which I accepted, along with the quick glance in my direction, as the reprimand she had intended. But the dismay had transmuted into a real fear. If I felt nothing for Henry of England, had I given up all that meant most to me in life for nothing? Was this bleak emptiness all there was for me?

But Henry, aware only of two pairs of eyes fixed on him, bright beneath their hoods, looked over towards me. The girls were so weary their skin was translucent.

'I'd forgotten how young they were.'

'Ten years and five,' I said. 'This is Marguerite and Blanche. They have proved to be stalwart travellers, but in truth it has become wearying for them. The days are long.'

'And your sons?'

I shook my head. At that moment it was beyond my power to summon up a concise explanation that would not overset me. I was more weary than I had thought.

'I understand.' And so that I would not have to explain, with all the grace that had failed me, Henry turned back to my daughters. 'I knew just such tedious journeys when I was a boy. Let's see what we can do. Do you like music, Blanche?'

Blanche nodded.

Henry looked about, brows meeting as he considered, until he beckoned to a page, a young boy who made up part of his entourage.

'Let me borrow your pipe, Sim.' From where it was tucked

in the lad's belt, a little carved wooden pipe exchanged hands, and was passed into the confines of the litter.

'They have pastimes of their own.' I felt the need to defend myself. Were my children not well provided for?

'Ah, but this one has the interest of novelty,' Henry replied. 'You'll see.'

We were accompanied for the rest of the short journey into the town of Exeter by some un-tuneful renderings. It was the giggles that meant most. And then inevitably a raised querulous voice and the sound of a slap. The piping died an instant death. Which made Henry laugh.

'I remember that too! My great aunt, Lady Wake, who was ever present in my own childhood, had a short toleration of music.'

How understanding he had been. I felt humbled, and touched beyond words by his concern. But it was not love. An absence of three years had undoubtedly proved to be far too long to keep alive an affection that had barely been given time to be born. Any nurturing had been by Lord Thomas and our own ultimate determination to snatch a future together. But determination was not love. And that after all was why I was here in this foreign country with my feet numb with cold and no sensation of love anywhere within me.

★

Exeter welcomed us with cheering through the streets. Oh, for a tapestried chamber, a bed with a good mattress and candles that did not reek of tallow. I was used to a level of luxury that did not include smoking fires, damp coverlets, water still icy from the well, and fleas. The populace, well primed with news and with ale, was vocal enough to bring colour to my cheeks although I knew the cheers were more for Henry than for me, their future queen. A foreign queen at that. There was something I needed to know.

'Do they know I am Breton by marriage? And French by maternal birth? Will they approve of me?' I asked Henry who rode beside me, acknowledging the well-wishing. I was not naive enough to think I would be welcomed with open arms. Any liking would be of my own making in this insular land where foreigners were habitually suspect. It might not be the easiest of roads for me. It would interest me to hear Henry's view of his foreign wife, more enemy than ally.

'It remains to be seen. You may have to woo them.'

Henry tossed the brief comment lightly into my lap. So he foresaw a degree of hostility: a difficulty, but not beyond my solving. Then, as I was considering ways and means of a Breton duchess winning over recalcitrant subjects, and even perennially morose ones like my lord of Worcester, we were come to the Bishop's palace, where, as a guest, I had nothing to do but stand in the centre of the episcopal hall and once again wait for my husband by proxy to come to me.

It was here, surrounded by cold stone and clerical minions, that, to my relief, as I watched Henry, at last memories began to flow strongly as *this* action, and then *that* one, this gesture, that particular turn of his head, urged them into life. There was the same energy, the same air of command, the same proud authority in his lineage that he wore without realising it. And the same love of garments to impress. Beneath the mud-spattered cloak, his tunic was panelled and pleated in close-woven blue wool. His boots might be encrusted but were of the finest leather. His hood was jewelled with rubies, as was the linked chain that defined his shoulders. So little had changed from the Henry who had been disinherited and returned to right a great wrong. Or so I thought.

But then I saw the thumbprint of age as he dragged off his hood and ruffled his hair which was cropped shorter than I recalled, and there were lines between his brows that had not been permanent three years ago. Nor had there been the shadow of grooves running from nose to mouth that, in the moment that he turned his head, endowed him with a decidedly saturnine look. And yet again, as Henry moved about the room, ever restless, I saw the same lithe athlete I had known. I imagined he would be the same successful combatant today at the joust where he had made a reputation second to none. The years had laid no burden on him at all.

And yet he *was* changed, I decided, as he gave orders to his men, conversed with the Bishop, listened to the complaints of Worcester, then clipped his brother Somerset's arm with a bark of laughter. Sometimes his tongue was like a blackthorn, sharp, precise, excusing none, until it became as smooth as a honeyed warden pear, inviting friendship, offering clemency. There was, indeed, only one man who drew the eye in that room. Only one dominant power. In those three years and more he had grown into his rank and made it his own, an impressive figure, more than worthy of his father's shoes. Henry might not wear a royal coronet, but it was as if its distinction gleamed on his brow. If he was proud as Lancaster, he was doubly so now. Even when he bowed to kiss the Bishop of Exeter's ring, he was the imperious King of England in every word, every gesture.

How little I knew of this man who in the eye of the law was my husband. This was the man to whom I owed my loyalty and my obedience.

A guffaw of laughter took my notice. What was it that would make him laugh? I had no idea. There had been little laughter in our experience together. How would I reach out and touch this man who was a stranger? What would I say to him after the trivia of welcome? Moreover, what would he think of me after our years apart? Would I see disappointment in his eye?

Marie de Parency was hovering to remove and dispose of my cloak, my hood, my gloves, and in true female style, as I removed them, smoothing my own skirts, twitching the short veil that protected the rolled silk chaplet, into some sort of order, I wished I did not look so travel-worn for this first meeting. Henry was far finer than I.

At last, Henry bowed.

'Your chamber is arranged, Madam. Your daughters and their nurse are taken care of. And your household.' Henry's smile became a grin. 'Your nurse has confiscated the pipe, but I'm sure we can negotiate for its return tomorrow. For a little while at least.'

Negotiate.

Negotiation was a skill in which I had competency. Was that what we must do now? Negotiate a new relationship?

'I would be grateful for a few words in private, sir,' I said.

'I expected no less,' came the reply. 'In fact, to my mind

it is imperative. We have waited long enough on the needs of others.'

He took my hand and led me to an anteroom that was empty of people and much else, sparsely furnished except for a carved cupboard painted with a frieze of prim saints, a prie dieu and a crucifix, although it had to be said that the tapestries were very fine, if not what I would have chosen for this occasion with their vivid seraphic scenes, sufficient to uplift the senses with anticipation of heavenly joy after death. Perhaps it was a chamber used by the Bishop, whose rooms we had just commandeered, for his private devotions. There we stood at last.

When we had last met in this fashion, Henry had kissed me with some passion, and I him. Henry had spoken of love, nor had I been slow in my response. The air around us had been bright with our desire to be together, even as we acknowledged that it could never be. Now here we were, man and wife before the law. But no kisses here. No easy words. Nothing but a shaking quagmire beneath our feet. We stepped as carefully as ambassadors of a hostile power, facing an unpredictable relationship.

'I should ask pardon for my late arrival,' Henry began.

'We were blown off course,' I explained unnecessarily.

'I was waiting at Farnham, expecting you to put in at Southampton. I raced west when I heard. Your couriers tracked me down.'

'Bishop Henry was certain they would.'

This was not the conversation I wanted. I wanted to know if he was gratified to see me here on English soil, if he had any reservations over this marriage upon which we had embarked in a fit of extravagance. I wanted to tell him that, although he might be assured, I was suddenly troubled by the finality of what I had done. What we had done. That I was not sure, and never would be unless we could revisit the past and all we had seemed to mean to each other. I needed to explain that I felt akin to the tapestry behind me. I seemed to be standing in a deep pit, steep-sided, with no angelic ladder to help me discover a path to paradise. What was worse, I had dug the pit myself.

I could not remember the passion that he had stirred in me.

Meanwhile, Henry was hunting for wine within the preserve of the painted saints. There was none, and since there were neither stools nor chairs for our use, Henry was soon standing in front of me again while the angelic throng rioted around us in their heavenly abode. But at least a cloak of honesty fell over us when Henry began to speak.

'I am finding it uncommonly difficult to initiate a conversation with you, Madam Joanna, despite the fact that you are by law my wife. Once, as I recall, I kissed you and pledged you my love until the day of my death. And you, Madam Joanna, were quick to kiss me and tell me that my love was returned in equal part.' A smile gleamed in his eye although his face remained severe. 'How is it that we have nothing to say to each other now?'

My lips parted to reply. Then closed. How disconcerting.

I could negotiate a treaty with this man. I could discuss the strengths and weaknesses of royal finances. I could certainly explain the intricacies of French policies, their search for power and ambitions to acquire more land. I could oversee and explain the state of domestic expenditure in a royal household. I could even begin negotiations for a royal marriage. I could be obedient and dutiful, supportive and loyal, forthright and well-informed, sure of my power; reliable for all those tasks a royal husband might ask of his wife, a superb helpmeet. I had done all of those things, been all of those things. I could do them all again.

But love? How could I talk of love? I had no experience of it.

'Are you well?' he asked as if he feared that my silence might be a remnant of *mal de mer.*

'I am, sir. And you?'

Holy Virgin! My mind scrabbled to express all the feelings that I had believed were there, in my heart, in my mind. In a moment of inexplicable trepidation I felt I needed Lord Thomas to interpret between us. I had felt closer to Henry when the wooing had been in Lord Thomas's surprisingly eloquent hands. Facing the reality of Henry's glittering eminence, I was at a loss.

This was no good!

'Henry…' I said.

'Joanna…' he replied, eyes gleaming again with perhaps a little mischief.

'I need to say…'

Say what is in your heart.

'Tell me what it is you need to say. And I will tell you what is in my mind,' Henry invited. He was not tongue-tied, but then he had already married a woman he loved. He knew the rules of this game far better than I.

'What I wish to say, what I wish to know, is…'

A figure, stepping quietly into the shadow of the carved arch of the doorway, took my eye, stilled my tongue.

Do you still love me, Henry? Because I am floundering in the unknown. The words I would have spoken faded into the air around us as Henry gave his attention to his brother, Bishop Henry.

'Forgive the intrusion, Henry.' At least the Bishop acknowledged me with a little nod of his head. 'I understand how difficult this is. But do we go on tomorrow?'

'Yes, we do. We've no time to waste.'

'That's what I said. It's just that His Grace of Exeter is planning to bless your arrival and your union with the lady in a High Mass. If we are to escape, we need your authority. He won't accept mine.' Bishop Henry shrugged, in no manner discommoded. 'One day he will, but for now it has to come from the King's own mouth.'

'Tell the good bishop what the King's own mouth is saying.' How it pleased me to hear Henry's exasperation, much like my own. 'Tell his grace that I am in a delicate meeting with the Duchess of Brittany. With my wife. With whom I have not had conversation for more months than I can count.'

Bishop Henry's face had stilled. 'There is another matter, Henry.'

'Can it not wait?'

'It cannot. Owain Glyn Dwr can never wait.'

Momentarily a frown touched Henry's brow, the jewels on Henry's breast glinting as he moved fully to face his brother. 'Does it need to be addressed now?'

'I'm afraid so.'

'I'll come,' Henry said, and to me: 'Forgive me.'

'Of course. Is there a problem?'

'Nothing that need give you concern.'

'Who is Owain Glyn Dwr?'

This gentleman was swept aside, Henry's hand flaring with a ruby, deep crimson at its heart. 'Just a temporary Welsh thorn in my flesh. Nothing that will spoil our marriage.'

But I thought his smile was thin and I swallowed a sigh. So much for our intimate exchange of thoughts, ended before it had begun. It should not have surprised me, for was not a sovereign's life at the beck and call of others? Henry was a new king with an impression to make. Nor, clearly, was he ready to let me into his confidence. I prepared to follow Henry back into the Bishop's audience chamber where the easy conversation had, in our brief absence, become something of a heated exchange. But Henry, instead of moving forward, suddenly came to a halt in the doorway, half-turning towards me.

'I know you had a hard journey. My people told me of the dangers you had to face to come here. I would not have had that for the world. I had hoped for a good landing, and for me to be with you when you set foot on the shore of your future home. Instead it was all hardship and unpleasantness, although even Worcester admitted you were a most courageous traveller.'

'I was well cared for.'

Henry's smile was wry. 'I can take no blame for the storms—I am not master of the waves—but I am sorry. Perhaps I should have postponed your coming until the spring and calmer seas. But I was in haste to meet with you again. I believed that you felt the same.' His chin tilted, eyes quizzical as he watched my reactions. His smile was quite gone. 'How hard it must have been for you, leaving your sons behind. I presume that was the King of France's doing?'

For the first time we were touching on personal matters.

'Yes, through my uncle of Burgundy. I was warned what would happen.'

'You know of course that it was indirectly an attack against me. A malicious ploy, to threaten you and so prevent your alliance with a man France sees as an enemy and a foul usurper. France will not enjoy the prospect of any formal alliance between England and Brittany.'

'Yes. I know it.' I could not deny it. 'My uncle of Burgundy did not think I would risk so much to come here to you.'

Henry took a step back into the room.

'Why did you not tell me? Why did you not tell me that such abhorrent pressure was being placed on you? It was not right that you should carry such a burden alone.'

A little warmth stole into my heart, that he should care, but I kept my reply businesslike, because that is what he wanted. 'Because the decision had to be mine. It would have been unjust to shuffle Burgundy's threats onto your shoulders, however willing they might be to take the burden.'

'A woman of integrity.'

'I hope so.'

'How do I show my appreciation for such a sacrifice? To choose life here with me rather than the care of your sons. Many women would not. I admire your courage.'

It unlocked my words, his care for me, his ultimate compassion.

'I was anguished. But I have no regrets for being here. If I appear less than joyful, you must put the blame on the effects of the lamentable voyage.'

'An honest woman and a strong one too. I knew I had not been wrong in my judgement.'

So I had been lacking in grace at our meeting on the road. I felt heat rise in my face as I sought to find words to make reparation, yet in the end I had no need of them, because Henry, astonishingly, understood.

'Do you think I have no intimation of all you have been through?' he asked. 'You could not be more wrong. Thomas de Camoys has proved to be a man of remarkable intuition, who reported your trials with no bending of his damned knee to my royal dignity. I know you have had no one to lean on. Now I give you permission to lean on me.' And he was striding back across the room, gripping my hands in his, clasping them together within the calloused shelter of his own. He kissed one cheek and then the other, then my lips. 'There is my promise for the future, superficial as it must be. Now I must deal with this matter of Glyn Dwr before my brother returns to drag me away.' He re-covered the ground to the door at a lope, before looking back over his shoulder. 'You are far more beautiful than Ambassador Rhys who stood as your proxy. We will make a magnificent union of it.' His smile was intoxicating, like a cup of hippocras on a winter's morn. Before it vanished as fast as it had appeared. 'I could have lost you to the storms before I had even found you again.'

Alone again, I watched as Henry departed to inform the Bishop of Exeter that his offer of a Mass was kind but not necessary, before addressing himself to his counsellors and knights who were still in hard discussion. Henry was not smiling now. It worried me that there were pressures on him of which I was not aware. But I would remedy that, as I would seduce the fractious English.

'I could have lost you to the storms before I had even found you again.'

Henry could never have known how important that declamation was to me. I would prove to be a good wife and an effective queen. Henry would, in his own good time, enlighten me as to the importance of this man Owain Glyn Dwr. And perhaps Henry would even find the time, and the inclination, to kiss me again. It might be that I would rediscover that moment of pure mystical happiness in the chapel at Nantes that had evaded me ever since.

★

'Where are we going now?' I asked, barely able to catch my breath.

Our royal party made its way, in a rush now, from west to east, through Bridport and on to Salisbury, where I managed another brief, almost private, conversation with Henry. A matter of minutes. Would our life together always be like this, with demands on his time and his ear, battering at him from every side? It had been difficult to get him alone to any degree, even though I considered myself to be mistress of manoeuvrings and organisation.

'Winchester,' Henry replied, reading a courier's delivery held in one hand, at the same time eating a mutton pasty grasped with the other, liberally spreading crumbs that were pounced on by the dark-brindled greyhound that frequented

Henry's heels. Nothing regal or imperious about him this morning. I had forgone the pasty.

'Winchester,' I said. I had expected London. Were not royal marriages performed by the Archbishop of Canterbury with all the sacred majesty and soaring arches of Westminster Abbey to give appropriate verisimilitude? That much I knew. It was certainly what I was expecting. As a Valois princess it was my due.

Henry heard my hesitation. He finished the pasty with a quick chew, licked his fingers and thrust the letter into his belt.

'We will be wed at Winchester. I have a debt to pay to Bishop Wykeham.'

'A debt?'

His smile was magnificently enigmatic. 'I wouldn't be where I am today without him. We will honour him with our presence. And now I need to give some instructions to my ever-glowering and dissatisfied lord of Worcester...'

It was clear that he did not intend to say more about the debt, or the instructions, whatever they might be. I was left watching his retreating figure, catching a brisk list of orders being delivered. I was left to ponder my situation. Once again Henry was walking away from me while I was being kept in the dark, growing darker by the minute.

When I wed John of Brittany, and I a young girl under the dominion of my father, it was an occasion of much rejoicing and expense, an opportunity for the aristocracy of Navarre and France to join with their Breton relatives, all encased in gold and jewels and damasked satin. I had been young and overawed, even anxious of an event that had not been my choice. My father's will had been my law. This marriage in England was my choice, at my behest, yet still I was anxious, now that the moment had arrived, when I had not thought I would be so. How could I be anxious about an event I had striven so hard to encompass? But would this place Winchester be sufficient for a royal wedding? My haphazard arrival gave me no intimation that it would have suitable grandeur.

Perhaps Henry was aware of my concerns for, having dispatched a squire to ride on ahead, he returned to where I still stood and continued as if there had been no interruption.

'Then, when we are wed, we will go to London and you will be crowned at Westminster.' He was still brushing crumbs from his sleeve. 'There you will receive all due consideration as a princess of the Valois blood.'

There was an astringency in that final observation, in the sharp glance. So Henry had noted my disapprobation at being escorted with no more ceremony than an item of luggage.

'I have no doubt of it, my lord,' I said with praiseworthy composure.

Oh, but I had. Too many doubts, as we were given orders to mount. I felt that I was part of a campaign in which I was not a priority. A situation that I might accept, if someone took the time to inform me. Henry rode off.

'The King is preoccupied, my lady,' Lord Thomas observed at my side. 'It is not an easy time for him.' Now why did I feel that he had been ordered to keep me company? He made, as ever, an eloquent apologist for my absent husband.

'I had noticed it.' A little flame of temper flickered in the grey morning. 'Perhaps you would explain to me why we are in such a hurry.' I turned my head to look directly at him.

For a moment Lord Thomas looked like a hunted man,

then came up with: 'Perhaps because our King cannot wait to make so beautiful a woman as yourself his wife, my lady.'

'Base flattery, my lord,' I replied briskly, without compassion for my companion who had coloured to the roots of his hair. 'All I know is that there are events pressing on us that no one is speaking of in my hearing. Including you, Lord Thomas. Are there untold difficulties in this kingdom?'

'No difficulties that cannot be solved, my lady.'

I turned a direct gaze on him. 'Is it to do with a man called Owain Glyn Dwr?' I saw the slightest widening of his eyes. 'Once you would tell me the truth, sir. Once I could depend on it.'

'Once I did.' Lord Thomas raised a hand in acknowledgement of the hit, abandoning subterfuge. 'Now you must ask the King, my lady.'

And I would. Oh, I would. As soon as the opportunity presented itself.

I felt that my life was running beyond my control, that my place in this new kingdom was on the periphery when I was used to being at the precise epicentre. In Brittany nothing was done without my knowledge or without my command. Here I had the strongest sensation, even though I had been in England for a matter of days, that I was being placed firmly into the role of obedient and decorative wife. I did not enjoy the sensation.

And what was it that was troubling Henry?

I would discover. As soon as I was married to him in the flesh.

Chapter 8

In the end it was so simply done, and yet with such magnificence. Here in Winchester I had my fanfare and heralds,
my celebration, all come to a glittering completion under
Henry's command. It was as if the nave of the cathedral had
been newly rebuilt for this very occasion rather than as a
measure of Bishop Wykeham's ambitions, the stonework
glowing, drenched in candlelight, echoing with precise and
measured plainsong. The responses of the nuptial mass lifted
into the arches and tracery as if angels themselves had come
to bear witness to our union.

And the festive throng that came to Winchester to
welcome me had duly impressed me, for it outshone the
aristocratic witnesses in Brittany in every sphere. The heraldic
emblems were those of the highest in the land. The titles rang
with power and earthly rank as the banners of the aristocracy
shivered in the cold air. The jewels set in gold chains were
just as good. And the damask. If anything the fur of sable

and marten on sleeve and collar was even more sumptuous, although many still favoured the outdated vair and miniver.

'They've turned out in style.' Bishop Henry, gold and red vestments ashimmer, cast an eye over the congregation. 'Nothing like a marriage to bind families together. Although it wouldn't have surprised me if some here present had found an excuse to stay in their ancestral home with the drawbridge raised.' His tone was more than dry, his lips twisting at some ironic thought.

'Why would they not come?' I asked.

'It has not been an easy few years.' Inadvertently echoing Lord Thomas, he moved his shoulders, a frequent habit, the silk rippling along its length to the floor. 'Our quarrelsome and ambitious lords are here in full panoply. Where they'll be tomorrow, and what they might be wearing instead of this superfluity of silk, I could not foresee.' He frowned. 'I wish I could.' Then the frown was smoothed over. 'But this is a day of celebration and not one for considering how I might dissect the past or trying to predict whether they have weapons and armour packed in their coffers beneath their wives' embroidered linen.'

An interesting thought. 'I would not expect you to approve of a scrying glass,' I said. 'Or the use of any means to predict the future.'

'As a man of the church, I do not, of course. Nor should you admit to such questionable knowledge, my dear sister.' Sometimes Bishop Henry could be grandiose beyond his years. I thought he donned it along with his episcopal boots. 'But sometimes even a bishop must consider that it would be useful. Ah! Now we begin…'

Did no one speak what was in his mind? I felt like catching hold of Bishop Henry's jewel-plated chasuble as he moved to take his place in the procession that might eventually form, but by then I was too caught up in it all to worry about the significance of the content of aristocratic coffers. Henry, striking in a full-length houppelande of deepest blue embellished with fur and gold stitching, was encouraging two young boys in my direction: similar in age, on the edge of manhood but still growing into their limbs and strength, they were confident, well-drilled for the occasion, and lavishly clad as befitted their rank. The boys bowed and addressed me with creditable demeanour under their father's stern eye.

'My lady.'

'We welcome you to England, Madam.'

'Two of my sons,' Henry said. 'The younger pair. John and Humphrey. Hal and Thomas are otherwise engaged on royal business in Wales and Ireland.'

Smiling, I extended my hand. 'I am honoured to meet you at last. Your father has told me much of you.'

'Welcome, Madam Joanna,' John repeated gravely. 'We are here to celebrate with you.'

'And enjoy the feast after,' added Humphrey.

Henry bent on him a frown, but it was an indulgent one.

'They'll make themselves very useful in pointing out everyone you don't know. Which is more or less every man and woman here. But don't believe all they tell you. They listen in to conversations far too much than is good for them.'

The boys grinned, so that I saw the look of their father, before their faces fell quickly into solemn lines. And as they merged back into the throng, I was forced to swallow hard.

They were much of an age with my own eldest son whom I would have wanted with me on this auspicious day. I fixed a smile and turned to Henry, searching for an innocuous observation to mask the fact that my heart wept. 'They are handsome boys.'

In spite of my practised dissembling, Henry saw my distress, for he took my hands in his, notwithstanding the very public place, and spoke quietly, without any artifice at all.

'I cannot put it right for you, Joanna. But I can give you another family. It's not the same for you as your own sons, but they are fine boys and I know you'll enjoy them, and they will like you. And perhaps in the fullness of time, we will have our own son. Neither of us is beyond the age of creating another child.' He paused for a moment, his brow marred by a little frown that might have troubled me if he had not merely asked: 'Would that please you?'

So much offered in that one speech. Henry had seen my need and answered it with such deft kindness, and with that offer the love that I feared had died a sad, gradual little death from absence and neglect, all the physical desire that had seemed to grow faint, like an illuminated letter fading on a badly prepared manuscript, all returned with the force of the waves that had washed me ashore, and broke over my head. It had not even needed the intimacy of a kiss, only the knowledge that our minds could entwine and exist as one.

All I could do was answer his final question.

'Yes. Yes it would please me.'

A smile touched his face, warming the planes and the opaque depths of his eyes, and in them I read all the love I remembered, a love that was re-lit in me. He had offered me his own sons to fill the space, a little, in my heart. And one day we might indeed have a son of our own blood, of our own flesh. It meant more to me than any gift he had given me of gold or jewels that now adorned the bodice of my gown. Here was a depth of compassion I could only have guessed at, and all the remnant of murmurings of doubt in my heart melted away.

'Thank you,' I said. 'I will care for your sons as I would care for the sons of my own blood.'

Which did not express the emotion that wrapped around my heart, but it was enough. My love for Henry was no longer faint with barely a breath to give it life. I made my vows in the holy light of Winchester in good heart and in joy, confident as I gave myself and my future into the hands of Henry of England.

★

'Since we are two people experienced in the demands of marital harmony and the marriage bed, we will forgo your advice and your company, my lords.'

Henry's command to those who enjoyed our marital feast was softly given but there was no gainsaying it. So no ribald jests, not even an accompanying escort complete with minstrels and music, all waved aside as the last dishes were eaten and the fair cloths removed. Henry and I were man and wife, proxy replaced by the sacred words and holy blessing of Bishop Henry in the presence of God. Even that had been fitting, I thought, for us to be wed by Henry's brother, since Bishop Wykeham, far advanced into old age, was too ill to leave his rooms. We had feasted and danced, given gifts and drunk toasts. John and Humphrey had pointed out the English proud and high-born. But now…

We were alone.

And my breath was catching in my throat.

'Will anyone find a need to discuss some matter of royal policy with you before dawn?' I asked, not wholly in jest.

Henry was in process of barring and locking the door.

'Ha! You would hope not! I defy anyone to break that without a battering ram.' He looked round the bridal chamber. 'Bishop Wykeham lives in good style. No wonder he could come to my aid.'

'How?' I asked, remembering. I was interested. And it would fill a little time until the demands of the marital bed took precedence. I was astonishingly nervous. We were indeed experienced, but I was not so confident in the affairs of love. I still did not know what to say to this man that were not affairs of government or inheritance or discussion of the weather on the morrow.

Henry rubbed his fingers together in the age-old gesture of the usurer. 'Money. I was in dire need. But this is not the time to discuss high finance. Or my dire lack of it.' He began to unbuckle his sword belt. Then stopped, hands dropping to his side. 'In truth, I feel that I no longer know you, Joanna. I feel like a bad mummer who has forgotten his part in the play.'

'While I have never known a part in this play to forget,' I admitted. 'I do not know my lines. How do I speak of love?'

Henry growled a laugh as he completed the unbuckling, and handed the belt to me when I held out my hands. 'The last days haven't helped. I'm sorry.'

'Nor do I know you,' I admitted. 'Do you realise? It is three and a half years since we breathed the same air. Even then our knowledge of each other was little more than a shared kiss.' I too could laugh a little now, the tightness beneath my bodice loosening. 'I feel like a young bride, innocent and ignorant of the arts of love.' And then, when I had placed the sword across the coffer, I said because it was in my nature to meet a difficulty head-on: 'I don't know what to say to you. It makes me nervous. I don't like it.'

Not so, my memory whispered. He has given you his sons as your own family. You know he wants you here. And when you look at him your body acknowledges that he is no stranger to you.

'Why talk at all?' Henry replied. 'I could embrace you instead, until you are less nervous. There have been too few kisses.'

I stood motionless before him. 'I would like that.'

'And it will be my pleasure. Although I have to say that you do not appear nervous to me.'

Henry framed my face with his hands and bent his head until his lips brushed mine in the softest of salutes. 'Welcome to your new kingdom, Joanna. And to your new husband.' Then he kissed me again, his hands sliding from face to shoulders in a smooth caress, so that my lips warmed against his. His arms moved round me to hold me in the lightest of embraces, and I sighed with some pleasure.

A noise disturbed the stillness.

Abruptly, Henry lifted his head.

And any thought of pursuing the kisses was demolished by a thump, a flutter and squawk from the fireplace, followed by a sudden displacement of air, as with a clap of wings a bird circled the room. I flinched automatically. Henry swore, watching the creature as it came to land with a clumsy swoop onto the top of the ornate prie dieu, where it sat and rustled its feathers in a cloud of soot.

'Jackdaw,' Henry observed dispassionately.

'So I see. They fall down chimneys at Nantes too.'

He was smiling at me, stirring my heart with delight despite the rude interruption.

'Well, my wife, it seems our kiss must be postponed until we can deal with this domestic issue.'

'Don't send for the servants!' I said, sharp as a blade, imagining our privacy destroyed for another hour.

'Certainly not. Now if you stand out of the way by the bed…'

Henry would have pushed me to take cover but when the bird attempted another circuit, I shook my head.

'I'll help. What do we do?'

'Catch it. Unless you want it flying round the room all night.' The bird was back on its perch. Henry was inspecting me with a speculative air.

'What?'

'That might serve.'

I clutched my veil, instantly possessive. 'I'll not sacrifice this silk or the gold stitching for a jackdaw.'

'Pity. It would have been just the thing. Then we must…' He looked round, ducking as the bird took another fluttering pass across the room. 'Throw me that,' he ordered.

A small tapestry gracing the top of a coffer. Large enough for our purposes, small enough to manhandle. When the bird launched itself again, I seized the cloth and pulled, dislodging a silver bowl to clatter on the floor, together with an unlit candle, a rosary. And when the bird momentarily came to land, its claws caught in the bed hangings, I handed the cloth to Henry, who launched it and himself at the bird. Snatching up a coverlet from the bed I went to his aid, ultimately pinning the panicked creature to the floor, bundling it in the cloth.

Henry crouched, holding firm. 'Do I wring its neck?'

And, seeing the spread of his more than capable fingers, I thought he might. I had much to learn. A man who had challenged his King and forced him into surrender would not necessarily be a man of compassion towards an intrusive jackdaw.

'Death on our wedding day? It sounds a bad omen.' I grimaced a little. 'I've a better idea.'

Finding a window that unlatched, I pushed it wide, while Henry thrust both bird and cloth through it. The jackdaw flew away into the darkening sky. Henry leaned out to watch the tapestry fall in a heap to the ground below.

'Someone will explain it tomorrow I expect.' He closed and latched the window, a little breathless.

'You have soot on your cheek.'

'And hands.' He grimaced, trying not to wipe them on the glory of his wedding finery. 'Fortunately we have been provided with the means to wash.'

It was a homely scene as I poured water, tepid now, from ewer to basin and between us we put Henry's appearance and the chamber to rights.

'It looks as if we have just indulged in our first marital

spat.' Henry replaced the silver bowl and candlestick with neat precision. 'We know each other far better than many a newly wedded couple. Look how well we work together to dispatch the poor creature. How domestic we are after all.' He finished, folding the square of linen. 'Now where were we?'

His smile was an embrace. I returned it. 'You were welcoming me to England and claiming your marital rights to kiss me.'

'Then let us continue.'

Once again he framed my face with his hands, still a little damp, and kissed my lips.

'My sentiments, my dear Joanna, have changed in no manner since the day we stood in the chapel in Nantes and I told you that I loved you. I am now making up for lost time.'

And he kissed me again.

It was like a feather stroking over my heart, softening it, minute by minute.

'As I said that I loved you,' I replied when I was free to speak.

'I said that I would choose to wed you, if I could.'

'And now you have.'

I pressed my lips against his. Then laughed as a jackdaw feather floated down between us, from where it had been lodged in the roof beams.

So too did Henry laugh. 'Well, that's the tender bit over and done with. All we have to do now is fulfil the physical consummation—and then learn the good and bad about each other as fast as we can.'

'Is there bad?' I asked.

'Assuredly. Sometimes I have a chancy temper.'

'I know that. I heard it. When Richard disinherited you.'

'I can also, I am told by my family, be too domineering for my own good,' he continued. 'How could I be other than proud, raised by my father to know that the great Lancaster inheritance was mine?'

'So am I very proud,' I admitted.

'I know that too. Everything to do with your Valois antecedents, I expect. What else have you hidden from me?'

'I am of a managing disposition. I like my own way.'

'From past experience, I think I had guessed that.' Henry grinned.

'And I can be irritable when I don't get my own way.'

'Then I am well warned.'

By this time we were sitting on the edge of the bed, sharing a cup of wine that I had poured, the heady spices filling my senses, spiking my awareness of my surroundings that had come into clarity as if I were seeing everything with new eyes. Bed, tapestries, polished wood, prie dieu and crucifix, edges all sharply delineated. And Henry. I looked at him over the rim of the cup as I took a sip, seeing the candlelight fall across this features, highlighting the hollow of cheek, the flare of nostril, the impressive line of his nose. Furthermore I was suitably dazzled by the leaping gold leopards on the breast of the close-fitting white silk paltock that had been revealed after he stripped off his houppelande.

'I expect that as King you too have become used to managing affairs as you see fit,' I said.

Henry's glance sharpened as he took the cup from me.

'When I can. God's Blood, there are those who would do all in their power to hinder me.' He took a hearty swallow.

'But you will be victorious.'

'Oh, I will. Because to fail will mean this country—a country over which I now have a God-given duty of care—will be rent from top to bottom by war and violence.'

'But you will not fail.'

'It is still in the balance.'

How serious we had become, in the mere blink of an eye, as Henry drank again. There was a darkness in him, in his observations, which unsettled me, so that I felt moved to place my palm on his chest to absorb the steady beat of his heart as the exigency of the jackdaw was retreating. Which caused Henry to retreat from whatever malign image troubled him, to draw the back of his fingers lightly down my cheek, before linking them with mine, holding our hands thus lightly intertwined against his chest.

'Will we be compatible, do you suppose?' I asked.

'We'll make a good fist of it. I think we will argue.'

'Why?' I had rarely argued with John who had been of an amenable disposition.

'Because I suspect we are both as strong-willed as each other. We are both used to enjoying power. It will take a little time to come to know each other, so that the rough edges of conflict can be made smooth.'

What an imaginative way to look at it. And realising that he would understand, I decided to make a confession.

'When the seas were at their worst, when I thought we might founder, I thought that it might be God's punishment on me, and that we were never meant to be together because it was not God's will. It seemed to me that God would call me to account because I had abandoned my sons and my Regency of Brittany. I thought God might never bless me with happiness because I had placed this before my duty to others.'

What I could never have foreseen was the effect of my confession on Henry, whose brow promptly snapped with precision into a solid black line. My hand, still enclosed in his, felt the muscles of arm and chest tense.

'And would you also presume that God would see fit to punish me for Richard's untimely death by taking your life? Is that what you would say? Sometimes it is in my mind, that I must make recompense for Richard's end at Pontefract Castle.' His voice was suddenly raw, as if this was a debate that had troubled him often. His fingers tightened around mine like a vice. 'For a vengeful God to demand your life as the price for my sin would be the harshest punishment I could envisage.'

I moved my free hand to his sleeve. What maelstrom had I stirred here into life? It was like a storm-cloud suddenly appearing in a cloudless sky. Henry's hand covered mine where it rested, so hard that the rings dug into my flesh. Eyes wide and dark, he appeared to stare into my thoughts, as if he might find an answer there to the question he had proposed. So Richard's death was a shadow on his soul. I dare not ask his own part in the demise of the late King at Pontefract, from self-inflicted starvation, it was said. In the end I replied sharply. Anything to return us to the closeness that we had enjoyed.

'I would not presume to say any such thing, my lord. My

concerns were for my own sin of betrayal. How would I condemn you to God's judgement, in a matter of which I know nothing? I ask pardon, if it is needed.'

I felt the tension drain from him, as fast as a summer storm could dissipate, and he raised my hands to his lips.

'It is I who should ask pardon. Your coming here to me was right in every way, a fulfilment of what we had discovered in each other. You must believe that.'

And I breathed out slowly, for we were once more sailing with a fair wind and an even keel. The circumstances of Richard's death had been set aside, at least for now.

'I believe it. I believe it now. I am destined to be here with you.'

'I have always known what I wanted, since the day I heard that Duke John's death—God rest his soul—had freed you. I kept an image of you in my mind. To take out and hold.' Henry's smile was wry. 'Like a holy image.'

'I am no saint,' I admitted, still wary of that disconcerting change from light to dark.

'None of us is. What changed your mind? Was it my head-long dash across England to rescue you from Worcester's dour conversation? I swear the imprint of that saddle will be on my arse for the next decade.'

Which made me laugh, the irreverence of this man who was a soldier as well as a king, but I shook my head. I would not tell him why. It was a special moment that I would keep close in my heart. I did not think he would understand how important his gesture had been to me.

'What do we do tomorrow?' I asked instead.

'Tomorrow we go on to London. Your coronation in

Westminster Abbey is all arranged. Then, unless the news from…' He changed direction with a smoothness I might have been forgiven for missing. 'Then, fates and errant jackdaws permitting, I will take you on a tour of Kent, so that your new subjects can see you, and you can see them. But first there is tonight.' He stood, at the same time bringing me to my feet. 'We will disturb these fine sheets of Bishop Wykeham's and make our lawful marriage a physical one. If it please you, my lady.'

'It pleases me greatly. And since you have dispensed with my ladies in waiting—are you handy with laces?'

'Of course.'

Of course he would be. He had been married. A good marriage. A generous, loving marriage if all the tales were true, cemented when they were very young and only destroyed by Mary's untimely death. Which made me say, unusually sensitive for me perhaps, for I felt it was necessary to acknowledge what he had once had, and lost, and that I was too old and experienced in the ways of the world to be jealous of this poor dead girl.

'I am sorry that I am not Mary.'

His brows rose. 'So you are kind as well. It is nine years since Mary died. I loved her and I'll never lose her from my memory, but that was a different life. It pleases me that you are here in my arms, and eventually in my bed when I unfasten this obdurate sleeve, and that you are yourself. That you are Joanna. And now we've talked enough about past and future. Now is the present and it is all ours. We will make our own memories. To task, woman. Help me here. And then I'll help you. If we can dispatch a panicked jackdaw through a small window, we can unthread a lace or two. And more.'

What I saw in his face, in his steady regard, was all that I could wish for. There was the love, diamond-edged, diamond-bright. All I had longed for, yearned for, was confirmed as the candles burnt down and our love was expressed without words, simply in a long smiling acknowledgement of what had brought us together.

'I love you, Henry,' I whispered at last.

'I love you, Joanna.'

So long it had taken us, but we were where we wished to be. Henry's fingers interlinked themselves with mine and I knew I had truly come home.

Were we not experienced in what might pass between man and wife in a marriage bed? I knew the stretch of thigh against thigh, the slide of flesh against flesh, the joining and conjoining. I did not lack in confidence as I unpinned and folded the precious gold-stitched veil, no longer in fear for its life. But of this marriage bed I had no experience.

My knowledge was that of care at the hands of a man who came to my bed with calm respect. Henry came to my bed with passion and need. It burned in him. It set alight to my own. My experience was that of a brief fulfilment, one that did not always touch my senses or my needs. Henry had stamina in his athlete's body to rouse and rouse again a desire in me that complemented his own in fervour. My senses were subsumed in the wonder of it. I knew of the caress of affection. Henry's caresses were those of a conqueror who had waited long for this day. But I was not his conquest.

Rather we matched kisses and caresses until our energies were suffused with mutual delight.

'Disappointed?' I could feel Henry's confident smile against my hair as I rested against him.

'Only that it is finished,' I said, hiding my own smile.

'And who's to say that it is?'

Henry's hand travelled delicately over my hip, and I shivered.

No, it was not finished.

Whatever it was that troubled Henry was dispatched as ruthlessly as the jackdaw on that night. At last he slept deeply. It pleased me that I could give him peace of mind as well as pleasure, and that my husband would wish to remain at my side until dawn when he renewed his exploration of my body. Another gratifying experience, even more that the physical consequences of my years of childbearing, which I felt in all honour bound to confess, presuming that he had not noticed, did not undermine his appreciation of me.

'You are the prime jewel in my crown, Joanna. You are unblemished in my eyes.' Which glinted in the cold winter sunlight as he expressed a rare accolade, and not a little mild mockery. 'Do you doubt me? I think I have proved it well enough.'

I smoothed my hand over his nobly gained scars. 'You have proved it beyond all my imaginings,' I agreed, and sighed against his shoulder.

In the following days I would persuade him to tell me. Who was Owain Glyn Dwr? What was the issue with Richard's death that had left so heavy an imprint on him?

Tomorrow and tomorrow. For now my mind and heart

were at rest, all due to a man who loved me and had not given up on me. Now I must set myself to learn what manner of man this was, and return his love with my whole heart. Here was a new life, a new beginning, where we might, together, make of England a country of wealth and peace and greatness. It would be a new experience for me with the foundations of that life set firm in love. I admitted to a deep excitement as the new day beckoned.

Chapter 9

Summer 1403: Eltham Palace

The clerks scratched with their pens, the only sound to break the silence in the muniment room at Eltham Palace. Henry prowled in their midst as, soft-footed, I opened the door. It was the first time that I had explored this chamber and seen him at work since I had settled here with my two girls and Philippa, Henry's younger daughter; the elder, Blanche, was already wed to the Elector Palatine as part of Henry's dynastic plan and so beyond my jurisdiction. Since the three girls were much of an age and enjoying their own household, I was free to explore. So here I was in Henry's domain.

Although a man who had made his name in the tournament, in military campaigning or in the hazardous demands of a pilgrimage to the Holy Land, Henry looked every bit at home amongst the evidence of day to day business of the realm, the musty smell of parchment, the dancing dust motes that clouded the air. I could even imagine ink on his fingers, and might have smiled at the thought of the King of England writing his own receipts, except that I thought there was an abstraction about him. An imprint of concern as he read a document, rubbing the bridge of his nose with fist.

Henry looked up, his expression indubitably austere, but by now I knew the fire that burned beneath the restraint that guarded all his actions. His gaze touching on mine, the austerity broke and his face lit in a smile that relit the new, bright desire within me, that still had the power to amaze, to astonish.

'Joanna.' He redirected his prowl towards me. 'I hoped you would come.'

'You asked to see me, my lord.' More formal than he in the company of a half dozen scribes, more aware of my dignity. Intimacy was reserved for times when we were alone. But I too was smiling when he leaned to plant a kiss on my cheek. It was a sweet moment.

'And to your benefit, lady. I have documents for you to read.' Lightly snapping his fingers to the nearest clerk, who scurried, Henry took from him and handed to me the documents. Or at least two of them. The rest were in the coffer on the table, surrounded by other rolls and codices and letters in tidy piles. Henry, I had learned in the short time since my coronation, enjoyed organisation in his work. Everything was where he could put his hand to it. We were, I decided in a little leap of pleasure, much alike.

With a gesture from Henry, the clerks receded like a wave, making us a space.

'This is yours.' His hands closed around mine as I took the charters.

'Another gift?'

Because he had been up betimes to attend Mass before breaking his fast, a habit I had learned was the order of his day, I had not seen Henry that morning. Now here he was, slouching a little, close enough for me to touch if we had been alone, the lines of his face softened with pleasure. I could see myself reflected in his eyes, my hair tight braided, demurely covered with an embroidered veil, not flowing virgin-loose as it had at my coronation.

'Why did I not remember that my wife was so beautiful?' Henry had said before the ceremony, twitching a fall of my ermine cloak into place. 'Your hair is the colour of my favourite stallion. Or the polished wood of my lute.' For a moment he had wound his hand into the dense wood-dark mass of it, before restoring it to appropriate neatness, and leaving me to experience my coronation alone, as was my due.

It had been a glorious occasion when the sceptre was placed into my right hand, the gleaming sphere of the orb with its jewelled cross in my left. Such powerful symbols of my individual authority. Such a scene of personal achievement as finally the Crown was placed on my brow by Archbishop Arundel, Henry's closest friend who had accompanied him back from exile, and the superb Earl of Warwick, fighting as my own champion, defeated all comers in the festive tournament. A day of such satisfaction and joy, culminating in Henry formally presenting me to my new subjects.

'My beloved wife, Queen Joanna.'

The cheering as he introduced me to the crowd was gratifying.

But I would never wear my hair again unbound in public. Queens, after all, must observe appropriate gravity.

'Another gift,' Henry repeated now, interrupting my remembering. 'With less glitter than the gems you are wearing, but still of great value.'

My fingers toyed with the sapphires and pearls that garnished the amulet pinned to my bodice, but the heavy seals of the documents drew my attention strongly, informing me that these was of far greater importance to my new status as Queen than any jewel, no matter how valuable. I knew what it must be, had been anticipating it, and I would be interested to see exactly what value my new husband had placed on me as his consort. Returning one roll to Henry, I flattened the other under my hands, letting my eye scan down the page. It was new and soft under my fingertips, the ink barely dry.

I read. I had expected much, but not quite this.

'My dower,' I observed coolly at the end as if there was nothing of note. Nothing to shake me, with this evidence of Henry's regard for me.

'Your dower,' he repeated. 'Do you approve?'

'How can I not?'

For it was a quite magnificent sum. Quickly I read the salient points once again, of my value in Henry's eyes, knowing that it was more than flattering. The English Exchequer would pay to me the sum of ten thousand marks, every year, from the day of my marriage, until the lands that were given over to me raised the same sum in rents. Exchanging that roll for the second, I read the list of all the estates that would now be mine, to raise that sum of money requisite for my needs.

There they were, the manors of Woodstock and Langley, Havering-atte-Bower and Rockingham, together with the castles of Hertford and Leeds. All the traditional Queen's lands, as was my right, and so much more. Spreading throughout the length and breadth of the country, all in all it was quite breathtaking that such provision had been made for me. It was good to be appreciated, for my Valois and Navarrese connection to be recognised, acknowledged with a dower appropriate, and more, for any Queen in Christendom. With this money for my personal use, I would make an impressive consort for Henry. I would keep a household fit for my rank as I would entertain lavishly this English aristocracy I had yet to come to know. No one had better experience than I of the importance of outward display to keep restless nobility loyal to the Crown.

And was I not fit to sit in royal counsels? Henry had welcomed me with extraordinary generosity. Now I must repay him.

'A list fit for a Queen,' I said. 'How can I express my thanks?'

Henry restored both documents to me, at the same time as he took the opportunity to brush my palm with the tips of his fingers. I felt my skin flush, not merely with pleasure. Would I ever be as unaware of servants as an interested background audience as he? I supposed that I would learn, and soon fall into these English habits.

'I could hardly have my wife suffering dire poverty,' Henry was saying. 'You will need moneys for your household and your own needs.' His gaze held a flattering appreciation as he took in my garments. 'I dare say the robe you are wearing cost the rents from the manor of Geddington for at least a twelve-month. I cannot have you appearing at Court in rags.'

'Nor shall you,' I admitted, smoothing the hand not clutching the rolls over the extravagantly rich overlay of silk of my new houppelande. 'I am very fond of clothes.'

'I have noticed.' His smile faded, Henry stretching his shoulders as if to rid himself of some irritant. 'Before God, it took some getting. I've had to hold off a barrage of complaint from friend and foe alike.'

I did not entirely understand. 'Why?'

He took the rolls from me and held them both, one in each hand, as if weighing them, as if they were ingots of gold. 'My Exchequer considers you to be an extremely wealthy woman in your own right. And so in need of a mere gesture from the English public purse, rather than a dower of greater value than any previous English Queen.'

So Henry had indeed been generous. But: 'Wealthy?' I considered my Breton income as Dowager Duchess, suddenly unsure of my footing. 'I am not without funds,' I agreed. 'That is true. But I am by no means a wealthy woman.'

My uncle of Burgundy had failed in his bid to rob me of my dowry. I had come to England with my Breton rent rolls intact.

'Are you not? I don't know your financial situation. It

was not something we discussed in our singular wooing.' He was regarding me solemnly. 'Perhaps I should have had Lord Thomas investigate your account books before he assured you of my intentions towards you.'

Was this English humour? Again that little brush of uncertainty disturbed me, coupled with a sense of displeasure that I had come under the critical eye of the English Exchequer.

'Perhaps you should have so instructed him.' I kept my voice as even as Henry's. 'I had not thought my Breton holdings to be a matter to be negotiated between us when you asked me to become your wife.' A new thought intruded. 'Did you need a well-dowered bride?'

'It was not my first thought.'

Which did not quite answer my question. Perhaps he now wished it had been. My initial pleasure in Henry's gift to me seemed to be leaching away, minute by minute, like whey strained through muslin cloth. What right had this English Exchequer to dabble in my own Breton finances? And did Henry believe me so lacking in honesty that I would hide my wealth from him, in the hope of inveigling more land and income to my own use? I was not so mercenary. I felt my spine stiffening, that I should be so suspect.

Nor did I care to discuss the matter in a room full of minions.

'I will show you the truth of my Breton dower, my lord,' I announced in a voice that drew the attention of more than one clerk.

'You don't have to.'

'But it seems to me that I must. If you will come with me?'

I turned on my heel, not waiting to see if Henry followed

me, but of course he did. Leaving the rolls of my dower to
the care of Henry's clerks, we walked side by side, in a silence
that was not quite comfortable, to my own chambers, where
I summoned a page to bring one of my travelling coffers
and its key. Whereupon I lifted the lid to reveal rolls and
documents, neatly arranged, much like Henry's.

'You are remarkably efficient.'

'Of course.' I ignored the suspicion of surprise. Henry must
learn what manner of woman I was too. 'I need to know
where my wealth is, where the rents are paid—or not paid.
But look at this.' I sought for and handed him a scroll. 'This
is an accounting of my income from Brittany. The rents I
should receive.' And then another roll, much handled. 'This is
the amount in rents that has never been paid to me for one
reason or another. There, so marked, is the sum that I and
my clerks have never been able to wring out of the men in
question. The culprits are listed below.' I watched him read,
resentment still simmering not far below the surface. 'I'll not
cry poverty, Henry, but I'm no wealthy widow come here
with the intention of bleeding England dry.'

If I was taken aback at the bitterness that suddenly larded
my tone, so was Henry who abandoned the accounting to
stare at me. 'I never thought you were. And I see that your
Breton finances are compromised. I am sorry for it.'

Fidgeting with the key, I was aware of nothing but the
fact that the closeness between us had been spoiled. Nor did
I quite understand how we had arrived at this uneasy place,
except that royal finance was at the bottom of it. And that
Henry's tight-fisted Exchequer had stirred the pot.

My expression must have been easy to read that morning.

'Have I angered you?' Henry asked, his hand brushing over my wrist as I retrieved the documents from him. 'Interfering in Breton finances that are no concern of mine?'

I might have thought he was lightly mocking, but his gaze was surprisingly stern, and I realised that I was frowning at him across the two rolls. I should not be frowning. Henry had fought to achieve my magnificent dowry for me and I must show my gratitude. Nor must I allow finance—either Breton or English—to become a festering sore between us that would undermine our new understanding. I would not have Henry frown at me as I was frowning at him. It behoved me to make reparation.

And since we were alone, I took a step and kissed him, as he had kissed me.

'What's that for?'

Henry was courteous rather than gratified.

'To show my appreciation for what you have done for me. To persuade you not to frown at me. And to persuade you to consider a favour I would ask of you.'

The relaxation in his stance, in the lines around his mouth, was palpable. 'Since you are still a new bride, how can I refuse?'

So I asked, hoping he would not take it amiss, but suspecting that he might. 'I wish to have my own council and administration for my dower lands and my income. And a place in which to house them.'

Which took Henry aback, casting some new emotion over him, evident in his voice.

'Is that entirely necessary?'

Should I not have expected it? Henry must see it as an

implied slur on his own fiscal organisation. Where I had intended to draw the single unpleasant sting, I had in fact let loose a swarm of bees.

'I think it is.'

'I had presumed that your affairs would be amalgamated with mine.'

I kept my reply smooth, as if it were a matter of little moment. 'I have always dealt with my own finances as Duchess of Brittany. Why change the habits of a lifetime? There is no need for you to be troubled by my Breton dower. I am the one to do it. I'll not burden you, Henry.'

Henry was not mollified. I could see it in the tilt of his chin.

'It is your intention, then, to keep close ties with Brittany.'

'Of course.' Why would he question this? Was this another unexpected morass in which I must step carefully, or be dragged unsuspectingly below the surface? 'It may be that I have left my sons behind, but I will not cut my ties with them completely. Would you expect that of me? I will always have Breton interests at heart, because they are the interests of my eldest son.'

'I suppose I should expect no less…'

I waited. And then to prompt the thought that had stamped Henry's face with contemplative lines: 'But what?'

I thought he would reply, and that I would not like his judgement, but something changed his mind, so that at last his lips curved into a reassuring smile of great charm.

'There are no buts, my dear. None at all. I mustn't forget that your son John will always retain a place in your heart.' He placed the rolls back in their coffer for me and locked it, returning the key to me, as if that would end the discord between us. 'As for your request, I will give you your council, and a tower sufficiently appropriate to house them and your records.' But there was the ghost of a frown again. 'I suppose if you keep some contact with Brittany, it will at least help to prevent war breaking out between us.'

I looked up sharply. 'Do you expect war?'

'No.'

'You would tell me if you did.'

'Of course.'

'And yet you see it on the horizon.'

'Perhaps.'

What a bleak little exchange. And there I was, frowning again.

'It is the duty of every ruler to guard his boundaries,' Henry said. 'There has been ill-will between English and Bretons since at least my grandfather's day.' His hands were fisted on his hips. 'Let's cry truce here, Joanna. Trade squabbles between our countries need not mean hostility between ourselves. As your own mother must have discovered.'

'I doubt my mother felt any emotion towards my father other than intense dislike. He was not a man easy to love.'

Which, to my relief, made Henry laugh. 'An understatement. And much unlike his daughter. Whom I find it impossible not to love.'

Which smoothed away all the wrinkles in the day. Had we not, without any difficulty at all in the end and an honest exchange of opinion, resolved the dissension that had disturbed the surface of our new marital pond, like trout rising to snap at unsuspecting mayflies? Henry drew my hand through his arm to lead me back to the muniment room.

'We will deal well together, Joanna.'

'Of course.' And then, because I would not allow secrets to lie undiscovered, 'Why is the English Exchequer being uncooperative over my dower?'

'The Exchequer is no longer uncooperative,' he stated, as if it was not a matter of debate. 'Your dower is secure.' His smile was warm. 'Whatever problems we have to face in the future, we will not allow our financial state to come between us.'

'No. Of course we will not.'

But it left me wondering what other problems there might be. What did Henry foresee that I did not? And I had noted the smart diplomatic hop from war to trade squabbles, bringing the whole down to a lower level of importance.

But then I was distracted, for Henry's good humour was all restored.

'Come and see what I have in mind for your new domain. I am in process of building a new tower. Is that fate, do you think? It is almost complete and will be most suitable...'

And I was impressed when he showed me the drawings, near to the gate to Westminster Hall. This would become mine, for the custody of all my affairs of business and the space in which I might house my own personal treasurer, my receiver general, my chancellors and my steward. As to who would hold the offices, Henry suggested English men of skill and experience who would ease my way into English politics. It would please me to meet and instruct John Chandeler, Bishop of Salisbury, as my treasurer, and Henry Luttrell, my steward.

With much satisfaction at the outcome of the morning's work, I flexed my fingers, jewel-heavy, decorative but practical. I would help Henry to rule, standing beside him as he became the great King I knew he would be. It had perhaps been a day of uncomfortable learning, but the lessons had been fruitful. We were both of a mind to drive forward to fulfil our own desires—many would say we were too set in our ways—but I had no doubt that with good sense any divisions born of our new alliance would be fast healed.

I kissed him lightly, in the spirit of my new learning, scribbling clerks notwithstanding, before leaving Henry to his dusty documents.

★

Pulling a fur-lined cloak around my shoulders, I shivered.

'Do I send for spiced wine, my lady?' Marie de Parency, my most loyal of serving women, was already summoning a page.

I shook my head. Undoubtedly there was a coolness in the air at the English Court, but one that had nothing to do with the refusal of a chilly spring to blossom into true summer. This hint of frost had developed, slowly, insidiously, and I could not doubt that it was directed at me. It would take more than a cup of hippocras to cure it.

I could not fault the correctness of how I was received in England. Respect was paramount. Deference all-pervading. I was bowed into every chamber I wished to use. I was greeted with fanfare of hautboy, shawm, sackbut and pipe at dinner. My beauty was lauded by Henry's minstrels, a little too unctuous perhaps—I was past the heady days of my youth—but it was flattering, and I thought my face not beyond favour.

'White as the lily, more crimson than the rose,
Dazzling as a ruby from the East,
At your beauty past compare I always gaze…'

What woman would not enjoy such appreciation? Sung in my mother's tongue, it added another fine layer to my happiness.

The brief discord between Henry and me over the matter of my dower had, it seemed to me, been effectively laid to rest.

But it was a cold acceptance from these proud English aristocrats in Henry's Royal Council. There was no corresponding warmth in their demeanour. A smile, for their courtesy was without fault, had the glittering edge of a blade, quickly sheathed. There was no laughter, more often a tight silence if I entered a chamber unannounced to take them unawares.

And occasionally, disturbingly, increasingly, there was no laughter in Henry either.

I considered the cause. There was the rebellion, of course, that had been rumbling when I first came to England, of which I had now discovered every detail, as every good wife should. Henry might not speak much of it, but I had made it my policy to discover all about Owain Glyn Dwr. A Welsh lord, this Glyn Dwr, who had proclaimed himself Prince of Wales and, with an army of Welsh behind him, was snapping at Henry's heels, promoting rebellion throughout that province far to the west, then crossing the border into England at every opportunity to stir trouble in the Marches. Had that not been the reason for our rush across country to Winchester and on to Westminster, the increasingly heavy discussions? It had certainly been the reason for the absence of Henry's son and heir from our wedding. Prince Hal, young as he was, had been in Wales at the head of an army, whilst Henry could not afford to take his eye off this malingering insurrection for one second. Even to wed me.

Henry should talk to me about this perennial thorn in his flesh, I decided. He had been too long alone, too long without a confidante to share his inner thoughts when he sat at ease with a cup of wine when the demands of the day were done. Who better in this role than his wife, a woman of some political experience? I would provide a solid sounding board for his plans and fair counsel for all Henry's deliberations. It seemed to me to be the most obvious of roles for an able consort to play, and entirely fitting for my temperament.

★

My anticipation that Henry would consider my words of fair counsel was to fall fruitlessly, with a reverberating crash, onto stony ground. A misapprehension on my part that was to be shattered with brutal simplicity when, riding through London one morning in the direction of Westminster, I pulled my horse to a standstill, fingers tight on the reins in something akin to shock: my head whipped round.

'Wait here!' I said to Marie de Parency and my escort.

There was a new head displayed for public disparagement on London Bridge.

Not an unusual occurrence, criminals frequently being called on to pay this most degrading of penalties, nor was I in the habit of inspecting them, but this one was chilling. I pushed my mare closer. This one I knew, and it roused nausea in the pit of my belly for I had not been forewarned. Here were the pale features with sunken eye-sockets and the effects of vicious carrion of Thomas Percy, Earl of Worcester. His hair tangled on his brow, rank with sweat and blood. The last time I had seen the Earl of Worcester he had escorted me from Brittany, before standing shoulder to shoulder, impeccably groomed in silk and fur and jewels on his breast with his brother the Earl of Northumberland and his nephew Hotspur, to honour my wedding.

The Earl would be a morose onlooker no longer.

Now he was horribly and gorily dead, and I knew full well the reason why. This was the terrible reality of civil war. In calamitous association with Owain Glyn Dwr, the great northern magnates of the Percy family, with all their allies and retainers, had risen up in arms against their King.

'Trusting them so implicitly was my mistake,' Henry had said, irritation investing his every movement as he prepared to depart. 'Rewarding them for past loyalties was an even greater one. Give them one purse of gold and they demand twenty. Gold that I have not got!' He finished buckling his sword-belt with crisp exactness. 'I have to stop Hotspur meeting up with Glyn Dwr at all costs. He's marching through Cheshire, collecting troops. I haven't the resources to fight two of them together. If they join forces the whole country will erupt in flames, taking me with it.'

So Henry had gone to war. Not a skirmish. Not a siege of some Welsh town or castle. Henry had left, not four months after our wedding, with the prospect of a fully fledged battle,

Englishman waging death-dealing blows against Englishman. Almost before the dishes from our Winchester banquet had grown cold, sauces congealing, Henry was summoning his retainers and levies, donning his armour, informing the Council of his intent.

My soul curled within me in dread of the repercussions, and I had said as much to Henry, appalled that this family that had brought Henry safe to his inheritance should now be engaged in bringing him to his knees. I did not need the experience of it to know that war within a country breathed disaster. Victor and conquered must find the common ground to live with each other afterwards, that much I could see. Re-establishing peace would be no easy matter if king and rebels came to outright battle with heavy losses on both sides. Even presuming that Henry returned the victor.

Henry must have read the concern in my face. 'We'll defeat them yet. I have Hal and his troops in Wales to call on.' His hand was firm on mine, and I caught it as he would have walked away from me to collect all the personal accoutrements necessary to kill and defend.

'When you win, Henry.' There was a warning in my voice. 'Show mercy to them.'

Henry's face and reply were equally uncompromising. 'I think not.'

Still I would make the case for leniency. 'Clemency is a fine attribute for you as King. It might be politic to win the Percy trust again when the blood and fury and dust of battle have all settled. To show them that you will deal within the law as a worthy ruler, bent on justice and honour.'

It was as strong an argument as I could make.

Henry's reasoning was even stronger.

'How do I show justice and honour to those who commit treason and break their foresworn oaths? They are out for my blood, so the penalty must be death. *Necessitas non habet legem.*' He frowned over the loose stitching on a glove. 'Do I need to translate?'

'No.'

It needed no translation, and I was exasperated that he would ask. Necessity has no law. There would be no compassion for Henry at Percy hands if they emerged victorious; for his part Henry saw his path as one of ruthless efficiency in obliterating his enemies, and clearly, if his last blighting comment was a measure of it, Henry's temper was running high. I tried again in measured tones.

'It is an uncomfortable policy to pursue. It might create more enmity.'

'What choice do they give me? How can it create more than I already face? Must I tolerate war in my own lands, between my own people, bringing bloodshed and destruction? Before God, I will not.' He hugged me hard against the unforgiving armour—'Keep the faith, Joanna!'—before letting me go, allowing me no more time than to return a brief kiss. Thus I was summarily abandoned, with nothing to do but wait, the lot of all women. My opinion, prudently offered, had been nothing but chaff to be dissipated in the stiff wind of Henry's convictions.

And so I waited. With votive candles and prayers and increasing anxiety.

Until, now regarding Worcester's battered, raven-scarred

head on London Bridge, my anxieties were answered unequivocally. But mercy? Had Henry been moved by my plea? Henry had shown none, news flooding in that all was effectively settled in a fierce and particularly bloody battle for both sides outside the marches town of Shrewsbury where Prince Hal and Henry faced the Percy levies. In the aftermath Worcester was executed for the treason he had undoubtedly committed, Hotspur cut down on the battlefield. No mercy here. Nor did Henry come home but instead marched north to bring Northumberland to its knees after dispatching Worcester's severed head to spread its message of treachery, while taking the grisly head of Hotspur to York, to reduce his father Northumberland through fear and grief. The rest of his traitorous body had been displayed in towns the length and breadth of the country.

No compassion then, and there would be some faces spectacularly absent from the ranks of Henry's councillors. Without doubt this campaign would instil fear. But would it heal and mend? I doubted it.

It was July.

Henry did not come home. I could not reach him, neither in my thoughts nor my dreams. I continued to light candles and offer prayers when from the north Henry marched into Wales. It was not until December, when Worcester's head was stripped of all flesh and frost was heavy on timber and stone that Henry rode into London and I was there, with the formidable bulwark of the Royal Council behind me, to honour his return.

And how conflicting my response to him.

This was a King returned to his capital as conqueror in

magnificent array. Henry might be fine drawn with lack of
sleep and food but his entry into the city was exquisitely
ordered to impress. Banners and pennons blazed with proud
Plantagenet colours in the cold air; the royal standard, fringed
and gilded, flew over all with its lions no less fierce than
Henry had been in battle. The royal livery breathed power
and authority, winter sun creating a shining pathway in
heavenly blessing.

Henry, riding with all his formidable experience at the head
of his private retinue as if born to rule, called to my heart.
Such power, such confidence, such conviction. Such beauty
as he removed his helm to receive the massed acclamation of
his subjects. He would annoy me, repudiate my considered
thoughts, he could set me at a distance, but my love for him was
immeasurable. As I watched him draw near, my senses were set
aflame by his smile for a well-wisher with her child, stretching
out his hand to her as he passed. Those hands that could master
the fragile strings of a rebec as easily as curb the energies of his
horse. Soon he would stretch out his hands to me.

But by now, after five months of parting, I was finding it
difficult to show any emotion at all in public. I felt as if I were
a pickled neat's tongue, the planes of my face unresponsive
to any emotion. Five months of absence and warfare were
a blight on any marriage. Old habits of reticence had taken
hold of me once more.

'You are right welcome, my lord.'

It was all I could manage, hideously formal, and I could see,
by the merest flicker of his eye, that Henry was disappointed
in me. The Council left me in no doubt that I should have
received him with hautboys, cymbals and rejoicing, but I

could not. When I might have fallen to the floor at his feet
in a wash of relief, all I could do was greet him in cool and
measured tones. The lessons of my youth had been too well
learned to gather him into some flamboyant embrace.

I allowed him to kiss my hand.

'We have missed you,' I said. 'We have rejoiced at your
victory.'

Henry risked a kiss to my icy cheek.

And then we were free to speak, the councillors bowing
themselves out of our presence, when it might have been
expected that formality would go by the board and we might
indulge in some warmer exchange of opinion, even if not
of an intimate nature.

There was no warmth.

'I saw Worcester's head,' I said.

'I thought you would.'

'Did you kill Northumberland too?' Where were my
words of love and longing? 'Has his head gone missing on
the journey south? Or did you leave it on the gates of York
with that of his son?' Oh, I was not temperate.

Henry's expression was beyond reading. 'Did you expect
me to execute him?'

'Yes. Why not eradicate the whole family?'

'I did not. Northumberland is now languishing under
guard for his treachery, to answer before parliament. His
punishment for raising arms against me will be parliament's
decision. He has taken oaths of fealty, so I doubt he will suffer
death. Does that please you?'

'Yes.'

'I could not let Worcester and Hotspur go free at

Shrewsbury unless they came to terms. I tried. By God, I tried, but Worcester made every excuse he could muster not to negotiate. If I had used them with mercy they would have been in Glyn Dwr's camp before I could draw breath after offering them polite forgiveness. It won't work, Joanna.'

No. Perhaps it would not. The Percys might be cowed but Glyn Dwr was stronger than ever and a French fleet was sniffing round the southern ports. I had learned a hard lesson. The security of England was more important than the law and in achieving it Henry could be pitiless.

'Have you a kiss for your long-absent husband?' Henry asked, his expression still as stern as if passing judgement on the absent Northumberland. 'Have you at least a smile that is a genuine expression of your love? For I believe you do love me, beneath that daunting exterior.'

And then he was smiling at me. He was within touching distance. He was safe and he was home.

'I cannot be less than daunting in public,' I said.

'But we are no longer in public. We are very private.' His fingers were lightly engaged around mine.

'We are in an audience chamber.'

'Which is empty. Except for the two of us.' His lips were pressed against my wrist, against the quick beat of my blood. 'And I have been apart from you for so very long.'

At last I smiled, my face softening, my senses melting, as I welcomed him into my arms, and when my own desired words still escaped me, I discovered those within the span of my own knowledge, and made amends with them.

'Let him kiss me with the kisses of his mouth; for thy love is better than wine.'

Henry replied from the same source, familiar to both of us.

'Set me as a seal upon thine heart, as a seal upon thine arm, for love is strong as death.'

My amends were well received, allowing us to discover much to reunite us in the sultry beauty and passion of the Song of Solomon. Henry was returned, he had shown clemency at the end, and I was glad.

★

'What's amiss?' I asked, when for the whole morning Henry had been locked in collaboration with his Council whose members looked as collectively disobliging as the statues above the great west door into Westminster Abbey. I had caught my preoccupied husband's attention by the simple expedient of awaiting their departure from the Westminster chamber, then taking a stool beside him at the table of business.

'Are we at war again? There is a furrow deep enough between your brows to plant a crop of cabbages,' I said, hoping for a softening of expression.

'What do you know about planting cabbages?' he responded. He regarded me as if from a great distance.

'Not a thing. What I do know is that a pall of trouble hangs over you. Are we at war?' I repeated.

There was that breath of a hesitation. One I was becoming used to, as if he might be considering whether to honour me with his confidence or not. So that when Henry placed his hands flat-palmed on the wood, to push himself to his feet, I grasped his nearest wrist, and tugged, to prevent his escape.

'I would like to think that I knew what was in your mind, Henry, rather than have to guess.'

Which made Henry settle back in his chair, with some resignation, turn to rest his elbow on the table and grin briefly. 'Then I must ask pardon, Madam. It is become a matter of habit to keep my own counsel.' So I had been right about that. 'Am I anxious? Sad, perhaps, at the death of a woman who had more influence in my life than she would ever know.'

I frowned a little. So it was a family bereavement that was gouging the lines. 'Not one of your sisters.'

'No. Duchess Katherine has died. In Lincoln.' His smile was wry. 'She was always there, in one capacity or another, throughout my life.'

I recalled her at Calais. Graciously friendly, wearing her new status as the Duke's wife with ease. There was no doubt that in that relationship love had triumphed over the overt hostility of those who thought such a marriage between the ageing Duke and his mistress to be unseemly.

Henry was continuing, in pensive mood. 'Her ending was a peaceful one. She missed my father beyond bearing.' And then, more to himself than to me, 'It will help to ease your dower situation with parliament and the Council. Some of Duchess Katherine's property will devolve to you.'

Which struck me as peculiarly insensitive from a man who was rarely thus. 'I would not wish her dead. For the sake of an estate and a house, however valuable,' I responded.

'Of course not.'

And I saw that any door on confidences that I had opened had closed again. But I had not come to discuss my dower.

'Do your ministers approve of me yet, Henry?' I asked.

Henry's eyes narrowed. 'Why would they not?'

Which was not helpful. 'Do they fear my intervention, seeing it as meddling? I will help you in every way I can.'

'As I know.' Henry had become brisk. 'As for my ministers, they need time to become acquainted with you.' Then, after an infinitesimal pause: 'And with how you see your role as Queen of England.'

I considered this. 'Is my role a matter of dispute between us?'

'You have to understand.' Henry was become even brisker. 'The Duke of Brittany allowed you considerable autonomy but here in England it is not in living memory that the Queen has engaged herself directly in the events of the realm. My grandmother Queen Philippa was a woman content to lavish her talents on her children and her household. She might hear petitions and dispense patronage but she did not deal directly with affairs of government. Richard's first wife Anne might have done so, but her death was untimely. Isabelle, of course, was a mere child. The only Queen of England the nobility will remember from family anecdote and experience was Isabella, wife of the second King Edward who meddled outrageously, undermined the King's power and dragged the country almost into civil war.' Henry's regard was not without compassion for my position. 'Not only that, Isabella became involved to an unfortunate degree with Earl Mortimer, siding with him against her husband the King. Her memory has done you no favours. It is thought by many that the best policy is for the Queen to be a self-effacing wife, highly decorative, with no demand on her time but to bear heirs for the kingdom and dispense charity.'

Which effectively put me in my place. 'I see. And is that what you wish? For me to be good and decorative and fertile, and nothing more?'

'No,' Henry replied without pause. 'I value you far more highly than that. So will my ministers. Give them time.'

I should have been satisfied. And yet I felt that Henry was a master of quiet dissimulation. Not trickery: that was not his way. But he could keep concerns as close to his chest as a swan would cleave to its single remaining cygnet.

I stood, preparing to leave him to his discussions when the shuffling of his returning ministers could no longer be ignored, but his hand on mine stopped me.

'Might I make a suggestion?' He did not wait longer than to read my raised brows. 'That you do not scowl at the members of my Council.'

'Did I?'

'They would think so. It is difficult to read a frown and set mouth as friendly.'

'But they resent my presence.'

'Only, as I have explained, because there is no precedent for it. Put your pride aside, Joanna, and smile at them. They will warm to you.'

Sinking back to my stool I saw the truth in it, of course, acknowledging that I had been unwise. I knew better than to engender hostility through careless handling. The path to successful negotiation was one of cool calm politeness, not snarling ferocity. My only excuse was that I was still finding my feet amongst the eddying of power in this Court where nothing was as it seemed.

'I have been wrong,' I admitted. I will remedy it immediately.'

I smiled at the returning counsellors. Some of them even returned it when I asked their pardon for interrupting the business of their Council.

And so I retired with a degree of accomplishment, yet in spite of his concurrence that I would be accepted and allotted a role at his side, I felt that Henry was still manoeuvring me, gently but even more firmly into the background. I had sensed it on the journey to Winchester. I sensed it even more strongly now. Music and passion would be shared with me, but anything appertaining to royal policy was slammed hard and fast behind a closed door.

I was not a woman to be shut out.

How unfortunate that Queen Isabella had left such an uncomfortable legacy for me. Nor was that of Queen Philippa any more acceptable. What would I do with my time if I were to mirror my life on hers, full of family and dispensation of patronage? I was not a woman to spend it in setting fine stitches.

★

My resolute smiles and friendly overtures towards Henry's councillors having no significant effect, matters quickly came to a head.

I was in process of traversing an antechamber at Westminster, one that I rarely used and one that at this precise moment was redolent with passion, where Henry's newly hung tapestries were of war and conquest, the hues bright and red with blood where sword bit into flesh. Yet no more hostile than the mood of the men who had gathered centrally to exchange their low-voiced conversation. I halted on the threshold, my page who carried my missal dragged into immobility by my hand clamped to his shoulder, my ladies staunchly frozen behind me. I might be on my way to hear Matins, but this atmosphere, these chance-heard opinions, wiped away any desire for immediate prayer.

I let my gaze travel the room. Since my own advent was not immediately recognised, the conversation continued. Low-voiced it might be, but it carried well. A sibilant hiss on finance. The harsh consonants of Breton. The short open vowel of war.

I would not hover in the doorway in my own palace.

Releasing my page, I walked forward, and since I made no attempt to creep, the discussion dropped into a potent stillness, like an axe through the neck of a traitor. The silence was absolute. Not even a scrape of shoe or rustle of damask sleeve. All eyes were turned to me. It was like treading through pools of venom.

'Gentlemen, my lords, I hope I do not disturb your deliberations.'

My lips smiled. My deportment was impeccable.

So was their response. They bowed, respectful to a man, as I walked the distance between them to the far door. Even when it was closed at my back, I felt the lowering cloud of their disapproval. I had been right about the chill, whatever Henry might say. Like the thinnest of ice on a puddle, but sharp enough to draw blood if one was unfortunate enough to have a thin skin. Nor could I broach the matter again with Henry. He would simply placate me with soft words, to wait until they knew me better.

How long would that take? A year? A lifetime? Would they finally find me acceptable as I neared my deathbed?

I would not wait. It was not in my nature to live with this covert disapprobation any longer. Moreover I knew who would deliver an honest answer, however uncomfortable it might make him, however distasteful I would find it. So deciding, I diverted from my plan of prayer and heavenly assurance, directing my steps in the opposite direction. Perhaps I was mistaken after all and the wintry temperature had everything to do with the undercurrent of unrest in the country rather than with me.

I hoped it was so. If I was a naive woman, I might have believed it.

*

I might have abandoned prayer for the occasion, but Henry Beaufort, enjoying his luxurious apartments, was on his knees before his prie dieu. Nor did he immediately rise when I was ushered into the room by his servant. Here was a man of presence and self-confidence, newly created Lord Chancellor of England and enjoying the glory of it. There was no doubting his abilities, or his ambition, but I decided that he would be a friend to me in my need for information.

Bishop Henry rose, crossed himself with a hand that glittered with gems, and genuflected before the crucifix. Only then did he turn, showing no surprise.

'Madam Joanna.'

'Bishop Henry.'

'Now why would you need to seek me out so early in the day?'

'Because despite your lack of years, a more astute cleric I have never met.'

Henry Beaufort, royal half-brother, Bishop of Winchester, Chancellor of England, was all of twenty-eight years old. He grinned.

'I will do my poor best. If you will sit…'

I sat while Bishop Henry poured wine for us both and took the carved high-backed chair opposite me.

'Well, then?'

I inhaled steadily. 'I wish to know how I am regarded. Here in England. There was much celebration when I was made Queen. I was lauded as Henry's wife. Warwick fought as my champion. Yet within a year the gilding has worn thin. Now, whichever way I turn, I feel the shadow of a storm-crow hanging over me.'

Bishop Henry pursed his lips. 'I could say that you are mistaken.'

'You could. But you won't. You will tell me the truth.'

'Then I could say that I think you should ask my brother to answer the question. It is—how shall I say?—a sensitive subject.'

'So sensitive that your brother won't tell me. He is polite and reassuring that I will be the most well-loved of queens when the English nobles come to know me. I don't believe him. I am treated with a cold distancing as if I were the carrier of the plague. I have been married less than a twelve-month.

What have I done? Is it some English custom I am ignorant of? Have I committed some grave solecism?'

He tilted his head considering, eyes bright, smile as dry as dust. He might be younger than my years, but I felt he could strip the flesh from my bones and read my entrails if he so wished.

'Why come to me?'

He looked as if he wished I had not.

'Because you will tell me. Henry denies it. Lord Thomas would be soothing. You will be honest. Even though I presume I will not like your reply.'

'No.' He took a sip of wine. 'I don't think you will. But it is quite simple. You are disliked. Quite spectacularly, in fact. You are probably the most unpopular royal bride for at least a century. You are considered untrustworthy because you are Breton.'

And no, I did not like it, as the brutal delivery struck home. The implied venom in the enlightenment momentarily took my breath.

'But I am not Breton. I am Navarrese. I am Valois.'

'Just as bad. The enemy, in effect.'

'But they knew that when Henry first broached our marriage.'

'Ah! But Henry knew there would be difficulties over your marriage from the very beginning.' Bishop Henry smiled knowingly. 'He was amazingly circumspect in his dealings with the Council.'

'You mean he kept it secret?'

'Indeed. Until the negotiations were complete and the deal done and you almost on your way. What the Council didn't know, the Council could not oppose. When your ambassadors arrived, and the Council questioned the purpose of the visit, Henry informed the Council that it was none of their business.'

So the whole wooing had been clandestine. I had known of his desire for discretion; he had made it plain enough. But to keep the whole affair hidden was more extreme than I had realised. I did not know what to think of this.

'Henry did not tell me of the extent of this opposition.'

'Perhaps he thought you would know without the need for his telling.'

'Yes, I was aware of some dissatisfaction. But not that the Council would rather Henry marry a daughter of the Grand Turk than marry me. Am I so naive?'

'I would never be so discourteous, Madam.'

'But you think I should have known.'

'If you ask my advice, yes. You must learn to look at this through English eyes. We have had years of dispute over who rules the sea between us.' He ticked them off on his elegantly jewelled fingers. 'Trade disputes, fishing disputes. Pirate activities. Breton alliances with France. It puts Brittany firmly on the shelf of those whom the English distrust. And your son is Duke of Brittany. Why would it surprise you if they look askance when you walk into a room or express an opinion?'

'I see. I suppose it is on the same level as Burgundy warning me of the consequences of my coming to England. That this marriage would be opposed by France. Then it seems I have been truly naive.'

No, I thought. Not naive. But ill-informed. I should have

done better, perhaps. And then the sharp thought, sharp enough to wound. Henry should have been honest with me, as I had been with him. I had warned him of Burgundy's open hostility. Henry might have hinted at disapproval, but he had given me no image of the true level of English disfavour.

Meanwhile, Bishop Henry inclined his head, his fingers stroking over the silver crucifix on his chest. 'It is an extra obligation on my brother that he could well do without. The pressures are building on him. He is beleaguered on every side.'

'But will your stiff-necked English necessarily like me more when they know me better?' I asked, not liking the idea of being one of Henry's problems, an albatross around his neck. 'I have done nothing to antagonise anyone. And yet I feel the frost in this Court is deepening. I know I don't mistake the chatter when I walk into a chamber. Any conviviality dries up like a well in summer. Will they ever find me more acceptable?'

I detested having to ask. England had acquired in me a Queen with high blood and status, acknowledged throughout Europe. My brother of Navarre had approved of the match. Why should past enmity between pugnacious fishermen sour my welcome? Better a high-ranking royal daughter than an unknown woman, or even an English girl, who would bring England's King no enhancement to his position. England should see me as an asset rather than a difficulty to be overcome.

'Why not?' Bishop Henry was as smooth as the silk of his robes. 'As you say, you have been here so little time. But you might consider…'

Something else for me to consider? I raised my brows extravagantly.

Bishop Henry laughed, showing his teeth. 'How unaccommodating you appear, Joanna, when you try so hard not to be. Tell me this. How many servants have you, waiting at this moment outside my door?'

'Seven. Six of my waiting-women,' I said. 'And one of my pages.'

'And how many of them are Breton?'

'Seven.'

'How many servants in your household are Breton?'

'All of them. Except for the handful of members of my Council, provided by Henry.'

'There's your answer. Your connection with Brittany is still very strong. Too strong.'

So that was at the root of it. That I had come to England with the women and people of my household who had served me in Brittany, and I had made no changes.

'And,' Bishop Henry pursued, 'would it be true to say that your confessor and your physician and your cupbearer, not to mention your sempstress and your daughters' nurses are also all Breton?'

'Yes.' And seeing the direction of his questions, I tilted my chin despite the heat I felt along my cheekbones. 'And I'll not dismiss them.'

'Then you will continue to fall into disfavour. You are expected to put English interests first.'

'Which I will. All the members of my new council are English. My treasurer is English. My steward is English. That is enough. I'll not dismiss those who came to serve me.'

Bishop Henry's brows arched as beautifully as mine. 'If you are of a mind to be intransigent…'

'Perhaps I am.' And then, because it was uppermost in my mind: 'Why would Henry not tell me this?'

'At this precise moment, Henry has other priorities than the nationality of your servants. You might consider, Joanna, when you are mulling over all the rest, that the sum of money Henry negotiated for your dowry was greater, as far as I am aware, than that given to any other queen in the history of this country. It is a mark of my brother's high regard. If you will accept more advice, you should perhaps consider how you spend the money when parliament is showing its disapprobation of royal expenses. Your extravagance can only weaken Henry in his attempt to find accord with Council or parliament. It would receive much praise from the Royal Council. I expect they would smile on you if they saw your lifestyle being more frugal.'

'Curb my expenditure? As I recall, there was no curb on the expenditure for my wedding feast. What did that cost Henry?'

The Bishop winced delicately. 'Far too much, many would say. But as for you, Joanna, if I might be forthright—perhaps the ordering of Flanders linen is not good policy.'

I bridled. 'Flanders linen is of the finest.'

'And most expensive. As I imagine is the sable pelt around your cuffs. And as for the purchase of wine and other comestibles from your previous home at Vannes…' Bishop Henry's nose narrowed with disapproval. 'Such luxuries could be purchased in England.'

I stood, angry now, at such a personal level of disapproval.

'And how do you know what I order, or from whom I order it?'

'Gossip, lady. Only gossip. But I swear it's true.' For a moment he considered me. 'Will you take some advice?' And before I could reply, 'My brother does not give his confidences easily, a habit that of late has become more pronounced. They have to be teased out of him, gently like a whore's kiss. Or excavated with a hatchet.'

'And which method do you propose that I use?'

'I will leave that for your discerning eye, Madam Joanna. But I would use a hatchet. It's quicker.'

I did not like the gleam in his eye as I placed my untouched cup of wine on the coffer and left him to his interrupted petitions to the Almighty. Well, I had asked for the truth had I not? That I did not like what I had heard was no fault of Bishop Henry's, but it left me unable to make polite conversation as if it had never been said.

On the threshold I paused to bow my head. 'I will consider your advice, your grace.'

And what a wealth of new knowledge for me to digest. A dislike of all things Breton. Extravagance. My unwillingness to employ English women around me. I had not given any of this a second thought, merely continuing my lifestyle as I had managed it in Brittany. And as I returned to my chambers, flanked by my despised Bretons, I wished Henry had been more open. Was it lack of courage in him? I did not think so. Consideration for my sensibilities? I had thought we had a marriage that could withstand honesty.

Perhaps I had been wrong on a number of fronts.

I could no longer ignore the level appraisals as I traversed the rooms and antechambers. They were sufficiently Medusa-like to turn an unsuspecting onlooker, even an English Queen, into stone.

★

My first instinct was to pack my travelling coffers before sending a message to my husband that I was returning forth-with to Eltham, where at least my daughters and Philippa would smile as I walked into a room. They would enjoy my company, showering me with questions and demands. Still undecided, I considered my household, looking at it with Bishop Henry's jaundiced eagle eye. The pages, servants, musi-cians, the women who dealt with my laundry and mending, my ladies in waiting. Yes, they were all Breton. A sin of omission rather than commission. It had not entered my mind to take an English woman into my service when I had so many who knew my ways and worked with cheerful competence. What had my mother done? Had she kept her French retinue when she became Queen of Navarre? When I had become Duchess of Brittany, had I not brought my own people from Navarre? Of course I had. Eventually I had employed Breton ladies as the need arose. I could recall no outcry over the speed or lack of in forming my new household.

It was all a storm in wine-cup. And if so, to brood at Eltham would do nothing to calm the waves. I was not good at silent brooding.

Thus my second instinct: to remain at Westminster and do what I did best: immerse myself in my own affairs and the business of my finances. They had been long neglected, some ends that were uncomfortably loose needed to be mended. I would be here when Henry was less preoccupied. Meanwhile I would spend my time wisely and effectively. If nothing else I would make it plain to these English subjects that they had a Queen capable of applying herself to business, far more than a decorative consort, incapable of appreciating the needs of this country. And if my garments were made of the finest linen and silk, edged with the finest fur, I would show the English that I was worthy of that expenditure.

It might also be that I should accept Bishop Henry's needle-sharp advice and consider the composition of my household. To add a cluster of well born Englishwomen would not come amiss and might help to allay suspicions that I was beyond accepting good advice. It would be good policy to show my appreciation of the wives of Henry's noble families.

In this satisfactory turn of mind I immersed myself in the fiscal dealings in my tower where it soon became clear to me that, in respect of my Breton dower, there was one obvious step for me to take. A sensible decision all round. And so I began to dictate to William Denys, one of my English officials.

'It is my will that my claims to the sum of seventy thousand livres due, as dower income from my marriage to John de Montfort, Duke of Brittany, together with the annual rent of six thousand livres on lands in Normandy, as listed below, will be transferred from me and placed under the jurisdiction of my son John, Duke of Brittany, for his use in perpetuity.' I paced as I spoke. 'Signed and sealed by my hand on this day in the year 1404 at Westminster…'

'If there is any single step that you might take, to make

the English dislike you more than they already do, Madam, it is that one.'

A damning observation. The dictation dried on my lips as I turned slowly.

'My lord, I did not expect you.'

'Unfortunately, as I am made aware.'

Henry waved my people, suddenly all ears, back to their work. His expression was not one such as I had come to know. Here was anger. Here was frustration. Here was stark debate in his eyes.

'Do you need me?' I asked, as wary as a rabbit below a circling buzzard, an experience I did not appreciate. 'I thought your time today was required by your Council.'

'It is.' His gaze swept over my clerks who, heads down, hands busy, were astonishingly industrious. 'Perhaps I have neglected you. Perhaps I should have made myself more aware of what you and your fiscal officers are doing.'

'I am overseeing the disposition of moneys that are mine. I have the right.'

Now his gaze was on me. 'Is it your right to give it to your son?'

I resented the tone. I resented the arrogantly raised brows. I resented the presumption. My reply was suitably caustic.

'Why should I not?'

'Why not indeed? Shall I tell you how I see it?'

I waited in silence.

'You brought nothing to England. You brought no financial advantage. Nothing that could be put to good use for England.' How gratingly cold his voice, like the fall of a portcullis. How grim his face, as if facing an enemy on the battlefield. As if I were one of the Percys at Shrewsbury. 'I did not ask it of you. I wanted you, not your wealth. But here I find you granting away what you have to be used in Breton policies.' His voice now fell to a harsh croak. 'I cannot believe that you are so politically unaware, Joanna. By sending these rents to your son, it is pouring money into the pockets of Burgundy. And what do you suppose the Duke of Burgundy will do with it? Burgundy has no love for us. He'll rub his hands in joy when he receives this godsend, plotting how many ships he can supply to spearhead an invasion of England.'

How did I respond to this accusation, that I would wilfully put money into enemy coffers? Pride was a shackle on my tongue. Quick anger, that I had been accused and judged, was a harsh curb. I would not be told what I might and might not do with my own dower. Let Henry so judge me.

'I trust that my uncle of Burgundy will use the rents for the good of Brittany, my lord,' I said. 'So that my son, when he comes of age to govern, inherits a state of some wealth and power.'

'I forbid you to do it.' A reply I should have expected.

'Forbid?'

I held his stare with my own. And in it Henry read my denial.

'Do you wish to be held up for even more hostile criticism?' he asked. 'I was given to think that your present unpopularity disturbed you.'

'You have been talking with your brother.'

'Yes.'

ANNE O'BRIEN

I did not like that he had been discussing me with Bishop Henry. 'Why did you not tell me that my Breton associations were a matter of disgust to your subjects?'

'I did not think I had to. Could you not see it for yourself?'

Pride and anger took me in an even tighter grip. 'I thought I was a valuable wife for a man who has usurped his throne. A man who needs to improve his standing in the eyes of the rulers of Europe. A Valois princess, sister to the King of Navarre, would be a considerable achievement. It seems to me that I have misread my worth.'

While the atmosphere in my tower room positively crackled, I waited for the lash of Henry's retaliation. It did not come. Instead, accents biting:

'You might have proved to be a better wife, more acceptable as Queen of England, if your damnable Breton subjects had not within the last three days put themselves into a state of outright warfare against us.'

'They have not,' I breathed.

'Do you say?'

'If you mean trade skirmishes, have they not been in existence since as long as anyone recalls? There have always been such disputes between our two countries.'

'And I see you side with Brittany.'

'No, I do not. That is not what I meant and...'

Henry's hand flashed and gripped my arm, fingers as biting as his voice.

'It's not important what you meant. By God, Joanna, it's not a mealy mouthed matter of fish and cloth this time. What the Bretons are doing at this very moment is signing treaties with the Welsh! The bloody Welsh and Owain Glyn Dwr!

And, by God, if that isn't enough, the Bretons have joined up with your precious Valois connections to make landings in Wales. Yesterday, God damn them, they launched a raid on Plymouth which we were hard stretched to beat off.'

I did not ask if it were true or claim disbelief. I knew it must be so.

'And you are sending sources of income to your son,' Henry continued, dripping scorn from his tongue to scald me. 'You'd be better making use of your high-born connections that you are so proud of in negotiating a truce.'

'I have no power in Brittany. I gave it all up for you.'

'You do have power. More than you know. If you send your son rents to strengthen Breton efforts on behalf of Glyn Dwr you are stabbing me in the back. And what's this?' He picked up a detailed list awaiting my approval, surveying it with a clench of his jaw. 'Wine and furs, is it? An order for supplies from Vannes. So my brother was right. More money in Breton coffers to fund the war against us.'

There was nothing I could say in my own defence. Nor would I, even though shame had begun to lick around the edges of my defiance. I doubted Henry would have listened even if I had.

'I worked hard for a dower for you, and achieved it against all the odds,' he snapped. 'You might show some appreciation by not supporting Brittany at every move.'

The blood had drained from my face. 'Are you regretting it? Am I not worthy of it?'

'Oh, yes. Your connections are beyond value to a usurper.' In bitter irony Henry picked up my prideful words. 'Or I would not have worked so hard to get it for you. You came to England with nothing to our benefit. No treaty. No land. No money. This is how you repay me.' His voice dropped so that none would overhear. 'I have enough enemies, Joanna, without my own wife adding to their number.'

Every sense froze into disbelief.

'I am no enemy of yours,' I said.

Tell him. Tell him the truth.

But there was no opportunity. Nor was I of a mind to do so.

Henry cast the order for commodities on the table with a contemptuous turn of his wrist before striding from the room, leaving me to deal with an anger as cold but as viable as his. Yet beneath it all I castigated myself for my foolishness. Pride had driven me. Pride had allowed him to think the worst of me. I should have been honest, but instead I had given him due cause to suspect that I was playing a part in financing Breton-French attacks on behalf of the Welsh traitor Glyn Dwr.

But I could not forgive his berating me as if I were a lowly clerk. Nor could I believe that he had accused me of being his enemy. With dismay and defiance in equal portion, I completed the transfer of rents, singed it, sealed it, and ordered it to be sent to my son. Henry thought the worst of me. So be it.

The joy of my wedding day seemed many months ago. It was, in a painful way, a relief when Henry pleaded business away from Westminster. Since he was absent from my table and my bed I was not compelled to think of what we could possibly talk about.

Chapter 10

Once again, with what was becoming an uneasy regularity, Henry donned his armour and prepared to lead a campaign into Wales where the stronghold of Carnarvon, dangerously undermanned, was under siege.

He saluted my fingers. 'God keep you, lady.'

'May the Blessed Virgin smile on you, my lord.'

After our difference of opinion over my Breton rents, our demeanour was as polite, as carefully courteous, as that between ambassadors negotiating a truce, where good manners must be preserved at all costs but with little hope of a friendly outcome. Royal policy reached my ears in droplets, like ice melting in a slow thaw. Or through women's gossip. Should I, Queen of England, learn of a siege in Wales or another Breton attack on the Isle of Wight from the chattering of my women?

'Do you have any demands of me, my lord?'

'I've left all in Bishop Henry's hands. And Archbishop Arundel's.'

Which rubbed even more salt into my wounds, for once more I was left sitting on the margins of events where I was no more than an onlooker. Was I not Queen, invested with orb and sceptre and Crown, anointed with holy oil? It was my right to be Henry's confidante and adviser. It was my right to stand at his side.

Henry continued to turn a blind eye to my rights as wife and consort.

'Do our lives spin in separate circles,' I asked, unctuously sweet, 'meeting only when the arc of yours collides by chance with mine? Is that to be the pattern of our days?'

Henry's eye was not indulgent.

'That sums it up fairly well, as things are. The arcs, as you put it, will collide in the second week of December, at Abingdon where we will celebrate the birth of Our Lord. If you will make arrangements to meet me there. I have a need to meet with the Royal Council in January. And after that I have summoned a parliament for the new year.'

'So a brief meeting, I collect. At Abingdon.'

'Yes.'

'After which our perfect circles will spin on alone,' I might have said, but I did not since Henry was already too distant to hear.

Irritation became the ruin of my days, annoyance the strident companion of my nights. And when I could not sleep, there was the fear. Military campaigns could so easily result in death.

'You are as intransigent as each other,' I thought in a

moment of weakness as, moodily, I rejected one rolled chaplet and demanded another.

Which I promptly denied with vehemence. Henry was the intransigent one here, unused to allowing a woman access to his closest thoughts and his policies.

As for this Royal Council that seemed to approach every matter with a gauntleted fist, and this parliament that demanded to be heard, how should I deal with them? Was Henry so powerless that he must dance attendance on them? I did not think that the King of England must bow the knee before his subjects. Was he not King in God's name? It did not seem to me that the man I had come to know in Brittany, the man who had moved heaven and earth to woo me, the man who had returned to England to reclaim his inheritance with such fervour and dedication, would become a cipher in so short a time.

Who held power in this country? How would I ever learn it if Henry was unwilling to open the journal of his days for me to read?

★

On the surface Christmas at Abingdon was a splendidly festive affair, enhanced by an aura of family: the presence of all four of Henry's sons as well as my daughters. I might have more than a brief acquaintance with John and Humphrey but this was an opportunity to meet Hal and Thomas, both young men who had already had their taste of warfare. Thomas was full of lively humour, Hal more reserved. And suffering, beneath the austere demeanour that cloaked his young shoulders. His greeting was courteous but not effusive.

I doubted he would ever be effusive, but I was not deterred. I knew how to deal with growing boys.

Except that Hal was no longer a boy. He was a young man blooded in battle. By the Virgin he was! It was a terrible blemish for a young man to carry, a blow to his pride as much as to his flesh.

'Will you allow me to help you?' I asked when we had a moment's privacy between the religious observance and the feasting. No point in pretence; the boy was in pain.

'And how can you do that, Madam?'

So he would deny any such need, a normal reaction from a youth who had a dignity to uphold. It was natural that he would reject my approach, a mere well-meaning female, with tinctures and potions tucked in her sleeves.

'One of my household,' I ventured, 'Mistress Alicia, the nurse who has the care of my daughters, is skilled in dealing with the aftermath of severe wounds. She has salves and ointments, of great value, to encourage restoration of the flesh.'

Hal visibly stiffened. 'There is no need. A soldier must bear the wounds he suffers in battle. My father's surgeon John Bradmore has done all that can be done.'

'Master Bradmore saved your life, I have no doubt. But I think there is a need, if only to relieve the pain. I know that you were greatly hurt and I think it still troubles you.'

I could see it in his eyes, the constant dragging hurt of a deep wound, as I offered a more direct comment that would influence this controlled future king who was destined to bear such a terrible wound, for the arrow head that had found its mark, from one of the Cheshire bowmen in the Battle of

Shrewsbury, had been lodged deep within the bone of his cheek. It was a miracle that he was alive.

'No one doubts your courage, Hal. You do not need to suffer. Also the salves will restore the quality of your skin, so the wound becomes less obvious.' I placed my hand on his arm, risking rebuttal, knowing, as did he, that nothing would ever fully mask so hideous a scar. 'Let Mistress Alicia try what she can do. An ointment of Wood Betony will do no harm and may do much good. Nor will it hurt you more than you have already been hurt.' I felt him relax a little beneath my fingers and smiled at him. 'Pride should not stop you. I am not your mother and can claim no authority over you, but I know all about the pride of young men. I have my own sons. Will you allow Mistress Alicia to come to you? No one else need know but you and she.'

I would not talk to him of the properties of hemlock and henbane, difficult herbs, witches' herbs to bring death and terrifying hallucinations. He did not need to know. Hal might balk at their usage but in the right hands they had the power to alleviate the most severe of pains. I could concoct a tincture, the sharp taste disguised under the heavy sweetness of honey. Mistress Alicia would administer it as carefully as any nurse to her charge, to allow this impressive prince a good night's sleep.

After a moment's thought, Hal smiled, his sombre face lighting as if from an inner candle. He was much like his father. 'My thanks, Madam Joanna. I am grateful for any help that will make my future wife not look on me with horror.' He took my hand and kissed my fingers, and then my cheek, admitting: 'You are very kind. Sometimes the pain is still great. I will let Mistress Alicia come to me.'

If Henry learned what I had done, he said nothing, allowing both Hal and myself our privacy, for which I was grateful. I thought that neither father nor son would appreciate the content of some of my manuscripts.

'You look sombre,' Henry observed in a moment's respite after we had returned from a hectic hunt through the meadows and he helped me dismount. 'Too much hunting?'

I shook my head, already turning away.

'You miss your sons. That's it, isn't it?' It made me stop and look back.

'Yes.' Briefly, very briefly, for I still had not entirely forgiven him, when he put his arm around me I rested my head on his shoulder. 'Celebrating the New Year without them is always difficult.'

'I am sorry.'

It helped, that smallest acknowledgement, so that the tensions between us retreated from the knife edge on which they had been balanced. There might even have been a restoration of warmth between Henry and myself, but it was a fragile thing and needed nurturing. Whatever problems dogged him, Henry had not escaped them for the birth of the Christ child. Barely were the Twelfth Night junketings over than Henry was heading back to Westminster. No nurturing was possible.

'Do I accompany you?'

'If it is your wish.'

It seemed to me that he did not greatly care. He was stacking documents, handing them to one of his clerks.

'What are they?' I hoped for a reply.

'Proposals for a tax, to be raised on the value of land-holdings.'

'Will parliament and the Council accept them?'

'They must. There's a lot hanging on it.'

Nothing more.

'Will you be busy?'

'Yes. You could go on to Eltham with the girls if you would find that more comfortable.'

I went to Westminster, of course. And once there I asked Baron Thomas, newly returned to Court after the military success against the Percy rebels, 'Who rules this country, Lord Thomas? Parliament, Council or King?'

'A heavy subject, Madam, for so bright a day.' He looked startled at my forthright approach with no gesture towards polite welcome. Whereas he kissed my fingers with punctilious grace.

'Heavy for any day. Who holds power here?'

'It is a matter of balance. Discretion is needed in all things, Madam.'

'The answer of a born diplomat and courtier, Lord Thomas. Are you avoiding my question?'

'Possibly, Madam.'

He bowed and walked away. And I realised, after all he had done for me, I had not even had the courtesy to ask him about his welfare and that of his children. I had disappointed him, and I was regretful. I did not like to be thought discourteous. Neither could I afford to alienate the friends I had in England. There were few enough of them.

But discover more I must. Since Henry was as close-latched

as a cleric's purse, and Lord Thomas obdurately loyal, I must make my own arrangements.

★

I had sent for him. Bishop Henry, resplendent with the intricately linked chain of Lord Chancellor gleaming. I thought he sighed as he walked into my private chamber in the Tower, for once, at my arrangement, free from clerks and officials. He sat neatly on one of the clerk's stools, one leg crossed over the other, his velvet cap poised on one knee.

'I have the strangest feeling that you have a request for me.'

'Don't worry. I'll not ask the impossible.'

Although perhaps I did. Perhaps he would refuse, Queen or no Queen. I did not know the precedent for this, but I could guess. The Bishop smiled. I returned the smile with dulcet charm. We had come to a remarkably good understanding.

'I have come to realise that I know nothing of how this country is governed,' I said plainly. 'It is becoming a weakness for me, this not knowing. I need to learn more, rather than being cushioned by those who tell me it is not their place to inform me, or who do not understand why I would wish to know. Henry is either silent or absent. Or just angry.'

'Understandable.' Bishop Henry shrugged. 'How may I help?'

I told him.

'No.' He refused without even taking a breath.

Why not?' I was determined not to be refused.

'There is no precedent for it.'

'Does that mean it cannot be done?'

I poured a cup of ale for him.

'Not quite,' he admitted. For a moment he sat in contemplation, running a finger around the rim of his cup. 'Alice Perrers, the old King's mistress—our grandfather—broke the precedent, but that was only because she had been accused of witchcraft and was summoned.'

'That is hardly likely to be relevant to me.'

'No.' His brows levelled ominously. 'I will not arrange it. If you were discovered, your reputation for meddling would be rolled even further into the mire of foreign relations.'

'Meddling? I do not meddle. In fact, I would like to meddle, as you so inelegantly put it, more than I am allowed.'

'And that's the crux of the matter, my dear Joanna. It is thought that you might indeed meddle. We do not think kindly of Breton meddling at this moment. Hand in glove with the Welsh.'

'I know. The bloody Welsh.' I remembered Henry's cold fury.

'Exactly. So I will not.'

I persisted. He could not refuse for long.

★

'Stand there. Don't move. Don't shuffle. Don't even breathe.' Bishop Henry's hand was heavy on my shoulder, his voice soft but authoritarian in my ear. 'If you are discovered we're both up to our necks in hot water.'

'Will not even your dignity as bishop and Chancellor save you?' I whispered back. I felt a breath of nerves on my nape, but I had got my way.

'I might survive the approbation. It will do *you* no good at all.'

I stood, dark cloaked, dark hooded, in the shadow of a screen set up by some clever means by Bishop Henry in the side gallery to the rear of the Great Hall at Westminster. I could see little, but I would hear all, and I found that I was trembling. Never having seen Henry dealing with matters of government in this formal setting, I did not know what to expect, but would it be so different from John and his dealings in Brittany? I prayed for a good outcome, even though I did not know what that would be. And I prayed for an understanding of what it was that drove Henry so that he slept little and worried much.

Here Henry was meeting with the parliament he had summoned. In my mind's eye I could see him, striding into the chamber, footsteps echoing, then taking the royal throne in this magnificent setting. His figured houppelande would fall in majestic folds to his ankles, sleeves and cape edged with royal ermine, his burnished hair clipped around with a golden coronet. I might not see, but I could imagine as silence fell, taut and severe. This parliament would be impressed. It would be cooperative, amenable to Henry's request for taxation. It needed Henry's steadying hand on the reins of power to obliterate insurrection and so ensure England's future greatness.

Here I would learn. Here I would gain a sense of Henry's calm assurance, his clear authority, his unquestionable right to wear that coronet.

And did I learn?

Oh, I learned it well, retreating even further into the shadows.

What a lesson it was for me as the next hour unfolded.

What an appalling education in humiliation and degradation. It was an essay in calculated insolence, impossibly damaging to Henry's dignity and majesty as King as the Speaker issued parliament's demands. The words might be honeyed in respect but this was all artifice; their intent was vicious. This body of subjects, summoned by Henry, proceeded to question Henry's spending, his taxation, his choice of advisers, even his right to rule England. Henry was ordered by this recalcitrant parliament to reform his lifestyle and practise economy. He was advised to discuss every matter of business with his Council if he wished to enjoy peace in his realm. His request for taxation based on landholding, for which he had held out so much hope, was thrust aside until parliament was satisfied with Henry's response to their demands. Their demands!

It was a stunning rebuke from subjects to their King.

Throughout it all, even when his right to rule was actually questioned, Henry responded with clear argument that nothing could shake.

'It is known to the whole realm that I am the true heir of Lancaster. I was chosen by all the lords of this realm to be its governor and its King. I have the right to rule this country as I see fit.'

It was to my mind an irrefutable argument. I stood in stunned silence, absorbing his pain as he answered every attack, but to no avail. I could not see Henry but I understood, from the low level timbre of his voice, his anger at what this parliament was demanding from him: that Henry's royal accounts be subject to public scrutiny.

How could he tolerate such defiance, so much rank

disaffection? Standing as motionless as the pillar at my side, I wondered at his apparent weakness. Was it merely a matter of financial dependence? But was it not in the interest of England to destroy the Welsh rebels once and for all? Surely they would see the need. If I were Henry I would dismiss this rabble of Englishmen who had no respect for their ruler, and summon another parliament.

If I were Henry…

But then, I was not, and could not understand how this had happened, that he should be supported so strongly, so effectively, against Richard, yet within four years here he was forced to face such rampant disobedience, such defiance at the hands of his own parliament.

As my heart beat in compassion for him, Henry's hopes of taxation were rejected out of hand. The insurrections and incursions that tore England apart weighed nothing against parliament's hold on Henry's purse strings.

And here was the measure of my new knowledge. Now I understood Henry's silence, and I understood the dogged protection of his close family, his friends, who closed ranks around him. Now I understood his reticence to involve me. Like the lock of my ivory coffer, where the key clicked neatly, cunningly, into place, all became clear to me. This was his burden to bear, his task to restore England to peace and fair rule, even when thwarted by this ill-mannered, disloyal body. What a terrible weight for him. And even worse that he could not, would not, share it with me.

For what man of Henry's imperious nature would admit to his wife that his parliament was beyond his control? What man of pride would confess willingly that his authority, sanctified by God, was under threat from a power apparently greater than his own?

And then, when I thought this parliament's defiance could get no worse.

A pregnant hush. A rustle of leaves of parchment. A new voice.

'We present a petition, Sire. That in the interests of our security at this dangerous time of imminent invasion, all French persons, Bretons, Lombards, Italians and Navarrese be removed out of the palace.'

The words rolling off the man's tongue with such relish fell into my mind with all the clarity of a herald's summons to arms. By what right did this parliament make this demand? Of course Henry would refuse. He must refuse.

'I will consider it,' Henry said, voice flat, without expression. A voice of compromise that chilled my blood for I knew full well the target here. My household. My servants and ladies in waiting. The petition might wish to rid England of French and Lombards and Italians, of whom there were many amongst the mercantile interests in London, but its primary aim was to rid the Court of the Bretons and Navarrese. My own servants. This parliament would dictate the composition of my own household. And Henry had not refused it.

From compassion, my emotions leapt to bright anger. This visit of mine, dangerous as it might be, had proved more than an education. It had opened my eyes to the true relationship between Henry and his subjects, whispering in my ear as the members stood in a rustle of cloth and a shuffle of leather.

They might well wish to be rid of you too.

Bishop Henry came to collect me when the Hall was emptied, the session at an end.

'Let's move fast. Was it worth it?'

'It was a despair of enlightenment.'

'So now you know. But don't tell Henry of this little escapade. His temper is slow and infrequent, but it can be brutal when roused. I've no wish to bear the brunt of it.'

'I think it will be on my head, not yours.' I squeezed his hand. 'But he will never know. How could I tell him that I had witnessed his ignominy?'

'You could not.'

I felt scoured of emotions, but now I understood to some degree the power battle in which he was engaged. I also understood the unwillingness of Henry's friends to reveal the extent of his political weakness to me. And clearly I played some part in it, for the hatred of Bretons was far stronger than I had ever appreciated. The powers assaulting Henry from all sides would well threaten the security of his throne, but more damaging than that to my mind, and far more crippling, this had been a very personal attack on his pride, his royal dignity. His honour, which so strongly coloured the man he had grown to be. How could the proud Lancaster heir ever support such overwhelming disgrace?

He deserved my complete allegiance in the face of so much hostility. He deserved my participation in every facet of government.

★

Use a hatchet, Bishop Henry had advised, so here I was, not to cajole but to demand.

'If your Royal Council does not trust me, Henry, give me something to do. Give me some authority. Allow me some power of my own. If you show that you trust me, it will show your hide-bound subjects that they can trust me too.'

Putting aside my cloak, allowing him a little time to recoup, I discovered Henry gone to ground in a distant chamber, where he studied me thoughtfully. It was a spare room of cold stone, perfect for a conversation between wary antagonists; a room without luxury or decoration, unlike Henry. Still impressive in blue and ermine but the coronet discarded, his hair giving the impression of a windblown disorder from restless fingers, he was seated at a wide table, surrounded by documents, the greyhound somnolent and curled at his feet. Perhaps my timing was not as sensitive as it might have been given the morning's parliamentary débâcle, but I could see no hope of improvement. Why wait another day, a week? Better to tackle this abyss between us, that was growing deeper and wider by the hour. Henry's stare was unnerving, but I would not be unnerved.

'If you do not wish to put the delicate matters of finance into my hands,' I continued, unable to resist a barb of my own, 'then give me the negotiations for Philippa's marriage with the royal house of Denmark. That should fit suitably into the role of a mere woman.'

A breath of silence. Then:

'So you want to help?' Henry's tone was as discouraging as his speculative regard. 'Forget the wedding. Get the God-forsaken Bretons to enter into a peace treaty with us. Or at least a truce. That should do it.'

He brought his fist down on the parchment spread out

before him. A diagram of the structure of a new cannon, lethally menacing in its bold lines. A fitting subject, I thought, to blast the parliamentary opposition out of existence. I could understand Henry's ire, even if it was directed at me. I was after all the nearest object to attack.

'You wish me to open negotiations with my son,' I said. 'I can do that.'

Which offer he waved aside, the parchment rolling up, hiding the diagram. Henry, I saw, had been drawing it himself. I had not known of his interest in cannon.

'With Burgundy breathing down the young Duke's neck? What hope of a successful outcome, when Burgundy is hand in glove with France? I suppose it is impertinent of me to expect it of you.' He frowned as a thought returned to him. 'You could of course stop sending the Duke rents.'

Well, I had dug my own grave there, had I not? I was in no frame of mind for confession. Even though Henry promptly took my silence for guilt.

'There's nothing you can do, Joanna. Deal with your own household. That will be enough.'

It was damning. Bishop Henry's hatchet was failing, but I was in no mood for the whore's talents. Neither was Henry. Promptly, I lost all patience.

'So it's not only your ministers who do not trust me, Henry. It appears to be a complaint that is contagious, like a virulent rash. You do not trust me either, do you?'

His brows had levelled, flattened, much in the manner of those of Bishop Henry. 'I trust no one in the present climate.'

How neatly he had slid round the edge of my accusation. 'You have not answered my question.'

'Because I don't know the answer to it.' He spread out the diagram again, anchoring it wide with his fists. 'I trusted the Percys. They stood for me when I returned to England. They raised their retinues to fight for me. I thought they would be the backbone of peace and stability for me in England, holding the north and west in my name until my sons were older. I gave them my trust, and what did they do? Rise in rebellion against me because my gratitude did not support their ambitions. I misjudged the extent of their ambition.'

'But the Percy insurrection is destroyed,' I said.

'Northumberland lives still. And now it seems that I have misjudged my own family. Even my own blood is potentially aligned against me.'

'Your family?' Now that had caught my attention.

His expression was not encouraging. 'So now I trust no one. In future I alone will deal with the threats to my kingdom.'

'But you cannot do it alone.'

'I must. Let me read this to you. And before I begin I should perhaps explain that I am intended as the infamous moldewarp, the mole.' His lips twisted in disgust on the word, sliding a document towards him with one finger as if to touch it was anathema. 'A creature that creeps on its belly in the dark. Am I a mole? I am a son of kings, of Lancaster, God help me!'

He began to read, hard and fluent, now prowling as he read, as if stillness were impossible.

'A Dragon shall rise up in the North—the Earl of Northumberland himself—which shall be fierce and shall declare war against the Mole and shall give him battle. This

Dragon shall gather into his company a Wolf that shall come out of the West—my present adversary Owain Glyn Dwr— that shall also begin warfare against the Mole, and thus shall the Dragon and the Wolf bind their tails together...'

'Henry!' I stopped the flow, astonished at the tenor of what he was reading. 'What is this?'

'A prediction. A prediction of my downfall at the hands of my enemies. An open invitation to insurrection.'

'From whom?'

'Does it matter? It was written down at the beginning of my grandfather's reign, so I am told. The Prophesy of the Six Kings. The sixth king after King John will be the last. I am the sixth king. I have been reminded of it by some malign hand. Let me continue, my dear wife...

'Then shall come a Lion out of Ireland...'

'And who is this lion?'

'Edmund Mortimer, son of my cousin Philippa. Royally born. Plantagenet born. He was taken prisoner by Glyn Dwr two years ago, then promptly compounded the problem by marrying Glyn Dwr's daughter, by God! Now he has ambitions of his own, as I always suspected. Did I not say that my own family was digging hard at the foundations of my power?' Henry returned to his furious reading. 'So Mortimer shall fall in company with them, and then shall England tremble.' He took a breath. So did I at the fire in Henry's eyes, turned on me. 'The despicable Mole shall flee for dread, and the Dragon, the Lion and the Wolf shall drive him away. The land shall be partitioned in three parts; to the Wolf, to the Dragon and to the Lion, and so it shall be for evermore. What quaint terminology. But clear for any man with wits to understand.' He refolded the sheet. 'There you have it. And you talk to me of trust. My kingdom to be partitioned by three of my subjects—and one of them my own blood—while I am to be dispatched. In the face of this, what trust is possible?'

'Do you believe it? This prophesy?'

'Whether I do or not, the dice seem to be stacked against me,' he said with a breath of a laugh that had no humour in it at all. 'Tell me what you see, Joanna, here in England. What is it that fills my days?'

He expected an answer, so I gave it. 'Northumberland and Glyn Dwr.'

'Exactly! All I need is cousin Edmund Mortimer added to the fray. And since he is as close to Glyn Dwr as it is possible to be, their tripartite union against me as soon as Northumberland is free from restraint is not a step I would argue against with any conviction. This prophecy is a conflagration waiting to devour the kingdom. So as I said—whom do I trust?'

'You trust me.'

He regarded me. What was he thinking behind that magnificently impenetrable stare? It made me tremble.

'I do not distrust you.'

'I swear that you have more regard for that animal that shadows your heels.'

'Don't bend my words, Joanna. I have enough on my platter without your insecurities.' The hound, Math, sat up, disturbed by our raised voices, so that Henry stopped momentarily in his perambulations to smooth a hand over her ears before flinging himself back in his chair, turning once more to the harbinger of death beneath his hand.

I was summarily dismissed.

Hatchet abandoned, I stalked from the room, leaving him to his deliberations, but not before I had acquired the prophetic warning, reading it at my leisure when the door to his chamber was closed against me. As I took in the cunning depiction of Wolf, Dragon and Lion, it made me understand how hard-pressed Henry must think himself to be. I had not realised how much he feared for his kingdom. Now it was becoming clearer, illuminating his most deep-seated fears. Whatever the level of truth in this prophesy, it posed a terrifying threat with its magical foresight.

Returned to my chambers, I consigned the document to the flames, watched it curl and fall into ash. Would that it were as easy to destroy the damage it could cause, for events were conspiring to ensure that Henry trusted me as little as he did the Lion, the Dragon and the Wolf.

How would he see me?

The Snake from across the Sea, I supposed. The Serpent, the ultimate symbol of treachery and mistrust since its advent with the apple in the Garden of Eden.

How it hurt. A knife in the flesh. An arrow in the heart of my marriage; all I had dreamed and hoped for in those days of my wooing was ephemeral, disappearing like mist under a noon sun as reality laid its hand on me.

Be patient, I urged, despite the pain. Henry will solve the problems of Glyn Dwr and parliament. Of Northumberland and Edmund Mortimer. The Dragon, the Wolf and the Lion will be destroyed as Henry emerges triumphant to disprove this meddlesome foreseeing. And when he does, one day there must surely be room for negotiation between

England and Brittany to restore peace. One day we will have time to sit and talk again and share that love that brought us together. And that I knew, more clearly than all the rest. The love that had brought me from Brittany to this marriage must not be allowed to become nothing more than a shimmering illusion under the weight of politics and distrust. I was no Serpent.

I trust no one.

What a disturbing admission to hear from his lips.

Even though I understood Henry's bleak scepticism, I could see no way forward for us. Unless I apologised to Henry. Or he apologised to me. But for what would we apologise? It seemed that fate had stacked the scales against us, as the prophesy had stacked the dice against Henry.

★

I was singing, dolefully, suffering a delayed sense of guilt.

> '*Go heart, hurt with adversity,*
> *And let my lord thy wounds see!*'

The door to my private chamber was pushed open, causing me to look up from where my fingers plucked at my lute strings with a melancholy that echoed my heart. When I saw that it was Henry standing just within the door, holding an object in the crook of his arm, I smacked my hand down to still the tune. I would not wish him to know that I was labouring under any form of regret. I wished I had been playing a spritely Burgundian dance.

But Henry knew the song well, and with a neat switch of words, after closing the door against the ever-inquisitive Math, he completed the couplet.

> 'And tell her this, as I tell thee,
> Farewell my joy, and welcome pain, until I see my lady again.'

He did not need the lute. He could hold a tune perfectly, which irritated me even more. His ear for music far outstripped mine.

I dismissed my women who were sitting in various attitudes, stitching or merely engaged in some desultory exchange. Their eyes had sharpened at Henry appearance, but this would not be a conversation where either of us would want an audience. I watched him, unable to sense what he might say, a failing which was becoming a habit. I waited until the last of my curious women had crossed the threshold and Henry closed the door softly behind them.

'So you have abandoned your construction of a death-dealing weapon,' I said. 'Your aim against those who displease you, if you were to fire it yourself, would be excellent. I can only trust that I am never in your sights.'

No apology from me here. I was unbending. Unsmiling. And yet I raised my hand in some sort of greeting because I knew what good manners were. 'You are welcome here.'

Henry's expression was as reserved as mine, his eyes unwavering. 'I was not sure that I would be. Forgive me. You deserve better than you got from me.' He did not move from his stance by the door. 'It is not your fault.'

'That I am Breton by association? No. It is not. I hope that you will remember that.'

'And I hope that you will remember that I am not always my own master.'

My heart shivered with the memory of that disastrous confrontation with his subjects in parliament. I could not tell him that I had seen his humiliation, even though I longed to ask why he had allowed it.

'So I understand,' I said.

Neither of us moved. There was no path to reconciliation here. Well, for the sake of my own conscience, I would make it easy for him. Or at least not as difficult.

'Will you come and sit with me? Or is this a mere passing visit between the formulating of policies beyond my knowledge with your ministers? If so I accept your apology.'

He approached to stand, looking down at me from his impressive height, a frown in his eyes, the box, for that is what it was, still awkwardly cradled in a hand that was far more used to wielding a sword.

'Are you regretting coming to England, Joanna?'

If it was a plain-speaking that shocked me, I gave no sign, and gave back measure for measure. 'Sometimes, yes.'

'I'm sorry for that.'

'I try to be adaptable. I know the pressures on the ruler of the realm. I don't expect you to dance attendance on me.'

'We won't always be so beset with confrontations.'

Still disconcertingly grave, he took my hand and raised it quite formally to his lips, as he used to do when I was still a wife and he a widower without an inheritance. 'I remember why I wooed you. And why you came to England. We have had barely more than a year together. Do we accept that our love is of a lesser importance than affairs of government?'

'Yes,' I said. And when his brows rose: 'You said you enjoyed my honesty, so I will tell you. I feel I am treading on perilous ground, that if I step off the narrow path, I will sink without trace in a quagmire that will destroy the foundations of what I thought we had. We have had so little time to build on those foundations. No time at all, in fact. How many hours in a day, in a week, do we spend in each other's company? To talk, to exchange ideas. Even to laugh together. I accept that men and women of our status must put duty first. I have lived with that all my life. It was instilled in me since the day of my birth. But, by the Virgin, I sometimes feel that I made a bad bargain. Sometimes I wish...'

I stopped, disturbed by what I had just admitted.

Henry was equally stunned. Then: 'Don't stop now.'

'Then this is truth, Henry. I gave up everything for you. Home, children, my authority as Duchess of Brittany. I have received little in return. I am used to having power at my fingertips, but here I have none.' I raised a hand to halt his predictable intervention. 'I don't expect to rule, of course I do not! But I am not allowed to employ the skills that I have, not even to your benefit. I feel that I am under scrutiny from your English lords from the moment I emerge for Mass to the time I remove my veil at night, and I don't measure up to the image of what they would like their Queen to be. Probably genteelly silent and prettily self-effacing, sitting within her women, utilising her hands and mind to nothing more innoc-uous or strenuous than stitchery and lute-skills. I am worth more than that. As for us—you and me, Henry—we meet so infrequently that we have to renew our acquaintance every time we do. I am living in a state of betwixt and between, unsure of my role, certainly unsure of my acceptance. So yes, sometimes I regret coming here. There is a chasm growing ever wider between us.'

'We must not allow that.'

'No. For even when we are at odds, I have a need to be with you. This estrangement hurts me beyond bearing. But I swear I cannot find a bridge to cross this divide. When I try, you retreat in smart order. Or chop down the bridge supports.'

'Whereas you, Madam Joanna, are equally quick to set fire to the planks. It hurts me too.' He hooked a stool with his foot and sat in front of me, all in one fluid movement. 'Shall we try again?'

'Yes.' And after barely a moment's thought, because that one accusation, that I was funding Burgundian hostilities, had hurt more than most: 'I should tell you, Henry—even though it does not sit well with me—that I did not tell you the whole truth. I did not send viable rents to my son. I would never fund Breton campaigns against England. Nor would I ever support Burgundy's ambitions.' I paused, seizing my courage, for I had indeed been at fault. 'It was not what it seemed, and I was not honest with you.'

Henry's brows twitched, his mouth set again. We were still not on a safe path. 'It might be better if we did not return to that point of dissension.'

'But listen.' At last I put the lute aside, carefully on the floor. 'All I sent was a tally of the rents due to me that had never been collected. Nor ever will be, I expect, since I failed in all the years of my marriage. Those rents will not aid Breton coffers, not at all. The landowners are famous for their resistance to their overlords. They'll not pay unless an army descends on them.' I saw the surprise, the sudden relief. 'I should have told you, but I was too angry. The truth is that the rents I gifted to my son are well-nigh worthless. I suspect there is insufficient income from them for Burgundy to purchase a new horse.'

Henry considered this.

'And I was too impatient to discover the truth.'

I lifted my shoulders, let them fall. 'You didn't know. But you would not have listened anyway. So I let you believe the worst of me.'

'Leaving us both martyrs to a misunderstanding.'

'Yes.'

Seated though we were now, close enough for intimate conversation, so close that I could count the faint lines that might deepen if he smiled, we were still stepping cautiously around each other. Our love was still so new, so uncertain, and now furiously undermined. Placing the box at his feet, Henry lifted my lute, his fingers producing from its strings a ripple of beautifully plangent chords, so beautiful that they awoke my senses, forcing me to swallow.

'Don't shut me out, Henry,' I said, snatching at control.

'Sometimes I must. I have brought you a peace offering.'

Exchanging the lute for the little box, he offered it, carved in ivory, placing it in my hands, where, turning it so that it glowed in the light, I stared at the exquisite workmanship.

'It is beautiful.'

A virgin was in process of entrapping a unicorn, its proudly horned head resting delicately in her lap, while a pair of lovers sat under a tree with a spritely falcon to keep them company.

'I have never seen a unicorn,' Henry observed conversationally.

'And I, of course, am no virgin.'

'So you are unlikely to satisfy my curiosity by being able to entrap one for me.'

A little ripple of humour, of shared delight in this fine object that we could both admire. How long was it since we had experienced that? I found myself smiling at the virgin, and then at Henry, who smiled back, with such gentleness that all the hard ridges that seemed to encase my heart were softened.

'I will pretend if you wish,' I said, laughing a little, relief pouring over me.

His hand was possessive on mine. 'No need. We'll leave the unicorn for another day. Open it.'

So I did, and lifted out a double-sided comb enhanced with courtly couples amid luxuriant foliage, exchanging chaplets in a garden of flowers. If the little box was a delight, the beauty of the comb was exquisite.

'It belonged to my grandmother, Queen Philippa,' Henry explained as I examined it. 'I think she brought it with her as a young girl from Hainault. I managed to save it from my sisters who coveted it. I would like you to have it. And, my lady, if it is your will, I think I would like to make use of it.'

I looked up, surprised, for tenderness had been in such short supply. What I saw in his face made me respond:

'It is my will, my lord.'

Thus when I unpinned my veil and removed my chaplet,

Henry was as good as his word, applying the comb until my hair flowed loose and shining over my shoulders, and with it all my anger melted away. For while he combed we talked. Of this and that, of trivial, day to day happenings. All to remind us that love was still alive, even if it had been cooled by the unforgiving wind of thoughtless handling; of power and politics and civil war.

When my hair was smooth enough to please the most critical of my women, I poured wine for Henry and offered him a platter of preserved plums.

He eyed them.

'I presume they come from Brittany. I suppose I should refuse them, since I took you to task.'

'I would be sorry if you did. They are the fruits of my home at Vannes, and they are willingly offered in a spirit of reconciliation.' I continued to hold the platter towards him, temptingly. Bishop Henry's hatchet had gone awry, but there were indeed other methods to seduce a handsome man. 'These plums, from what were my own gardens are, by repute, extremely potent in rousing dormant passions.'

Did they have such a reputation? I had no idea, but on the spur of the moment it seemed to be a worthwhile ploy. As indeed it was. Henry promptly ate one. And another.

'I think you should eat one too,' he remarked. 'Or perhaps a half dozen.'

So I did. Between us we finished the plate. Our kisses were sticky with the sweetness. Was the reputation of my preserved plums from Vannes well-deserved? Oh, but it was.

Our reconciliation moved on to more intimate moments than eating plums and the combing of my hair. Our energies completely ruffled its gleaming length, and in so doing, with no regrets at all, laughter and love and physical desire were restored to us, and with it the bright magic that we had allowed to escape our grasp. All was eloquence and poetry, when we had the breath to be poetic, until Henry murmured against my throat:

'There is something I should tell you, Joanna. Something I should have told you before now.'

'And what is that?' For a moment, caught up in the unexpected hint of strain in what seemed to be a hovering confession, I was anxious rather than diverted.

But Henry sighed, slow and languorous, defusing my fears, his words muffled against the little hollow below my ear. 'Tomorrow and tomorrow will do. Or even later.' He sat up, pulling me with him. 'I never regret that you came to England,' Henry said, incongruously stern despite his unclothed state. 'You are all I could dream of, hope for, in a woman to share my days. To walk with me through joys and travails.'

It was all I needed to know. Tomorrow would do well enough for any confession, whatever it might be. I thought it would be of no moment. And yet I wondered what it was that he had needed to tell me in a moment of emotional passion.

'I love you,' I told him.

It was all I needed to say. We were magnificently reconciled.

★

Until I received a document, delivered by an official minion to my council in the hour before noon on the following day.

'Madam.' Steward Henry Luttrell was holding it out to me. Not a long missive, as I could see by the single folded sheet.

'Is it from Brittany?' I asked, busy with an accounting of the previous month.

'No, Madam. From the Royal Council.'

I saw the expression on his face. I saw his unease.

'Have you read it?'

'I have, Madam.'

I took it, my senses aroused for some level of provocation. What business did the Council have with me? Unless it was to do with my dower. Master Luttrell's sanguine expression said otherwise.

I opened the folded sheet and read the briefest of content. No petition this, as presented before Henry. This was an order, to me, couched in terms I could not mistake.

I refolded it. Sharpened the folded edge with my nail.

Steward Luttrell hovered. 'Madam? What is it you wish me to do?'

'Not a thing, Master Luttrell. Where might the King be at this hour of day?'

Chapter 11

He was not easy to find, but eventually I located him in the ordnance chamber, contemplating a list of weaponry with his Master of Ordnance. Spread before him was once again the diagram of Henry's cannon. Except that Henry had abandoned his artillery and was perusing a document, running his thumb over his chin as he read, a gesture I was quick to recognise. From the set of his jaw he was not pleased with what he read. Only pausing until Henry's official had melted into the background, I cast my communication from the Council before him. I would try to be conciliatory, even as my belly leapt with anger at what had been done without my knowledge. If I had not been present at that parliamentary session, I would have been entirely ignorant of what was planned. Of what was now demanded with the full force of law.

'I have received this,' I said, my tone luminous with distaste. 'You knew, of course.'

It is required, by order of the Royal Council, that those within the Queen's household who are Breton or Navarrese be dismissed. Of those who accompanied her to England, the Queen will be permitted to retain one lady in waiting of her choice.

I had re-read it again since that first revelation, a thrum of dismay running under my skin.

I could not believe that they had done exactly as they had threatened. Removing my whole household. Was their leaving me with one lady in waiting supposed to reconcile me, a sop to my undoubted fury? I was to be isolated. Forced to employ English servants not of my choosing. I would not be dictated to. I would not. I would not accept that those who had served me for so many years should be dismissed at the will of parliament and Council. And yes, perhaps it would have been good policy on my part to have employed English men and women, but did I not so employ them? Every important official in my council was English. Furthermore, had I not accepted the value of Bishop Henry's advice, acknowledging the good sense of employing Englishwomen? But in the fullness of time, from my own choice. Not at the dictates of a parliament, issued in a tone that had absolutely no recognition of my regal standing.

And then there was Henry. Henry who had loved me and wooed me anew with his grandmother's comb and fine words. And then betrayed me.

'You knew about this, didn't you?' I repeated as Henry slowly retrieved the sheet and read.

Of course Henry knew of it. I will consider it, he had said. But I had never thought that he would concur quite so readily or agree to such a whole-scale pruning of my people.

'Yes,' he said.

'Why did you not tell me?'

'I did not think they would act so swiftly.'

'And you will allow this travesty? Why do I have to do this?'

Why should I have to surround myself with English women and servants who certainly had no respect for me as French and Breton? Would it cost me any less to employ a coterie of Englishwomen than it would to keep the Bretons I knew well? I did not think so. But clearly Henry did not accept my annoyance.

'I see no problem. Simply employ English servants instead. Then there will be no question of their loyalty and no inspection of your household.'

It was as if a cold hand gripped my heart. So here was the essence of it. It appalled me that I and my people should have become the object of such suspicion.

'So that's the issue. Their loyalty to England. Are they suspected of being in the pay of Brittany? Of acting as spies?'

'You are too extreme. We have to understand the Council's fears.' Of course Henry would support the English view on this. His combing my hair with such tenderness had made no difference at all. 'Surrounded by Breton ears as we are, who knows what matters of policy might be leaked to Brittany and so to the Welsh? And to the French. It's a matter of security, Joanna. It is not intended as a personal insult.'

'To me it is a matter of my comfort, my disposition of my people. And my authority as Queen. I deny that any one of my household is guilty of passing valuable information to those who would attack us.' And suddenly I saw deeper into this attack on my people. 'Have I been blind? Am I too suspect of being complicit in such treachery, through my Breton servants?' I tilted my jaw. 'Am I so accused of treason? How dare they make such groundless charges.'

'They make no such charges.' And Henry picked up on the most salient point in my complaint. 'It is merely a matter of the protection of the realm, in which sphere, Joanna, you have no authority.'

Whereupon I threw caution and conciliation to the winds.

'And neither, it seems, do you. Are you not able to protect your wife from such encroachments? The Council might as well accuse me of treason! What manner is that in which to treat a Queen of England? Even out of common politeness, I would have expected a personal request, not an order in Council.' I gestured to the Council's dictate. 'I resent such an order.'

Henry's reply was bleak. 'It has to be done, Joanna.'

I stared at him. 'Who is King here?'

'I am King. Do you even know what that means?'

'Very likely not, since you effectively balk at my ever discovering.'

'Then here it is.' His hand clenched into a fist over the letter that he still held. 'This is what it means to me to be King. I am fighting for my Crown. For the security of my country. For the inheritance of my sons. And if that means compromise with parliament, then that is what I must accept, because this damned recalcitrant parliament, as you put it, and the Royal Council, will have it no other way. Even my life is at risk.'

'I do not know that.'

'How would you? Now, if there is nothing else to discuss…'

I stalked through the antechamber, as I so often seemed to stalk, my maids pattering behind, turning at the stair that would lead me to my private chamber. Snatching at a folded sheet tucked into a gap in a window frame. And then, seeing another that had been slid behind the corner of a tapestry, I acquired that too, curiosity rife and for a moment replacing exasperation. Even before I had reached my door I had smoothed them flat, read them. They were exactly the same, written in the same hand with the same seal, and the content, brief though it was, made me shiver with its implied threat. Furthermore as I frowned at what was unquestionably treasonous, I knew where I had already seen such a document. Sweeping on my heel, dismissing my women, I retraced my steps, opening the door on Henry without notice, but not before acquiring another folded sheet, heavy with dust, blown by a draught into the corner of the stairwell.

'You did not tell me,' I announced.

Leaning across the solid lines of the cannon, forearms braced, Henry looked over his shoulder. 'Tell you what?' He was no more accommodating than when I had left, so I held out the three letters.

'These. And before you deny it, you have one too.'

Certainly without artifice but with a definite air of annoyance, Henry slid the crumpled document from where he had placed it, out of my sight. 'Yes, I do. It was sent to parliament. There are others in circulation, all over London, all from the same source.'

'Someone has had a busy few days of penmanship.'

'They have indeed.' Henry showed his teeth in a grim

smile. 'And believe it or not, the threat in this fair screed is far more lethal than any unsigned and unproven prophesy.'

There were letters, purporting to be from Richard, the King whom Henry had challenged for the throne. Richard who had died in Pontefract. But not so! He was, Richard announced in a firm and lively hand, safe and well in Scotland, waiting for his English supporters to rise in revolt against Henry the Usurper, to welcome him back to his throne and his Crown. The signature was his. The seal was his. Or so they appeared to be. This was a personal invitation to insurgency by King Richard the Second.

'What is this?' I demanded.

'A clever forgery. Or not so clever. It doesn't matter. Those who wish to believe it will do so. And the reason that I did not tell you, is that I really did not need to have this discussion.'

'But I do. I presume it is untrue.'

It horrified me that Henry would hide this conspiracy from me, that he would disguise a threat of so personal a nature. Meanwhile, while I tried to preserve a sense of moderation, that the threat could not be as lethal as I imagined, Henry was speaking low and fast, as I had learned that he did when anger simmered on the rim of boiling over.

'Richard is dead by starvation. But which of his erstwhile followers will believe it, if they are intent on rebellion? All I can do is summon Richard's keeper at Pontefract Castle to swear that he is dead and his body witnessed. Not that Richard's followers will accept such a confirmation. I can already hear the blast echoing from one end of England to the other. Would I not pay the man to keep his mouth shut if Richard was indeed alive? Was not the coffin empty of Richard's body when I arranged for it to be buried at Kings Langley? Short of opening the tomb and displaying his maggot-ridden corpse to public view, I have no answer to this malevolent riddle. Perhaps I will do just that…'

At which his temper, usually under such expert control, was lost in spectacular fashion, Henry screwing the offending forgery hard in his hand before hurling it across the room where it bounced against the wall, dropping down onto an array of swords. While the thought came to me, and one that was by no means new, that I did not know the role Henry had played in Richard's death. Had he played any at all? In the face of this passion I would not ask. I did not want to know the answer.

'And, once again, I am under an obligation to answer to parliament,' he continued. 'I have to satisfy them that this is a lie.' Henry had begun to stride across the room and back again, oblivious to the weaponry that lay in ordered formation. 'Do you not realise how viciously damaging this letter could be? If I cannot prove it to be false, nothing more than a malign attempt to undermine my position, the whole country will rise to the rallying cry of King Richard is Alive and we will be back in a sea of blood and destruction up to our necks. Parliament is already demanding that I release Northumberland from imprisonment as a sign of my goodwill.'

I watched him as he wheeled round to come and stand before me, to snatch up two more of the letters and destroy them, tearing them across and across, dropping the pieces at my feet. Now, here was indeed danger, here was no wild imagination. Here was a carefully constructed campaign to call together every disaffected strand in the country to rise up and overthrow Henry, and Henry, full of glittering energy, was beyond anxious. My heart beat slow and hard as real apprehension laid its hand on me, unpleasantly clammy in the mild air. My blood was cold in my belly, but my own temper began to heat because Henry had chosen to deny this plot, and Henry appeared so helpless to stamp it out. As I too was helpless. Easy to destroy a letter of intent, reducing it to powerless scraps on the floor; more difficult to stop a descent into blood and death on a battlefield.

Why was it that my own sense of fear and impotence should reduce me to such white-hot anger? I chose the obvious target for my attack.

'And you will release Northumberland? Even though he is guilty of treason?'

'I think I have no choice,' Henry said, calm returning. 'I have an instinct for survival.'

'Survival! But at what cost? I would not do it. I would not bend the knee to parliament over a matter of such blatant treachery. Northumberland is guilty by his own words. I know that I have advised clemency in the past, but do you simply release him, even though he smirks at your weakness? I would have more pride than to accept such a demand.'

'But you, Joanna, are as proud as Lucifer.'

His expression was shuttered, his voice raw, all the love we had so recently shared held in abeyance. And I flinched. Had not my father been described in exactly those same words, which was to my shame, but there was no turning back now. My reply was unfortunately intemperate. 'And you are not?

Why should I not be proud? My ancestors have been ruling Navarre since...'

'Since mine were Kings of England.' The interruption was biting. 'I might be a new king. And a poor, unworthy king in the eyes of your Valois cousins. I might have wrested a crown that was not mine to take. But I swear there is as much royal blood in my body as there is in yours. I am the heir of Edward the Third, and of Henry the Third through my mother's blood. I am no base-born upstart.'

And I was ashamed at my presumption. But no less angry.

'I do not know you.' Never had I thought to make such an admission.

'No, you don't.'

A silence enfolded us, so searing that it could be felt like a barb in the flesh. There we stood, like pieces on a chessboard frozen into stalemate. No hope of our minds meeting.

Until Henry took the last remaining of Richard's letters from me and spread it over the sketch for the cannon. 'Both weapons of war, in their own way, both with the power to kill,' he observed. 'It seems that the clouds engulfing our marriage are equally black with foreboding.'

'And a torrent is imminent. I am afraid it will sweep us away.'

I became aware that Henry was regarding me, as if he were engaged in a personal debate, in which the outcome was uncertain. My heart plummeted like a stone into a well. I did not think that I wanted to learn more. I had too much to absorb about this troubled state and, more pertinently, this troubled man.

'Is there something else I should know?'

'There is. So let us pre-empt the torrent, even if it does sweep us away. For better or worse, there is someone you must meet. I think it should be now.'

This I had not expected. 'Why?'

'Because we have become enmeshed in so much suspicion and distrust.'

'And who is this person I must meet? Will it heal the wounds we inflict on each other?'

'I doubt it. But it needs to be done.' He took my hand, refusing to allow me to resist. His grip was strong and uncompromising, as was his voice. 'Come with me, Joanna.'

I allowed myself to be manoeuvred from the room, Henry pulling me with him. Was this the strange confession that he had almost broached in the aftermath of desire?

'Why do I think I won't like this?'

'Because it's the truth. You won't. But as things stand between us…'

'Can it make them worse?'

'It depends how magnanimous you can be. If you cannot, then…' He stopped, so that I too halted, and found myself grasped by the shoulders. And there I saw Henry's own uncertainty, but equally his determination. 'If you cannot accept, you are not the woman I had thought I had married.'

I flushed with dismay.

His fingers flexed as he released me, but not before he surprised me by placing a kiss between my brows. And perhaps I recognised some dark humour there. 'I am finding a need to bare my breast before you, Joanna. I seem to have been baring it often of late. Too much for my liking.'

I could not smile. I was too anxious about what this new revelation would be.

★

Coming to the decision that nothing could be gained by postponing this meeting, it was carried out with purpose. Henry escorted me with a firm hand and even firmer stride as he directed me towards a part of the palace set apart from the royal chambers we used, a set of interconnecting chambers that were, it seemed, self-sufficient. Once a nursery, I thought, where nursemaids and servants could care for the royal offspring in well-appointed rooms away from the frenetic bustle of the Court. But Henry's children had long outgrown such needs.

All was quiet behind the first of the closed doors. Who lived so sequestered a life here?

We traversed two antechambers with no words exchanged, until Henry opened a third door and gestured for me to enter. Before us, the small sun-warmed chamber with doors opening off in two directions, contained all the detritus of an indulged childhood, carefully managed. Folded linen. Playthings. A pair of singing finches in a cage hung in the window. I recognised the busy atmosphere immediately from the infancy of my own children. Here was a nursemaid who stood from where she was stitching and curtsied as we entered. And on the floor at her feet a child engaged, with utmost concentration, in threading acorns onto a string.

Until he heard our footsteps. Whereupon he scrambled

to his feet, and would have rushed forward if not restrained by the young woman's hand to his shoulder.

'Let him come,' Henry said with a smile, releasing me.

The boy launched himself at Henry. Before collision, he remembered, lurched to an unsteady halt and bowed with quaint and unsteady decorum, while Henry sank to his haunches, reaching for the child's hand, drawing him close.

'I have been eating,' the child announced.

'So I see. Your tunic bears witness to it.' Henry cast a look in my direction, brows raised. Brows that suddenly showed a marked similarity to those dark bars in the undeveloped face before me. 'This, Edmund, is Lady Joanna. She is my wife.'

The child dimpled with a charm of which he was unaware. It struck hard.

'This, my lady,' Henry was continuing, supremely bland, 'is Edmund. He is my son.'

The likeness was striking. It delivered a blow beneath my ribs so that I had to swallow hard.

Edmund bowed. 'I have a knight and a horse,' holding out to me a wooden toy.

'A very fine knight,' I agreed, taking the offering. I was used to young boys, even though my heart was bleeding.

'He is a very fine knight,' the boy repeated carefully. Retrieving the toy in an instinct of possession, the child ran to where the sun poured through the window, where he knelt to make the horse leap with a loud clatter along the warm boards.

I waited for what would come next. I had no idea what I would say. Whatever I had expected, it was not this. So this was the reality of Henry's confession, neatly slid aside until tomorrow and tomorrow. This was what he had not told me in all the days we had been together. This was it, and I really did not want to know.

'Is all well here, Agnes?' Henry was asking, as if unaware of the turbulence at his side.

'Yes, sir. He grows well and begins to know how to behave.'

'It's time I employed a tutor to teach him his letters.'

Henry walked slowly across to the child, to crouch again and indulge in some exchange which made the boy laugh, then returned at the same steady pace and led me out, while I strove to control all I wished to say. All I wished to know. I could not speak before the child or the servant.

'Edmund is my son,' Henry repeated when we stood facing each other in the little courtyard with its pots of herbs and clipped bushes, out of earshot of the household. A place of peace where the general hubbub of a royal palace carrying out its daily affairs did not carry and even the sound of the birds was muted.

I was not at peace.

I inhaled against the constriction in my chest, the sharp scent of rosemary filling my senses but offering me none of the calm I might have expected from so powerful a herb. There was only one issue in my mind. How could I withstand this? Raising a hand I touched Henry's cheek, as if in affection, as if re-affirming a shared and deep emotion, except that in my heart was all shadow and none of the substance of it. This revelation had, without doubt, shaken me, scattering all my certainties that were already under attack.

'I am trying, Henry,' I said calmly, 'to work out his age.'

'No need. I will tell you.' As my hand fell away, Henry

made no attempt to capture it as once he might. Severe and unyielding, despite the latent heat of the warm stones that surrounded us, he stood alone. 'Edmund was born three years ago. In early summer. Is that what you wanted to know?'

As I thought. As I feared. So the child was conceived in the autumn of the year that Henry had returned to England to take back his inheritance. While I had been worrying about the state of his health and his immortal soul as he engaged in a revolt to take a crown that was not his, Henry had been indulging in intimate relations with some unknown woman. A mere handful of months since he had declared his undying love for me, he had consoled himself with the kisses and embraces of another. While I had yearned for him, fretted for his safety, Henry had taken a woman to his bed. And here was the evidence. A child, obviously recognised, clearly loved, carefully nurtured.

'Was the child born here in England? Or in France before you left?'

How cold my voice. Every inch of me seemed to be encased in a robe of ice despite the sun warming my shoulders through the heavy silk. All my previous doubts and debates were as nothing compared with this. They all fell away under the weight of such a betrayal.

If you cannot accept, you are not the woman I had thought I had married.

Henry's words floated on a sudden burst of bird-song from the stone coping of the high wall above me. But was I? I did not know.

'In England,' he said.

'At least it was not before you made your farewells to me

with such fine words. Although I would be interested to know how long afterwards. Your passion for me was apparently short-lived.'

'I'll not make excuses for what I did, Joanna.' Clipped and short. Henry was as close-governed as I.

'Nor do I ask you to. We were not wed, so your life was your own to direct. And his mother?'

'She is dead. Fortunately I discovered the child before he disappeared into a knot of relatives who would have kept him. I brought him here.'

'Was she your mistress?'

'No. We had no long-standing agreement.'

'Did you love her?'

'No.'

'Have you made a practice of sleeping with passing women?'

'No.'

I could not prevent the catechism, question after question, none of the answers capable of healing the wound he had dealt me. And I realised what I did not know. Another blow that would bring me to my knees, if Henry assented.

'Do you have a mistress now?'

His gaze on mine was unfathomable. 'No, I do not. And have no intention of taking one.'

'Then at least I can be grateful for that. Who was this woman? A wench from a tavern?'

'No. She was no tavern whore.'

'I did not mean that. It does not matter.' And I flung away from him, horrified by the surge of absolute despair.

But it did matter. Oh it did. In that moment when the

sun warmed my shoulders and the herbs cut into neat edges gave off heady scents of summer, I was as cold as winter. I had believed myself to be in love—and it to be reciprocated—while Henry had enjoyed a relationship elsewhere. My thoughts became as bitter as the rue that grew along the edge of the path, its sharp perfume disturbed by my skirts.

'Edmund is my responsibility,' Henry was saying as I attempted to gather together the rags of my dignity.

'Of course he is.' Would I expect any other response from Henry to a child born out of wedlock? He was not the man to abandon a child. It made me feel no better. 'He is a charming boy, impossible to dislike.'

'If you cannot accept him, if you cannot accept my past, then we are destined to enjoy an uncomfortable marriage.'

'Enjoy…? You have damaged me, Henry. I did not expect such evidence of lust between love's declaration and marriage. At best an inconvenience. At worst a deadly sin.'

'My life has not been without sin. But that is not new to you. And I think Edmund's begetting is not the worst of them.' His observation was lightly made but the emotion that coloured his eyes, as I looked back over my shoulder, was far from light. 'A man who usurps another's crown, whatever the justification, is destined to carry the burden of it until the day of his death.' Henry paused, but when I thought he would say more to enlighten me, he dropped the subject with: 'As you say, that does not excuse my sin of lust. I thought you should know.' He paused again, before asking once more the pertinent question. 'Are you capable of compassion, Joanna?'

'I must think about it.'

And Henry left me to make my own way back to the royal apartments. He was in the end as angry as I, his spine as stiff, his shoulders as rigid, while I turned my back, so that I need not watch him walk away from me. I had not handled that well. But, indeed, as I abandoned the courtyard to the pleasing hum of bees and a flitting butterfly, I could not think how I could have made it easier for either of us.

What would be our future together now?

★

I kept myself to myself. My council could deal with my ledgers of finance without my assistance. I cancelled an audience with a deputation of merchants who were hoping for my approval of a consignment of fine sables. Furious with Henry, angry at my own undisciplined response, I could settle to nothing, even though the thought intruded that this was in essence a matter of little account, not worthy of my consideration or my contempt. How many years had Henry been alone since the death of his beloved Mary? Almost a decade now. It would be unrealistic to expect a man of Henry's calibre to embrace chastity. Who was I to castigate him for sins of the flesh? And I flushed as I recalled asking him if he made a practice of sleeping with passing women. How could I have been so vulgar? But disappointment can lure a woman into the crudest of observations.

Two lines of a popular song dropped into my mind.

Love like heat and cold pierces and then is gone;
Jealousy when it strikes sticks in the marrowbone.

The marrow of my bones? That was the least of it. The sharp thorns of jealousy were lodged in every inch of my flesh.

But think, Joanna, I urged, trying for a futile objectivity. At the moment of his invasion with a handful of friends, when he would fear failure, resulting in either death or imprisonment, might he not be driven to submerge his fears in the arms and flesh of a willing woman? A woman who was there and warm and flattered by the attentions of the Duke of Lancaster, while I was far away and closed off to him through unyielding marriage vows. It would be unjust to condemn him for a night's lapse from the high code of morality, before the probability of battle and an unknown future. When marriage to me was not even a speck on his horizon.

Are you making excuses for him? My conscience nudged uncomfortably.

I was, for I could not accuse him of lack of responsibility. Henry would care for the child. He could have abandoned him to the charity of others. It was not unknown. Even to arrange for Edmund to be brought up by someone far from Court would have been a simple matter to arrange. But Henry had brought him here with formal acknowledgement and a duty to raise him as was fitting. More than duty—for was there not an affection between them? It had sparkled in the air in the nursery where the child had laughed with his father.

Who was I to condemn Henry for his acknowledgement of his son?

Yet, in my betrayed heart, I did.

The clash and clamour of past weeks continued to reverberate in my head.

My conviction that I was loved, wanted, desired shuddered into rank oblivion, the conviction that had brought me here through storm and disapproval wavered. Where was the linking of heart and mind that had brought us together in the first place? Every day it disintegrated a little more, as the edge of a tunic would gradually unravel with day to day wear, fraying beyond redemption, with no opportunity to re-stitch and mend it. Henry had combed my hair so that I had trembled with desire, before introducing me to his son born from a moment of physical lust.

Henry had another son on whom to lavish affection. Whilst I...

Emotion caught me unawares; an old theme it might be, but it still had the strength to fill me with grief. Henry had another son, while I had had to leave my sons behind.

But that was not what ate away at my control, sharp-toothed, visceral. My thoughts refused to obey me, instead picking up on that new thought, full of pain, full of disappointment. For was that not at the centre of my unwarranted anger towards Henry and this illegitimate child? There it was, stark as a shadow at noon.

There was no much longed-for sign of my bearing a child for Henry. There would be no child of our love. It was a devastation that I had not admitted, even to myself, until now. I had not realised how much I had hoped for this. Jealousy of this poor, dead, unknown woman who had borne Henry's son became an arrow-storm to strike me anew. Henry had another son, but not by me. My petitions to the Blessed Virgin had failed to receive her blessing. I remained barren.

Hoping for a distraction, I took the steps down into the gardens, so recently a scene of disharmony, so recently abandoned by both of us, where I now heard my daughters engaged in some exciting pursuits of their own. For a little while Marguerite and Blanche sat with me on the bright covers spread by their nursemaids, although it was an effort for me to concentrate on their chattering. It was a relief when they leapt to their feet and raced off along the path.

'Edmund!' Blanche called.

And I looked round. There was the child again with his nursemaid, the sun bringing to life the russets in his hair. In that moment of uncertainty, of cowardice, of blinding regret, I wished I did not have to face this small son of Henry's who had kindled the fires of jealousy so strongly, simply by his existence. It had been my intention to keep my distance.

The boy escaped his nurse to run towards my daughters, calling their names. So they already knew each other. Watching as the girls drew him into a game, much as they would have accommodated their youngest brother, tolerant of his lack of skill at catching a ball, letting him match his steps to theirs when they ran, laughing with him, I considered that they had never talked to me of him. Perhaps they had merely accepted him, simply another occupant of this palace that they had come to call home. It made a bright picture, as the boy galloped across the grass, shrieking with delight, reminding me of my own son Richard, so that I could not watch, and turned my face away.

'With your permission, my lady.' It was Agnes, standing at my shoulder.

It was in my mind to dismiss her, but I did not. 'Of course. Come and sit.' Which she did, with some unease as if she feared a catechism from me. But what to ask? Did I not know enough. And yet…

'When did the child come here?'

'As an infant in arms, when his mother died. I was employed to care for him.'

Agnes looked over at her charge, with pride.

I too watched him, the boy's laughter ringing out as he fell and rolled in the grass. 'What will happen to him?' I asked, without thinking.

'My lord the King plans that he will go into the church when he is grown.'

It made good sense, an obvious road to promotion for a younger son. Or an illegitimate one. Perhaps Bishop Henry would take him under his wing. Bishop Henry knew all about the insecurities for illegitimate children, even those of royal blood. As a son of Duke John of Lancaster and Duchess Katherine, before the hallowed sanctity of their marriage and his own acceptance before the law, Bishop Henry's future had been dependent solely on the recognition and generosity of his father.

The intricate game finally drew to a close, the girls returned breathlessly to me and Agnes took Edmund off. Then the boy came running back to me.

'I am Edmund,' he reminded me, in case I had forgot. A very familiar line appeared between his dark brows.

'I remember you, Edmund.' You might have been mine, I thought.

'I did not say goodbye,' he informed me carefully, as he had been instructed.

How not to smile? 'No, you did not. But it didn't matter.'

'Agnes says that I must be polite. I am the King's son.'

'So you are.' I rose and took him by the hand to lead him to where his nurse awaited him. Until he dragged against my arm, raising memories of my own small children in the past.

'I have dropped my knight.'

Liquid anxiety bloomed in the eyes turned up to me for help. No, it was not Richard he reminded me of, but Henry. The russet-tinted hair, the straight nose, the darkly marked brows. As he grew the child's jaw would firm with strength of purpose. I found that I was staring at him, a desperate longing invading my heart. Until Edmund squirmed to release his hand, so that, through that unexpected ripple of pain, I smiled down at him. Henry rejected my offers of support, but I could remove the sadness from his son's face.

'Then we must find our knight. He will not be far away.' I led Edmund across the grass. 'There he is.'

Edmund pounced in the long grass, before returning to slide his hand with utmost trust into mine.

'Thank you, Lady Joanna.'

So he had remembered. Kneeling beside him, I dusted the debris from his hose where he had earlier fallen in the grass. And when Edmund placed a hand on my shoulder to steady himself, my heart beat with a single stroke of acceptance.

'I have a hole in my knee,' he confided, inspecting the tear with a deep frown, making my heart clench a little.

'It is not a very big hole, Edmund. Agnes will mend it for you.'

The frown was displaced by an infectious beam. It had not been difficult to call him by his name after all; his smile was so thoroughly engaging. Almost I lifted him into my arms, as I would have lifted Richard, but I ruffled his already ruffled hair and sent him off.

As I watched him go, utterly disturbed, with the sun breaking into golden facets in my eyes, I saw the figure at the end of the garden and did not have to blink to recognise it. Of course. Henry had come to find me. He could no more allow this very personal shadow to hover about us without an attempt at healing any more than I. There was no hesitation in me. I walked towards him and we met where earlier we had exchanged such recriminations. Now the singing birds were witness to a softer meeting as I offered my hands, as I acknowledged one salient indisputable fact. Henry had chosen to share knowledge of this child with me. He had humbled himself, admitting his fault, handing power into my hands to forgive or denounce. I could do no less. It reduced my own pride to rubble.

'I am sorry, Henry.'

'No sorrier than I.'

Henry's eyes were bright with understanding. 'Can you accept him?' was all he asked.

I tried to keep my reply light. 'It would be impossible not to. My daughters treat him as a brother.' Then I could be inconsequential no longer for the longing was heavy in me. 'Forgive my intolerance.' I swallowed. 'Forgive my jealousy.'

'I deserved your ire.' He raised my hands, kissing my knuckles very gently. 'I need to tell you that, although Edmund's existence must seem like a betrayal to you, his begetting was not. To my discredit, he was not conceived out of love. My love is for you.'

My regard was steady on his. 'Conceived out of a soldier's excess energies in a time of war.'

'Something like that…'

I touched my fingers to his lips. 'There is no need to explain. I understand.'

As I did, as I must. It had no bearing on what we had together, on what we had become to each other, as I had at last accepted. As I must accept. The finches and the busy insects paid us no heed as Henry kissed my lips with reverence, brushing an inquisitive butterfly from my veil. But a reticence remained between us. Beneath the physical pleasure there was a hindrance against which we might still stumble if we did not have a care. I knew that there were thoughts in Henry's mind that were not open to me, while I could not tell Henry of my desire for a child. Not yet. But one day I would when affairs of state pressed less onerously on his shoulders. If such an unlikely eventuality should ever occur.

★

Invasion had become the talk of the Court when, with the turn of the year, a French fleet was gathering at Harfleur. The news was enough to spur Henry into action. Since he had no money to ready an army or a fleet, a brisk round of royal castles and defences in the south became a thing of urgency to ensure that they were strong enough to repulse any landing. Despite our recent reconciliation, despite our soft words and rapprochement over the existence of Edmund, this would prove to be an emotionally charged farewell.

·I had taken up my position on the steps leading down into the inner courtyard, resplendent in velvet and fur and embroidered gloves against the grip of January cold. The royal escort was present, mounted and heraldically blazing, banners and pennons making a brave display, but Henry was not. Minutes passed. When Henry still put in no appearance, I walked across to Lord Thomas de Camoys and John Beaufort, where we were soon to be joined by Humphrey who, at fifteen and sullen, was ordered to remain behind. I was sympathetic to his adolescent restlessness. I too, to my chagrin, was not wanted.

'I would like to accompany you,' I had said, walking with Henry to Mass on the day before he would leave, seeing no real reason why I should not.

'It would be more politic for you to remain here, as things stand.'

Henry was staring straight ahead. Familiar exasperation shivered my veiling.

'How do things stand?'

'On the cusp of invasion. I am sorry, Joanna, but it would be better if you did not ride into one of our ports with the invading force looming on the horizon.'

It was not my physical security that concerned him. It was the fact that Breton ships were joining the French attack against England. Henry and I might be reconciled as lovers, but events across the sea were conspiring against me, and I was no closer to winning a place at Henry's side in affairs of state. I bit down on a sharp reply, but only momentarily.

'Do you still not trust me, Henry, not to pass state secrets to my son the Duke?'

'*I* trust you. The English in the path of the Breton invaders intent on pillage and destruction might consider that they have cause to be undecided.' He was even brisker than usual.

'I have done nothing to give reason for their suspicions.'

'You don't have to *do* anything. Your association is enough.'

Neither one of us was pleased with the other. My hand closed on the hardest object I had, the reliquary pinned to my bodice, one of Henry's gifts on the occasion of our marriage, and gripped it until my fingers ached. There was no reasoning with him. I might consider our love to be the single shimmeringly brilliant gem in my jewel coffer, but there were so many other treasures capable of adding to the whole sparkling effect. If Henry would only accept my talents and my strength, what a superbly shining crown we would make for England.

'You are a stubborn man, Henry.'

'While you, my love, are deliberately provocative. It will be better if you remain here where you will be safe.' I looked back, lips parted, as I began to climb the spiral stair ahead of him, prepared to ask him if he truly believed me to be under threat, but at the top he took my arm to draw me precipitately into the chapel. 'If you wish to be of help, pray for a fast peace negotiation between our disparate families.'

'Of course. Do I not spend my life in so petitioning the Blessed Virgin?'

'Then the Lady will doubtless be receptive to any request you might make.'

I chose not to reply to so acid a response, but here I was to witness Henry's departure, because to absent myself in a fit of pique would have been discourteous. My smile for public consumption was rigidly bright, my stance uncompromising as the perfect English consort.

There was Henry's favourite horse, one of Lancaster breeding, chafing now at the bit. Once, in the early days of our love, Henry had compared the colour of my hair to its satin sheen. Now saddled, bridled, a cloak was thrown across the whole to cover the beast from withers to tail, the gilded stitching brighter than the wintry sun. It kept my eye. Henry might be ostentatious, but the cloak was too grandly formal for this rapid gallop round royal defences. Henry would surely not wear it. At the animal's head was Elmyn Leget, one of Henry's most capable squires, together with his head ostler.

Where was Henry?

There he was, loping down the steps, Math bounding to greet him with noisy joy. Striding across the courtyard, Henry handed a fistful of documents to one squire to pack into the travelling coffers, whilst seizing felt cap and gloves from another, and nodding to the squire who held the horse's reins, acknowledging his brother John who strolled over towards him. Immediately, with a bow and a flourish, Elmyn stripped off the cloak, folding it over his arm, and the ostler ran a soft leather cloth, which had been tucked in his belt, over the glossy surface of the saddle. Usual enough I supposed, until, after a final all-encompassing swipe of the leather, the ostler buried his nose in the cloth to sniff loudly. He tested the surface of the saddle with his thumb, head tilted. And for that moment it seemed that every eye in the courtyard was on him, including mine. Including Henry's.

We waited.

With a saturnine grimace the ostler addressed Henry

who clapped him on his shoulder. A coin exchanged hands. Sweat gleamed on the horse's coat. The entourage returned to its own affairs, and Henry mounted. It was as if it had been done many times before. A ritual. But enough to catch my interest.

The cloak was carefully folded and packed into one of the wagons.

At this point in the proceedings, Henry deigned to notice me. He raised his hand in recognition. And I reciprocated as he manoeuvred his horse towards the steps where I had taken refuge out of the way of the general mêlée.

'God go with you, my lord.' My voice was clear and strong. My smile perfect as I presented my hand.

'And with you, my lady.'

Henry raised my hand to his lips. Courteous, attentive, but his stare was inimical, his hands already gloved so that the touch was impersonal, his lips a bare skim before I was released. I was no longer smiling.

'When do you return?'

'By the end of the month.'

'I will look for you, my lord.'

'I will send a courier, to keep you informed of where I will be.'

'I will be delighted to know.' How hard it was to keep the edge from my replies. 'God Speed. I will petition the Blessed Virgin to smile on you.'

'Which is more than you do, Madam.'

Henry bowed, signalled his escort to precede him, snapped his fingers to the hound and drew alongside Elmyn and his brother without a backward glance.

All very neatly done. Exactly as I had wished, apart from that final, painful little stab. I wished my heart did not feel as if it were crushed by a heavy slab of marble. It was as if we were hostile forces, withdrawing after a failure to negotiate suitable terms, only to re-engage at some future date. It would not hurt if I did not love him so much.

I turned to go, for it was in my mind to return to my accommodations before Henry had ridden through the gates, ashamed that I should be so churlish, but I was past making excuses to myself or to Henry. Instead, recalling what had taken my interest, I gripped Lord Thomas's sleeve before he could mount and follow.

'Explain the ostler and the saddle to me. Is it an English ritual?'

Lord Thomas might have stifled a sigh. 'No, Madam. It is not of long standing. But it has been thought to be a necessity.'

'Why?'

A pause. 'A matter of security, my lady.'

'And how would that be?'

This was making no sense. Lord Thomas hesitated again.

'Tell me,' I demanded.

'Because there was an attempt on my father's life,' Humphrey announced.

My eyes flew to his. Then to Lord Thomas, who picked up the tale, since there was no help for it.

'It was before your marriage, in the first year of this reign. There is no need for concern, Madam. As you see, we have taken precautions.' Lord Thomas fidgeted with his bridle as if wished he were gone. 'It was the matter of a poisoned saddle, the leather impregnated with a substance that would have killed the King in great agony if he had ridden ten miles.'

'What was it?' I asked.

Lord Thomas shrugged his ignorance. 'Fortunately it had a harsh aroma that pervaded the smell of horse and leather and so was discovered. We make sure there is no possibility of a repeat performance. As for the substance used…'

But I knew what it was. There in the sunlit courtyard I considered my knowledge of the poisons to hand in any well-stocked garden. Witches' herbs, all of them, with potent uses against an enemy. Henbane, to call up evil spirits. Black Hellebore to rouse a violent frenzy in the most well-mannered man. Belladona, the Deadly Nightshade, bringing forgetfulness and death. And then Monkshood. Wolf's Bane. This was undoubtedly what the assassin had used, a paste from the deadly Wolf's Bane, for indeed it was deadly, rapidly absorbed through the skin, whether contact with seeds or stem or root. Whoever had applied it to the saddle had not intended Henry to live long. It was what I would have chosen if I had wanted a man dead yet keeping the hand of death secret.

'I did not know of this attempt,' I said.

'He would not tell you. He would not worry you.'

'There was also the metal contraption that was secreted into my father's bed to spear his vitals,' added Humphrey with some relish. 'But we think that wasn't true. Just a rumour.'

'And what did your father say to this metal contraption that might only be a rumour?' I asked, by now thoroughly jolted.

'That it was none of my affair and I must hold my tongue,' Humphrey said.

'Some fear-mongering by those who cry "King Richard is Alive" and would drive the kingdom to destruction by so doing,' said Lord Thomas to dampen Humphrey's ardour and reassure me. By now I could not mask my horror.

'And then there was...' Humphrey began until Lord Thomas choked it off with a hand heavy on the boy's shoulder. But it was all I needed.

'How many attempts have there been on his life?' I demanded. 'How many attempts which Henry has seen fit to hide from me?'

'Apart from in battle?' Lord Thomas was calculating rapidly now that the cat was out of the bag. 'There was the one at Epiphany—in the year that he took the throne...'

'I know of that...'

'Don't forget the Countess of Oxford's plot to invite a French invasion and bring back Richard.' Humphrey's sullen demeanour had completely dissipated.

'Did your father tell you of that one?'

'No, I heard about it from the ostlers. The Countess is first cousin to the Percys. She has an axe to grind against us. The French were to land in Essex, but they didn't come. And Richard is dead anyway.'

'And when was this?'

He shrugged inelegantly. 'Three months ago or thereabouts. They tried to land in the Isle of Wight but were driven off. We'll not let the bloody French set foot in England.'

He was astonishingly laconic, until he recalled my own French connections, at which his youthful features flushed to the roots of his hair. But his discomfiture was of no account to me. Henry had said he was fighting for his life, an assertion

I had brushed aside as an exaggeration. But this was not in any way an exaggeration. With these conspiracies as well as the revolt of Glyn Dwr and the Percys, and the planned involvement of French troops, it was a miracle Henry had not been brought home to lie dead at my feet. It was a miracle that he had lived to wed me in the first place. The metal contraption of Humphrey's telling might only be a rumour, but who was to say it might not become a reality? As for poisoned saddles…

The threat of violent death was suddenly very close. I grasped Lord Thomas's sleeve again as he put his foot in the stirrup.

'I presume that Henry thinks it might be someone in his household who anointed his saddle. So that he must take precautions every time he mounts a horse.'

'It's possible, my lady.'

'Must be, I'd say,' added Humphrey.

And I remembered, as sharp-cut as if he stood beside me. *'I trust no one.'* And then, *'I am fighting for my life.'*

I had not understood. I had wilfully not understood, and Henry had deliberately kept his own counsel.

'Who can he trust? Once he would have said that a Percy lord was the best friend he could ask for. But that was before the bloodbath of Shrewsbury.' Lord Thomas swung into the saddle with all the vitality of a man less than half his age. 'Better to be safe than sorry. All we can do is protect him from plots and take care of the royal saddlery.'

I felt guilt sweep through me as I stared blindly at Lord Thomas's departing back. I knew Henry faced opposition, but I had not known the threats to be of so widespread or of so personal a nature. I knew nothing of the Countess of Oxford, a Percy cousin, and her plottings. I should have made it my place to find out from other, better sources than the ostlers. I had been too busy regretting Henry's unwillingness to allow me access to his private concerns. I had been neither supportive nor understanding.

The French invited to invade England by this Percy cousin? Another excellent reason why I might be hailed as the most unpopular of Queens.

And why had Henry not told me any of this? Because it was in his nature to be protective. What was it that he had said in the chapel only the previous day? It will be better if you remain here where you will be safe. And I had thought it merely a matter of the English despising their Breton mercantile adversaries, while Henry had closed his mouth like a rat-trap so that his fears of yet another attempt on his life and mine would not be transferred as an equal weight to bear down on my heart.

'By the Virgin!' I said aloud, astounded once more at the overweening pride of men.

'Madam Joanna…?'

I came back to the busy scene of the courtyard to find Humphrey staring at me with some species of concern. 'I did not mean to worry you,' he said gruffly. And then as if he could read my mind, 'My father would not tell you. He never does. He keeps his thoughts to himself, and he would not wish to cast a shadow over your life. He takes precautions, and he would think that was enough.' He hesitated. 'He has increased the guards at Eltham when Philippa and your girls are there. And when we spend Christmas there. No harm must come to you, you know. He values you highly. We all do. You are very kind. My father said I must not worry you. I'm sorry if I have…'

It made me want to weep.

'Thank you,' I said. 'Don't worry—I'll not tell him that you broke his confidence. It is good that you did.'

I felt like ordering a horse to be saddled to ride after Henry, but that I could not do. I must harness my guilt until he returned to me.

Later, much later, when the events of the next turbulent days had rolled out, when all became clearer in my mind, I was to return to this moment. To Henry's deliberate secrecy. To his constant fears for his own safety and that of his family. How could I, knowing the difficulties of a ruler holding a state together, of holding tight to Crown and power, how could I have been so blind to what he was facing? From family as well as from enemies, and it was the treacherous undermining by his family that bit the deepest and drew his heart's blood. Facing deep plottings and insurrection from those he should have been able to trust, Henry needed all the courage in the world to raise his head above the parapet. But that is what he did, day after day, to hold this country securely in his hands and preserve some semblance of peace.

Why had I not seen? Because Henry had wilfully intended me to be blind, to protect me, to preserve my peace of mind. The poisoned saddle was a deliberate attack against Henry. A chance arrow when hunting, a skilful thrust of a sword in battle, might both end Henry's life, but his sons too had been threatened at the Epiphany tournament. Henry would see it as a matter of pride to protect his family. Knowing Henry, as I now did, he would bear the burden of it from one year's end to the next, but I must not be allowed to worry.

And no, I had not noticed the increase in armed retainers at Eltham.

But oh, I should have done so. I should have shared the problems. Could not a wise wife inveigle her husband into telling her the inner secrets of his heart? Instead I had withdrawn into pride and haughty anger when my finances came under scrutiny and my Breton servants were threatened. I had been as much in the wrong as Henry.

Proud men were not always willing to listen to the counsel of women. That would change. Had Henry never read the wisdom of Madam Christine from Pizarro? I would ensure that he did. I would belabour him with the pertinent passages if necessary, between Mass and breaking our fast.

Proud Queens, it seemed, must also change. As Madam Christine observed in her writing under the patronage of my uncle of Burgundy, a wise woman should avoid oppressing her men-folk, since was that not the surest way to incur their hatred? She would best cultivate their loyalty by speaking to them boldly and consistently, and with wisdom.

I sighed. Madam Christine's beautifully written *City of Ladies* was a rare essay of good advice to any woman. But first Henry must return to me in one piece. And where to start? Promoting peace in my own marriage, the erudite lady would doubtless advise.

I became aware of Humphrey still fidgeting at my side. With my new insight, I wondered: 'Did your father leave you here to have an eye to my safety?' I asked.

At fifteen years he was the same age as his older brothers

when they had already been experienced in the field. Now Humphrey was concentrating, more than was necessary, on the departing baggage train.

'No, my lady, there would be no need. You are in no danger.'

I did not believe him. He was as adept at dissimulation as his father.

I patted Humphrey's shoulder. 'We must endeavour to entertain ourselves, it seems, in your father's absence.'

He looked askance. 'What is it you wish to do, Madam?'

'Would your father object if we try out his young hounds? It's good weather for it.'

A glint appeared in Humphrey's eye as if he had been rescued from unimaginable boredom. 'He might say they are still too young.'

'He will not know, nor will we put them under any pressure. I think a gentle lope along the water-meadows will do them no harm at all.'

He did not hesitate. 'Let's do it.' His eye slid to mine. 'I think I should tell you, since you know the rest of it. My father carries a bezoar stone. Even at home.'

'Does he now?' An item of magical properties, to guard its owner from the effects of poison. 'Tell me more, Humphrey.'

So it happened that I was still standing on the steps with Humphrey as Henry rode out through the gateway. I saw him stop, wheel his horse and look back, Math obediently at his horse's heels. Henry was too distant for me to read his expression, or he mine, but he raised his hand, palm towards me in a little gesture of peace.

Don't go! I longed to shout after him. Don't leave me with so much unsettled between us.

But that is not how we did things.

I raised my hand in the same acknowledgement. When he returned I would talk to him. I would make him talk to me.

Chapter 12

The day of Saint Valentine, when the birds of the air discover their mates and swear their true love, according to the writings of Geoffrey Chaucer, back in the reign of the now assuredly dead King Richard. An auspicious day for my reuniting with Henry, some would say. I wasted no time in my travelling to Kennington when Henry's courier informed me that he would be there.

I was strangely nervous but I held my emotions under restraint as I was received with honour and escorted by the chamberlain to where Henry was waiting for me in one of the family chambers. The weariness of travel was on him, I saw immediately as I entered. For once he was not busy with cannon or finance or any other urgent affair. For the first time since I had known him, his hands were not engaged with pen or book or weapon of war. Rather, simply sitting, hands loose on the arms of his chair, head resting on the back, Math at his feet, he had been staring beyond the window towards the south, suspended in a strange calm that was not a calm at all, as if he were waiting for something. Or someone. His face was thinner. How could that be? We had been apart for barely a month, but he looked pared down to bone and muscle. Then the long moments of introspection were set aside, the air of hard-strung tension dissipating as the greyhound rose to greet me. Henry's mouth softened, but I could not call it a smile.

'My lady.' He rose as the chamberlain closed the door quietly at my back, and bowed.

'My lord.' I curtsied.

For some reason the occasion demanded the formality. Perhaps it was the setting. The room Henry had chosen had no fire, no soft comfort. The painted tiles and the carved window arches patterned with fitful sunshine were the only decoration.

'When did you arrive?' I asked, stretching my hand to his.

'Two days ago.' He touched my fingertips with his own, lightly, impersonally.

'And were the defences against the Bretons as you would have wished?'

Henry acknowledged this with a winged brow. 'Against a full-fledged French invasion? No. But we will do what we can. Enough of that. I invited you to come here because there are things that need to be said between us.'

'Which is why I am come to be with you.'

St Valentine, I decided, would find it hard work to cast his shadow over this moment.

'Do we sit, or do we face each other in combat?' Henry asked.

'We sit. I am not here to fight with you, Henry.'

'Nor I with you. Then come.' His hand was warm around mine as he led me to the window seat where he seated me beside him before casting an oblique glance in my direction. 'I have not even kissed you yet in greeting.'

'I noticed the omission. But, then, I have not kissed you.'

'We have much ground to make up.'

Which we did, with no difficulty. His mouth was warm and firm on mine, lingering a little on a sigh of pleasure that I shared. Perhaps I had been too apprehensive about this meeting. Perhaps all was possible.

The latch on the door clattered. Without warning, the chamberlain hovering behind, a dishevelled youth staggered in before he managed a cursory bow. Henry looked across, frowning at the intrusion, but the squire's demeanour and weather-stained livery were sufficiently arresting to halt any rebuke.

'My lord...' The lad fell to one knee, before pushing himself upright with some effort, hat clutched to his chest. With a concern I had discovered to be so typical of Henry, he was across the chamber and at the squire's side before his knees could buckle again, grasping his arm, while I procured a cup of ale, of which the lad gulped down a mouthful, wiping his mouth on his sleeve. He was unaware of the dust that smeared his chin and cheek. 'There's danger, Sire...'

'Be calm, man.' Within the conflict that had just invaded the room, Henry's voice was gentle. 'Hugh, isn't it? Take a breath or two. Then tell me.'

'Yes, my lord. I'm come from Windsor, sent by the Constable.' The young man was in control now, and the words came, fast but true, and spine-chilling in their implication. 'It's the Mortimer lads, my lord. They're there no longer at Windsor. They've been taken by their guardian, my Lady Despenser. Their door was secretly unlocked…' He dragged in a breath, took another gulp of ale as his voice croaked. 'Her ladyship's riding west to Abingdon with them. The lady's tenants are up in arms in support of her. The Constable said you must be told. At all costs.'

I listened, absorbing the critical elements that could cast England into another maelstrom. The pallor of the squire, the urgency of his delivery, his eruption into the room, held no surprise for me. I knew about this situation and its lurking threat against Henry. There was indeed no secret to it. Lady Constance Despenser and her brothers Edmund of Aumale and Richard of Cambridge, all offspring of the Duke of York, and thus Henry's first cousins, had been guests at my wedding at Winchester. I knew them as part of Henry's extensive family, enough to exchange a Court conversation with them. But this alliance between Mortimer and York presented one of those complex problems of inheritance that existed in every family. And this one had the potential for dragging England down into civil war. The young Mortimer boys, Edmund and Roger, had a claim to the English throne that could threaten Henry's own.

Complex and threatening indeed.

For Edmund and Roger Mortimer were direct descendants of Lionel, Henry's uncle, second son of the old King Edward. Which, with King Richard dead, might for some put the blood claim of these two boys to the English throne before Henry's own. Except that their royal descent was through a female line, Lionel's daughter Philippa, which for others removed them from the reckoning. Edmund, now fourteen years old, was Earl of March after the death of his father; his brother Roger was two years younger. A dangerous age if any discontented Englishman might consider the young Earl of March a more suitable king than Henry. Or a useful puppet.

Henry had placed the boys at Windsor under lock and key, in the care of his cousin Lady Constance Despenser. Better to have them under his eye than at large, where ambitious men would be more than willing to make use of their royal blood. Except that now, according to the squire, a conspiracy had cast up another treacherous situation, from within his own family.

It raised in my mind the old mischief-making prophesy, with Henry as the despised mole, threatened by the Lion, the Dragon and the Wolf. For the Mortimer uncle of these two lads was the self-same Mortimer, the Lion from Ireland, in close alliance with Owain Glyn Dwr. A complex situation indeed for me to work through but it was as clear as day that to have the Mortimer boys in the hands of their ambitious uncle and the Dragon Glyn Dwr would hack away at Henry's tenuous hold on the country.

'And they are heading west, you say?' Henry was asking, still astonishingly calm.

'So the Constable thinks, my lord.'

'And then on, if I know Constance, to South Wales. To join up with Mortimer and Glyn Dwr who will be awaiting their coming.'

The squire was not expected to reply. Moving to stand at his side, I acknowledged the true pressure that Henry lived under. Every day. Every minute. His whole family seething around him with insurrection and ambition.

Who indeed could he trust?

'So they have a start on us,' Henry was saying.

'Yes, my lord. It was discovered early this morning, before dawn. They must've gone late last night. I rode as fast as I could.' No wonder the squire was close to collapse. It was more than a score of miles from Windsor to Kennington. 'I would have been earlier. My horse near foundered.'

'You were a brave lad,' Henry assured him with a hand to his shoulder. 'It was well ridden. It may be that you have saved us all from bloodshed.'

Then all was action. What did our differences matter, or our first tentative kisses, when these two royal-blooded boys had been seized to make mischief for Henry? While I dispatched the squire to the kitchens for food and warmth, Henry shouted for a page who was sent running to raise his brother John Beaufort from wherever he might be in the palace. Who arrived forthwith, to be advised briskly of how he would be spending the hours of this day and the next:

'Take a small force and get after them, John. Stop them. The boys must not be allowed to fall into the hands of their uncle or Glyn Dwr. Not at any cost. If they do they'll become pawns in a bloody game from which none of us will emerge with our necks intact. Send news to Windsor of how you go.'

No further explanation was needed. John was gone, issuing orders as he went.

I waited, although I knew what Henry would do, even as for a moment he thought, head bowed, arms folded. Then:

'I'm for Windsor. To find those involved in this accursed plotting—not that it will take long, for I see my cousin Richard of Cambridge's hand in this as well as that of his sister. I'd hoped I could trust her with the boys' safety, but she has been lured into the Mortimer camp. I doubt I could have foreseen that.' He lifted his shoulders, a resigned little gesture, but there was no resignation in his planning. Conviction laced every word. 'Once I know what's afoot, I'll see what needs to be done to secure the country from attack. It may be they've invited the French to advance their planned invasion, in which case the Council must be informed. All ports must be kept under surveillance. Then I follow after my brother. Although I know I can rely on him to make best speed.'

Exactly what I thought he would do. Henry was a leader of men, a man of action. He would no more sit at Kennington and let others patch the wound than he would remain within his pavilion if there was a tournament to be fought or an enemy to be brought down. I was forgotten, our need to talk pushed to the back of the shelf with the cobwebs. As it should be.

As it would not be. The days of my sitting on that shelf were long gone. I knew exactly what was my role now. 'I'm coming to Windsor with you.' The words had already formed in my mind, except that Henry was halfway through the door, sword and sword belt in hand, concentrating on the hours ahead. In a sharp wounding, redolent of disappointment, I could imagine what his reply would be. 'What need? I'm not sure what you can add to this.'

'Henry!'

He turned his head, expression gravely thoughtful, as if some intriguing fact had caught at his attention through all the driving need to summon his escort and be on the road to Windsor within the half hour. Then, with a line between his eyes that might have heralded a smile in less fraught circumstances, he turned fully and stretched out his hand across the space to me.

'Come with me, Joanna.'

I looked at him, at the hand held open, palm up in invitation, while I savoured those four short words. Only four but of vast significance in the journey we were making together and that had faced so many unexpected hazards. For the first time Henry had asked me to stand beside him, to act with him against this most bitter of enemies.

'Do you mean it?' I asked, unwilling to grasp what might, in the next breath, be snatched away. Any emotional charge still made me wary.

'Yes. I mean it.'

There it was. Henry was asking me to play a role that was not one of mere ceremonial, and I knew, when he found time to smile at my hesitation, that it was not my experience that he needed. He wanted me, his wife, to ride with him to Windsor and be with him when he set in motion the events to destroy Mortimer and his Despenser cousin. This was a very personal invitation that we should not be parted in this moment of extremis.

I hesitated no longer. Without a word I was striding across the chamber.

'It will be a long and fast ride,' Henry warned.

'Then find me a good horse.'

He gave a bark of a laugh. 'I won't wait for you.'

'I won't expect you to.'

I placed my hand in his, closing my fingers around his as if we were making a contract.

'Thank you, Henry.' So simple but so intimate a gesture from two people equal in thought and word. 'So now we act together. It is time that we did.'

His grip tightened around mine, acknowledging all that I did not say. He said it instead. 'Yes. It is more than time that we did. I should not have waited so long.'

We might be faced with yet another insurrection, with the threat of yet another war on English soil, but my spirits soared like a summer swallow.

★

No time for further talk or gestures, intimate or otherwise. We saved our breath and pushed on with barely a halt for a mouthful of wine and to breathe the horses. With the bare minimum of escort the King of England could move fast when he had to. I knew Henry kept me under his eye, but he did not humiliate me with too demeaning a care. Indeed there was no need for his concern. The horse was good and I was used to travel, choosing to ride astride, skirts bunched and anchored firmly.

What a strangely bizarre interlude it proved to be as we rode together, our minds at last in tune, as if we were playing from the same sheet of music, so that the harmony twined and meshed. Henry's issues were my issues. A closeness enfolded us, even though we neither spoke nor made overt contact, except when Henry touched my arm to draw my attention to some unforeseen obstacle. We were together, and England's future lay in our hands. It might be a time of unparalleled danger but, perversely, I was happy, an emotion that simply chose to exist within me. I had never felt so close to him. When, once, Henry looked across at me, it was with a depth of understanding for the enormous step we had chosen to take, so that I knew his experience of this hectic ride was the same as mine. But I merely grimaced, asking only when he drew rein, the grey towers of Windsor coming into view: 'Will John be in time to stop them, before they reach Glyn Dwr in Wales?'

I was breathless. I knew that it was imperative.

'I pray God he is.'

'And I.' I shifted in the saddle. 'I will offer up a novena. As soon as I get off this creature.'

At least it made him look less grim.

'Thank you for coming with me.'

'You could not have stopped me.'

Henry stretched out his hand to tuck a wayward strand of hair, now wet and matted for at some stage it had begun to rain, within my hood.

'It matters more than you can ever know,' he said.

For a brief moment of the brightest happiness, I held his gloved hand against my cheek, and then we rode on.

★

At Windsor I was an irrelevance to the greater scheme of things, but in the hours that followed I would have been nowhere else. It was a lesson in government watching Henry at work when faced with unimaginable pressures. Some fast questioning of the Windsor household revealed the depth of a conspiracy that had been in the plotting for some months. Now it was racing to its fulfilment. Duplicate keys had been made by some treacherous locksmith to access the boys' chamber. Lady Despenser had fled west with the boys.

And then news came in from John. The quarry had reached beyond Abingdon. He hoped to apprehend them before they crossed into Wales but time was of the essence.

With a map spread on the table before him, his fingers tracing his cousin's most obvious route, Henry considered this.

'What do you do now?' I asked when his ponderings continued.

'It's as we thought. They've dispatched a courier to France, pleading troops and money for the Mortimer cause. It's in my mind they'll make a push for the eldest—Edmund—to become king. Do I have an army strong enough to stop them if France becomes involved?' His eyes held mine as he admitted the depth of the crisis that was unfolding before our eyes. 'I do not. If caught between French troops from the south, Glyn Dwr from the west, the Earl of Northumberland levies from the north, I can't hold this country together.'

'Then we must stop the courier.'

'Yes. And I need to warn the Council.' Letting the map roll itself up, he sought for a piece of parchment. 'I need a clerk. Why can you never find one when you want one?'

I picked up a pen which I proceeded to sharpen. 'You have one.'

'So I do.' His hands were warm on my shoulders as I pulled up a stool. 'Will you write this?'

He began to dictate. Slowly for my comfort, standing behind me to read as I wrote. Information for the Council on the conspiracy. Orders to keep an eye out for the courier in London. To apprehend him. To close all ports.

When complete, Henry scanned it, took the pen from me, and scrawled at the bottom of the page his final instruction in his own hand. To watch the ports.

'The Council must set out patrols along the south coast at all costs,' he explained as he wrote the one line. 'An invasion at this juncture would be disastrous. It would destroy everything I hoped for. All I have worked for.' Below, he signed it with his initials as he was wont to do. Then frowned. 'I forgot to bring my signet. It will have to go unsealed. I doubt it will be questioned.' He looked across to where I still sat, pen still ready. 'What will you do?'

'What do you want me to do?'

'I need you to be at Westminster, to be in direct communication with the Council. If—when—I find them I'll send the boys back to Westminster under guard. Into your keeping. I'll send Constance there too. She needs to be confined. Will you do that for me?'

There it was, at last, the very essence of trust, allowing me to step within the confines of his life. When he could trust no one else, he could trust me. It coloured the air in that room with gold, filling my lungs with its value, but my reply was pure business.

'I'll be there. I'll take care of the boys. It's not their

fault—they're young and vulnerable. And I'll be sure to keep Lady Despenser close. She will not abscond again.'

I was already donning outer clothing and close-fitting cap for what would be another long journey. We both knew there was no time to waste.

Henry nodded. 'Keep it all quiet. I want no rumours to add fuel to this fire. The Council will know what to do. I'll come to you at Westminster.' He folded the letter. 'I'll send this on with a courier.'

'No need. I'll take it. I will stand surety for the lack of a royal seal if I have to. I'll see that the Council begins to act.'

Henry's hands closed over mine as he gave the orders into my keeping. What to say? No time for anything but the immediate.

'Be safe,' I said.

'I will come back to you,' he replied. And then, surprising me: 'I could not have managed this so speedily without you.'

'I am very sure that you could!' Well versed in Henry's capacity for detailed and efficient strategy, I did not need flattery. Here was a threat to be diffused. I knew that he could do it. And would do it.

And I was rewarded again with a glimmer of a smile that warmed the sternness. 'Perhaps I could.' Followed by a hard fast kiss that made my blood beat in my wrists. 'Never doubt, my virtuous and noble wife. Your value to me is inestimable. Your price to me far above rubies.'

And then I was on my way to Westminster, holding Henry's appreciation of a virtuous—and a capable—woman close in my heart. I had taken that final step to be with Henry, staunchly at his side, and we both knew that it would not be the last. This was why I had come to England. This was the shining pinnacle of my ambitions to fuse love and acceptance in Henry's governing into one intricately braided whole, as close-knit as I braided my hair every night. Now my task was to reach London and prevent the outbreak of a dangerous conflagration of uprising and invasion. Fear and accomplishment were strange bedfellows, but I undertook my mission with confidence. I did not even stop to say my promised novena. I discovered that it was perfectly possible for a woman of determination and grave anxiety to pray on horseback.

Henry had proved that he trusted me. It was as fine a benediction as I could ever imagine.

★

'We would see him dead. He has no viable claim to the Crown. The boy Edmund Mortimer, Earl of March, is the true heir since Richard is dead. We would make Edmund Mortimer king.'

A final denunciation from a vengeful woman before I directed her to the chamber where she would sleep under guard. Thus Lady Constance Despenser, Henry's superbly untrustworthy cousin, face raw with passion, here at Westminster in my keeping.

'Henry will be interested to hear your excuses when he returns,' I replied. 'Is there ever any excuse for treason?'

Yet Henry had taken up arms against Richard. It was, as I acknowledged, all a matter of pragmatic balance.

'There is every excuse, my dear cousin-by-marriage, when the man who has the Crown has denied Edmund Mortimer his rightful claim.'

I was unperturbed. 'You have failed and you will pay the price for putting the peace of this realm in jeopardy,' I said, every word as weighty as any Queen of England might pronounce.

Lady Constance had all the Plantagenet pride, and a decided flounce, as she strode to the door. And her parting shot, as malicious as any that had come before it:

'And what will Henry do to me? Have me starved to death in some distant castle?'

'He will not.'

'There is every precedent for it. As you must know very well.'

I gave a little shrug as if her words did not disturb me, as she has intended that they should.

'It was your choice to oppose Henry. Now, since you readily admit to treason, you must be prepared to face the judgement of the law. You should have known better, Constance.'

Constance's smile to me was pitying. Richard and his death while incarcerated cast a long shadow, particularly for Henry.

Constance Despenser and the Mortimer heirs had been overhauled in their flight to freedom and treason and a lethal Welsh alliance by John Beaufort's fast riding company, then returned to Westminster where I awaited them. I wasted no time on them, knowing in my heart that this was not for my dealing. I might wish to stand at his right hand, but Henry must make his own depositions with this treachery within his family. Yet I had no fear for the boys. Whatever the shadows surrounding Richard's death, Henry had shown himself capable of magnanimity to those who opposed him. If he could pardon Northumberland for raising his standard against him in war, he would not be less compassionate to those of his own blood. I had no doubt that the Mortimer offspring would be returned to some soft confinement until better times.

The boys, silent and near exhaustion, were settled in a chamber. So too was Constance Despenser, biting in her fury at being thwarted, but for whom I had no compassion. I listened to her vitriolic outburst, where I learnt considerably more than I already knew. I might be horrified by her confessions, but also magnificently enlightened.

Time stretched before me. Now that the most urgent threat to peace was laid to rest, I had my own priorities, equally urgent to my mind. All I had to do was wait for Henry, at which I was become greatly skilled. It seemed that I had been waiting for him all my life.

I picked up my embroidery, setting perfect stitches, my ears alert for his arrival. The border, glimmering with peacock and pomegranate hues, grew steadily under my hand which did not tremble. At my feet curled Math, reluctant but resigned since Henry's absence left the greyhound bereft.

'So you once sat at Richard's feet. You made a crafty decision in cleaving to Henry instead,' I informed her. 'I too made an excellent choice. The time has now come when all must be made plain between us. This day will colour the rest of our life together.'

I must not falter. I must not step back from this. I chose a length of silk of gold that shone bold and fierce in the candlelight at my shoulder. So must our words be tonight.

Bold and fierce in our reuniting. I would not allow this opportunity to be tainted by Henry's reticence or my own impatience. What was it that he had said? As proud as Lucifer. My heart shivered a little for I knew it to be true. But that could change. It was too painful, too heart-wrenching, to continue as we were. As I snipped the length of gold, I prayed that Henry thought so too. We must both be prepared to meet on a line of truce. Then, God willing, we could step over together.

At last. I set the stitching aside as sounds reached me. Henry was come, the room enclosing us as the latch clicked into place. How I loved him. How I needed this time of conciliation, as I thought he did too. He might have ridden as if the devil was on his heels but there was no sign of weariness on him as he crossed the tiles, painted with their flamboyant flowers and meadow creatures, to where I sat. It was as if the events of the past hours had destroyed all his doubts, to set his blood racing with a true commitment to the future. To England's future and our own. Had he not preserved England from a conflagration? Had he not prevented more bloodletting, more death? The immediate threat, pawns in such innocent form as two young boys, had been removed from the board and sent to bed. Henry's eyes were alight with victory.

For a long moment Henry simply stood, looking down at me and I, hands lightly clasped over the embroidered panel in my lap, returned his steady gaze. Until, surprising me, intriguing me, he tossed his hood and gloves to the floor at my feet, in the age-old symbol of defiance, in challenge on the tournament field. And it was a challenge. I saw that too underlying his triumph. To undermine the rebels who would disrupt his rule was not the only battle he would undertake this day. Eyes no longer veiled, expression no longer guarded against me, he was Plantagenet to his arrogant fingertips. No soft lines, no laughter, brows a forbidding dark bar, energy pulsed from him. Henry had known it as he had raced through the night to be here. We would face our private demons at last.

I tilted my chin and waited.

But when Henry wheeled round and strode back to the door, apprehension bloomed. Had I read him wrongly after all? But it was merely to usher Math out of the room and turn the key in the lock. There would be no interruption tonight to this domestic conflict as he strode again to face me, every action governed.

And so I rose, carefully setting aside the stitching, the gold silk still unused, yet I gave no trite expression of greeting, wife to husband. Following the demands of my heart, before Henry could speak, I stepped over the hood and gloves to meet him in the centre of the chamber, where I placed my palm squarely where his heart beat beneath the thickness of his scarred brigandine. Where I felt it leap a little. His emotions were not as governed as he would have me believe. And so my heart leapt too. I was fighting here for my future. My happiness. My contentment. *Our* future, happiness and contentment. It was in my mind to win.

Although the lines on Henry's face softened infinitesimally, yet he neither smiled nor spoke. This, after all, would be a skirmish to the death. It slid into my mind, an unsettling little thought. What would I do if we failed to find some firm rule by which we could live, which would allow us to love and rule together? I did not know. Thus we must find it and ensure it was inscribed in letters of gold.

'Well?' I asked, because he was King, and thus it must be I who broke the silence.

'It's a long time since you have placed your hand on my heart,' he said. A little dagger thrust with the skill of an expert combatant.

'Then I have been at fault.' I would acknowledge it. But then I turned the dagger towards his breast. 'But how can I indulge in such intimacies? We barely spend enough time together to destroy the barriers we have built up between us.'

And Henry raised his hand in recognition of the hit. 'Both of us being so skilled at constructing those barriers.' A breath, before he spoke what was in his heart, and in mine. 'Sometimes I feel that they are impenetrable walls between us. I think we are both at fault.'

Still he stood without moving, waiting for me.

'I agree, if we are apportioning blame,' I said, and repeated: 'We are both at fault. And yet I felt that we had breached those walls, when I rode with you to Windsor.'

Henry's heart settled into a steady beat, as if that was all that he had wished to hear.

'Welcome home,' I said.

And Henry, at last, raised his hand, to place it over mine, before lifting them both, lacing our fingers into a clenched fist between us, resting it lightly against the velvet cushioned metal plates of the brigandine.

'It's a long time since you have done that,' I said in deliberate mimicry.

Henry smiled. We both remembered the jackdaw.

I continued my attack, for here still was a threat to our happiness.

'Why did you not tell me, Henry? Why did you not tell me of the threats against your life?'

Whatever he had expected me to say, it was not that. I saw it in the darkening of his eyes, and he would have shaken his head in denial. The image of the dagger once again gleamed between us, and I would use it. I would not allow him to escape into a cold-planned retreat, however good his reasons might be in the masculine pattern of his thoughts.

'And here is yet another conspiracy, another attempt to rid England of her King,' I continued. 'You can't keep silent about something that will affect us so greatly. Your son Humphrey is a fount of knowledge. I have used him shamelessly, enough to know that your household and family are rabid with disloyalty.' I gripped our joined hands tighter until our knuckles gleamed white. 'You can deny nothing, Henry. I should tell you that I know about all the plots to have you killed by one means or another. I know about the ineffective Countess of Oxford. The metal contraption in your bed that probably never happened except in the lurid imaginations of your stable lads. And the poisoned saddle that quite clearly did. A particularly nasty stratagem worthy of my un-lamented father. But I learned none of this from you, my dearest love. How could I not know of such goings on under my very feet? Why did you keep silent about something so pertinent to us?'

His heart under our joined hands was no longer steady; his grasp forced my rings into my flesh.

'And this new conspiracy,' I continued, ignoring the discomfort, 'this planned attack on Eltham at Christmas is certainly a matter for my concern.'

His nose thinned as he inhaled slowly. 'So Constance told you.'

'She revelled in it. How her inestimable brother and your dear cousin, Richard of Cambridge, had hoped to be standing beside your tomb by now. He had it all arranged. A neat little ruse to rid this country of you and your blood when we were celebrating the birth of the Christ-child. Nothing easier. A group of paid assassins to scale the walls of Eltham between one feast and the next. She has no regrets for what she and her brother would have done. There's nothing like ambition and treachery to bring out the worst in families, as I well know.'

'It was discovered and prevented before it could come to fruition.' Henry's demeanour was quite untroubled, but my rings were still hard pressed. I forced myself not to flinch as he explained: 'I did not mean that you should know about it. What use in worrying you with something you would probably never hear about?'

I studied the stern set of his mouth. Here was an unde-monstrative man with such pride. To accept criticism from me was far harder for him than to face an opponent with a lance and a desire to spill his blood in the lists.

'I understand about families who will strive against each other even unto death,' I said. 'I know of that. Who better than I? My Valois cousins are drenched with blood. Did you think I would not understand, and blame you for your family's treachery? I would not.'

Henry retaliated fast. 'Why should you spend your days in fear of your life, when there is no need? Would I have my wife looking over her shoulder in her own home? I took a sacred oath that I would protect you and keep you from harm. I swore that, if I could, I would give you happiness. And if that means keeping the truth from you, then that is what I would do. I keep my promises, Joanna.'

I felt a little lick of temper, but curbed it under a flat observation.

'You, Henry, have been less than honest with me.'

'You did not need to know.'

'But I did. I do have a need. Because I am your wife. You had no right not to tell me. Do you not understand? Because I love you, any threat to you is mine to know.'

Which effectively silenced him.

And then all control escaped me at the thought of Henry's body at my feet, riddled with wounds, masked in blood, as I stepped unsuspectingly into one of our chambers. 'How dare you keep silent! I had to find out about the saddle from Thomas de Camoys!'

'So Thomas couldn't keep his tongue between his teeth.' The bar of Henry's brows had become heavier still. 'Then since you've discovered so much—here's the truth of it. There were enough strains in our marriage, without assassination lurking in the corners of your chambers.' And he pulled abruptly away, releasing me, retreating to the vast arch of the fireplace. 'There are so many complexities between us,' he said. 'And I'm sorry for it. Perhaps I should never have…'

'No!'

I was across the room in an instant. I would not allow him to regret our marriage. I would be no martyr to Henry's impossible honour. I took hold of his arm, so strongly that he turned to look at me, arrested by my vehemence, as I had intended.

'Don't apologise for bringing me here, Henry. I could not tolerate that. I came because it was my wish to be your wife. I came of my own free will, against much opposition. This marriage was of both our making, for good or ill.'

I felt his appraisal touch lightly on my face, and with it, surprising me, pleasing me, a brush of his lips. 'I love you beyond words, Joanna. My desire is to spend my life with you. But sometimes love and desire have been pushed into the background, like a tapestry, beautiful in itself, but merely a furnishing that decorates the room where more important action must unfold. I cannot cast aside my duty and loyalty to this country. I accepted it when I took the Crown. England must come first.' Henry lifted his shoulder as if the burden was indeed a heavy one. 'You of all people must have known that. A good king does not have the freedom to put himself before his country. That's what Richard did, to England's sorrow. And to my own.'

'I do know. I do accept.' I took his hands, holding them as if he were lord and I his vassal, intent on making my own promises. 'I love that in you,' I said. 'Your assurance, your dedication. It is what drew me to you. It is no detriment to my love.'

'And I admire it in you. The pride and the passion.' Once again, without our realising it, our fingers were linked. 'Some days when I awake, I half expect you to be gone. You, along with all your infuriating Bretons, to interfere again in Brittany's problems.'

'I will not do that.' The air of the room was softening around us. We had not exchanged such thoughts for so long. Perhaps we never had, and therein lay the problem. 'I will never do that,' I repeated. 'I will never leave you. I will rid myself of every one of my Breton household if it will mend the Council's hostility towards you.'

Again I was released as Henry traversed the room. But this time I would not follow him to close the space. This time he must come to me. When he leaned to snuff a guttering candle, in bitter, wifely mode I stooped to pick up the hood and gloves he had flung at my feet, smoothing them and placing them aside, then his cloak that he had draped, still sparkling-wet from rain, over a stool by the door. I folded it likewise, smoothing the fur edging, because I was at a loss.

'You don't have to do that,' he said.

'I know I don't have to do it. I know, Henry!' Reason was not working. A woman might need infinite patience to deal with a man of Henry's calibre, but on that day it was not mine to apply. Temper might do it, and indeed suddenly my throat was clenched with it. 'We could send for a page, a squire. A body servant. The members of the Royal Council. Archbishop Arundel of Canterbury himself, who is more friend to you than I am. We could be surrounded by people, all of whom would do the job much more efficiently than I. When do we ever get time alone, to become more than chance acquaintances who believe that they might love each other? Our wooing was with a stretch of sea between us. In the years since we married—and so few of them—you have been in my company less than my confessor. The demands on your time are great, which I accept, but it is war or parliament or Council. Yes, we have had Christmas at Eltham, but even there we share the time with family and friends. And so our marriage contains more thorns than perfumed rose petals. By the Virgin! We never have time to pick the roses.'

I saw him stiffen. 'You know what is demanded of me as King.'

'Who better? But what I also know is that I expect him to communicate with his Queen. If we are to make anything of this marriage…'

'If we are to make anything of this marriage, you must work for me, not against me.'

'How can I when you push me away? Am I incapable of helping you? When you invited me to accompany you to Windsor, I thought that you trusted me at last, and I rejoiced in it. I thought that for the first time there was a true unity to be savoured. To be celebrated. But now this new threat of assassination. It frightens me.'

'I am remarkably hard to kill, it seems.'

'For which I must thank God. You must talk to me, Henry. You must tell me of the clouds of intemperate ambition that hang over you and threaten your very existence. If you don't, how will I know?'

The smallest of smiles, even if it was wintry. 'I will write you a list.'

I was not smiling. 'I don't need a list. I know the difficulties that hedge you about. I have discovered them for myself, without your help.'

'Do you truly know? Who does? Who sees beneath the Crown and orb and ceremonial sword?' And suddenly Henry's anger matched mine. 'Who sees the reality behind the trappings of my kingship? "King Richard is Alive." The clarion cry of every rebel in the country. I cannot lay it to rest while there is insurrection in Wales. We are open to attack from France and Brittany along our southern reaches. And my coffers are empty. Do you understand the true weakness of my position?'

It had been engraved on my soul. I would never tell him of that day I had seen parliament humiliate him with its defiance and its demands. I shook my head in utter frustration when all I could do was watch unfathomable pressures build within this man who would follow his own path until the day of his death.

Yet it was as if my hopeless gesture unleashed a torrent. For, once begun, Henry talked. He talked as he never had since those far off days in Vannes when words had come more easily to him. I did not interrupt, but simply sank to a stool, to sit motionless with the damp cloak in my lap, absorbing every nuance of victory and failure, letting him tell it in his own manner.

'My blood is royal—of that there is no dispute. My claim to the royal inheritance is pure and true—but the anointed King of England was Richard. So how did I become King, when I was not born to it? This is how. I removed the Crown from Richard's head and it was placed on mine by the lords of this realm. I was acclaimed by them. There it is, Joanna.

A subtle but very tangible difference that casts a permanent shadow over my power. I am not my own man.' He opened his hands, palm up, staring at them as if therein he would see the answer to the problems that hemmed him in. As no doubt he did. 'My hands are so often tied because I haven't the coin in my coffers to free myself from parliament, or to wage an effective war against those who refuse me their obedience. Do you know what parliament demands, as a price of their cooperation in raising taxes. Power over me and over the decisions I make, because ultimately the Crown of England was in their gift. It is a humiliation too great.

'You speak of apportioning blame. Before God I feel it like the weight of the sky, forever pressing down on Atlas's shoulders. Am I not to blame for the unrest and bloodshed that threatens to ruin this land? Am I not to blame that I cannot heal and settle the lives of those who have given me their loyalty, by destroying those who see it as their life's work to destroy me? If they cannot accept me as King, there is no hope for the greatness of this land that my father and grandfather revered. This land to which I too have dedicated my life.

'Do you know what was planned? Of course you do. Did I not read the prophesy to you? A tripartite division of England, between my ferocious adversaries. The Dragon, the Wolf and the Lion. Northumberland would take the north, Glyn Dwr the west, while the rest would be apportioned to Mortimer in the royal name of his nephew who is asleep somewhere in this palace. Thus England carved up for the ambitions of others. I cannot let that happen. But how can

I diffuse this malevolent scheming when I am unable to either fill my coffers or win the loyalty of my own family?'

So there it was, impressing me all over again; Henry's utter dedication to the life that chance had placed at his feet, and that held me in thrall. And also the burning sense of failure. The treachery of family turned against him that preyed on his mind more heavily even than the betrayal of the Percys ever did. I felt his grief, his helplessness, all the vehement emotion written in his face. In his fists clenched at his sides.

'How does a King explain such a débâcle to the woman he has made Queen?'

All I could do was stretch out my hand, keeping my voice level so that he would not know how poignantly he had touched me. 'He does not have to explain. The Queen feels his despair. But knows that he fights with every sinew in his body to make it right. The Queen knows that there is no weakness in him.'

'How does a man explain his grief to a wife whom he would love and protect until the day of his death?'

'How does a loving wife not understand? How does a wife not take the burden of it into her own heart?'

'Sometimes it seems to me that I have to gird my loins for another battle when I come home, where I would simply enjoy a little peace.' His voice was raw with sudden anguish.

And I nodded, my fingers clenched hard in the fibres of the cloak. 'We have been deaf and blind to each other.'

Then he was beside me, kneeling, taking the cloak from me, casting it in a heap on the floor so that there was no distance between us and his fingers could linger on my cheeks.

'You must not weep. It is unnerving to have my strong wife weeping.'

'I do not weep.' I had not realised, but the tears were there for Henry to wipe away.

'No, of course you do not.' And he kissed away the dampness of which I had been unaware with such tenderness after the onslaught of despair. He held me in his arms as the emotion settled around us, like the ash falling silently, harmlessly, in the hearth. So we remained for a little time.

'What do we do now, my wife?' Sitting back on his heels, it was a question that had only one answer.

'We destroy the barriers,' I said.

'A major undertaking, requiring a siege engine and cannon.'

'Unless we open the gates. In which case it is not impossible.'

'No. Not impossible at all.' He was watching me, absorbing every nuance of the words we spoke to each other. 'Then here, as I see it, my dearest love, is what appears to be at least one key to the lock. I promise to confide in you.'

'I will be your confidante and your conscience, if you will. And I promise I will be sensitive to English policies.'

He laughed softly, a sound I had so rarely heard of late and that brushed my skin with desire. A soft knock sounded on the door, almost apologetic. Henry raised his brows. I shook my head. Leaning to kiss my hair, Henry walked soft-footed to the door. But he did not turn the key.

'Yes?'

'My lord.' A youthful voice, one of the pages.

'Is there a war?'

'No, my lord.'

'A fire in the kitchens?'

A startled pause. 'I don't think so, my lord.'

'Then go away. Whatever it is can wait until the morrow.' And when there was a scratch of nails against the wood. 'Take Math with you and feed her.' When he looked back over his shoulder, there too was the gleam of humour that I had so much missed. 'We have made a start. A small one, but one worth the doing.'

I returned the smile, knowing that we were, at last, as one. Whatever the problems without, we would hold to this precious time together. Tomorrow the repercussions of Constance's treachery would demand Henry's mind and his body. But tonight he was with me. And then he was kneeling before me again, as any troubadour's lover before his lady.

'Be with me, Joanna. As if we were making a new start, with you arriving at Falmouth in the heart of the worst storm for decades.'

'And you far away in—I have forgotten where you were.' Laughter was beginning to be reborn.

'Be with me. In spirit. In mind. In heart,' Henry said, while my hands were held secure in his so that I could not have escaped even if I wanted it. He kissed my palms, as a lover would kiss his beloved, and all my doubts melted.

'Be with me, Henry,' I repeated softly. 'In good times and bad.'

'Let us hold firm against the world.'

'And together we will bring England to the glory that you foresee.'

I slid to my knees to face him, eyes on a level. How easy

a thing it was to plight our troth, all over again, with an embrace and a kiss that did much to drive the shadows away.

'Are we too weary to seal the deed?' I asked.

Henry's eye held the glint of steel. 'I'll have you know I am in the prime of my life.' Then, practical to the last as we walked together to the inner chamber where there was the promise of a good bed: 'Work with me, Joanna.'

'What do you need from me?'

'A truce with Brittany.'

So the world had not quite gone away. It never would, but I could bear that.

'Then I will do it. If your sons are old enough to go to war, mine is old enough to make peace. But that can wait for tomorrow. And I must ask a boon from you in return.'

'Hard bargaining, Joanna?'

'Good policy, rather.'

Henry kissed me. 'Tomorrow.'

The time for talking was over.

We were reserved, a little reticent. The strains and tension between us were too great to be overcome with a single caress, a touch, a casual word of love. Not even a blaze of passion could destroy the distance that had insidiously grown until it was a vast expanse of ice and snow, blanketing the landscape. Now we would make a new road, with care for pits and crevasses. We would walk it together, supportive of each other, and find our way as the obstacles melted away.

Thus it had of necessity to be a healing, and so it was a slow coming together. A leisurely divesting of clothing, a kiss to shoulder, to throat. A slide of fingers along arm, over muscle and sinew. Over swell of breast and thigh. It was a re-acquaintance with what we knew we would find. We were in no doubt of it. The love was there to be rediscovered, if we were of a mind to do so, as we were. Henry would never again close the door of his love or his governance against me.

And it was with the gentlest of wooing that Henry taught me about love all over again.

'I want a child, Henry,' I murmured against his shoulder, when our first breathtaking steps along that joyful path had been made, when all was laid out for our enjoyment and my mind was free to voice the one lingering void in my life. 'Another child. With you. Soon. Before age takes its toll.'

'Then that is what we will do.'

All our reservations gone, Henry applied himself with power, with knowledge. With his flair for awakening every pulse in my body.

'I think we could say that we have gone a good way to destroying the walls and bastions between us.'

Whereas I had been thinking of roads and pathways, Henry was engaged in warfare, but that was a man's view of love. I hid my smile against his throat. Now we must rebuild what we had cast down. With walls of honesty and truth. With bastions of love. We would surely do it. We had arrived at last at our safe-haven, the linking of our fingers a symbol of what we could achieve together for England's greatness.

★

Henry's gift of reconciliation to me? Not a book. Not a jewel. No amulets or glittering collars. Nothing of intrinsic value. Instead a hard-headed, deliberate negotiation with the Royal Council. My household must be diminished, that I must accept, but Henry put the argument for leniency. I was allowed to keep twelve of my most valued servants. Meagre stuff but a gesture I had not expected and which caused me much quiet rejoicing for of the twelve were my most loyal Marie de Parency, and Mistress Alicia.

Henry had fought for me and overcome parliament's strident objections to the Breton hoard, at what cost to his pride I was never to know, but with a clear mandate in the manner in which I might express my gratitude in kind, I wrote, sending a fast courier to Brittany, to my son. After an affectionate greeting, I stepped seamlessly from maternal to diplomatically ambassadorial:

> It is in my mind, John, that a truce between England and Brittany would be of value to both our countries. The present alliance between you and the King of France, resulting in attacks against England, distresses me. Your father held England in great affection, as he did its King. He would not approve of your aggressive stance against Henry.

And his response, more ducal than filial:

> I regret your distress, maman, but English piracy continues to harass my trade and gnaw at my profits. My sailors are in constant fear, my cargos under threat. I am advised, maman, that there is no optimism at present upon which to base a truce with your husband.

I regarded his words, in no way discommoded. Did I detect the influence of Burgundy here? A brief but pertinent conversation with Henry over the boon I required from him had the desired result and gave me the ultimate weapon I needed.

I wrote again.

> *It is a sign of puissant ruler, John, to consider all possibilities to bring peace to his country. I am certain that you will not turn your back on this offer of an olive branch. My lord Henry has released to me the Breton prisoners who were caught raiding along the coast of Devon. Without a truce between us, they will, and rightly, remain incarcerated in England, to their grief and your detriment. It is in my power to release them, on promise of future good behaviour, as part of a lasting truce between our two countries. A Duke of Brittany of your good sense would see the value of this.*

I awaited the outcome. Not for long.

I smiled as I issued instructions. The Bretons released, the truce made, parliament might snarl at the loss of their prisoners into my hands, but the Royal Council appreciated the end to debilitating warfare, these edgy lords assuring me of their goodwill. Receiving their less than effusive thanks with grace, it was as much as I expected. From Henry, in the new spirit of our restored harmony, I expected much more.

'What would you choose to do, Henry,' I asked, as we broke our fast, 'if the day were your own?'

'Watch the casting of my cannon.' He said it without thinking, until he read the heavy silence on my part. 'I presume you would rather I did not.'

'I think you should spend it with me.' Knowing Henry as I did for an inveterate lover of casting the dice, innately unable to resist a challenge, I seized the well-worn ivory pair that were never far from his hand and shook them in my cupped palms, preparing to release them amongst the detritus of crumbs and fruit parings. 'If I win, it is my choice.'

'And if I win it is the cannon.'

I threw the dice. Grimaced speculatively. A depressingly low number.

'I can beat that.' Chin propped on his interlinked fingers, Henry grinned.

'I expect you can.'

Henry shook, and threw.

I sighed. 'It has to be the cannon then.'

Henry was watching me.

'What?' I said.

'I've changed my mind. I will read poetry to the beauty of your face.'

'And where will we read this poetry?'

'In your chamber. Where there is the most comfortable bed I know, if the power of words, by some mischance, begins to weary us.'

I watched him solemnly. 'I could accommodate that.'

'Then we'll visit the casting of my cannon tomorrow.'

'Perhaps.'

Negotiation in all things. Love in all things. Kisses were no longer a rare commodity, with or without sugared plums. The tangled web of my emotions was smoothed out into a long shining skein, like my hair, under Henry's combing.

'I doubt we will change overnight,' Henry said, ruefully as

he left me, to deal with a rumour of uprising in the north, about which he had done his best to provide me with every nail and bolt of detail. 'You look happy.'

'I am.' I tucked my hand in his arm. 'I am valued. I am loved.'

Music was restored to us too, in the words of Bernard de Ventadour, that most vaunted of troubadours:

> '...more joy I have in my heart and I must sing,
> As all my days are full of joy and song,
> And I think of nothing else.'

There was a limit to our laughter. Henry sent Lady Constance Despenser to answer for her sins before the Royal Council. Her brother Richard of Cambridge was dispatched to the Tower of London to teach him better manners. The Mortimer boys returned to their restricted freedom at Windsor.

As for the locksmith who had made the counterfeit keys that released the Mortimer boys, he paid for his treason with his clever fingers, and then with his head.

There was a limit to Henry's tolerance after all. And to mine for Henry's enemies. I stood beside him as he signed the order for the traitor's death. I no longer argued the efficacy of clemency. Henry's safety was paramount, for England and for me.

Chapter 13

June 1405: Eltham Palace

The letter came, delivered to me, at the end of a hot June.

To be given into the hand of Joanna, Queen of England.

I had no anxieties even though Henry was once more on the well-beaten road to war. It was written to me in his own hand. He must have found himself with a moment of unexpected leisure.

'Don't expect to see me before the end of the year,' Henry had said when he rode *ventre à terre* from the Garter Feast at Windsor in April to light yet another fuse to blast Glyn Dwr into submission. 'Or even hear from me,' he added. He might have sounded apologetic if he had not been consumed with fury. His farewell kiss was brisker than I had come to expect since the healing of our wounds. 'I suspect there'll be no time for writing.'

Henry had already sent his cannon on ahead. This would be a fully fledged campaign to restore the fragile peace which was once more being undermined. Within me, as once again I waved him farewell, was a hard knot of resignation. I knew well how to live alone, with quite enough to occupy my mind and hands, yet I felt an unease at this precipitate departure, an unease that intensified when a sudden shaft of April sunshine, thin and insubstantial as a candle-flame, slid across Henry's body, his features. He looked older, a wolf during a lean winter, intent and purposeful, full of energy, but with the passing of years refining him and greying his pelt.

I did not want him to go. I did not want him to be far from my care. But then, as it had always been, the decision was not mine to make, and I chided myself, for Henry still lacked far more than a twelve-month to his fortieth year. The gloss of age was merely a trick of the light.

Henry must have read the disquietude in my face, for he took the time to hand his reins to his squire and exchange another word with me, so that the image of advancing years fled completely, replaced by the Henry I knew, vivid and determined, driven by untapped energies.

'You can write to me if you wish, of course,' he suggested.

Grim humour was allowed to force its way through his anger.

'But I won't know where to find you.'

'Then we must remain apart in body.' He raised my hands, first one and then the other, to his mouth in formal adieu.

'But not in mind or spirit. You are with me always. God keep you, Joanna, and I'll be at Eltham for Christmas.'

'And may He shower His blessings on you too.' Then as he turned to recover his reins. 'Henry…'

He looked back, impatience stamped on every inch of him.

'Take care,' was all I said.

It was the worst fear of any wife, that her husband, departing with battle in mind, might not return except on a bier. Before he could mount, I tucked a silken packet in the neck of his tunic where I knew his crucifix would rest.

'Don't fuss, woman! What's that?'

'A protection,' I said.

'Do I need it?'

I would not say that I knew about the bezoar stone to ward off poison that would be secreted somewhere about his person. This was vervain, the miraculous holy herb, to keep enemies at bay in battle, as well as guarding against the more mundane problems of fevers and the effect of dog-bites. Vervain was my favourite remedy for all needs.

'Yes,' I said, patting the riveted metal plates beneath the fine covering of his brigandine, not expanding on its properties. 'I considered Black Hellebore, to keep you safe from wolves, but you are unlikely to meet such creatures.'

'Unless they are of the two-legged sort and called Percy.'

Mounting, issuing instructions, he was gone in a welter of armour, fine horseflesh and heraldic glory, while my heart sank. Christmas was far in the future.

Now this letter, delivered to me in the overwhelmingly female household at Eltham with Marguerite and Blanche and Henry's daughter Philippa. I turned the document in my fingers. Since Henry had taken the time to write to me, I presumed it was good news. Perhaps he had brought the venomous Earl of Northumberland to heel after all.

'Is he at York still?' I asked the courier.

'No, my lady. The King was at Ripon when I left.'

So not far from York. 'Is Northumberland still in the field?'

'Yes, my lady. Or he was when I left and my lord the King was planning an advance against him.'

For by now, Wales was not the only burr beneath his saddle. In the north the Earl of Northumberland had predictably raised a new rebellion, forcing Henry to abandon Wales and ride the breadth of the country to deal with him. Faced with the Tripartite plan of the Dragon, Lion and Wolf to carve up England between them, exacerbated further by the addition of the treacherous Archbishop Scrope of York who had dared to raise an army against his King, determined to add God's might in driving Henry from the realm, Henry was equally intent on stopping them and ruling with an iron fist.

Why would he write to me at so crucial a moment? Climbing the spiral staircase to the little oratory Henry had had constructed, a place where I would find privacy in the bustle of the palace except for the severe painted faces of saints and angels, and where I might sense Henry's presence with me, with my heart racing from its normal beat, I broke the seal and prepared to discover what he was doing.

To my dear wife,
There is no need for any concern.

Which was kind of him. Heart settling, I read on, prepared to feel his thoughts entering my mind across the miles.

> I am at Ripon where I have been for the past week. Archbishop Scrope is dead, by my hand. Unfortunate but necessary. England must learn that high office, whether clerical or secular, will not exempt a man from punishment if he raises an army against me.
>
> It is my intention to march north to deal with the knotty problem of Northumberland. His castles should be no match for my cannon, but the stronghold of Warkworth might be intent on defying me. I don't envisage a long campaign, before I turn my attention back to Glyn Dwr.

So at least I knew where he would be for the forthcoming months, and I knew his thinking, even if his execution of an archbishop filled me with some unease.

> I am writing to set your mind at rest if news reaches you, as it may from other quarters, about the reason for my choosing to rest at Ripon. Any suggestion of a major blow to my health is no more than a gross exaggeration spread by my enemies. I was laid low by a brief ague on leaving York, but am now restored due to the offices of Master Recoches. I am in good health and within the week will march north to complete the campaign against Northumberland. I ask that you will pray for success in our campaign against those who would disrupt the peace of our kingdom. My thoughts are with you and my heart is in your possession, my much loved wife. Always.
> Henry

So there was the reason for this communication. Oh, Henry! Relief strong, I found a need to laugh a little despite the painted faces around me looking askance. Was there ever a man who feared for his health more than Henry? He was the only man I knew who kept an astrolabe in a coffer beside his bed, so that his physician might work out the position of the stars for the most efficacious taking of healing potions. Which other king travelled, even the short distance between Eltham and Windsor, with his personal physicians and surgeon in attendance? For a man who had spent his youth in the tournament field, he had an astonishing care for his life. Or perhaps that was the reason. He had seen much death from wilful neglect of symptoms.

A brief ague. A fever, then, and not to give cause for concern. But he had thought about me and did not wish me to worry. Henry's consideration was a blessing, a staunch reminder that I was in his thoughts even when he was far away. And perhaps I was wrong to laugh. A King must retain his strength in the eyes of his people. A King must represent the epitome of power and authority. I could accept his intense concern with all things physical.

For a moment I studied the letter where the letters, bold and upright, gave no hint of ailing health. All I had to worry about was Northumberland and the bloody outcome of a battle, if that is what it would take for Henry to settle the north into obedience.

I must put my faith in vervain, Henry's cannon and the Blessed Virgin's grace.

And meanwhile there was the matter of Philippa's imminent betrothal to the King of Denmark to consider. I took myself from the oratory, turning my back on the angelic throng, to a happy discussion of clothes and jewels for the young bride with three enthusiastic girls on the brink of womanhood. A far cry from Henry on the battlefield.

But how brief my reassurance, my heart tumbling from hope to dismay, for when I rose next morning it was to discover a second courier awaiting me. A second letter. The superscription from the hand of Master Louis Recoches, Henry's favoured physician. Any light-heartedness was stamped underfoot when I saw that the courier was more than weary from hard riding.

'When did you leave Ripon?' I asked.

'Yesterday, Madam.'

Here was urgency. Gesturing to him that he should sit—which he refused to do, which worried me even more—I tore the sealed sheet apart. If Henry's physician was writing to me there was just cause.

> *Madam,*
>
> *I find a need to write to you, despite the fact that my lord the King has forbidden me. I am assured that you have the King's best interests at heart, and I have decided that you must know. The King suffered a grave attack to his health when a few miles from York. A conflagration that rendered his skin red and blotched. The pain he suffered was of a severe nature and could not be soothed by any remedy that came to my mind, forcing my lord to take refuge at a small manor at Green Hammerton, and then a further week at Ripon, where the symptoms gradually faded.*
>
> *I tell you this because I have no hope that he is cured.*

Merely that the disease is in abeyance. Furthermore you should know that those who were with him were shocked at the virulence of the attack, and despite all my efforts, the word has spread amongst those of treasonous persuasion, who would still cry 'King Richard is Alive' to make trouble for our King, that it was an act of Divine retribution for the execution of Archbishop Scrope. It has to be said that the two events—the execution and my lord's illness—occurred on the same day.

It is my belief that you should be aware of these happenings.
Your loyal servant,
Louis Recoches.

This was disturbing. This was more than disturbing, that Henry's physical trials should be interpreted by those who wished him ill as a Godly punishment for a political act. Keenly aware of just how Henry's mind worked, I knew this rumour, like some malevolent creature, would creep to fix its talons into his mind; that his thoughts would be as troubled as his body.

'How was the King when you left?' I demanded of the courier, still resolutely standing as immovable as one of my gate-posts despite being in dire need of food and ale and rest.

'Well , my lady.'

'Was he still planning his campaign in the north?'

'Certainly, my lady. Within the week. My lord the King was most enthusiastic to attack my lord of Northumberland's castles.'

Which sounded good enough. If Henry was campaigning

what need for me to fall into a trough of despair? And yet here
was a warning I should not ignore. I liked Louis Recoches. I
trusted him, as did Henry. Old in years, a fountain of practical
common sense, he had been physician to the late Duke of
Lancaster and was a much revered member of the household.
What had persuaded him to disobey Henry's instructions
and tell me of his fears?

Only, as he must see it, an emergency.

Dismissing the courier at last towards the kitchens, I
ambled towards my chamber, my thoughts with Henry so
far away from me. A burning of the skin. A great pain. A great
fear. If I was with him now, I would talk to him, reassure
him that Archbishop Scrope's death had been well earned
by a man who dared to raise his banners against his King. I
would ease his conscience.

But I was not with him now. I was too far away to match
my mind with his and argue the case until he was at ease
again. Never had the distance between us seemed so great
as they did on that bright summer morning.

Be calm, I urged. Be sensible.

Back in my chamber I recovered Henry's letter from my
coffer to reread. Yes, the handwriting was firm and flowing
with no indication of weakness or lasting pain. Henry could
not be so very ill if he could inform me of the wellbeing of his
beloved cannon and his campaign against Northumberland.
Master Recoches was merely being cautious, for which I
should be grateful.

How long would it be before I could see Henry for
myself? Christmas at Eltham was far too distant.

And with that thought, a sharp stab of sorrow struck

unexpectedly, and with it was resurrected, not for the first time, the acknowledgement of the one continuing lack in my life. Henry and I might have been reconciled in love, in body and in spirit, but no child had been conceived of our happiness. Were we not both proved fertile? Edmund stood as proof of Henry's potency and my courses coming regularly, I knew that I still had the power to conceive. Perhaps at Christmas, at Eltham, where there was time for celebration and joy and for physical pleasure, our greatest desire would be achieved.

I tapped Henry's letter against my hand, thinking that it might be good policy to investigate by what manner of means a woman, who no longer had the fertility of a young girl, might encourage conception. It might be good policy to consult my books of herbal potions, and Mistress Alicia whose knowledge was monumental in such affairs.

I sent my thoughts, swift as a rock-dove, towards the north and petitioned the Virgin that she would give Henry health and success. And bring him home.

★

'Thank God that year is over.' Henry trod into the entrance hall at Eltham, a joyful Math at his heels, a squire and two pages carrying various items of documents, armour and clothing. 'And pray God there's not another like it.' He stood for a moment, looking round at all those who had gathered to celebrate with us. 'I've missed being here at Eltham.'

'Eltham has missed you too.' Smiling, I walked forward. 'We have all missed you.'

Hands touching, and because we were surrounded by

household, dogs and various offspring, we kissed formally, one cheek and then the other. Christmas at Eltham. It had come at last and I was overjoyed to see Henry again. The days of celebration and festivity stretched ahead, full of promise, full of happiness, and most of all delight to have Henry back within my keeping.

I cast my eye over him, looking for any signs that might serve as a warning. I took in his stance, his expression, the set of his shoulders. Northumberland's rebellion had been ruthlessly put down with ferocious energy. Against Glyn Dwr there had been less success, but would resume in the spring. Since Master Recoche's warning it was always uppermost in my mind but I could see no evidence of pain as he bent with easy grace to pat Math as she nudged his leg to attract his attention.

Henry took off his roll-brimmed cap, tossing it to one of the pages, at the same time running his hand over his hair. It was thinner than I recalled, more close-cropped. Henry caught my eye with a little grimace. Oh, the vanity of men. I would tactfully say nothing, merely look out a remedy for hair loss.

'Not that I hold out much hope for an improvement in the New Year,' Henry was grumbling as he dealt similarly with his gloves and dragged his campaigning cloak from his shoulders.

'Why not?'

'I've issued writs for a new parliament in March. How can it not be contentious?'

'Finance?'

'When is it ever not?'

'I forbid you to worry about parliament until the new year,' I said, determined to put the tension in him to flight. 'But not now. Now your time is mine, when your family do not commandeer you.'

It was my pleasure to see his face soften from lines of frustration. Shooing the dogs away, and the servants, pleased to have their lord returned to them, I drew his hand through my arm to follow his sons and the girls into the family apartments.

Henry tensed. Halted, every muscle in his body braced.

I stopped too. 'What's wrong?'

'Nothing at all. Just pleased to be home.' Leaning, he smiled, planted a kiss on my lips, linked his fingers with mine and let me pull him slowly towards fire and wine and family chatter.

Where Master Recoches had joined us. Who was staring at me. I did not like the quality of that stare. But that too could wait. I would talk with him later if I thought it necessary.

Henry lowered himself into a chair, as if days in the saddle had taken their toll, accepting a cup of ale as he gave his full attention to the family news, particularly Philippa's enthusiasms over her approaching marriage, and while I cast a subtle but eagle eye over him. I thought he looked tired, but no more than a King might, after a year of diffi-cult campaigning and the general horror resulting from his summary execution of Archbishop Scrope. The lines of strain around his eyes would soon smooth out with good food and some fine days of hunting and Twelfth Night games of which he was inordinately fond. His hair might be short cut to his scalp but he was still a handsome man. I presumed there had been no recurrence of the symptoms in June and since Henry chose not to speak of it, I took his lead and I let it lie. If there had been some problem, I thought that he would have told me. Henry was back and as news was exchanged, laughter frayed the edges of absence and it was as if he had never been away.

After an evening of dissecting the pernicious campaigns of Glyn Dwr backed by his French allies, before they were banished for good, it was time to retire. Hal, still cruelly scarred but his face much redeemed from those early days after Shrewsbury, continued to devise means of dealing with Glyn Dwr, becoming more imaginatively vicious as the wine in their cups dwindled. The girls gossiped over Philippa's forthcoming betrothal to Eric of Denmark. We left them to it, as I walked at Henry's side, imagination leaping ahead. It would be good to be together again. After days of preparation, my chamber was a haven of clean linen and scented pillows. A perfect place for a harassed King to find sanctuary from the world in the arms of his wife.

And if I had strewn my sheets with the fragrant leaves of the lemon balm to aid conception, who was to know? Who was to make comment, other than Mistress Alicia who had prepared the noxious draught, if I had drunk the distilled flowers of the gillyflower, noon and night for four weeks, to render me fruitful. I was full of hope.

At the door to my chamber Henry came to a halt where, in a strangely deliberate gesture, he turned to look at me. 'It's good to be back with you, Joanna.'

His austerity was a surprise. I might have expected him to push me into the chamber where he would embrace me with a fervour. But no, there was nothing untoward here. It always took a little time to ease back into intimacy after a long absence. Both reserved in nature, we could not simply drop into a closeness. It had to be earned, renewed, recalled through a chance word, the touch of a hand, of lips, of eyes, like a new wooing between new lovers. It would all come about. I had no fears that we would soon be at ease with passion restored.

'It is good to have you back,' I returned lightly. 'It has been a long parting.'

I placed my hand against his chest, as I had before, a tender gesture, a promise of what I hoped for. Henry's muscles tensed. I felt him actually hold his breath and resist.

'Joanna…'

He paused. I tilted my head, a silent question, still unconcerned. Henry smiled a little. Yes, it was always difficult after a long parting.

'Forgive me, Joanna. I would sleep alone tonight.'

It was a shock. Concern leapt into life. I could find no response that was not foolish, yet still I said it.

'Why?'

Unusually, distressingly, his eyes slid from mine. I could not recall Henry ever being uncertain or insecure. Reticent, yes, but not lacking in confidence. His directness was one of the attributes I most liked in him. But then his gaze returned and held mine, flat and uncompromising, as if he had made a decision with which he was not comfortable but which he would pursue to its bitter end.

'I am weary. I would be no good to you as a lover.'

Which I could understand. More or less.

'Could we not just sleep in the same bed?' I asked. 'I am reluctant to let you out of my sight.'

'I am not sleeping well. I am restless. It would be better if we were apart.' He kissed me softly, but on my brow rather than my lips. 'Just for tonight.'

I could think of nothing to say other than, 'If that is your wish, Henry. Do you need me to organise a sleeping draught?'

'Not necessary. Master Recoches has already supplied me with what I need.'

As he turned to walk to his own private chamber, I stretched out my hand to catch his arm, to draw him back, but he had moved beyond me. Perhaps he even quickened his pace. 'Good night, Joanna. May God keep you in his infinite mercy.'

Which left me standing, arm uselessly outstretched.

'Sleep well, Henry.'

I heard when Henry closed the door. The lock clicked into place very softly. How could such a soft action, so unthreatening a noise, hurt so greatly? For a little while I stood where he had left me, my arms at my side, tempted to simply follow him. To knock and demand admittance—but he was weary and did not deserve that I pester him through sheer disappointment.

So we spent that night apart.

And the next.

And the next, when Henry did not even try to find an excuse, and I was becoming too humiliated to ask the reason. I had meant to touch delicately on his thinning hair. Did I not have to hand the root of the *lilium candidum*, pounded small with honey which would restore hair to its youthful glossy thickness? But Henry kept me at arm's length as surely as if he wielded a lance. It proved to be impossible to have an intimate conversation with a man who locked his door or kept himself in the centre of the family crowd, where discussions of male vanity and virility were forbidden. Again, heart-breakingly, I felt thrust out of Henry's life. Irrelevant. Isolated. Unwanted.

And without doubt it was deliberate on Henry's part.

A strange species of panic began to inhabit my mind with all the possible reasons for Henry's rejection of me. Since our estrangement we had been as close as a walnut in its shell, but now, now it seemed to me that Henry would ride a dozen leagues and wrestle with a dragon rather than spend time alone with me.

And the crux of my worry, the one that coated me in despair. After that one impersonal kiss on my brow, when Henry denied my bed, Henry never touched me.

Where lay the problem? Was it me? After all the difficult paths we had trod together, after we had overcome the storm and tempest and the sucking ooze of swamp and mire, had Henry simply fallen out of love with me, wishing he had never embarked on that astonishing wooing? Even more distressing, it seemed to me more than possible that my increasingly distant husband had met another woman capable of giving him more pleasure and less challenge than I. Fast growing Edmund was evidence of just such an occasion, when we had been apart. I had thought we were reconciled. I had thought I had come to understand Henry's driving needs and he had accepted the sharp edges of my character. I had tried so hard to smooth them into tolerance.

In those days of festive pleasure and celebration at Eltham I was forced to face the truth. I was rejected as a wife in all carnal sense.

Quicksand once more moved under my feet. Henry no longer returned my love. My lemon balm and tincture of gillyflower to enhance pregnancy lay gathering dust in their phials. My root of Madonna Lily, supreme remedy for loss of hair in its tight-lidded pot, began to dry and curl at the edges.

Meanwhile I watched him for any evidence of the state of his mind, like a female hawk watches its errant young. I could not fault him. During the day he was in good heart, courteous, quick to laugh and encourage the family in festive excess. He sang. He dressed in rich velvets and damasks of past years when we acted the old myths and legends. Charming, friendly, affectionate, he seemed prepared to sink readily into the demands of this festive season.

But here was the difference. Henry did not ride out with the young ones when they hawked or hunted, on the pretext of business spending many hours in the muniment room, buried with his steward in documents and rent rolls. Or he retreated to the mews where he kept the company of his young hawks. He did not dance. He did not participate in the ferocious and rowdy game-playing.

Frustration was a wild beast within me. This was not how we spent Christmas. Christmas was a time for family. But Henry was ignoring his own precedents.

And to me? How did my husband, my lover, respond to me? As outwardly as charming and friendly and affectionate as to the rest of the family, but there was an invisible wall between us through which I was not allowed to pass. Henry had a myriad of excuses to prevent himself being trapped in a room alone with me.

My despair grew. But so did my pride. Why must I persist when it was as clear as the heart of the cabochon diamond Henry gave me as a New Year's gift? Henry did not want me near him. I could humiliate myself with rejection no more. I found that I was withdrawing further and further into my old reserved self. I no longer even tried to tempt Henry into intimacy.

Until, that is, the evening when he thought no one was aware of him, when we were all concentrating on the dolorous take of Tristan and Isolde, acted with great verve by Hal and Philippa in the velvet robes and peacock feathers of Edward the Third's Court. In that moment, Henry's face was drawn in an agonised torment, as if sleep had become a stranger to him and his thoughts were raw with pain.

And I was watching.

Sleeping apart from me was not solving the problem for him. Insurrection in England might well keep him from sleep, but I was convinced that there was far more than Northumberland's machinations on his mind. I steeled myself to make yet another attempt to draw him into confession.

'What's Northumberland doing at this moment?' I asked with apparent mild interest, coming to sit by him, setting a little trap. 'Plotting new conspiracies?' Since Henry was still up to his neck in non-festive business, I saw no need for me to hold back.

From which he escaped with perfect equanimity and smooth if acerbic handling. 'Spending this festive season at Alnwick, I expect, considering how he will govern his new realm after dividing it with Glyn Dwr and Mortimer. And I don't expect he is being forced to discuss it with his wife.'

Which put me firmly in my place, and rather more sharply than I had expected. No more traps from me, then. But eventually I reached the limit of my tolerance.

'Henry.' Rising early, knowing his habits as well as I knew my own, I had intercepted him as he descended the spiral stair from early Mass in his oratory. Since he was alone, and I seated on a stool at the foot of the stair, I spoke without preamble.

'Tell me what is amiss.'

'Nothing is amiss, Joanna.' There was no attempt at a smile. I thought it took him an effort to meet me face to face. I might even have suspected him of trying to walk past me when I stood and stepped in his path.

'I do not hesitate to say that you lie,' I said, grasping the nettle.

I saw the chain on his breast rise and fall as he took a breath.

'You must not worry.'

'How can I not worry?'

'All will be well. All will be well.'

'No, all will not be well, Henry. How can all be well when you banish me from your bed and will not talk with me about anything more meaningful than the lack of seasoning in the venison pottage or the fascinating fact that John is growing so fast that he needs new shoes every time he blinks?'

Henry's eyes might narrow as if I had dealt him a physical blow, but his reply was as unemotional as all his recent replies.

'It is better so.'

'Better? Henry— 'Yes, I would ask him. 'Is it your health?'

'No.'

Well, that was a strong denial. I sought for another reason, snatching at thoughts that raced through my mind. Anything that could have a trace of logic attached to it for this distancing.

'Have you taken some vow of chastity? Is that it? To atone for Scrope's death?'

'No.'

'I could understand if you had. Although I would not necessarily agree with such a course of action.'

'I have taken no vow.'

So I would ask. The one question I feared to ask:

'Do you no longer love me? Have you no wish to spend time with me?'

And how crudely immature that sounded to my ears, so that I flinched inwardly, becoming brisk as I hid my humiliation. 'I would rather you tell me if that was so. I can withstand the death of your love. But this permanent uncertainty is cruel.'

His eyes remained still on mine. 'I love you as much now as I have always loved you.'

I felt a little roll of temper. 'Then why will you not talk to me about what it is that keeps you so far from me? Why will you not show me that you love me? Why will you not even allow me to touch you?'

I took a step towards him.

And as if in proof of all I feared, to prevent any chance that I might launch myself at him with fervent kisses, Henry retreated one deliberate step.

It was a moment of horror. Of impossible despair. The distance between us, barely more than the length of a longbow, seemed to me as wide as the sea between England and Brittany, and this time I could not cross it, because he would not allow me to do so.

I summoned all my hauteur.

'I understand. You have left me in no doubt, have you?'

His silence was a reply in itself. This time it was I who stepped back.

'Don't worry, Henry. I will cause you no further discomfort or embarrassment by importuning you when it is clearly not what you want from me.' I raised my chin, all Navarrese and Valois pride. 'I was not raised to lavish unwanted emotions. I'll not force myself on you again.'

Henry's face was white beneath the bronze of the summer campaigns. 'You misunderstand me.'

'Misunderstand? How can I possibly not understand, when you would rather spend even five minutes with your miserable hawks and hounds than with me. How can I misunderstand that you lock your door against me? I am not witless, Henry. If you love me still—as you claim—then it has to be some sort of misplaced vow! And I have to say I doubt it. It is in my mind that you love another woman. There is plenty of evidence of such in your family, is there not? It is cruel in you not to tell me.'

'Don't badger me, Joanna.'

A heat of temper flickered between us to match my own, but now mine imploded from fire to ice.

'No, Henry. I will not badger you. I will leave you to your own inexplicable devices. It would be too humiliating to do otherwise. You are safe from me. You may lock your door with impunity.'

And I left him. Every nerve in my body trembled for what I had done. At a complete loss, for still I could not let this lie, I sought out Bishop Repingdon, one of our guests and Henry's confessor.

'Has my lord the King taken some vow of abstinence?'

Startled, he blinked. 'Not to my knowledge, Madam. He eats well enough.'

'It was not his intake of food that was in my mind.'

'I have no knowledge of any vow, Madam.'

Bishop Repingdon regarded me as if I should not have the impertinence to ask, but vows were not unknown to gain God's forgiveness. Why would Henry not tell me if he had so committed himself to God's grace?

I must find my answer elsewhere.

'Is the King ill?' I demanded of Master Recoches after I had hunted him down in his herbarium, a discreet little room where he stored and prepared his potions. In my uncertain mood I might even have thought that he too was hiding from me.

'The King is as well as can be expected,' he intoned, his hands clasped tight around a pottery bowl, fingers white on its edge as if he would crush it into pieces.

'What does that mean? You were concerned for him when you wrote to me.'

I thought that he paled slightly. His eyes were wide. The bowl looked in even greater danger of being crushed. 'The King has responded to treatment, my lady. I was wrong to worry you.'

'So there is nothing that should make the King act in any manner unlike his normal behaviour.'

'No, my lady.'

The obvious thought crossed my mind.

'Has the King warned you not to speak with me?'

Master Recoches swallowed. 'No, certainly not, my lady.'

Which fervent response deepened my suspicion that Master Recoches had indeed been ordered not to share his knowledge.

'I hope you don't live to regret your silence,' was all I could say, a weak parting shot. I could not afford to make an enemy of him. If he would not, I could not make him. Just as I was unable to make Henry.

As soon as Twelfth Night had been marked with mummers and minstrels, before I could renew my campaign against him, as if I were a desperate virgin I decided crossly, Henry had summoned his entourage, ordered his coffers to be packed and was preparing to depart, leaving me in a state of perplexed and sharp anxiety. Our leave-taking was notably public and emotionless, whilst I hid the fact that I was fractious and worried to death.

'Where are you going?'

'London. Keep in good health, Joanna.'

'And you also, Henry.'

He bowed over my fingers. No more, no less. He did not even salute them.

For a pair of lovers it was a miserable attempt. I watched from one of the towers as his cavalcade disappeared from view. Not only had we not conceived a child together, we had not shared a bed. As for the potion to render Henry's hair once more thick and lustrous, I had pushed it into the baggage with terse instructions to Henry's squire to get Henry to use it. The squire could not do a worse job of it than I had.

I had no idea when we would meet again.

It seemed to me that we were all mummers, all masked, playing a part in mystery where we had no knowledge of the ending.

Chapter 14

It was July when the courier brought me news that iced me to the bone despite the summer heat, fear stalking down the length of my spine.

It is urgent that you come, Madam. My lord the King is at Walsingham in Norfolk. His health is a cause for grave concern. It is my belief that you should be here. A wife should be with her husband at such times as this.

Without even waiting for the packing of my travelling coffers—they could travel on after me—I was mounted and, with only Marie and the smallest of retinues, I was on the road from Eltham to Norfolk within the hour, the letter from Master Recoches tucked in my sleeve. If in the past he had been ordered by Henry against communicating with me, he was now in a mood of righteous defiance and professional excuses. Brief it might be, but his letter had the capacity to spur me into action.

I had never visited the sacred shrine of Walsingham, yet I knew of its reputation for miraculous cures from its holy wells. For the comfort that the Virgin granted to childless women.

A sardonic humour touched me. Once I would have considered petitioning the Virgin at Walsingham for my own need. Now I accepted the futility of it. I had long since consigned the lemon balm and gillyflower potions to the fire in disgust, along with my hopes that Henry would ever desire me again. But what was Henry doing at Walsingham? Unless he was in dire need of a cure that Master Recoches could not provide.

My heart was a leaden weight in my chest that grew heavier with every mile I covered.

I arrived there, in the midst of crowds engaged on pilgrimage, women of all ages and degree, clad in silk or well-worn wool, all seeking the Virgin's intercession. By now I was half expecting to be chasing a wild goose, finding that Henry in restored health had gone on to King's Lynn, but he was still there in the ecclesiastical accommodations commandeered by such a notable visitor, with a reduced household and a lurking Master Recoches. When I arrived in the sun-warmed little courtyard with its dovecote, a cat sunning herself with a litter of lively kittens, and the all-pervading scents of lavender, the usual clutter of pages and servants, immediately fell silent. Of Henry there was no sign, which I hoped was good news. He was obviously not laid low by some dire affliction. But the silence was ominous. I dismounted and beckoned to the physician, who approached and bowed, looking both worried and surprised to see me so soon.

'Well, you have put the fear of God into me, sir. And I am come.'

'So I hoped, Madam.'

'Where is he?'

'In the church, Madam.'

'Why did he come here?'

'To seek a cure, Madam.'

And at last my anger took flight under a scrape of true fear, as fine-tuned as a lute-string in the hand of a master. As lethal as a new-honed dagger's edge.

'So your skills are failing you. I think we need a conversation, Master Recoches. And forget that the King told you not to break any confidences. It seems that we can hide this no longer and I demand an explanation. Since my lord the King is reluctant to give it, the burden falls on you. No excuses. You will tell me everything. And you will tell me what you are doing to remedy the problem.'

The physician bowed again. I thought he wished that he had not summoned me.

It was a long and painful conversation, desperate in tragedy, destroying all remnants of my irritation. I stood and listened, absorbing every word, recognising the effects such symptoms would have on Henry. I was filled with remorse that I had not known.

'How would you, my lady? My lord the King did not want you to know. He would have found it all too demeaning. He would do anything to abjure your pity.' He paused. 'Or your disgust.'

I could find no reply to that.

I left him and sought out Henry.

★

I stood in the church, still in my travelling clothes, and allowed my eyes to become accustomed to the darkness after the bright outer world. Gradually forms took shape, the nave stretching before me towards the transepts, where I eventually walked, stopping on the steps that would take me into the chancel. For there was Henry, kneeling before the high altar. I waited. I would not disturb him for the world, not with the weight of my new knowledge on my heart, but when he had finished we would speak.

Minutes passed. Henry prayed, proudly upright as if he would deny the state of his body, only his head bent as he made his petition. Anyone ignorant of the situation would see a man in good heart and health, seeking guidance of the Blessed Virgin. Now I knew better. And it was confirmed when, at last, he stood. That is, as I saw even at my distance from him, when he struggled to stand. When he limped slowly along the length of the chancel between the choir stalls with their darkly carved creatures and angelic minstrels, favouring his right leg. Here was something far more serious than thinning hair and blighted vanity. Here was agony. Yet he would walk the length of that holy place without aid of either servant or staff. No King of England in Henry's eyes showed weakness.

Forcing myself to remain motionless, even though anxiety was building in me with his every step, I absorbed the moment he recognised my cloaked figure at the foot of the chancel steps. And as he continued to approach, I watched an array of expression touch his face, one after another. From horror. Through frustration. To acceptance. To fear. And perhaps, finally, to relief.

I could have wept for him, but this was no time for excess emotion, from either of us.

Henry at last stood before me. Our eyes caught and held, both accepting that this was the moment when neither of us could avoid the truth.

'Master Recoches, I presume,' Henry said. His voice held its habitual easy timbre, displaying none of his physical weakness.

'Yes. Do you blame him?'

'Yes. I wish you had not come.'

Henry's face was as unemotional as his voice and untouched by the years. His competent, square-palmed hands firm, his fingers flexible as they clenched around his belt. Had Master Recoches been misled in his reading of Henry's illness after all? But I had seen the pain, the halting step. I had seen the fear in Henry's face.

No. I knew the physician had not been wrong to any degree.

'Why would I not come?' I asked softly. 'Why would I not come to the man I love? And who I believe loves me? Do you not want me to help you bear this time of trial? You should have asked me, trusted me. Did you think I would turn away from you?'

Momentarily he closed his eyes to break the contact. And then opened them so that I could read the fire, the sheer determination of will.

'I wish you had not come, Joanna.'

'Are you ashamed of physical affliction?' I asked gently.

'Yes, if it is God's punishment,' he replied.

'It is not. Are you not a good King?'

'The Crown was not mine to take.'

'You made a better fist of it than Richard ever did! And if it's Archbishop Scrope that troubles your conscience, to commit treason, as he did, is punishable by execution. You need no excuses there.'

'I cannot talk about it.'

No, he could not. Not now perhaps. Not here. But one day I would make him face his terrors. And I would be there to face them with him.

In ultimate compassion, I stretched out a hand to touch his arm. There was no mistaking his reaction this time, the flinch, the deliberate avoidance, so that my hand met thin air. How had I been so blind in the past? Yet I moved closer, touched his hand instead, which he allowed.

'Take me to your accommodations, Henry,' I said softly. 'Let us assess this together. Let me give you comfort.'

'If I told you to go back to Eltham, I don't suppose you would.'

I did not deign to reply, and from somewhere deep within me, I excavated a smile.

And to my relief Henry's mouth curved into at least some semblance of the same, and walked with me.

★

It was a plain room he led me to, a monkish cell, as one would expect in a monastic establishment, but not without some touches of luxury for a noble visitor. The tapestries decorating one wall were particularly fine as I would expect, souls cast into torment in the fires of Hell. The pilgrims made them wealthy after all. But Henry had no eye for such admonitions to live a good life under pain of everlasting damnation, and neither did I. There was enough pain in this room, between the two of us, to furnish every room in Hell.

As soon as the door was closed against the world, whereas once Henry would have taken me in his arms, now he walked away from me, his limp even more pronounced since appearances were no longer necessary, and stared beyond the open window towards the sacred shrine of Our Lady where miracles were known to happen. His arms rested for support on the carved stonework at either side, his face drawn in utter fatigue.

'When did that happen?' I asked carefully, still uncertain of his mood, even his willingness to tell me.

'April,' he replied tersely.

Two months ago!

'Did you think I would not wish to know? That I would not come to you and help you in any way I could? I know our marriage is young in years, but I thought that we had a profound depth of understanding of each other.' His shoulders tightened under my stare. 'I did not expect to be kept in the dark over a matter which is so personal and so agonising for you. I am your wife, Henry. A wife of your own choosing. If I could do nothing else I would pray for you.'

He turned bitterly, grimacing as the pain took him.

'You did not even give me the grace to pray for you,' I whispered.

It spurred him into what might have been a confession, had I been a priest.

'What would I say to you, Joanna, that did not humiliate me beyond bearing? I am a man who has spent his whole life in travelling, in fighting, in riding in the lists. A man who could oversee the vast Lancastrian possessions from the saddle. A man who could lead an army into battle. My reputation is that of a man who never lets grass grow beneath his feet.' He took a breath. 'When parliament opened in March, at my own calling, I couldn't ride. What sort of man does that make me? I could not even climb onto the back of a horse to travel the short distance between Windsor and Westminster. I had to make excuses for my lateness in attending the opening.' His voice grated with hitherto suppressed fury at his own inabilities, as once more he turned from me, hiding the agony as best he could. 'To get there I had to be rowed up the Thames in a cushioned barge, as if I were in my dotage. Before God, it all but unmanned me!'

'But you are better now,' I suggested, although it was a moot point. 'You can ride now.' Anything to make him turn and look at me again.

He did not, addressing instead the bright clouds and a flight of doves come to settle in the dovecote.

'If you mean I am on my feet—then yes! But look at me. I'll never be well again, Joanna. I'll never ride into battle. Or even at a tournament. As for a Crusade—it was predicted that I would die in Jerusalem. Did you know that? It will never happen.'

His despair dropped hopelessly into the silence of the room, like pebbles cast into a well.

'So you came here, hoping that the Holy Wells would bring a cure.'

'There is no cure.'

'There might be,' I persisted, fighting against the desolation that smote my ears.

But Henry's thoughts had moved on. I should have expected it. 'How can I oppose the ambitions of Glyn Dwr and Northumberland, when I can barely lift a sword? How can I impose peace on this war-torn country? I no longer have the strength, Joanna. My will desires it, but my body no longer obeys.'

At least his thoughts were moving out beyond the walls of this room. I would work on that, encourage him.

'Do you have the money to do it? To raise forces?'

'Yes. The clergy have given me a grant. And I have raised a loan. I can get troops in the field without difficulty.'

'Will your sons not lead your armies in your name?'

'Of course. Hal and Thomas are both more than capable.'

So pride still lived. Whatever the ignominy inflicted on his body, his mind was clear and working steadily. 'Then you must do that. You must give them the authority in your name. Until you are well again.'

'By the Rood, Joanna.' He covered his face with his hands. I had never seen him so distraught. 'Sometimes the pain is beyond bearing.' It was a cry from the heart.

'We will remedy that.'

'I doubt that you can.'

It was in my mind to cover the space between us, to take

him into my arms, to smooth away his doubts with kisses and soft words but we were far beyond that. Henry was walled up behind the implacable stones of his failure to fulfil his duty and physical suffering. All I could do was wait, and react. Preserving a calm countenance against all the odds, while my soul wept for him.

It was Henry who broke the silence. 'I have acknowledged Hal as my heir.'

It struck as nothing else, as I realised where his mind was going. How could I have known that his fear had become so deep-seated, so final? I could in that moment have shrieked my frustration at this man whose strength I could not break. Whose determination to suffer alone, a burden on no one and nothing other than his own resources, was without flaw, like tempered steel. Instead I braced myself, becoming predictably brisk and managing.

'You will live for many years more. We will be together and we will overcome this. You will ride into battle again and put paid to Northumberland and Glyn Dwr.'

'Do you say?'

He turned, at last he turned to look at me. There was strength there in his face. But also fear.

'Lock the door,' he said.

I tilted my head in surprise.

'It is time that you knew.'

And as I obeyed, slowly he began to unfasten his belt. With awkward movements he drew his short houppelande over his head, followed by the linen of his under-tunic, dropping them to the floor.

'Stop…!' I said, aghast. Seeing his intent.

Henry continued, stripping off the linen undershirt with inexorable purpose.

'You don't have to do this…'

'I do. I must. I was wrong to hide it from you, and I can hide it no longer. Here is the extent of my affliction. Can it be anything other than God's punishment?'

There it was, revealed for me to see, Henry standing, arms loose at his side, making no attempt to hide the hideous disfiguring. For Henry's skin, once so firm and smooth, so tactile under my hands when physical love held us in its wanton grip, was fouled by lesions. His body was a landscape of abrasions, of ulcerations and contusions, transmuting his skin into a thing of horror. Of nightmare. His face and his hands, his forearms, had been spared, but his body was inflicted with the most terrible wounds.

Nor had I noticed that he had lost so much flesh from flanks and thighs. But then how would I? Henry had not allowed me to see.

'Look at me, Joanna.'

If I needed any sign of his courage, it was in those four words. Henry's body was ravaged, but he had allowed me, at last, behind the screen that he had erected for so long.

'Is it worse?' I asked, striving to appear unmoved when my throat was full of tears. The lesions that leapt and cavorted down his torso continued beneath the drawstring of his braies, which Henry had not removed. 'Was that why you would not come to my bed?'

'Yes. It is worse. I could not inflict this ruin of my body

on you. I did not want to read disgust in your face when you walked away from me. Would not any woman lock her door to keep such as monster as I have become at bay?'

'I am not any woman, Henry.'

Risking a rebuttal, I stepped close, placing my hand, soft as a whisper, on his shoulder where the wounds were less angry, slowly so that he might retreat if he wished.

'I wish you had told me, but now you have. You do not disgust me. You never have, and you never will. The man beneath this terrible affliction is the same man I left Brittany to follow here. The same man I wed. You must not shut yourself away from me. My dear love, you must promise.'

And I thought he would but, eyes darkening with what could only be fear, Henry stepped back to break the contact. 'I think you should not touch me. I have heard it called leprosy.'

If he expected me to run from the room, he was wrong. I pursued him, placing my hand once again where it did least harm, to keep his mind in tune with mine.

'Would you forbid me to show my love, my faith in you and your inner strength? Master Recoches swears that it is not leprosy, of which he has some experience.' I spoke the dread word out loud again between us. 'I have talked with him. He is hopeful of a cure.'

Henry was not convinced. 'He seems to have run out of ideas. But I have dipped my hands in the waters of the Holy Wells. Perhaps the Virgin will have mercy.'

I stooped to recover his under-tunic and cast it lightly over his head. Together, we replaced all his clothes as if I were a squire aiding his knight to ready for the battle ahead, a prescient thought I decided grimly, until at last Henry was restored, looking little different from the man I had kissed and who had kissed me at Nantes.

But the mind of this man was not the same, rather full of dire foreboding.

'I see death. I see death reaching out to me, Joanna.'

I would not consent to such bleak anticipation. 'No. There is still hope. It is not leprosy but some lesser contagion and we will fight together for your life. There are pilgrimages to make, other remedies to try. I can help with the pain. I will not beckon death and darkness onwards, Henry.'

That night, at my insistence, and since I confiscated the key to the monkish room, we shared Henry's bed and I held him in my arms. There would be no need for fragrant leaves of lemon balm. Instead:

'Drink this,' I ordered, having sent Marie to discover the contents of Walsingham's extensive kitchens and talk with their skilled nuns. The juice of the mystical mandrake root, may the Virgin be blessed, had a reputation for deadening the worst of pain and dispensing the gift of forgetfulness for at least a few hours. 'It will dull the pain.'

Too weary to resist, he did not demur but drained the cup. And I thanked God that we had reached an understanding, as I prayed for Henry's deliverance.

He slept through the night in my arms, while I kept vigil. Until eventually I too slept.

When he awoke to find me awake beside him, we shared the blessing of the morning sun and our unity once more at the beginning of a new day. Henry looked rested, his features relaxed and smooth.

'Thank you, most beloved of wives,' he said. 'You are my light and my hope in this dark corner of my life.'

It was as moving to me as any declaration of love.

'We will fight to keep both light and hope alive, most beloved of husbands,' I said. 'You will not be alone in this battle. We face the foe together.'

He rose and stood, straight and tall, as if strength had been renewed. The gift of sleep was a gift of grace from the Blessed Virgin. As for his tarnished conscience, I would polish it to gleaming silver.

★

From Walsingham Henry and I travelled together to where we bade Philippa a slightly tearful but happy farewell on her part at King's Lynn, on her way to her marriage to make her Queen of Denmark. No one would have guessed that the King's mind was not wholly on the splendid alliance for his daughter, master of outward appearances that he was. His body might betray him but his mind still had the force of a battering ram. Philippa was dispatched with gifts and garments that would have been the envy of any Valois princess and, steeling himself, Henry was able to embrace her as a father would embrace his beloved daughter. That he needed copious draughts of a decoction made from the bark of the White Willow, no one needed to know but Marie who once again commandeered the kitchens and the herb garden of the Benedictine Priory where we stayed in King's Lynn.

After which we made our plans, with reluctance on my

part but acknowledging Henry's need to take control of his life. The disfigurement was no worse, his leg was stronger and the draughts of White Willow kept the agony in manageable proportions.

'Where will you go now?' I asked.

'Westminster. And Parliament in October.'

'Then I will ride with you. Can you ride?'

'Yes. My leg feels more at ease.'

'There.' I kissed him, not the first of kisses we had exchanged that morning. 'I told you that you needed me.'

'The solace of a good wife.'

'And, even better, a dose of White Willow.'

'I'll not deny it. You have given me hope. You have all my gratitude.'

Clothed as he was, restored to some suppleness of movement, it was hard to believe his affliction. Henry looked rested and alert as I handed him belt and sword, allowing him to complete the task.

'Remember that no one will know of your weakness. All your subjects will see is their King, a man of power and royal presence.' He was placing a gold coronet on his head, in preparation for a formal leave-taking with the worthies of King's Lynn. 'There is no shame, Henry. All I see is the courage you display in bearing it without complaint. God is merciful and will not punish a King who only desires good for his country.' It was all I could do to ease his conscience, a monumental task all in all that sometimes I thought might be beyond my capabilities. 'You must remember to eat well and sleep well once you are out of my sight.'

'How would I dare to do otherwise?' We touched hands,

fingers linked. 'I swear you have spies behind every pillar, to report my every action. And now we must go.' With the old agility he strode to the door, so that my heart lifted as he stretched a hand to lift the latch.

He never did lift it.

Without a word, without any element of warning, with no sense of distress, Henry crumpled to the floor at my feet.

'Henry!' I was kneeling beside him in an instant, turning him, turning his face which was as pale as the death he feared. His body lay inert, heavy. Through the thickness of his garments I could not even feel his heart beating. Bending over him, I tried to feel his breath on my cheek. It was barely a whisper. Perhaps I was imagining it, and he was not breathing at all. Was this it? Was this the death he had feared, stalking us without mercy, separating us for ever? How could it have struck so fast? There was so much that I still had to say to him.

'Holy Mary, Blessed Virgin.'

I gripped Henry's hand urging Her to listen. But I must do more. On my feet, I dragged open the door and shouted.

'I need help. I need Master Recoches.' One of the household servants fled at the urgency in my voice, and there was the physician kneeling beside me.

'What is it?'

He shook his head, going through the same motions with ear and fingers that I had done over Henry's lifeless figure.

'Well?'

'Patience, my lady!'

I had no patience. My belly was cold with fear.

'It is *une grande accesse*, Madam. A sudden and totally debil-itating attack.'

'Is he dead?' I forced the words out loud. My lips were stiff with terror.

'No, lady. Despite appearances, the King lives. He will recover.'

His calm assurance shocked my suspicions into wakeful-ness. 'Has he suffered these before?'

'He has, Madam. On two occasions.'

'You didn't tell me about this.' Abandoning any pretence at dignity, I punched his arm with my fist. 'How could you keep silent? Is there anything else you have conspired not to tell me?' Fear leapt to conquer all my new-won hopes.

'No, Madam.'

I did not believe him. I no longer trusted him.

'We must have the King moved. Immediately.' And the thought came to me. 'Do his servants know?' How would Henry bear the degradation of his household seeing him in this state of complete helplessness? But I could see no alternative. We needed help. We were long past the days of careful discretion. Anointed King Henry might be, but we had need of physical help. As I made my decisions, I read Master Recoches's silence as one of guilt.

'So they know? Have they seen him in this condition?'

'Yes, Madam. They know.'

I was the only one who did not. But no time now for anger.

'Then you will arrange for the King to be carried to his bed. And while you are doing that, you can consider any other details of this affliction that you have not seen fit to tell me.'

★

Henry lay on his bed, as unresponsive as the dead, while I sat and counted every tiny, shallow breath, dreading that every one might be his last. In recent months I had feared so often for his life, at the hands of assassins, on the battlefield. I had prayed for his skill and insight to avoid the weapons of his enemies. Now his life hung in the balance and not all his skill or insight—or mine—could protect him. I was helpless. Hopeless.

'Will he recover?' I demanded for the second time, or perhaps it was the third, when the hours passed and there was no change except for the movement of the sun, the lengthening of the shadows. Would Henry's life ebb away with the onset of darkness? I feared it. I could neither eat nor drink, only sit in a vigil of terror.

'When will he recover?' I persisted, my composure all but shattered.

'I cannot say, Madam. It was never as long as this.' Master Recoches hovered at my side like a bird of ill-omen. It was clear he knew as little as I.

'How long before? An hour? Two?'

It was now more than double that. Quadruple indeed. The morning had passed into afternoon and evening drew on.

'Do something!' I was beyond politeness.

'I pray, Madam.'

'We all pray. I had hoped you could do more.'

I had never prayed so hard, my fingers counting the beads

of my rosary. Dismissing the physician, who was not sorry to escape me, I sank to my knees. Paternosters and Aves, again and again I counted them in prayer as I sent petition after petition to the Blessed Virgin.

'Blessed Virgin, hear me.'

This was no ailment that could be assuaged by the cooling draught of White Willow or the soft hand of forgetfulness from the mandrake root.

At last as dusk merged into the dark of night I leant my forehead against the edge of the bed in growing despondency.

'Have mercy on us, Holy Mother. Intercede for us in our sin, now and in the hour of our death.'

There. I could do no more than commit him to the care of the Queen of Heaven. I must make penance for my intolerance of Master Recoches. I must attend to the needs of the rest of the household who would be waiting, like me, to hear of a death…

'Joanna.'

A breath of a voice stirred the warm air. I looked up, hardly daring to move, the rosary falling onto my skirts, before sliding to the floor with a little clatter.

'Henry.'

His eyes were open, aware.

'I feel as if I have just returned from battle.'

'I think you have.'

'Am I still at King's Lynn?'

'Yes.' Relief surged as it became evident that his mind was crystal clear, his thoughts lucid. 'Do you remember? We sent Philippa off to her marriage.'

'I remember. How long ago was that? I am thirsty.'

'Only two days.' I rose to pour a cup of wine, sending the page who was sleeping outside the door for Master Recoches as I did, before returning to lift him, pressing the cup against his lips, and he drank.

'How long have my senses failed me?'

'Not long,' I lied. Were we both capable of subterfuge, one to protect the other?

Henry swallowed the wine, painfully. 'This is not the first time,' he said.

'I know.'

He pushed to free himself from my support, to sit unaided, swinging his legs to the floor, as if to prove that his weakness was a temporary thing. And it seemed to be so, for with the wine, colour had returned to his cheeks, dispelling the grey pall.

'We will stay here,' I said, 'where you can rest for a little while.'

He looked at me. 'I know what I wish to do.'

'Then tell me.'

'I will go to Bardney.'

It was not what I had expected. 'Where is that?'

'To the north. Near Lincoln.' He acknowledged my astonished regard. 'There are relics of St Oswald there,' he explained, 'his bones, which are said to work many cures for those on the point of death. Perhaps he will have mercy on me.'

'I will come with you.'

'There is no need. I have work to do there.'

It hurt. And he must have seen it.

'I am not incapable, Joanna. These attacks on my body,

it seems, are momentary things. I can't control them, but when they leave me I can still work.' I saw as he gathered his strength of purpose around him once more, as if he were donning breastplate and basinet, cuisse and sabaton, for battle. 'Will you help me stand? I am the son of my father and my grandfather. I have a duty to my kingdom, and an honour to uphold my name. I must be worthy of my forebears, and of the position I hold. I will not sit, cosseted and blanketed like an old man for death to claim me. There is much for me to do in this kingdom and I will accomplish it.'

With some little effort, he was upright, his innate regality once more restored.

'Is there nothing that I can do for you? How will you travel?'

'I have a brass saddle to support my limbs, that allows me to sit upright and ride as if I was a young knight at the joust again.' His smile was heart-wrenching. 'I have to be a man amongst men.'

Which did nothing to remedy the hurt even though I knew he had hoped to comfort me.

'What about Glyn Dwr? And Northumberland?' Not that I cared greatly at that moment, but the affairs of state would not stand still.

'They must wait until I put myself right with God and gain salvation. Only then will I have the strength to face them and bring them to submission. Until then I trust my sons to hold the peace in England. Hal and Thomas will stand for me.'

So there it was, written in Henry's hand. He would go to Bardney and I must allow it. All I could do was to make a final plea. Henry had enough to bear without my weeping in despair on his shoulder. He had more faith in St Oswald's relics than I had. St Oswald had not sat for hours beside Henry's inert body.

'You must keep me in your confidence.' It was all I could ask.

'I know. I can no longer hide it from you. Nor can I bear it alone.'

I sighed. 'Yet you will try. At least allow me to kiss you farewell.'

It was a kiss of great tenderness. I had a need to hold him, but could not: to journey every step of the way with him, but that would dishonour him. I must let him have his way, and return to me when he could. How would I bear the not knowing? I could only rely on royal couriers and Master Recoches to tell me the truth. I had no confidence in Henry sending for me when the next attack struck him down, as we both knew it would. What if he did not recover the next time? What if this was to be the final time that we stood together on this earth? Never had I felt so helpless.

Henry's thoughts were following the same path.

'If I die before we meet again, my dearest love, know that you were the finest part in my life.'

As emotion gathered in my throat against my will, I touched his face, still miraculously untouched by the lesions that disfigured the rest of him.

'Don't you dare die!' was all I could manage, whispered against his hair, and then we walked together from the room.

★

Henry and I embarked on a new beginning. A new campaign. An outright war. Not against the rebels in north or west.

Not even against the members of parliament that continued to strike at Henry like cats spitting over a mess of fish. But against a foe we could neither see nor bring to battle.

St Oswald proved not to be efficacious.

A succession of new physicians of repute were engaged to replace the ageing Recoches who had lost my confidence. I scoured the great seats of learning in Italy, bringing doctors to England to use their talents to rid Henry of this curse of pain and physical degradation. David Nigerallis of Lucca, Elias de Sabato from Bologna, and Pedro de Alcobaca. I ordered the services of the eminent surgeon John Bradmore who had saved Prince Hal's life at Shrewsbury, who had removed the arrow head from his face with such skill. I tapped the knowledge and the skills of my ageing nurse, Mistress Alicia, whose mind was now sharper than her fingers when dipping into salves and potions. Peony against the falling evil. Chamomile to soothe a troubled mind. Yarrow to heal pernicious wounds of the skin.

We applied them all. We would leave no stone unturned.

I consulted my precious books.

'I swear you are poisoning me,' Henry growled as he downed yet another new draught, the bitter infusion of Bugloss to lift his spirits.

'I swear I am not. Be brave. I have another two remedies, pounded and sieved and mixed with red wine.'

And when the new ones failed to heal his suffering flesh, I resorted to the old ones, the ones with powerful properties but dread reputation. My beloved vervain with its magical powers. Rosemary to keep evil dreams at bay. And of course Periwinkle for good measure, with its ability to ward off evil spirits. No house where Periwinkle hung over the door would contain witchery. I would protect Henry from attack within this world and without. Nothing would stand in my way.

The fear of leprosy, that most pernicious of diseases, continued to haunt us. Rumours of Henry's ailment abounded at Court, like mushrooms in a damp autumn.

'Tell me the truth,' Henry demanded of Pedro de Alcobaca.

I held my breath for the reply. If it was leprosy, then it was Henry's doom. There would never be a cure.

'It is not leprosy, my lord.'

'You are very certain,' I observed, fixing him with my eye, refusing to allow him to slide into lies and half-truths. We were past the days of polite untruths.

'I have studied it, my lady.' Gravely, his dark Portuguese features compassionate, he waxed into detail. 'Your face and hands are untouched, my lord. There is no numbness to your hands or feet. Your eyes are keen, my lord, as is your mind. I swear that it is not leprosy.'

It was a relief, of sorts.

'It may not be leprosy, but is a judgement from God,' Henry said more than once. Which was a reflection of his despairing mind even when he drove his body to fulfil his royal demands.

So I would ease his mind too with herb infusions. I would drag him back from the brink of despair.

Henry never shut his door against me again.

'For I will assuredly summon a servant with an axe to destroy the lock!'

But there were some nights, and days, when Henry must face his worst battles alone, racked with fatigue and distress and pain. I allowed him that solitude to muster his inner reserves against an uncertain future, hovering outside his door until I sensed that he was ready to communicate with me again.

★

We sank lower into despair, a circling descent into a vortex of pain and hopelessness, when Henry was unable to travel at all, not even by river. When a moment of insensitive encouragement, suggesting that he walk with me in the herb-scented gardens, roused his temper to blistering heat.

'Walk in the garden? Why would I do that? Jesu! Once I could sprint from here to here,' he gestured expansively with his arm, a movement that made him gasp in agony, 'faster than my hounds. Now I can barely crawl from bed to chair. And don't lie to me. Don't fill me with soft hopes that we both know will never come to pass. I am dying, Joanna. We both see it. We cannot pretend that it is not so. But by God I'll go to my death in the manner in which I lived.'

The raw fire of arrogance had not dwindled.

'Forgive me,' I said softly. 'I was at fault.'

I never belittled him again. I never humiliated him. I let him set his own pace. We accepted what was clear to everyone, living the good days, tolerating the bad when pain ruled. We could have entered into a major pretence that this was not happening, that there were days of true healing. That Henry would recover and we would live out our days together.

We could not. That was not the way of it, for either of us. In those black days we faced the best and the worst together. But sometimes physical pain was not the worst of it.

Parliament, seeing the decline of the King, effectively stripped Henry of his power.

'I am to be put under supervision, as if I were a child,' Henry raged. 'The sort given to Richard as a ten-year-old boy. The Royal Council will overlook all matters of government, every decision that I might make. As if my mind was as destroyed as my body. As if I am incapable of stringing two logical thoughts together.'

'Could you not refuse? Could you not stop them?'

The reply was a silent snarl. 'Our household expenses are to be reduced. We have been told, with utmost reverence of course, to go and live quietly in the country. By God!'

So, since parliament as ever had the whip hand in matters of finance, live quietly in the country is what we did, at Leicester, at Kenilworth, at Woodstock. While the Council became a creature of Prince Hal's making, meeting under his auspices, obedient to his wishes, with the dread word abdication hanging in the air between us. Henry would not discuss it, and I did not push him beyond his strength. The Crown was his to dispose of as he saw fit.

How strange, it came into my mind. When I had first become Queen of England I had had ambition to wield regal power, as I had in Brittany. I had planned to share Henry's affairs, anticipating it with pleasure, and had resented the lack of opportunity. Now the authority had been removed from both our hands so that we were compelled to a life of quiet retirement, as if old age had made of us an irrelevance. Power had passed into the hands of the next generation where Hal was already experiencing the intoxication of royal authority. Yet I would have exchanged every power in God's universe for a restoration of Henry's good health.

Meanwhile Henry learned to travel by litter, until travel of any description became a thing of the past. I learned patience. I learned that love must sometimes be silent, an agony of waiting and tolerance when Henry could not even bear my presence. Our love became a matter of hands touching. A brush of lips. A conversation, a plangent moment of lute music, a page shared and enjoyed from a book. Love was a union of minds and we learned to live without the physicality of desire. We rode out no more, we did not hunt. It was as much as Henry could do to visit his hawks in the mews. I had a wooden perch carved and arranged so that his favourite birds could sit in his chamber, to be fed on chicken if that was what he desired.

I would have fed them on roast peacock if it had given Henry pleasure.

We had good days. Another truce with Brittany was duly signed and seemed likely to last despite the cynicism on both sides. Hal's incursions into Wales left Owain Glyn Dwr a helpless outlaw. Northumberland finally met his treasonous end on the battlefield at Bramham Moor. Mortimer too was dead, in Hal's effective siege of Harlech. The threat of the Dragon, the Lion and the Wolf had come to an end at last.

My daughters Marguerite and Blanche, young as they

were, were married to men of European rank and title and so
flew the English nest that had nurtured them. Baron Thomas
de Camoys took another wife, Elizabeth Mortimer, cousin to
Henry and widow of ill-fated Harry Hotspur who had met
his death at Shrewsbury. An advantageous marriage for both,
and for Thomas a strategic alliance to a woman of Plantagenet
blood, although I suspected Henry of shackling his suspect
Mortimer cousin to the most loyal man he could find. I had
to be happy for Lord Thomas. They seemed content enough
together with Elizabeth soon loosening her seams and Lord
Thomas anticipating another son.

Small steps of achievement, of happiness. These were days
when Henry felt restored, hope renewed.

'The despised moldewarp has won that battle after all,' he
observed, lifting his cup of ale to toast the future. 'My son
will at least inherit a country rid of war and intrigue.'

But then there were bad days, for death touched us too.
Henry's much loved Blanche died, giving birth to a son who
rapidly followed his mother into the grave. John Beaufort, as
close as any brother could be to Henry, left this life.

As for my own grief, my own son Gilles was struck down
with barely eighteen years to his name. So much promise
wiped out by some nameless fever when he crossed the
channel to visit me. Marguerite, my dear Marguerite took
her last breath so soon after her marriage to the Vicomte de
Rohan. So much death. So much pain. These were days that
must be weathered, when the anguish of our separation from
our family was as great as Henry's physical suffering. Those
were the days when we shut ourselves away and mourned

together. Even Henry's favoured greyhound, Math, reached the end of her allotted years to give him much grief.

And during all these months Henry could no longer bear to be touched to any degree, other than his hands and face. We slept apart and I accepted it, waiting outside his door at dawn until he could summon the control to master his features and admit me with words of welcome and love, for engulfed as we were with loss and desolation, the bond that held us tightened with every hour, every minute. With the dread threat of separation stepping ever closer, we shared and tasted every morsel of this scant meal that time still allowed us. We met each day with a light touch of hands and lips, expressing our love in word and thought, brilliant as jewels. In simple acceptance, impermeable as granite, of what we could still experience of joy in music and poetry. We never expressed the finite quality of our life together.

Until one morning.

'My regrets are as numerable as the stars in the heavens,' Henry said, strong enough to climb the spiral staircase to attend Mass in his oratory. The incense still hung in the air around us, shrouding the silver crucifix on the altar in a cloud of mysticism, as he struggled from his genuflection to his full height.

'There is no need for regrets,' I replied, uncertain of the direction of his thoughts. His eyes were trained on the suffering Christ, his own expression less harrowed.

'But there is. I am so sorry that we will never have the child we had hoped for.'

I thought of saying that I would never give up hope, but I could not. It was no longer possible to encourage, when the encouragements became hard lies. Henry, turning his head, must have seen it in my face, for he gripped my hand hard. 'We must accept it.'

And so I had. 'We have enough children of our own,' I assured him.

A pain, a hurt, a grief. I would never let him know how much it remained with me. Henry had his own agonies without mine to drive him into deeper despair.

I wept alone, that we would never achieve this symbol of our love together.

But then I vowed to weep no longer. In the depths of this abyss of horror and despair, I came to a new calm steadiness. After all, there was no further for either of us to fall.

Chapter 15

September 1411: Eltham Palace

'I don't think you should be doing this,' I said.

Tactlessly, perhaps, but Lord Thomas de Camoys, who continued to be my eyes and ears at Court, had warned me, and I did not like the direction affairs were taking. I could see nothing but unnecessary and prolonged trouble for Henry and for England.

'I did not expect you to approve,' was Henry's unhelpful response.

'I think it would be bad policy,' I continued undeterred.

'Your opinion on this matter is irrelevant, Joanna.'

It was short and sharp, Henry's jaw clenched, the line between his brows etched today with frustration as much as with pain. I should have learnt to keep my tongue between my teeth when I could all but see temper snapping in the set of his head, in the tension in his knuckles. But at least

Henry was alert, his mind active, his moods of depression set aside. The morning cup of White Willow, now necessary to get him through the next hours without excruciating agony, his skin afire, had been pushed aside.

'Are you strong enough to lead such an expedition?' I asked. 'It will mean days at sea and in the saddle. Would you condemn your body to such excess?'

'Am I not King?' Typically, when faced with royal policy, Henry ignored the state of his body. 'Who else would lead an army into France?'

I knew the answer to that. So did Henry. I chose not to answer it since it would be less than diplomatic in the circumstances. It was like trying to walk on egg shells without crushing them into tiny pieces.

'But it's not your policy,' I said.

'God's Blood! I know it's not my policy!' The irritation slithered between us. 'But my authority to determine the direction of England's involvement in Europe seems to have been snatched out of my hands.'

Which was another issue I would not pursue.

Henry was sitting at the table he had had erected in his chamber so that he could work without the need to negotiate the antechambers and stairs to the room he had once used. The surface of it was covered with documents and maps. Henry had a pen in his hand and a frown on his brow.

'And do we have the money to launch this expedition?' I asked with caution.

If we lacked money, it would keep Henry from engaging in so questionable a campaign. For once I prayed that the coffers were empty and parliament unyielding.

'It seems that we do. The Council is keen to go ahead.'

Worried beyond thought, I promptly abandoned my determination to be circumspect. 'And can I guess who has persuaded them?'

'We don't need to guess,' he growled.

For here it was: the policy that distressed me. The Duke of Burgundy—now my cousin John after my uncle's death—was soliciting England's help in the civil war that was tearing France apart. Burgundy was in open conflict with the Duke of Orleans and his followers, the Armagnacs, both of them intent on personal power building since King Charles was incapable of holding his aristocrats in check. To tempt Henry to commit troops to the campaign my cousin of Burgundy was offering the lucrative gift of four Flemish towns, as well as his daughter as a bride for Hal.

'Look,' Henry said, gesturing with sardonic drama. 'It is all prepared. Ships, grants. Even the damned pennons are painted. The standards embroidered. That's not one of them is it?' He scowled at the embroidery that lay neglected on my lap, but did not wait for a reply. 'Even my bloody bed is made ready for transportation. Hal is, if nothing else, efficient.'

For that was where this policy had received its backing. It was a sensitive area for me, to step judiciously between Henry and his heir, but I was becoming practised at it. It was not, after all, the first time I had seen such a dichotomy of interest. Since Henry's increasing physical fragility, Hal had taken his place at the meetings of the Royal Council to drive his own vision of England's future. The Council itself had been gradually reformed, Henry's friends replaced by those loyal to his heir. Henry's authority was under attack, quite wilfully, from his own son.

'So you will go,' I said carefully, this tragic conflict between King and Prince clear in my mind. How could he even contemplate an invasion of France? Every instinct cried out to forbid it. I would wager his being unable to walk onto the ship unaided, yet at the same time my intuition warned me that I must not interfere at this juncture.

'Yes, I'll go. I'll defend our base at Calais. And then I'll see which way the wind is blowing.'

I could ignore it no longer. 'And will you face Hal when he pushes for more, for a full-scale campaign into the heart of France? What will you say to him?'

'What indeed.' Henry sighed, tossed down the pen and downed another gulp of the White Willow. 'You see this as clearly as I do. You see which way affairs are moving. Can I stop them?'

Which gave me freedom to speak. 'Yes I see it. And I don't know if you can stop them.' I feared Henry was not strong enough to do it.

'Neither, by God, do I!'

I folded the embroidery—'It is not a royal standard'—and moved to stand behind him, a hand light as a breath on his shoulder. 'What does your heart tell you to do?'

'My heart tells me…'

As if conjured up by our conversation, there was a brisk knock at the door. Hal entered, Bishop Henry following. They bowed, but I felt their courtly demeanour hid something that would not be to Henry's advantage. Like the velvet skin of an apricot might hide the danger of a poisoned fruit in the hand of an assassin.

'Son and brother. And both together. To what do I owe the pleasure?'Through the cynicism, I felt Henry tense under my hand.'Help yourselves to wine. I would rather not stand. As you see,' Henry gestured at the mess of documents in front of him,'the campaign to support Burgundy against the Armagnacs is underway.' And when, refusing the wine, Hal and Bishop Henry exchanged glances:'What is it?You may as well tell me since you are obviously deep in some conspiracy.'

'Let me lead it, sir.'Tall and straight, with all the vibrancy his father lacked, Hal, impossibly impressive despite the ruined face, made his demand.

'No.' Henry's reply was gentle. I knew what it took him to keep it so. 'I will not give you permission.'

'Why not?' Hal leaned over the table, twitching one of the maps so that he could see it. 'I have been soldiering since I was a boy. I can lead this expedition to victory.'

'If we go to war, I will lead it. It's not a policy I like, but I'll be damned if I abjure my right to lead England into a fully fledged war.'

'You trusted me in the past. Why not now?'

I saw the quagmire lurch before our feet. Henry too weak, too proud; Hal too impatient, too insensitive. Their relationship was always on an edge, tottering, clinging to polite recognition. Without due care it could fall and be destroyed. Well, for Henry's sake I would remain silent no longer. I took a step, so that I stood halfway between them, in the line of sight of both.

'It is not a matter of trust. Your day will come, Hal,' I said. 'This is your father's campaign.'

He barely glanced at me. 'It is mine too. Or do you intend to give the command to brother Thomas?'

So here was jealousy too, another deep-seated emotion. I stepped in again.

'Your father has no intention of giving up the command to anyone. I am sure there is room for you to plan it together.'

'All I need is your authority.' Again Hal's reply was for Henry, not for me, but the slide of his eye was now in my direction. It was not friendly.

'It might be good policy,' Bishop Henry advised with smooth interruption, 'to let Hal take over.' He had stood apart, but now came to join the group round the table. 'Your health is still not restored, Henry. It is well known.'

'He is much restored,' I found myself saying, even though I did not believe it. I could definitely see which way the wind blew here, and it was working itself into a storm.

Hal let the map, which he had lifted to hold to the light, fall. 'The duty is mine. Do you want the truth, sir? Your wife will not give it, but I will. And your brother. You can no longer apply yourself to the honour and profit of the realm. But I can. Therefore, as your heir, the authority to take England into war should be mine.'

Silence. A silence that seared the air I breathed.

Slowly, Henry stood, until he was as straight as his son. Only I could see the effort it took.

'And whose opinion, that you have seen fit to deliver to your King, is that?'

'Mine. And that of the Royal Council.'

'And what else does the Royal Council say, in its wisdom?'

'There it would be good sense for you to give the Crown to me. To give it now. To abdicate.'

I saw the blood drain from Henry's face. Here was poison. I felt my hands clenched into fists at my side, yet I kept my tongue.

'Let me rule.' Hal leaned on the table, as if proximity would win the day. If the atmosphere had been tense before, now it crackled with conflict. 'Where is the Crown?' As if it might be sitting on a coffer, to be snatched up. 'Give it to me and I will bring England to greatness.'

'I will not.'

'The Council will support me.'

'I will never abdicate the Crown I won and have worn with God's grace.' Henry's glance at me was fierce with denial. 'What have you to say, Joanna? I can't believe you do not have an opinion on this.'

Denial, yes. I saw fear there too.

Could I not see both sides to this tragically unfolding clash of wills? Henry would never go to war again. I had only to look at him to see it. But it was his pride, all that he had left to him from the power that had brought him to the throne; that I could not destroy. Hal had the right of it, but for me to argue against Henry in this family arena would make an uneasy relationship even more untenable. I did not want to be at odds with the heir to the throne. To have Bishop Henry as an enemy would not be good policy.

I looked at Hal. At the Bishop. And then at Henry, my dear love. My only love. Loyalty was a hard path to tread when faced with truth. But love gave my steps grace.

'This is what I would say.' I replaced my hand on Henry's shoulder, resisting the temptation to grip hard, to give him strength in a confrontation that boded ill. 'The Crown is yours, my lord. To do with as you wish.'

As simple as that. It could be no other way. I would have to deal with Hal's disappointments and Bishop Henry's political cynicisms later. But I could not support them against Henry at this critical juncture.

And Henry's voice was stronger than I had heard for weeks, as if my will had fused with his, so that he spoke with a dreadful precision. 'If you came here this morning to hear my opinion of this piece of insolence, Hal, then you have it. It is not in the remit of the Council to decide who will wear the Crown. Nor is it in yours.' His eye took in both son and bishop. 'There is no more to be said.'

'But you cannot have considered, sir.'

'I have considered, gravely. The Crown is not yours to wear, Hal. One day it will be. Then the manner in which you wear it will be your own. Today it is mine.'

They departed in a cloud of sharp-voiced dissatisfaction. I followed, into the outer chamber.

'Hal…'

He wheeled round. 'My father does not have the strength. I am his heir. I will take the burden of government from him. And you should persuade him, Madam Joanna.'

He looked at me, challenging me to dare to question him, while I, once again, attempted to conciliate as best I could.

'You will do as you see fit, Hal, but don't leave the King out of your discussions, even less out of your ultimate decisions. We both know that you hold the power now, but you still do not have the right to do it. The Crown is not yours, however much you might wish it were so.'

Hal's brows levelled at what he saw as my temerity.

'I know you are negotiating with Burgundy,' I said, 'which is against the King's wishes.'

'It will be good policy.'

There would be no swaying him, but I did what I could. Perhaps I could persuade him towards more subtlety. 'It may be so, Hal. It may be that I agree with you, if it comes to a choice between supporting Burgundy or Orleans. What I cannot support is your defiance. I am not your enemy, Hal. You must do as you wish, but all I advise is that you don't alienate yourself entirely from your father.' But then I hardened my tone. 'I forbid you to distress him. It is not necessary.'

Hal retraced his steps with a little shrug, to salute my fingers. 'I know you are no enemy of mine. But I have ambitions to fulfil, and am of an age to fulfil them.'

'As you will. One day. But it will not be today.'

It was the best I could do.

Hal considered, then gave a brisk nod as he masked his dislike of my assessment, even managing a bleak smile. 'I will take your advice, Madam Joanna.'

When he strode away I called out so that he halted, turned, while I chose the words that hurt me in their utterance more than all the rest. 'All you need is patience, Hal. It will not be long. We both know that.'

He bowed. I knew he understood.

Returning to Henry's chamber, it was to find him in the act of striding across the room, astonishingly agile in the white heat of rage, teeth bared in what was not a smile, to open the lid of a coffer. From it he removed the Crown, flinging its soft leather wrappings to the floor. I had not known it was here, that he could not bear to keep it out of his immediate possession. Now he held it firmly aloft, using every ounce of his strength, as if he would place it on his own head.

'What did you have to say to my son, out of my hearing? You can be honest now, rather than diplomatic.'

'I was honest. I said nothing to Hal that I would not say to you.' I was not disturbed by the challenge in his stare. How similar father and son were, if they did but know it. 'The Crown is yours to dispose of as you see fit.'

'The Crown of England. My Crown.' He regarded it, turning it so that light caught and burnished the gems, setting rainbow prisms to dance across the tapestries. 'I won this Crown, when all it stood for had been dishonoured by my cousin Richard. I brought justice and fair judgement to England. I brought honest government. I had hoped to bring peace and prosperity to a country respected by every state in Europe.'

A flash of blood-red ruby fell across his face.

'And I have failed.'

'No...!'

'My Council and my own son would take it from me.'

It was in my mind to go to him, to deflect such self-condemnation, but the warning in the turn of his head stopped me before I had even taken a step.

'How many attempts have I faced to take the Crown from me? Too many to count: Northumberland, Scrope, Glyn Dwr. So many willing to rise in rebellion. And now it comes to this. My own Council would move against me. My own son and brother would conspire to dethrone me.'

All I could do was stand and listen in mute compassion as Henry poured out the guilt that had lived with him for a decade. It crashed around us like the breaking of a storm that I could only stand and absorb. Had I not always known that it had been eating away at his conscience? Oh, I had, but never had it been spoken until now. Never had I accepted Henry's culpability as I did now.

'Was I wrong, Joanna? Was I wrong to take hold of fate and wrest my inheritance from Richard? Was I wrong to take the Crown too? There are those who say it should never have been mine. It was Richard's and I brutally dispossessed him. Is this God's punishment on me, for taking a Crown that was not mine to take? Is this God's judgement for Richard's death, locked away in Pontefract?' His voice was thick with emotion. 'Before God, Joanna, that deed weighs on my conscience. It always has.'

And there at last was the question I needed to ask, and so I did.

'Were you guilty of Richard's death?'

He looked at me, the Crown of England held high between us.

'Yes.'

There it was, frightening in its starkness, and yet although I acknowledged his guilt, I could not add my words to his self-condemnation. I knew why it had to be done. What ruler was not aware of the need for pragmatic action, however despicable it might seem? And so Henry had conceded to Richard's death, inarguably a despicable act, but with the best of intentions to rid England of a suppurating sore that would drain her strength and drag her down: the presence of a living, deposed king, the source of every rebellion.

'I thought you might be,' I said, but there was no accusation in my voice. I knew the need for blood on royal hands and I would not condemn him. Not at this final juncture. It was not my role to stand in judgement. His own self-condemnation was enough.

'Could you doubt that it was my order that sent Richard to his death?' Henry asked. 'Oh, it was not my hand that struck the blow, but it was at my instigation that he went to his grave. There was no self-inflicted starvation. I made the choice, that if Richard lived he would remain a real and dangerous threat to this land that I love more than the breath in my body. The country supported me. The lords gave their assent. But yes, the blame is mine, and out of it I snatched this.'

The Crown, the symbol of so much pain, of so much glory to those who wore it, flashed and glittered with baleful fire.

'Do you see the ironic twist of it?' Henry continued, his eyes ablaze. 'It is not my enemies who have brought me low. It is not Northumberland or Scope or Glyn Dwr. It is not my ill-wishing cousins. It is God who has finally called me to account. God has inflicted this terrible suffering on me in reparation for my murder of Richard. For, before God, I am truly guilty.'

For the first time Henry had told me the naked truth, and seeing in his face a plea for understanding, I gave it unstintingly.

'God has also given you the courage to withstand this pain, and I will never leave you to suffer it alone. Look at what you have achieved,' I said. 'You are an acclaimed monarch, with heirs for the future. Your enemies have been defeated. Scotland and Wales are no longer strong enough to threaten you. France is embroiled in civil war. You have friends in high places. I see no failure here.'

It was as if a burning sore had been lanced. The anguish drained and, without hesitation, Henry placed the Crown on his head, and for that moment the years too rolled away. The young man who had fought and struggled and made himself King was reborn, all authority and regal bearing were his again as the light through the window gilded face and jewels alike.

I did what seemed appropriate. I bowed my head in acknowledgement.

'My lord. My King.'

'I am honoured, my wife. My Queen. My soul.'

It was the final bonding of our love, born out of pain and guilt and conviction. Our eyes held with all the promise and glory of a future that we both knew we did not have.

His breath was laboured with the emotion of the moment, until he raised the Crown again, as if it had become too heavy for him to bear on his brow, placing it gently on his table amidst the documents, where the jewels continued to wink and gleam. So beautiful. So deadly.

'I will not do it. I will not relinquish this Crown. The Crown is mine. What right has any man, certainly not my own blood, to dispossess me? Only death will take it from me. Where do you stand in this, Joanna?'

It was heartbreaking.

'With you.'

'I would like to be certain of this.'

I walked across and kissed his lips.

'I stand with you. I always have. Even when we were estranged.'

'I thought you would agree with the policy against the Armagnacs, and that it should be Hal who led the expedition.'

'I think it might be a useful alliance. I dislike Orleans's ambitions to seize the French Crown for himself. But I agree with no policy that will drag you or England into a war that would bring you no advantage. As for this.' I took up the royal Crown. 'This needs to be kept safe, for when you wear it again, with all the ceremony of a King before his Council.' I placed it back in the coffer, wrapping once more folded around it. 'What will you do about your son?' I asked as I closed the lid once more to restore its power to the dark.

'I will challenge his power. He has to learn that a king's power is a duty, and cannot be laid aside, until the day he lies on his deathbed and takes his last breath.'

'And that, we pray, will be years in the future.' Placing my hands on the closed lid, I stood upright and turned to face him. 'Hal hides it well but he does not like me.'

'Hal does not realise the value of a strong-willed wife.' Henry's eyes were gleaming as dangerously as the gems in the Crown, now hidden. 'What would you do in my place? What would be your next step?'

I considered this. How good it was to talk policy, as we had done in the past. I knew exactly what I would do.

'I would dismiss this Royal Council that is ripe for mischief. I would do it immediately.'

His smile was a little wry, but quite conspiratorial. 'I can't do it today. But by God, it's the best piece of advice I've heard for a long time.'

'I would dismiss your ministers who are too ready to fawn on Hal and do his bidding. I would select where loyalty is guaranteed.'

'A woman after my own heart.'

I thought. No, he was not strong enough to lead an army into Europe. His spirit might be stronger but not his body. What would he say to my next advice? Nothing gained, if I did not have the courage.

'And I would abandon the campaign too,' I said. 'Let Hal wage war when he is King. While you wear the Crown and see peace as a valuable policy, then follow it.' I watched his face, awaiting a possible explosion of anger. But perhaps not. 'Do I order the unpacking of your travelling bed?'

His eyes held mine. Would he agree, or would pride rule?

A smile spread across his increasingly gaunt features.

'I will do that too. Have the bed unpacked. I regret I am too weak to make use of it.'

We linked hands. We were at one. The days of our antagonism were long gone.

★

It was as if the Prince's challenge to Henry, the vile threat of abdication, had resurrected a full-flowering of life within Henry's wasting body. Energy renewed, seizing control as he had been unable to do for so long, he took a barge to Westminster and met with parliament, speaking powerfully, as it was told to me by Lord Thomas, demanding their three-fold loyalty and duty and obedience to their liege lord. As for the treacherous Royal Council, it was simply not summoned. Henry had resumed his powers as dramatically as if he wore the Crown from dawn to dusk. There was a flamboyance that had been long absent.

'Though nothing will resurrect my hair,' he groaned, nor for the first time, rubbing his fingers over his close-cropped scalp.

'But I still have remedies we have not tried,' I suggested, thinking of the many and varied properties of Southernwood mixed with fat and ashes that Henry would dislike intensely, as I dropped a kiss on the forlorn remnants of a once lustrous display. 'Although some of them have an unfortunate pungency...'

He grinned. 'I think you will have to love me without,' he said, for was he not sure of my answer?

'As I do,' I concurred. 'But I am willing to pander to your vanity, even though it is a sin.'

I smiled at this, as I stitched. It had become a compulsion with me, this new tapestry that I was creating with such ferocious energy, as if the figures that grew and capered beneath my needle were a true reflection of Henry's resurgence. As if I could trap the vibrancy of the tapestry into Henry the man, to build a bower of powerful emotion to defend him from attack by the malign forces that assailed him. And so I created the flowery meadow, the backdrop to my vibrant lovers, every flower speaking of the lasting power of love, while the expedition to bolster the Burgundians was dismantled. Although I saw the bitter acceptance in Henry's face, it was fast replaced with vigour that he was once more in command of his government, where it was better to use words than a sword. Was it not good policy to stand back from this war?

'If we support Burgundy, it will hack at our relations with Navarre and Brittany,' I advised. I had thought much over this proposed dabbling in French politics.

'Not to mention my subjects in Gascony who are in alliance with Orleans and the Armagnacs.' Henry set his signature and seal to yet another document of intent.

So it was done. No man would again undermine Henry's authority.

And as he grew in confidence, casting off the debilitating pain, I began to stitch the man I envisaged standing in my meadow, tall and strong, arms outstretched towards the space that would be occupied by the lady. I would stitch a falcon with a fierce eye on his wrist as an emblem of his nobility and his latent aggression in the arts of love. Meanwhile I clothed him in red, such as Henry might choose, his cloak fur-lined with ermine. Eventually I might stitch a collar in gold onto his shoulders.

At Westminster, far from my meadow, Henry began to wipe the past clean of insurrection as he looked ahead. A new Council. A new Treasurer. A new Chancellor. Men appointed that he could trust as the old disobedient guard was swept away.

'My previous Councillors will not be pleased,' he observed.

'Then reward them with gifts or titles for their past services,' I said.

And so he did. He did not look or sound like a king who had failed when he travelled to Windsor and presided over the Garter Celebrations. There was a new power about him, a new repose: an acceptance of this gift of renewed health. His keeping of the seals of Chancellor and Treasurer in his own hands was sufficient testimony to his single-minded sense of purpose, before handing them to men of proven loyalty, Archbishop Arundel and Sir John Pelham.

In my meadow, my tapestried lover was complete, the

falcon bright-eyed, and, satisfied, I turned my attention to the lady, to the sumptuous folds of her gown in my favourite blue, as she sat beside the stream. What would she hold? A flower perhaps, offered to her lover as she offered her love.

As her ermine-lined cloak fell into its folds under my direction, with a vital switch in policy, Henry, in the interest of keeping old alliances firm, gave his support to Orleans and the Armagnacs, awarding control of the English army to his son Thomas. With inevitable results. Henry and Hal were even more estranged, but Henry would not be moved.

I stitched late into the night, as if the completion of this work would destroy the antagonism between King and Prince. As if my close stitching on the flowery meadow would hold the country from disintegration. The lady gained life with a sly smile, her little dog springing up at her knee as her lover approached. His hood was the same hue as her gown. In glowing russet, I stitched my lover's hair curling luxuriantly to his shoulders.

Rumour said that the Prince was planning bloody rebellion.

'He will not. He is just young and angry,' I said, hoping it was so.

Henry grunted. 'Hal must learn the royal burden of duty and service, to me and to his country.'

'Then speak with him.'

So Henry did. A dramatic interlude with discordant voices behind closed doors, where I awaited the consequences from without. Not even I would have intruded on them as, father and son, they hammered out their differences. There was no place for me there as I well knew. Whatever it was that passed between them, whether it be an exchange of brutal words with the emotional threat of a dagger as was whispered by servants and counsellors alike, they were reconciled to a degree. No one would know the truth of it, but abdication was not discussed again. No doubt Hal was simply biding his time.

My needle moved to the creatures in my meadow, a trio of gambolling rabbits with their voracious appetites. Symbols of physical love, they grew in fine detail as they raced through the flowers. And as my rabbits grew in bright-eyed liveliness, joy and hope, such simple emotions but so elusive, soared within me. Sometimes so strongly that I must protect the fine linen from the unexpected fall of tears.

I did not weep. There would be time for weeping soon enough, and it was not now.

The new indomitable strength continued to direct Henry's mind, even as his body betrayed him. But even here he was granted grace. My prayers, hopeless as they seemed to me, were answered.

'Stop stitching that everlasting masterpiece for a moment and come with me.' Henry took my hand and led me to his chamber in the middle of the day. 'I discover that I have a need of you.'

I did not understand. 'With whom would I negotiate now, on your behalf?'

It was a gift I had still used when Henry needed soft words to cushion a harsh policy.

'No negotiation, lady.' He drew my hand gently through his arm as we traversed the antechambers, slowly as he required. 'Or perhaps I should negotiate with you. For permission to claim you again as my wife.' I felt him tense beside me. It was not an easy request for him to make, but he did. 'If you can bear my wasted body. If you cannot, I will understand, and accept.'

Now I understood. Perhaps the Blessed Virgin had answered my prayers after all.

'I can bear it.'

In seemly fashion Henry kept his linen undershirt—for my sake—but our ardour was renewed although not without pain for him as we came together. Henry's flesh roused, his spirit flared, maybe a sad glimmer of its former power but enough to prove his love for me, and I gloried in it.

My touch was as insubstantial as starlight. His hands framed my face as his lips traversed my cheeks in light kisses as he braced himself against the predictable agony. What sacrifices love demanded, even when the fire burned brightly in him, in both of us. On that day, Henry gave me every gift within his power, with all the grace and courtesy of which he was capable, creating memories for me which would shine with everlasting brightness when, at some point specified by heaven in the near future, I would be imprisoned in loneliness. He knew it and so did I.

Next morning we hunted, Henry bright-faced, renewed in spirit and in strength, revelling in the speed of the hounds and the bold courage of the quarry, a full-grown stag, that eventually turned at bay to face its death. I could not watch the kill. The bowing of its regally tined head, the sweat-matted coat, the sheer terror of exhaustion in its blurring eye, held too much prescience for my liking.

And yet I was not without hope. For a time I put away my needle. My heart was lighter, my hopes for the future strong, so that I no longer needed to bury my fears in the picture I stitched. My lady still had an empty hand.

Chapter 16

'I have a great desire to visit the Holy Land one more time.'

Once Henry would have marched to the window, to look out towards the east, in the direction of the golden city of Jerusalem. Now he had no energy to squander. Now all he could do was lie on his bed and relive the days of his youth when he had prostrated himself before the Holy Sepulchre, imagining the scenes replayed on the embroidered tester above him. My heart hurt for him as I bent my head over my needlework so that he could not see the pity. I was stitching again. The lovers in their meadow were almost complete, but as they leapt with renewed life before my eyes, Henry sank into frailty.

'I know you do,' I replied.

'I wish to see Jerusalem once more. Do you know? It was predicted that I would die in Jerusalem.'

'I know that.'

If I could have transported him there by some magical means, I would have done so.

'And if I were young and my body as strong as my mind, I would go tomorrow.'

I looked up to see that he had turned his head and was watching me, his lips curved in a faint smile. I returned it. There had been no child of our final coming together but our love remained the lodestar to illuminate our path.

'I know that too. And you would have no compunction in leaving me behind to do it.'

What's more I knew that Henry had commissioned ships to take him by sea on this much desired pilgrimage to throw himself on the ultimate Divine compassion. They were more or less built. Not tomorrow, but by the summer months they would be ready, allowing Henry to fulfil his great ambition. He had not discussed it with me, anticipating the force of my reaction. Henry could still surprise me by the formidable strength of his will. Even now.

'Will you come with me?' he asked.

'Yes.'

The lines of his face softened in memory. 'So will you take to the sea once more to make the pilgrimage?'

'We will go together.' I pressed my lips to his brow.

'We will need pennons and banners again.'

'I will embroider you a magnificent banner.'

And he sank back on the bed with a sigh.

We knew it would never happen, that our promises were empty ones. The ships would never leave our shores and Henry would never make that final obeisance before the Holy Places. Jerusalem would remain a golden memory from his youth.

And yet, defiant and determined, a final meeting with parliament had been planned.

'Will you be well enough to go?' I said, increasingly anxious, trying hard not to condemn any such attempt as ridiculously foolhardy, as he lay breathless in his chamber at Eltham, his wasted chest barely rising to mark each laboured inhalation. It was December, the days short and cold with hard frosts. No time for a sick man to be travelling.

'Yes.'

'Wait a little while, until you are stronger.'

The young minstrel, William, perched on the window seat, allowed his fingers to pick softly at the strings of his lute so that a favourite melody of Henry's touched the air and hid the harsh gasps for breath.

'I will do it now,' Henry growled. 'Whatever you or Hal might advise.'

I had abandoned telling him what he must and must not do. And I knew why he would be there at this parliament, for had he not summoned it to meet on the third day of February, the anniversary of his beloved father's death? It would be his final meeting with the body of men who had so often undermined his desire to rule well, and he would dedicate it to his father.

'Hal is no longer a threat to you,' was all I could say. Their rapprochement had been a lasting one.

I watched in silence as Henry pushed himself from the bed and straightened to his full height. With crown and robes he would still make an impression of Lancastrian power.

'Do I accompany you?' I asked, knowing the reply, regretting it.

'No.' As decisive as ever. 'I'll come back to you here afterwards.' He raised his hand to still the lute. 'My thanks, William. Leave me now.' And as the boy bowed and walked to the door: 'You're still growing. You need new shoes.'

The boy turned and grinned, a bright moment in that sad room.

It was I who walked to the window to look out, moved beyond thought, so that he would not see the moisture on my cheeks. Even in the midst of all this, he could think of his minstrel and his youthful turn for fashion.

So I must let Henry go from Eltham alone except for the servants of his household, not to Jerusalem but to London. It was what he wanted, and England wanted it too. The country was waiting for the death of its King, waiting with breath held, servants whispering in corners, matters of government held motionless like a pike in aspic.

'What is the mood in London?' I asked Baron de Camoys who had made the journey to visit us. 'Do they know?'

'It is a time of expectancy,' he replied. 'There is no anxiety. We have our heir. It is merely a matter of waiting on God's will. All is at a standstill.' He touched my arm, as a friend would show compassion. 'You look weary, my lady.'

I smiled at him. 'Come and talk to Henry. Don't encourage him to overtax himself.'

Lord Thomas stayed an hour and I left them to talk. When he emerged I was waiting for him.

'No. It will not be long,' he said softly. 'And I thank God for it. For both of you.'

We both understood.

On the night before his departure Henry slept fitfully,

drifting in and out of consciousness. His final letters of policy had been written and signed, and I lay beside him on his bed, the palms of our hands the only flesh allowed to touch. And through that most insubstantial of embraces we spoke of the imminence of death.

'Joanna…' I rested my cheek against his head when I saw that it was what he wanted. 'We may never be together again.'

'No. If you insist on wearing out your strength, it may bring the end quicker than either of us desires.'

'But I do desire it now. And you should too. How long can I live through this pain?' He looked up at me so that I could read all that he refused to say. 'It is too much. I no longer have the will to fight.'

The White Willow no longer worked its magic. Nothing did. The tapestry which had seemed to bear such potency under my needle had been packed away. I would never finish it.

'You fought hard all your life. A courageous knight, a courageous King. The end will come when it is God's will.'

'I have been blessed. The day I met you at Richard's ill-fated nuptials set my feet on a path to much happiness. I hope I gave you joy too.'

'More than I ever hoped for. You have been my laughter and my tears. My joy and my sorrow. I too have been blessed. And will be until this life ends. We will be reunited in the next world. I swear it.'

'Your love for me was magnificent. You left everything for me…'

'Because, God forgive me, my love for you, insubstantial as it still was in those early days, was stronger than my love for my country. Stronger than my devotion to my children. or my family.'

Henry had fallen asleep and did not hear my reply, but I completed it anyway.

'Yes, it was a magnificent thing. It still is.'

I kissed him and tucked a religious talisman into his sleeve, a silver medallion such as a pilgrim might collect as a token of his faith in miracles, the Blessed Virgin smiling beneath the canopy of heaven, her baby son on her lap. I would make sure it was with him when he left me. My own attempts were at an end but the Virgin might still give him ease, or simply the strength to withstand. Was it wrong for me to want it, when Henry looked on death as an ultimate blessing? I would pray with him that it came fast and gentle.

That night I left him to the ministrations of his own body servants. The indignities of care would not be made worse for him by my presence. On the following morning, from some deep well of dedication, Henry sought and found the strength to travel from Eltham to Westminster while I dressed for this farewell as befitted the Queen of England in blue and white, damask and ermine, Lancaster colours. There was every attention to detail. The jewelled collar of my wedding day with its motto *Soveignez* sparkled on my breast. The great clasp with its ruby anchored my veil to the coif that contained my pleated hair. I would honour my husband the King.

Determined to the last, Henry walked to the riverside with only the arm of Lord Thomas for support while, standing on the steps of the landing, I curtsied deep and low at his approach, as befitted the occasion.

'Farewell, my lord. God keep you in his overflowing mercy.'

His hands light, weightless on my shoulders, without speech Henry held me quite still for the length of a dozen heartbeats, his tired eyes locked with mine. Then he kissed my lips and without further farewell he left me.

Now seated with cushions at his back in the royal barge, as a cover was cast over Henry's limbs, thin rays of winter sunshine appeared between the racing clouds to set the red and blue and gold ablaze. There was no warmth to it and I shivered, but surely it was an omen. A good omen as the lions of England snapped sinuously above his head in the playful breeze. God would give him comfort at the last. And Henry held up his hand so that the rays fell on the silver talisman. He had it with him after all.

To Lord Thomas, as he too stepped aboard, I said: 'Take care of him for me.'

The boatmen shipped their oars and pushed off, falling into a well-practised sweep. I remained motionless, my eyes on Henry's until tears blinded them and he was no longer in my focus. I knew that he had taken the Crown with him in its coffer. He would pass it to his heir when the time came.

When the time came, as it must in a matter of days.

How could I not be with him when that moment arrived?

I lifted my hand in a final gesture, palm raised as we had once acknowledged our love, flesh separated by the iridescent glass of a window. I saw Henry do the same. Our minds remained united. It was a comfort.

★

It was Lord Thomas who fetched me. Who sat, silently, at my side through that seemingly endless journey by water. He had not needed to tell me why he had come. My finery packed away, I was clad in thick travelling cloak and hood, my breath white in the cold air. What I wore now was an irrelevance.

'Does he live?' was all I could ask.

'Yes. But for how long…'

As he held my hand, more friend than subject, for that is what he had become, I willed the miles to pass as I willed Henry to live just one more day. I would not be thwarted. Henry would not die without my seeing him one more time.

When I arrived at the Abbot of Westminster's lodgings, where he had been carried when his strength finally gave way, Henry was lying by the fire, on some makeshift pallet. Ignoring the little crush of people who had come to witness the passing of a King who was greater than he knew, I pushed through to where he lay, Lord Thomas making the passage easy for me. Hal was there, and Humphrey.

Henry's eyes were closed but I thought there was a serenity that he had not known for many years. Perhaps not of the body, but of the soul.

'He will be pleased you are here,' I said to Hal.

'We have spoken.' He welcomed me with habitual reserve, but I thought that he was not unmoved, and I kissed his cheek.

'Have you made your peace with him?'

'My father exhorted me to live a good life, while I promised to pay his debts.' There was the remnant of the spare humour I recalled in him when he was a barely a man.

'And you will do it, as I know. He has given you a great inheritance.'

'Do I not know it? On my honour, I will not squander it.' His mouth, seemingly always stern, twisted a little. 'I did not always make things easy for him, did I?' Then, before I could reply, surprising me, he took my hand and raised it to his lips. 'I acknowledge your care of my father, of all of us. And I acknowledge your good advice. As your son, I will ensure the comfort of your future life here in England.'

His gentle consideration touched all my emotions, nor had I an appropriate response since it presaged Henry's death, but it was a comfort.

At my feet, Henry moved restlessly, eyes open. In them as they fixed on me I could read the relentless pain, but he still managed the ghost of a smile as, Hal forgotten, I sank to my knees. Hal could wait.

'You came,' Henry whispered.

'Lord Thomas brought me.'

It might have made me weep to see this shadow of the man I had known, but his eyes burned with an intense fire and I realised that this was to be his final achievement. He saw death at my shoulder and had no fear of it. Had he not made his confession at the Shrine of the saintly Edward the Confessor? He had been kneeling there at the moment of this final collapse. There would be no more resurrections. Assuredly he would receive God's ultimate grace.

Henry slid back into unconsciousness. It did not matter for, tasting the power of the future, we had made our farewells at Eltham. There was nothing more to say as I sat on the floor beside him, refusing all offers of cushions or wine for my comfort as we waited for the inevitable, and I remembered. When he had left me at Nantes, I had refused to sit on the floor in mourning. Duchesses did not so demean themselves. Now it seemed only right that I, Henry's Queen, should be here. If Henry would die on a pallet on the floor, I would sit with him, in the dust. We would be regal and glorious together at the end.

Henry opened his eyes.

'Joanna.'

His hands, crossed on his breast, were talon-like in his pain. I closed my own hands over them and pressed my lips to his forehead. Then his mouth. Reading a desire in his eyes, I lifted my rosary from my girdle and wound it around our linked fingers, before turning my head to locate the little travelling coffer. There it stood against the wall.

'Open that, if you will,' I directed Hal. And when he did, 'Bring the Crown here and place it where the King can see it.'

Which he did with rare grace, setting it at the foot of the pallet where the low-burning fire lit the gold and jewels with an inner resilience that seemed to illuminate the whole chamber. Henry's gaze thanked me as he found strength from somewhere, even though he could no longer stretch out a hand to touch the symbol of his earthly achievements.

'You are my greatest blessing,' he murmured. 'What exhortation do you have for me today?'

'Merely to be at peace at last. It has been a long time coming. You have earned it. And here is the Crown that will be yours until the end.'

'God will be merciful.'

An assurance in him that had rarely been there in recent years.

'God will be merciful,' I echoed.

'Pray for me.'

As I did, while his grip woke pain in me, the silver crucifix trapped between our palms, and I repeated the best, most heartfelt, comfort I knew.

'Hail, Mary, full of grace, The Lord is with thee.

Blessed art Thou amongst women.

And blessed is the fruit of Thy womb, Jesus.'

Henry's thread of a voice joined with mine, as it had so often in the past.

'Holy Mary, Mother of God, pray for us sinners,

Now and at the hour of our death...'

They were all there, his sons, his friends, but it was my hand he held, his grip whitening my fingers when the pain came upon him. They were all there, but it was my face his eyes rested on when the end came, when the final seizure robbed him of further speech. His gaze, tortured, anguished, spoke of enduring love. So did mine.

Until on a sigh, life departed. So softly, so effortlessly. All that vibrant spirit was no more. The man I had crossed the sea to be with, the man I had battled and loved and in the end preserved had gone from me for ever. The one true light in my life snuffed out like a candle under what I now must think of as a caring hand. I did not know what to do except sit beside him as his hands cooled under mine. Five and forty years seemed to be such a little time for him to bring England to peace and acceptance.

'My love. My dear love.' I no longer cared who heard my

wretched longing. A lifetime of discretion in public places bowed at last to loss and grief.

They left me with him for a little while.

And as the chamber emptied, settling into silence, I realised for the first time where we were, and so realising I found room in my heart for a strange joy. Henry had seen Jerusalem. I laughed a little, very softly, for the Virgin never abandoned us in our extreme need. Henry had died in the Abbot's Jerusalem Chamber.

No tears. I would not weep, but a grief I had never known before shook me. There in his hand at the last was the silver talisman I had given him, the Virgin honouring him with her constant presence.

The greatest blessing I could ever have asked for.

★

I returned to Eltham and haunted the empty rooms, finding no solace. For the first time in my life I was alone. Not only alone but lonely. Used as I was to men with whom I could discuss policy, the events of the day, the week, the year, there was no one. Our new King Henry would never discuss policy with me. I doubted King Henry the Fifth of that name would exchange matters of business with any woman. I had been blessed in my life with men who could see behind the frivolity of female garments to the intelligence and interest and experience a woman could offer.

Leaning against the door jamb of the chamber that Henry had liked the best of all, with its view over the river, I inhaled the stillness, thinking of my own children and Henry's. They were not here at Eltham, nor did I wish for them. My grief was too deep-seated to share, and I could not laugh. I would never return to my own tapestry. I could not envisage stitching those final fine details of my love for Henry and his for me.

Pushing myself upright, I continued to walk the rooms, the halls, the corridors, marvelling that, in spite of all the months we had spent here, there could be no sense of him. Neither in the air nor in the shadows where the stair turned, nor in the soft folds of the tapestries that I had brought from Brittany and which I now brushed with my hand as I passed. His prie dieu was unused. The rosary beads, all gold and coral, hung motionless, flat and unglinting, in the air. The missal I had given him, when I thought I would never see him again, was closed. I could not open it, and Henry never would. Never again. He was no longer here with me.

Except that I could easily be seduced. Once perhaps the soft hush of his feet at the rise of the stair caught my attention, but it was a cat scampering for cover. Probably the same source for nocturnal whisperings.

Your breath is gone. Your heart is still. Your eyes are closed. Yet I still breathe. My heart still beats. My eyes still see the void and shadows. How can that be? It is an empty world without you, Henry, my love.

I had thought that I might have a sense of him, here where we had spent such time together, but nothing. And I knew why, and could wish it no other way. Henry was at peace at last. Such pain as had tormented him, such guilt; I would not wish that on any man, certainly not on one I loved. What had it taken for this complex man to hold onto the Crown when his flesh screamed in agony and his body betrayed him?

His mind remained sharp and keen to the end. Impossible not to admire him, to pray daily for his recovery, but this was better. Henry was at last at peace.

God keep you at rest in his bosom, my dear love.

I could not weep. I had wept for him finally in the Jerusalem Chamber, all but flooding it with my tears when all had gone and I was left alone with the remnant of the King. Now was a time for strength and decisions, even though, behind the mask, I wept and raged at my loss.

What to do, now that my ties with England were severed? I considered in a desultory fashion.

Navarre, where I was born and raised. I had no strong memories of that Court except for my viciously wayward father. Family, yes, but too much time and distance between us.

Brittany? I would be made welcome at my son's Court, but to return to a Court where I had once held sway might not be to my taste. I would undoubtedly interfere. Best to keep my distance.

France, then. No, the strains and tensions of the Valois Court did not appeal.

I found myself standing in the centre of the magnificently appointed Great Hall, hands clasped loosely, feet undirected, thoughts uncontrolled, watching the sun bar the walls and floor with golden stripes. Like bars in a cell. A little shiver touched my nape until I shrugged it off. This was no prison. There was no curtailment to my movements. Any decision I made would be mine alone. No one could compel me to choose what did not please me.

Yet slowly I turned so that the sun's bars were behind me. They unsettled me.

Then footsteps approached behind me. Not the cat. Certainly no premonition of Henry. Firm and soldierly, perhaps not the youngest of steps, but they paced the painted tiles without hesitation. The voice too was confident, instantly familiar, that of a friend of long standing.

'I thought I would find you here, my lady.'

I turned back, oblivious to the disquieting stripes now broken up by the approaching shadow of the figure I knew well, and managed to stretch the unused muscles of my face into a smile.

Which Lord Thomas de Camoys returned with much more spontaneity. 'Let me guess what you are thinking, my lady.'

'I imagine you can,' I replied as I accompanied him towards the door that would give access to the gardens leading down to the river. Once there, a little wind blowing off the water and rippling the dense black silk of my over-sleeves, I faced him. 'What do I do now, Lord Thomas?'

'Why do you need to do anything? You have your dower lands. Enjoy the luxury of travelling round them and living where you choose.'

Practical as ever. 'I could, of course. Would Hal object to my remaining?'

'Why would he?'

Clouds had begun to gather so we retraced our steps. 'There will be no place for me at Hal's Court as Queen Dowager.' I frowned as the prospect took on a life of its own that I did not like. 'How old that makes me feel.' I was forty-four years old and on that day felt a hundred.

'As Queen Dowager there will always be a place.'

'Hal will wed soon,' I mused. 'His new wife will be pre-eminent in any ceremonial.'

I could imagine it. Being invited, tolerated, where I could be pushed into a corner and overlooked as a woman of no influence. I did not think the new King would necessarily be an advocate of Madam Christine de Pizzano. In his erudite mind he might give a nod to her in passing, but he would never allow me to sit in judgement, or even offer an opinion.

'A woman of your presence and birth will be invaluable to a new King, and a young one. Your experience can only be an asset to him in any negotiations with the Valois.' A pause. 'You could, of course, wed again.'

I wondered if he was serious. But of course he would be. I would still be a valuable commodity in the market for rich and influential widows. Nothing was further from my mind. We had made our way up the flight of stairs to the gallery where we lingered, Lord Thomas a silent companion, melancholy refusing to give up its grip on me, until surprising myself, I stopped and turned to him.

'What do I do, Thomas? Give me your advice.' I smiled. 'I recall asking your advice when you came to me as Henry's courier with words of love.' A laugh caught in my throat. 'And impatient exhortation...'

His expression stopped my breath.

'Joanna...'

So did the intimacy in his simple use of my name.

'Stay,' he said.

Lord Thomas was never less than punctilious.

'Stay, Joanna. I ask as a friend.'

I thought about it. Friendship. A sympathetic ear. An

acerbic opinion. A worldly-wise view of the Court. Why
not? He took my hand and enclosed it within his, more
used to wielding a sword than wooing a woman, but what
an admirable man he was. I would pretend that I did not see
the emotion in his eye.

'Will you, then?' And when I tilted my chin, still
considering. 'Henry would say stay,' he persuaded with
an unexpected grin that lightened the melancholy of the
atmosphere.

'So he would. As a friend, Thomas, I give you my reply.'

'I presume that means you will.' He released me. 'I think
you won't regret it. And now I must return you to your
women.'

He escorted me, with all the courtesy and chivalry I had
come to know in him, while at the centre of my heart, a tiny
nugget of warmth was fostered. I would stay in England. I
had a friend and one whom I could trust. I discovered that
it mattered much to me. I would choose to stay, to watch
and enjoy Hal make England the great state that Henry had
envisioned.

Chapter 17

September 1419: Havering-atte-Bower

'Visitors,' remarked Marie, bright with anticipation, as, slowing our horses, we turned into the stable courtyard. We had been riding in the autumn-tinted woodland, enjoying the passing of the seasons although the years flew too fast for me. 'Were we expecting anyone, my lady?'

'No. But visitors are always welcome.'

I was smiling, when once I had thought never to smile again. It was six years since Henry's death. Five years during which I had achieved some sort of balance in my life without him.

'Well protected, whoever they are.'

They were indeed. An escort of armed men sat their mounts in the forecourt of my mellow dower property at Havering, and although I cast my eye over them, they bore no livery. So an anonymous caller, and strangely disquieting in its way. I liked to know who approached my door. It would not be any one of Henry's sons, frequent visitors, for they would travel with heraldic emblazons to the fore, and Bishop Henry with everything but his mitre. Hal was in France. Nor was it Lord Thomas who would even now be walking towards me to help me dismount.

With my mare pulled to a standstill, I prepared to slide down, but then, for no reason that I could name, I chose to remain mounted, for the Captain was standing foursquare on the sweep of my steps, hands fisted on hips and frowning at me. I expect my brows rose. I was used neither to being frowned at by a mounted escort, nor to the lack of respect in his posture before my door. Then he was frowning no longer, but descending the steps to take my bridle and offer his hand.

'My lady…'

I noted a number of sumpter horses, unladen, and an empty wagon such as used for transporting my immediate necessities when I travelled to another of my dower properties. Was my visitor, come for a long stay, perhaps already inside and waiting for me?

'And you are?' I asked as I complied, shaking out my skirts, brushing a few leaves and petals that had attached themselves to my sleeves.

'Edward Holt, my lady.'

'Who is it that you have brought to visit me?'

There was the tiniest of pauses, barely recognisable as such, then: 'I have not, my lady. You have no visitor. I command these men, in the name of the Royal Council.'

My hand, collecting an errant piece of twiggery lodged in the embroidery of my cuff, stilled.

'The Council?' I was intrigued. I looked around at the empty wagon, but found no clue. Had I been sent something of value? Was it something to do with Hal? The Captain's face was a masterpiece of severity. 'Is there a message for me?' I asked. But if it was some news, would the Council not have sent a courier rather than a troop of soldiers? Perhaps they were simply en route to another engagement. I felt a ripple of pleasure. It might be that I was invited to Westminster to participate in some formal celebration. I would enjoy that. Life at Havering, part hunting lodge, part palace, with its patchwork of roofs and additions over the years, once the favoured home of Henry's grandmother Queen Philippa and in later years King Edward, suited me very well, but I was no Julian of Norwich, living as an anchoress, far from the company of friends and family.

'No message, my lady,' Captain Holt was replying. 'I am under orders.' Again, he paused, expression grave, lips tight pressed. Which should perhaps have warned me, but it did not, so that when he added: 'I am under instruction to confiscate your possessions,' it took me by surprise. The words fell on my ear inconsequentially, without meaning, nor was my mind quick to assimilate them.

'You are here for what purpose?' I asked as if he had spoken in a language I did not quite grasp.

'I am ordered by the Royal Council to confiscate your personal belongings,' he repeated slowly, stressing each word with care. And then when I simply stood and stared at him. 'I am to take possession of all that you own.' Another pause as if giving me time to realise the full scope of what he said. 'Including this manor of Havering-atte-Bower.'

The heat of the day drained away from me. It was still not making sense. My mind concentrated on the final statement.

'Am I to move from here, then?' I asked. My thoughts awry, even the intake of breath from Marie, who had come to stand at my shoulder, did not force my mind into line with what I was hearing.

'That will be arranged at another time. It is not within my remit.'

Well, I had other houses I could go to. Had not Hal given me permission to live in Windsor during his absence in France? Or I could go to my castle at Leeds. In any event, I would not be homeless. But now my thoughts began to concentrate, my mind to clear. Was I being turned out of Havering? That could not be. It was mine until my death. This was my dower.

'No,' I said. 'No.'

'I am under orders to inform you of this change in your condition, my lady.'

'My condition? On whose authority?' I demanded with all the authority of Queen Dowager. Already I had stepped around him to climb the steps to my home. They were my steps and this was the door into my manor. Without dispute, the land was mine and the buildings on it. 'There is no such authority that can deny my ownership of Havering-atte-Bower. It is mine by law.'

For a moment I thought there was compassion in the set of his mouth, but not for long.

'The Royal Council has issued orders to the contrary.'

I stopped. Thrust out my hand. 'Do you have written orders? I will see them.'

'No, my lady. I do not. I have to tell you, my lady, that your household—your servants and waiting women and grooms and all in your employ—are to be dismissed.'

I looked towards Marie in sheer disbelief. It was like being trapped in a nightmare, the strands of which would not be broken. Yet I would break them.

'You have no written proof of this order. On what grounds should so monstrous an order be given?'

'It is not within my power to say, my lady.'

By this time we had an audience, from stable and palace, for harsh rumour travels fast. It seemed that all eyes were fixed on my face, willing me to save them from the threat of being turned off from my employ before sunset, whilst I was still struggling with disbelief.

'Your household,' the Captain clarified his orders, 'will be given two days to find other accommodations, my lady.'

'And who will have my dower here at Havering?' I demanded, a flicker of anger at last fired by this cold disposition of my people, and of me.

'The King. It will be in his power to dispose of it.'

'But the King does not need it!'

It was mine. Why would Hal lay claim to so small a manor as Havering when the great palaces and castles of England lay within his grasp? Possessiveness swamped me with fury, blinding me to the stupidity of my statement, as I stood in the doorway as if capable of stopping a dozen well-armed, determined men from entering. Hal did not need Havering. This was all a mistake that could easily be rectified, if only I could see the way through this tangle of mistake and misunderstanding.

'I will not allow it. You have no power to do this.' Was my position not sacrosanct here in my adopted land?

But the Captain climbed to stand beside me, eyes on a level and without mercy. 'I must fulfil my orders. I would not wish to use force against you, my lady.'

But he would. He had what passed for the law and an armed body to enforce it. Suddenly I felt quite alone, shatteringly defenceless, unlike any previous experience in my life.

'I will not sanction this encroachment,' I said.

To no avail, as I already realised. I heard the approach of Marie's clipped footsteps, noting her hand on my arm.

'Let him by, my lady. We can do nothing.'

Which compelled me to gather my dignity into a hard, cold shell, and I stepped aside.

'You must do as you choose, sir.'

'Come with me,' the Captain ordered Marie with a brisk nod and, I thought, some relief. 'You can indicate the lady's personal property.'

So she followed, as I stood, straight-backed and disbelieving in my entrance hall, to watch the contents of my life being removed piece by piece from my home and carried out to the waiting transport. Quiet, efficient, it was encompassed with utmost speed: no rabble-driven plunder here but a careful working of the law, every item noted on a list by a black-robed clerk who stood at the door. Every item of personal property I possessed was taken while I watched in increasing frustration and horror, allowing it to happen because I simply could not prevent it. Coffers containing clothing and jewels. My lute. Chests that held my linen and precious mementoes of my life. My books. Henry's books that remained an integral part of my life. The unfinished tapestry upon which I had lavished such love and will-power to keep Henry anchored to this life. I could barely force myself to watch as they were passed into such rough yet careful hands, without leaping to prevent it. And there, tucked under the arm of one stalwart, was the cedar box that contained Henry's first gift to me, the silver-engraved ink horn and pen holder.

I stretched out my hand. 'Not that!'

Holding tightly, as if fearing that I would snatch it away, the soldier looked over his shoulder, to where the Captain was descending the stairs with the air of a distasteful task well done.

'Forgive me, my lady. There are to be no exceptions.'

I stepped back. It was lost to me. Everything was lost. It was as if all my life with Henry had been obliterated, loaded and strapped to the baggage animals. My horses were led out from my stables, saddles and bridles heaped in the wagon, all covered with canvas to protect the contents from the rain that had begun to fall. I had not noticed the clouds that had gathered to obscure the sun. The light in my own life had dimmed long since.

'Why?' I tried again, standing stiffly before the Captain, my voice level in command. 'On what grounds is this confiscation inflicted on me?'

'The Council will send further instructions, my lady. Tell your people to be ready to go in two days.'

He bowed, and they were gone, in a jangle of harness and a clip of hooves, silence gradually enveloping the house and its outbuildings. My household stood about in shocked inactivity. Even the birds seemed to have fallen silent. And when

ANNE O'BRIEN

I realised that they had taken my popinjay, I found myself laughing in what would only be unnerving lack of control, cursing those who had dealt with me with such ignominy. I hoped the popinjay would drive them to perdition with its senseless squawking. Except that they would probably wring its neck before they reached their destination.

I stopped laughing.

I walked from room to room. Oh, they were still furnished, lovingly cared for, the tapestries still bright, the little stools that Queen Philippa had used in her final years when she walked less, still in place. But everything of my own was gone, swept up. The manor looked as if it might be ready to welcome new guests, new owners, but everything that was mine had vanished. It was as if I had never lived there.

At one door that stood ajar—the final door that I reached—I halted. Already feeling bereft, I dared not go into my private chamber. But that would be cowardice. I stepped forward.

At least they have left me the inherited bed with its blue and silver tapestry curtains, I thought, a remnant of the earlier hysteria returning. But as for the rest. The room was graced only with a chair and a chest; a bare room for a chance visitor. They had taken all Henry's gifts to me. My psalter, my precious Book of Hours, even my rosary was gone together with my own prie dieu. Standing against the door frame, not wanting to step further, I viewed the scene of a very personal devastation. And then there was Marie at my side, looking at me wide-eyed, as if waiting for some outburst of anger or grief.

I was incapable of either.

'What now?' I asked, although what answer could she give. 'Do I have anything but the clothes I stand up in?' The hysteria threatened again, gnawing at the edges of my frozen inertia.

'It's not as bad as it looks,' she said, and drew me across the room to the carved chest that Queen Philippa had used, flinging back the lid. 'It's not much but the best I could collect together in the time I had. Then I sat on it while the soldiers picked up everything they could see.' She smiled grimly. 'Fortunately not one of them was prepared to push me out of the way.'

What treasures she had gathered together: a winter gown and cloak, items of personal linen and shifts and, Blessed Virgin, there were my Book of Hours and my psalter and rosary. And my tapestry of the lover and his lady.

'I hadn't time for more, my lady.'

'I am more grateful than you can ever know.' It was the tapestry that did it, and tears were close but I squeezed her hand and remained brisk. 'At least I can read and sew while I wait.' I looked at her. 'They will take me too. But I don't know where. I don't know why.'

'It must be stopped, my lady.'

'Yes, it must. And I'll fight every inch of the way to achieve it.'

My moment of weakness had died a rapid death. Yes, it must be stopped. I would have justice.

★

The meal still laid out for us in one of the parlours, still miraculously untouched by our visitation, was forgotten, appetite stripped away as effectively as my property, but I took a cup of wine while I considered, standing in the middle of the floor. Why would the King's Council take such an outrageous action against me? And yet the Captain had acted with such authority. What was clear was that I needed help. And advice.

'What will you do, my lady?' Marie asked as we went to discover my clerk to borrow pen and ink. I would not think of Henry's gift that was now languishing in one of the panniers on a sumpter horse.

'I'll send out a courier while I still have one. In fact I'll send two.'

And forcing my apologetic clerk to vacate his room, I sat to write two pleas for aid and information. Having written, I sent off a groom with instructions to waste no time in getting to Winchester. Bishop Henry would know, and would surely stand for me, for we had long healed the wounds of those days of Henry's suffering. A second groom was dispatched to Lord Thomas. Who else would I turn to?

And then all I had to do was let the hours pass as my household prepared to be cast adrift. But of course it would not come to that. I did not need either support or advice. All this was a mistake. My property would be returned to me forthwith. A mistake. An error of judgement. A misunderstanding.

My servants, silent except where they whispered in corners, looked to me with dismay. I smiled and reassured them as well as I could. All would be well.

'How can you be dispersed against my will? You are my household and in my employ. It is my choice to have you with me. We will wait for a visit from the Bishop of Winchester.'

But I recalled the early days of my marriage when, an

unpopular Breton bride, my servants had been sent home. I had had no choice then. Was this to be a repetition of my powerlessness in the face of the Council? But that was long ago. I was not unpopular. I was no longer seen as the enemy. Did I not have the King's confidence?

I felt a need for reassurance, but my confessor was away, travelling on a private matter. Confession would have been good, but my Book of Hours sustained me.

★

Four days I had to wait. Four days during which nothing more occurred to disrupt the placidity of life at Havering, except that we were all watching the road, ears tuned to the sound of horse and rider, and I was missing my favourite garments and even the popinjay. But as the days passed, it seemed to me more and more certain that there had been a miscarriage of justice. And being assured of that, I instructed my household to remain and continue their allotted tasks.

But I wished Bishop Henry would come.

At last one of the stable lads dashed into the courtyard to herald the news in raucous tones.

'Men coming! Soldiers!'

I leaned out of the window, disregarding any need for royal dignity.

'Is it the Bishop, Sam?'

'Can't rightly tell yet, m'lady.'

Smoothly, sedately, I made my way to stand within the wide door arch, at the top of the steps. If it was bad news, I would receive it with chilly composure. But of course, it would not be bad news.

It was not the Bishop. It was not Lord Thomas. Neither was it the Captain of four days ago. Instead a spare gentleman, richly clad, swung down from his horse and signalled to his escort of half a dozen liveried retainers to do likewise. I recognised both the man and the livery. Sir John Pelham, a courtier, born and bred to the last bone in his body. A man whom Henry had trusted to hold the seals of the Exchequer and with whom I had frequently conversed and who had served Henry well. So what had he to do with this? I waited, making no welcome when he came to stand at the foot of the stairs, and knowing with sharp instinct that this was not a visit I would enjoy to any degree, I had no compunction in forcing him to look up at me.

He bowed neatly. 'My lady.'

I inclined my head. 'Have you business with me, Sir John?'

'I do, my lady. I am come with a warrant issued by the Royal Council.'

'A warrant.'

The scene around me came into delineated focus, touched with brilliance, like sun on morning dew, so that it glinted like the diamonds in my marriage jewels that were no longer mine. So bright that it made me blink, the skin at my temples tight with a building pressure.

'Yes, my lady. I am come to take you into custody. You are prisoner of the Royal Council.'

When I had been told that my possessions and household were to be removed from me, the import of it had taken time to touch my understanding. No such lapse of time here. Oh, I believed it. I did not waste my breath in denying the possibility, in debating the rightness of it. And certainly when

I saw in Sir John Pelham's hand a document, red-sealed and heavy, I knew that he had come with all authority to take me prisoner. I might not understand why, but I could not deny the truth of what was happening within the confines of my own home.

Although fear rippled in my belly so that I had to breathe hard against nausea, I kept the mask in place.

'Do I invite you into my home? Or do I come down to you, Sir John?'

What it cost me to preserve my self-command.

'I will come to you, my lady.'

I turned and walked away from him into the entrance hall, hearing his light footsteps echo behind me. When they stopped, so did I, and turning, raised my hand, palm outstretched.

'Give me the warrant.' My eye travelled rapidly down the clerkly hand, then returned. Latched onto one phrase. 'What is this?'

'As it says, my lady.'

And I read again. And then again. Treasonous imaginings. I was to be taken as a prisoner for my treasonous imaginings. I was accused of seeking sorcery and necromancy in an attempt to destroy the new King Henry. I was accused...

'There is no truth in this.' My eyes snapped to Sir John's pale gaze. 'Who accused me of such impiety?'

'Your confessor, my lady.'

'My confessor?' I heard the tenor of my voice rise in utter disbelief. 'How can I accept that Father John would be party to something so abhorrent?'

Father John Randolf, my confessor, who had been with

me for more years than I could count on the fingers of my hands. A mild man, compassionate in earthly sins, but fervent in his desire to live a good life. He had heard my confessions, granted me absolution, comforted me when my destitution was at its worst, when grief overcame me after Henry's death. He had spoken to me of God's love and overwhelming kindness. Father John could never say such things of me.

'Your confessor, my lady, has made claims against you. They are there for you to read.'

And so I did. There it was. I read it aloud. I had 'compacted and imagined the death and destruction of our lord and King in the most high and horrible manner that could be recounted.' I swallowed hard. 'But that is witchcraft,' I said.

'Indeed it is.'

'I cannot accept this. And how can it be true? Think, man!' I strode to confront Sir John. 'The King has suffered no harm, to my knowledge. Is he not in the best of health?'

'Forgive me, my lady. Your acceptance is not necessary. Perhaps your methods to bring the King to his death were not as efficacious as you believed. That does not mean that you did not apply them to the King.' It had a terrible logic, uttered in Sir John's uninflected voice. 'Whatever the truth of it, I am here to disperse your household and take you into custody.'

Cool and calm and utterly unemotional, thus he announced the fate of the Queen Dowager of England.

I raised my chin. 'Where?' For a deeper horror than all the rest had come to rest in my belly. I foresaw a dungeon. A cold dark room. A trial. Was I truly to be accused and tried for necromancy? In that moment, all around me was black, a labyrinth of endless terror. 'Where are you taking me?' I demanded to know.

'You will go primarily to Rotherhithe, my lady. If you will be so good as to fetch travelling garments, I have a horse for your use. You will bring nothing else.'

'I have nothing else to bring, Sir John.'

I did as I was told. For the first time since a child under my father's unconcerned jurisdiction I must follow orders. Alone, I donned cloak and hood, taking barely a minute to survey what I was leaving behind; all the items that Marie had so cunningly secreted in the coffer were perforce to be abandoned. I was truly destitute. I was tempted to snatch up the rosary—I even stretched out my hand towards it—but the prospect of being searched for illicit belongings stopped me. Would they dare? I thought that they might.

Sir John Pelham awaited me below. It was clear that he had spent the little time in informing my people that they were no longer in my employ, for when I trod down the stairs, I was instantly surrounded. They kissed my hand, touched my cloak, even my hem. Mistress Alicia, my old nurse, wept. It should have been a comfort, that whatever they had heard of my plight, not one of them believed me capable of evil sorcery, but this was an audience with no voice. The Royal Council believed it was so, and they had still to pass judgement on me.

And here was Marie.

'I'll not leave you, my lady.' And to Sir John Pelham, my Governor, for that is what he was now become. 'I will be with my lady. I will go with her. It is wrong that she should be left with no one to serve her.'

'You will not, mistress. I will put you under restraint if

necessary.' Again the lack of emotion was chilling. Was it because he felt none, or because he had a need to cover his distaste for my alleged crime? I would rather he railed at me than pronounce: 'Now we leave. The sooner the better.'

Marie and I clasped hands for those final moments, for it came to me that if I were found guilty of witchcraft, Marie, the closest of my women, might too share the blame.

'Go to Bishop Henry,' I urged. 'He won't let you suffer for your service to me.'

Sir John's hand was on my arm, guiding me remorselessly to the door.

'We leave now, my lady.'

I stopped and looked at him, at his hand that intimated my new lack of freedom. 'It is not my intention to resist, Sir John.'

And so he released me, while I eyed him with contempt.

'I recall when you were a loyal servant to my husband, the late King.'

'Now I serve the present King, his son, my lady.'

Quite unmoved, impervious to any slight of betrayal, Sir John stepped back. Thus I walked out of my lovely manor of Havering-atte-Bower, a prisoner, under duress, even though I was helped to mount my horse with a curt deference.

'Sir John?' I asked as he mounted beside me.

'My lady.'

'You say that evidence was laid before the Council by Father John Randolf.'

'That is so.'

'Where is he? Where is my confessor now?'

Sir John did not look at me as he gave his animal the office to start.

'He has confessed to his own involvement in your spurious plots. He is imprisoned in the Tower of London.'

★

We rode in silence apart from the comfortable creak and jingle of leather and harness, unaware of the glory of the day. There was nothing comfortable about my state of mind. Blind to the autumn colours that had so entranced me, giving me such joy in my surroundings, the vivid yellow of the oak leaves hinted at the onset of death, the blood-red berries of the rowan told of poison. The feeding of swallows reminded me that they would soon be gone and winter would close down on us. And where would I be then? At Rotherhithe, a royal manor. Or somewhere much worse.

I would not think of the Tower of London with its confinement for traitors.

As we approached the river where we must make a crossing, the beat of horses' hooves drove a path through the tumult of my thoughts. From behind us, moving faster than we were, we were quickly being overhauled. My Governor motioned for his men to pull aside, but the approaching horsemen slowed to a walk and came alongside. The livery was instantly recognisable, the sight of it a relief. I would have cried out to him, unusually vocal in my relief that someone had come to my aid at last, but the expression on his face stopped the words in my mouth. With not even a single glance in my direction, Lord Thomas de Camoys saluted Sir John Pelham.

'Sir John. I need a word with the Queen Dowager.'

'My instructions are that my prisoner be conveyed to Rotherhithe without communication with anyone.' As Sir John raised his hand, one of my escort placed himself between me and Lord Thomas, leaning to take a grasp of my bridle.

'I care not what your instructions might be. I call rank here, Sir John.'

'You would challenge the Royal Council?'

Lord Thomas, frowning mightily, slapped his gauntlet against his thigh. 'Have sense, man. What harm will it do? Are you expecting me to ride off with the Queen in some ill-judged campaign to rescue her? Ten minutes of your time and you'll be on your way. Now give me—and the Queen—some privacy.'

Not waiting for a reply, using his weight, his undoubted authority, and his restive mount to push my escort aside, he laid hands on my bridle near the bit and hauled me and my horse to the far side of the road.

'Thank God, Thomas.' It was all I could say, and I held on tight when he folded one hand around mine.

'No thanks yet, Joanna. I'm not a rescue party.' He grimaced. 'I just needed to see you and know how you fared.'

'How do you think?'

'Keep your voice low.'

'I've been accused of necromancy, to put Hal's life in danger.'

'I know.'

'They say my confessor laid evidence. Is that true?'

'As far as I can tell, yes, it is.'

'And the Royal Council—do they believe it? I've seen

the warrant and the seals.' And then it struck me what it was that I did not know. What, in my rejection of all that had been said, I had not actually asked. Now I asked it. 'What is it that I am supposed to have done to the King?' And with a slew of bitterness I could not prevent: 'He seemed hale and hearty enough when he left for France. How can I have bewitched him to near death?'

'I can't tell you that. This is all I know.' Lord Thomas hauled on his reins as his mount, ears flattened, sidestepped in impatience. 'There is no detail that I can discover on the form of magic you used—are said to have used—but three witnesses have been found who will speak out against you and testify. Your confessor Randolf and two members of your household, Peronell Brocaret and Roger Colles. They are yours?'

It was a further unexpected blow. 'Yes. Yes, they are mine.' Their names and faces were as familiar to me as were all my household. It made it all the more unbelievable, unpardonable that they should have made such claims. 'Brocaret is employed by my physician. Colles is a clerk under the authority of my steward. They have been with me since Henry's death. I don't accept that they have given such a testimony.'

'Confessor, physician and clerk,' Thomas grunted, whether in disbelief or frustration I could not tell. 'Well, Joanna, all I can say is that all three claim knowledge. The Council is stating that it was Randolf who had the skill and the power to lure you into a plot to destroy the King. They have accused him of persuading you to resort to witchcraft. That's why they've locked him in the Tower. Until a trial's set up, I presume.'

'Of Father John? Or of me?' Thus I voiced my worst fears. And when Thomas shook his head: 'I can't condone that my confessor would admit something so patently untrue.'

'A man in fear of his life might do any manner of things.'

'Has he been tortured?'

Thomas lifted a shoulder. 'I know not. It's possible. Probable.'

'So I can do nothing unless I can prove my innocence. But how do I do that? When I don't know the form of my sin? I doubt there's any hope of my speaking with Father John? No, of course there isn't. Do I not know the way of such trials as well as anyone else? Keep everyone in fear and ignorance and hope the accused falls to his knees in confession.'

'There's nothing you can do until we know more.' Thomas must have seen the momentary flicker of panic on my face, and gentled his voice and his grip. 'Be brave, Joanna. This is not the end of the story.'

'Where are you going now?'

'To London. To see what I can discover. And I think it behoves me to talk to the Bishop of Winchester who usually has his finger in all manner of pies.'

Of course. Bishop Henry would know. But why not go higher than that?

'Thomas. Listen.' I was aware of Sir John becoming restive. 'Would you petition the King? On my behalf?'

'No point in going to the King.' He made no hesitation although his fingers tightened momentarily around my wrist. 'He's in France, and will be for the foreseeable future. If anything can be done, it's the Bishop we want. I'll see him. All you have to do is to remain stalwart.'

'Which is well-nigh impossible when they have taken everything I own apart from a change of clothing, and dismissed all my people. Even Marie. I have nothing of my own, not even my Book of Hours.' Dismay was in my heart yet I kept my spine straight, my chin firm. I would weather this storm with all the courage Thomas had hoped for me. That my beloved Henry would demand from me. That I, Princess, Duchess and Queen, had been raised to impart to my audience however small or large. I had never shown public emotion. I would not begin now.

'I have something here for you.'

As if it took no thought at all on his part, Thomas thrust his hand in the breast of his tunic and produced a rosary, pressing it to his lips, before sliding it into my palm, all as surreptitiously as a jester might magic a trick for the delight of a small child, but there was no joy here.

'It was my wife's,' he said gruffly. 'My second wife, God rest her soul. She knew about sorrow and hardship. She would want it to give you comfort. If comfort is possible this side of the grave. There seems to be little commerce in it today.'

Never had I known him so disheartened, the lines denoting his melancholic humour so deeply engraved, yet he could think of me. I pressed my hand with its burden to my heart.

'Be assured, I will make use of it. And make grateful thanks to your wife in my prayers.' Elizabeth Mortimer had died, leaving Thomas with another son.

'I have no doubt that you will.' As if regretting his bleak view of the future, Lord Thomas managed a smile of sorts as he gathered up his reins. 'Do not despair, Joanna. You will not be unsupported in this.'

And then with a nod of his head to Sir John, and a brisk gesture to his own escort, he turned his horse's head in the direction of London.

'Lord Thomas,' I called, on a thought, and when he drew back: 'Did you see this coming? Did you hear any rumour of this, for it was a shock to me?'

'I would say no. Yet in retrospect, the warning was there.' His mouth became a sneer. 'His grace the Archbishop of Canterbury certainly had a thought of it.'

Which, to my annoyance, was all he would say. His mouth shutting like a trap, he cantered off, leaving me and my gaoler to continue to Rotherhithe, where I was rowed across the Thames to the royal manor that I knew very well. And all the time I kept the rosary crushed in my palm, the crucifix digging in, as a talisman, the only comfort I had.

If anything can be done...

That is what Thomas had said, I recalled as the little grey waves on the river slapped against the side of the craft.

If...

I had hoped for confidence, for a bullish certainty, from Lord Thomas. In uneasy retrospect, he had neither. The Royal Council had a heavy hand when it chose to wield it. But why had that heavy hand chosen to fall on me? Innocent I might be, but the odds seemed to be stacking up against me. And why had Thomas been unwilling to petition the King? Surely there would be the obvious source for the truth of any plot against him?

Chapter 18

I disliked Rotherhithe.

I detested Rotherhithe. I hated it with a virulence. Oh, it was a charming enough royal manor with its walls and timber-framed structures, its outer and inner courts, and vistas over the river. Built by Henry's grandfather the old King Edward on the banks of the Thames where the marsh created a little island, Henry had had an affection for it. But this was one of the places where, in those latter years of torment, Henry had suffered greatly. Where pain had driven him to a frenzy of self-doubt and punishment for sins he had committed. Or even to my mind not committed. It was a place where he could not in the end find peace.

I despised it.

I was given the best bedchamber, Henry's own bedchamber, but hardly had I set foot in it than I demanded that I be accommodated elsewhere. Not merely to be diffi-cult and unpredictable, although the thought occupied my mind. In truth I could not bear to see the perch that the old King Edward had had made for his prized falcons outside the window. The perch that Henry too had made use of for his indulged favourites. The perch was empty which resurrected all my grief. Henry had not found peace there; I doubted it would be possible for me. I did not want the memories.

Every stone of Rotherhithe smacked to me of despair.

I maintained an unyielding expression when Sir John visited me in the chamber furnished for my daytime use.

'What do I do now?' I asked him with less graciousness than I would have ever used towards a subject in happier times.

'You wait, my lady.' He was equally severe. So this was to be the tone of our relationship. But what else could it be between prisoner and gaoler? I supposed I should have been grateful that he had not sent for me to present myself before him. Or had me dragged under guard. This was a cold distancing but at least there was no attempt to humiliate me.

'For what must I wait?' I asked.

'For the Royal Council to make its decision, my lady.' He stood with apparent stolid indifference, with no pretence of deference, eye contact rigidly held. His hand rested lightly on his sword hilt. It struck me that he was dressed for travel.

'What can it decide, Sir John? I have had neither a hearing before the Council nor a trial to weigh my guilt under these damaging charges.'

'That is what we wait on, my lady.'

So he would tell me nothing, but I would not make my incarceration easy for him. Was I to be a pauper for the uncertain length of my stay? I would lure him into some disclosure if I could.

'I shall have need of clothing, Sir John, if the waiting is long.'

'You will be provided with what you need, my lady.'

'Excellent!' I set my jaw. 'I want a psalter. And a missal, since I was robbed of my own. Surely if I am suspected of witchcraft, it would be considered good policy to provide me with means to save my soul. It seems I have no confessor to guide me. Do you provide me with a priest, to say Mass? I think it is the least you can do, if I am to remain here for any length of time, or my immortal soul could indeed be in danger from neglect.'

'I will provide all you need for the state of your soul, my lady.'

Anger was beginning to rise, at the effortless manner in which my imprisonment was being dealt with.

'I also desire the means to write, Sir John.'

For the first time his eyes were hooded. 'I consider that your writing of letters is not wise at this time, my lady.'

So I was not to be allowed to communicate. I swallowed against the burn of dismay. And not a little fear which I could not shake free.

'Will I, in your consideration, be allowed visitors during my restraint, Sir John?'

Which he thought about, lips thinning then curving into a tight smile. 'I consider that if they are worthy men, and approved by the Council, then it will be possible.'

I exhaled slowly in relief. There would be limits to my isolation.

'I need a serving woman,' I demanded.

'I will see to it.'

We eyed each other. Sir John bowed. But before he could make his departure:

'Do you not stay here, sir, to oversee the misery of my punishment?' I asked, anything to discomfit him. 'To beat me into submission so that I will confess to the Council forthwith and all can be put to rights?'

'No, my lady. I have duties at Pevensey, my own property.' He was already halfway to the door. 'I have arranged that you are not without comfort here. You are free of the rooms I have assigned to you. You are, of course, not free to leave. Guards will remain to ensure your compliance. Good day, my lady.'

Sir John inclined his head and strode out, clicking the latch softly with impeccable good manners but it was as if he had slammed it shut and turned a key on my freedom. Cushioned it might be, but imprisonment it was, all my actions dependent on the will of another. Sir John might offer me courtesy but it was as if it were smothered in hoar frost.

I rose from my chair to look out over the river to where men in boats had freedom to row with or against the tide, as they pleased. I had none. So I must wait. And pray it was not for long.

A knock at the door heralded a guard who escorted in a young woman. 'Your waiting woman, Madam.'

She curtsied. A pale-faced young woman, hair severely curtailed beneath a plain linen cap.

'Tell me your name.'

'Isabelle Thorley, my lady.' It was barely a whisper. Her

eyes never rose above the level of my shoes. Isabelle Thorley had obviously been warned that I had dangerous powers. I sighed. This was going to be harder than I thought.

'Do you play chess, Mistress Thorley?' It was my one hope.

'No, my lady.'

How fortunate then that I had not demanded from Sir John a chessboard.

★

The weather grew colder and wetter, and, contrapuntally, my spirits lowered.

I missed my confessor. I missed Marie. I passed the hours considering what it was that I might inadvertently have done, turning over and over in my mind all the things that a woman might do that could be construed as sorcery. The making of perfumes and potions. The tending of herbs for *potpourri* for winter use. For ailments of the household. That was not all, of course. I had tended to Henry's increasing need with draughts and balms to ease his pain. As I had made preparations to engender conception of a child. Some of my household knew of this. I had not kept it secret.

Was any of it witchcraft? I did not think so. Nor did I think Marie or anyone in my household was so involved in nefarious practices. Yes, I had the knowledge and skill to kill a man with a dose of belladonna, but knowledge did not imply intent. Yes, I had possession of the books with their instructions for the use of herbs both malign and beneficial, but possession did not dictate that I would ever turn my hand to necromancy. As for telling the future? Did my serving women? Perhaps they did in moments of frivolity, laughing over the outcome, decrying the choice of lover or admirer, hoping to see the outcome of a flirtation, in the pattern of rose petals scattered in a bowl of water during a full moon.

Nothing I had ever laid my hand to had been vindictive towards Hal. Nothing, I would swear it, could be construed as sorcery. I regretted his desire to take power from Henry before his time, but any dissension had been healed with Henry's death, our recent communication becoming gracious, considerate, even affectionate. Hal had been generous in granting me a role in his victory after Agincourt, inviting me to join the procession through the streets of London. And did I not so honour him, despite my own grief? For the dread field of Agincourt was not all celebration for me. It had robbed me of my brother Charles, King of Navarre. My son Arthur was taken prisoner, my daughter Marie's young husband Jean d'Alençon was dead. Such was the cost of war, glorious achievement for one, desolation for the other.

Hal had valued my willingness to set aside my mourning to honour his victory. I recalled his compassion and his gratitude as I donned royal colours and an ermine cloak, laying aside my black. Did that smack of enmity between us, so great that he would suspect me of foul play towards him? I was certain it did not.

Hal had been kind to me.

So why had Father John laid evidence against me? Had he indeed been tortured to extract his confession? And then the worst thought. Who hated me enough to encompass so vile an act, to inflict pain on another to ensure my guilt?

★

I was allowed visitors. Anticipation thrummed, for here came Bishop Henry and Lord Thomas together. Now I would learn the truth. But as they bowed low before me, neither man appeared to be rejoicing, bringing with them the cold of a late November afternoon, their respective visages as dark as the clouds banking across the river.

Bishop Henry shivered.

'It's not warm in here.' He frowned at the smoking fire. No, it was not warm. 'Are they looking after you well, Joanna?'

'Never mind that!' I walked forward to be enveloped into a hug, despite everything enjoying the aroma of cold outdoors from his rich clothes. The aroma of freedom. 'Have you come to set me free?'

Interpreting Bishop Henry's grunt of displeasure correctly, I stepped back, looking across to Thomas. I knew they had not.

'Unfortunately, no, my lady.'

'Then I presume you are here for a purpose. Will you fetch wine?' I asked my perennial guard who still lingered in the doorway.

'Send it with one of the maids,' Bishop Henry instructed. 'We have no need of a guard.'

'Sir John's orders, your grace,' my permanent shadow replied stolidly.

'His grace orders you to stand outside the room, man,' Bishop Henry responded. 'When you have sent for the wine. Unless the lady flies through the window, she will not escape.' Striding over, he shut the door on the man's back. And smiled wryly. 'Perhaps that was not the most politic of observations to make in the circumstances.'

'No, it wasn't.' My tone was acerbic even though I was delighted to see them both. 'He believes me a witch already. As does the girl appointed to act as my serving woman. The whole household of Rotherhithe make the sign against the evil eye when they walk into any room in which I might be.'

The door opened, Isabelle Thorley entering with wine and cups, placing them on a coffer, retreating in smart order.

'I see what you mean. She shuffles round you as if you carry the plague.'

Lord Thomas dispensed the wine.

'So you have no good news for me,' I stated.

'None.'

Bishop Henry sat in my chair, elbows propped on the arms, fingers steepled beneath his chin, while I demanded, since I had had much time for contemplation, too much time:

'Lord Thomas said the Archbishop of Canterbury knew of malign conspiracies against Hal. What did he mean?'

The Bishop squared his shoulders. 'Our Archbishop most certainly knew. He circulated letters against witchcraft in the week before you were arrested, that required English priests to pray for the safety of the King, whose life was apparently at risk. From the superstitious deeds of necromancers, if I recall his admonitions right.'

I did not know what to say, or even how to assess this new knowledge. And then, because it had been in my mind, 'Has my confessor been tortured? To get him to confess to my crime?'

'It would seem so.'

I had the grace to feel compassion in the midst of my anxieties.

'Will I be sent to trial?'

Thomas slid a glance in the Bishop's direction. 'We don't know. We wait on the decisions of the Council.'

'What does Humphrey say? Surely he has an ear to the walls of every member of the Council.' I knew that of all Henry's sons, Humphrey was in London.

'Humphrey is being surprisingly reticent,' Bishop Henry said.

It was like trying to prise a hazel nut out of its shell.

'So you can tell me nothing at all?' And when nothing was forthcoming from either of my visitors, men of power as they might be; when fear tripped its way along the skin of my arms: 'Why have you come then, if you can give me no hope for the future? All you have done is sit here in my chair, admit to ignorance, and drink my wine.'

Bishop Henry had the grace to blush, but it was Thomas who replied. 'We have come because you are alone, and need to know the worst as well as the best of it. There have been no detailed accusations made against you. We hear nothing of an attempt against the King's life. As long as it remains nothing but shadows, it is in your favour.'

'Witchcraft does not seem in any manner shadowy to me. Is the punishment for those guilty of witchcraft in England the same as it is in France and Brittany? In Navarre?' Another thought that had occupied my mind in the depths of sleepless nights. 'I think this might be the worst of it, so you had best tell me.'

'The punishments are various, Joanna.' Bishop Henry picked at the cuffs of his gauntleted gloves. 'Depending on the severity of…'

'For God's sake, tell me.' I was on my feet, all pretence at composure cast aside. 'The truth can be no worse than my fears. I'll not shriek and weep at your feet, if that's what you fear. When have I ever? Not even when faced with Henry's terrible burdens. I'll keep my anguish tight imprisoned. So tell me.'

And he did, without decoration.

'The punishments are various. Public humiliation. Imprisonment for the term of your life. Banishment. A public burning...'

Nothing that I had not already guessed. England was not much different from Brittany in aspects of the law against those who dabbled in sorcery. It was terrifying. But I kept my reply light, if caustic.

'Thank you, Bishop Henry. Your visit has been entirely worthwhile. You have frightened me to death. And so your advice?'

'Sit tight. We will do what we can.'

Without warning, my mind betraying me, I remembered the golden bars on the walls at Eltham after Henry's death. It had meant nothing, then, but now it seemed a harbinger of my present situation. I opened my mouth to remark on the strangeness of memories, then changed my mind. Better not. Events that foretold the future must be shunned, tainted as they were with necromancy. What an emotive word that was.

I could not sit again but paced the width of the chamber.

'Since you cannot help me, do I petition the King?' I asked, as I had asked once before.

And with the same reply.

'I advise not,' Bishop Henry said.

'Why not? Surely it is important that he is informed of what is being said? Would he not come to my aid if he knew my circumstances? I cannot believe that he would allow me to suffer any indignity.'

Bishop Henry's reply was gentle.

'Hal is preoccupied. His mind is full of battles and negotiations for a new bride. You must be patient.'

So was I preoccupied, and not at all patient, but I chose not to say. I had been sharp enough. I valued their visit more than I could say. I would not impose my ingratitude on them further.

'Perhaps when the King returns to England,' Thomas added.

'But when will that be?'

'Not until he is satisfied with the impending defeat of the French rebels.' He acknowledged my grimace with an encouraging smile that I tended to distrust. 'As you say, we have been of no real help to you today and can give you no comfort for the coming weeks.' He stretched out his hand to me. 'Come and sit. Let us at least enliven your day by telling you of what is happening at Court.'

So I complied, because there was nothing other for me to do, and we passed a half hour in gossip, salacious and otherwise, but our hearts and minds were not in it. The rank aroma of sorcery filled the room. I thought they were glad to go.

I was allowed, my guard in attendance, to descend to the wharf where my guests' barge was being made ready. How I longed to step into it, to claim my freedom, to return to Westminster and order my life as I had always done. Instead

I was constrained into allowing Bishop Henry and Lord Thomas to leave without me.

They bowed and kissed my fingers with grave diffidence as if they could read my longing. Yet I needed to ask once more:

'Can I presume that you know beyond any doubt that I am innocent?'

'I think you can presume exactly that.' The Bishop's kiss was soft against my cheek.

'I will not deign to answer such a foolish question,' Thomas said.

It was some comfort, I supposed.

They left me to stare out at their craft that sped over the little waves on the river as it took them back to London, until my guard chivvied me back to my allotted rooms.

I was not satisfied. I would find a means to petition the King. How could he not come to my aid, ordering my prompt release? Had he not a debt to pay to me? Had I not added my considerable weight to the negotiating of yet another truce with my son the Duke of Brittany only two years previously? Hal had been grateful, honouring me with Garter robes. Hal would not desert me. He knew my good intentions towards him.

And yet. And yet…

A doubt crept into my mind: a tiny grain of fear that doubled and trebled until it dominated every thought. Surely by now Hal would be well aware of my predicament, however great the demands of the French war. How could he not know by now that the Queen Dowager was in effect imprisoned for her attempts on his life? The Royal Council would have informed him. And if he knew, why did Hal not deny such a wicked untruth? Perspiration lay cold and heavy along the length of my spine, beneath the linen and velvet, as heavy as the fear that prompted me. Was it possible that Hal believed the calumny? If so, who had planted such vicious seeds of malice into his mind?

Helpless, my mind was exhausted from its useless travels through endless circles, that brought me back to the same terror, again and again. Hal must know. Hal had chosen to keep me under duress.

January 1420

Here come to Rotherhithe were three formidable men, the pennons of their escort straining in the wind of the New Year, as they rode into the inner courtyard. The fact that this deputation must have started out on its journey when the New Year festivities were barely complete, told its own tale. I could not believe that they had come merely to bestow some festive goodwill.

They made a grave trio. Bishop Henry, Humphrey, Duke of Gloucester, Lord Thomas de Camoys, three abreast in my solar. It was three months since my freedom had been taken from me. Three months since the vile accusations had been made, and my situation no different. The waiting, the constant anticipation that I would be summoned to appear before the Royal Council was becoming intolerable. Now, faced with their grim demeanour my long-held patience, hard won over the weeks, shivered and collapsed at our feet. Without offering a seat or a cup of wine, not even waiting until Thomas closed the door at their collected back, I addressed them, ignoring Sir John's page who, seated on a cushion in the warmth by the fireplace, continued to play inappropriate lovers' music on his lute. The words poured out, to my horror.

'I am prisoner here against my will. I am Queen Dowager of England, a princess of Navarre and Valois. I am innocent of all charges of necromancy, yet have been given no hearing. The charges have not even been presented to me.' My voice was low and bitter. 'And you look like a black-clad jury come to pronounce sentence. Is no one doing anything to discover the extent of my wickedness? I still do not know what it is that I have been accused of doing. So what is it, my lords? Has all been decided in my absence, without granting me my right of a trial before the law? Am I to face the ultimate penalty with flames to kiss my flesh? What is it that you have discovered, for in truth, I see that you have not come to rejoice with me.'

I was proud that there was no tremor in my voice. Every muscle in my body was governed. If they had come to pronounce on my death I would not shame myself or them.

Bishop Henry advanced to salute my hands, holding them between his own, as usual expensively gloved. Humphrey scowled. Lord Thomas preserved a dour countenance that I could not read.

'There is no need to discover more, Joanna,' Bishop Henry said. 'We now know all there is to know.'

'Then perhaps you will be good enough to inform me.'

'We think your constraint must last longer, Madam Joanna.' Humphrey was never one for soft words.

'Am I then found guilty?'

'No, Madam. How could you? There has been no trial.'

'I'm no longer certain that a trial, or lack of, will make any difference to my situation. You are not helpful, Humphrey. Why will you not petition the Council in my name? But I see that you will not.' It was not difficult to read his reluctance. Bishop Henry had already refused such a petition. 'If you two honourable men of my own family refuse, is there no one who will represent me?'

I spun on my heel to look directly at Thomas. Given his past service at home and in the battlefield, his close friendship with Henry and Hal, both father and son, I was convinced that he would have the authority to face the Council in my name. Ill-usage bloomed within me that he had not already offered. Now, silently, his gaze full of compassion, Lord Thomas shook his head.

To the accompaniment of the page's pellucid renderings, I lifted my hands, tight-fisted. 'Surely one of you has the courage to argue my case? Surely one of the three of you has the backbone to stand up to the Council's silence?' How I berated them, giving no quarter. 'You have the courage of a day-old rabbit beneath the talons of a hunting buzzard.'

'You need to understand.' Bishop Henry, ignoring my plea, and my less than flattering description, was leading me to my chair, trying to smooth out my fists, which he did, but I would not sit. The room was full of a black foreboding that grew minute by minute, playing on my nerves like Nicholas's youthful fingers still attacking the strings of his lute, which suddenly I could stand no longer.

'Stop that!' I said.

The music stilled mid-stanza.

'All I understand is that Hal would never be convinced of my guilt. We parted on the best of terms. And therein lies my salvation.' I dragged my hands free of the Bishop as he intoned:

'Hal knows you are innocent, Joanna.'

'So why am I here?' I heard my voice threaten to rise, and then the Bishop was pressing me to sit after all, with Thomas at his elbow, pouring wine, offering it.

'No. I don't want it.' I waved it away. 'What good is wine to dull the edges of this sorry existence? I swear that you have brought a miasma with you. It is not acceptable that I should be kept in the dark, however ill the news.'

For surely it was. It was as if the room was filling with the noxious stench of plague. I had been right to fear their news.

'Drink,' Thomas insisted.

'Well, I will!' Ungraciously. One quick sip, because it seemed the easiest action. 'Now tell me, for before God I see it is not something to give my heart comfort.'

It was Bishop Henry who pulled up a stool and sat to face me, hands planted on his knees, eyes on a level with mine, while Humphrey and Thomas flanked him, uncomfortably, studying the floor, or the tapestries. 'You should have seen this unfolding, Joanna. With all your experience and intelligence, it should have become clear. I certainly should have seen what was afoot, and have no excuse. Perhaps we are encouraged to see the best in my royal nephew, even when sometimes he does not earn our regard.' He fixed me with a straight stare. 'Tell me what you have, that Hal covets. Tell me what Hal desires more than anything in this world?'

'Victory over the French,' I replied. There was nothing new here. It was his one driving obsession, that every man in the country could have recognised. 'To pursue the policy that he began at Agincourt. I have no influence over that.'

'Perhaps not. But tell me this. How will our King achieve this momentous victory over the Valois?'

'Is this a catechism?' I responded. 'We all know the answer. By raising an army that is bigger and better and more effective than that of the French.'

Bishop Henry smiled grimly. 'There you are. You know all the answers. And how will my nephew do that?'

'By getting Thomas here to raise more money and more men. Which he is finding more and more difficult because...' I inhaled sharply. 'Because...'

It was like lighting a lamp in a dark room, so that all the shadowy corners sprang into life, every stitch and carving sharply defined. And in those bright-lit images were creatures I did not wish to see.

'Excellent, my dear sister! Hal is in need of a new source of wealth.'

My mouth dried. A rock was lodged in my throat. And it was I who reached out to my clerical brother. 'How could I have been so very blind? Because of course I have my dowry. Ten thousand marks in annual revenue.'

'You do indeed have your dowry.' Henry patted my hand as if he might console me, his face vivid with the excitement of political intrigue, even though it had been worked at my expense. 'Or you did have it. Look how much of England's wealth is tied up in your person. Our King is in need, at a conservative estimation, of forty thousand crowns. Am I not right, Thomas?' And when Thomas grunted his agreement, 'To dower his new French betrothed and pay for keeping his army at fighting strength until the French capitulate, your dower, granted to you by my brother, would solve all his problems. Do you see?'

'Oh, I do.'

'You have your dower lands too,' Humphrey added.

'I have them no longer!' Anger, sour as unripe fruit, began to flood through me as the enormity of what Hal had done struck home. And perhaps still a disbelief that this could be the truth. I regarded the Bishop in horror. 'Will he sell my dower lands? To raise money to pay his knights and footsoldiers?'

'It is my thought that he will use the estates to make gifts, dear lady. Land is an exceptional commodity when buying support. Hal will find it invaluable.'

'I cannot believe this.'

Nor could I. That Hal should treat me with so little compassion. Never effusive, never warm in his affections, yet never hostile. Oh, we had clashed over his ambitions when Henry was too ill to rule, but I thought that we had healed those particular wounds. Yet these men, politicians all, were telling me of Hal's rapacity. So great, so unprincipled that he would resort to an act of such injustice that any man of honour must condemn him out of hand. Had he so little affection for me after all? Was there nothing behind his precise exterior but a cold self-will? A selfishness beyond all belief?

'So what are you saying? In plain words,' I demanded. 'For I have a strong predilection for the truth and it seems to me the blackest condemnation of Hal that you could ever make.'

Bishop Henry hitched a shoulder, as if in regret, but did not hesitate to turn the knife in my sore heart. 'The King has instituted this accusation of witchcraft in order to take from you the land and money that he needs for the war. You were too wealthy to leave untouched. If you wish to know the source of the accusation against you, I fear it is the King himself. He desired to put you in a position of absolute weakness. He was the instigator.'

The poison that Hal had sown hovered in the air, filling my lungs with its grim residue. Breathing was suddenly difficult.

'Would Henry's own son be so unprincipled?' I asked. I could not accept that I had misread this splendid heir so completely.

'My nephew would use the word pragmatic,' Bishop Henry said. 'He would say that it was the obvious means to a much desired end.'

Yes, of course he would. Raised as a soldier from the earliest age, conquest and victory against the French had been the determining factors throughout his whole life. Now his dedication had placed me at the very centre of the royal strategy, threatening to blight the rest of my life.

'It is a ruthless and wilful act, based on sheer greed,' Thomas was saying. 'There is no excuse. But knowing is no help to you. It is impossible to change the decision of the Royal Council, unless Henry orders it. I'm afraid it all points to his never being persuaded to do that. He will wed the

French princess and by so doing claim the French Crown for his as yet unborn heirs. You, Joanna, are part of that plan.'

Bishop Henry released my hands but remained seated before me, a jaundiced expression tightening the corners of his mouth. 'All I can do is pray for a better resolution of the situation.'

'Pray! Do that! I hope it is efficacious.' They were all so infuriatingly calm, whereas I would never be calm again. Once more I squeezed my fingers into fists on my lap. 'We are all pawns in this vicious game. I presume that Father John is also innocent. And my poor hapless servants. For the sake of Henry's achievements in France we are all dragged into the foul detritus of the gutter. By the Virgin!' A memory slid into my thoughts. 'And I suppose that our revered Archbishop is all part of the plot, ordering his clerics to preach against the dangers of necromancy. How well the King laid the foundations, spreading fear through the whole country so that no one would be at all astonished to hear that the Queen Dowager herself, for some inexplicable reason, wished to do away with her step-son. If the Archbishop of Canterbury saw witches scurrying under every stone that was lifted, then I must be as evil as they say.'

Ungovernable fury was rippling dangerously close to the surface, but beneath it a grief. All my servants had been turned off from my employ. Some subjected to atrocities I could not contemplate. My own reputation dragged into the mire. All to put money into Hal's hands to fund the French war and a new wife.

'And I loved him, as Henry's son. How could he punish me in this manner? How Henry would grieve if he knew. I am almost relieved that he has passed beyond knowing the vile deed his son is capable of!'

'It's deplorable,' Bishop Henry agreed gently, gathering my fists into his large hands as if he could contain my anger and grief. 'But you will not be the first woman to suffer in this manner. Tell me a better, a more effective way to remove a powerful woman. A wealthy woman. One who already has a history rife with rumour and superstition. As a political move, it is superb.'

My grief was banished. 'Would you defend him? Would you sit before me and tell me that your nephew is merely a superb politician?'

'No.'

And as the implication of the Bishop's words drove home, I dragged my fists from his grasp: 'I don't take your meaning.' And then: 'I hope I don't take your meaning.'

Bishop Henry did not even have the grace to show regret. His face was as stern as if I were the worst sinner in his flock. 'Is it not true, Joanna, that your father possessed a most unenviable reputation when dealing with his enemies?'

'My father? I can think of nothing good to say about my father. But how does this have bearing on my life? On this accusation of black heresy and sorcery? I knew my father's vicious character but not this.' I looked round the trio of visitors. 'What is being said of my father?'

'It is said,' Humphrey observed, 'that King Charles of Navarre used necromancy to rid himself of any man who stood in his way to power.'

I stood. 'Who says?'

'There have always been rumours.'

'Rumours! Since when did a man need witchcraft, when he could readily use poison or a paid assassin with a handy dagger to achieve his ends? To my knowledge my father was prepared to use both. I will never defend him for he brought too many good men to their death. But necromancy? People might talk of it, but I deny any evidence. Nor is there evidence against me, his daughter. Do I keep a grimoire beneath my pillow and robes of sorcery in my clothes press?'

Bishop Henry was unmoved. 'All you say might be true. But your father's grim reputation does not help you. Nor do you need a text of magic. Herbal knowledge is sufficient, in which I—and others—are aware that you are well versed. You must see that is so.'

A cold, clear statement of fact. I was caught in the net of Hal's weaving, my father's cunning hand with poison and cold steel, and not least my own acquired proficiency. There was no escape from it.

I sat, allowing the thoughts to swim in my mind, inspecting their ever-changing pattern, considering new designs that could save me from this débâcle, but never creating anything that could rescue my floundering spirit. My visitors remained silent too, allowing me my privacy for this terrible reflection. They had had time to consider the hopelessness of it all. It was new to me. Thomas walked behind me to place a hand on my shoulder as if that could comfort me. And perhaps the warmth of it did a little.

'So knowing all of this, and accepting it because I must, what do I do?' I asked at last, allowing Bishop Henry to take my hands again.

'There is nothing you can do. The Royal Council will only release you if—or when—Hal changes his mind.'

Hal was not known for changing his mind. My fate appeared to be sealed, and my freedom with it. Rising I went to stare out at a scene that might be mine until the day I died. Walls and turrets, barred gates and guards to prevent my escape. Since it was too bleak to contemplate, I returned slowly to stand with my messengers of bleak despair.

'I have never received such a remarkable New Year's gift.'

Humphrey shifted uneasily: 'Victory in the French war is of vital importance to us.'

'Oh I know,' I returned. 'I suppose that I should admire your support for your brother. But don't try to persuade me that England's greatness and a French bride are worth my degradation. You'll not succeed and I'll not think well of you for trying. I pray your brother's young wife has a better experience at his hands than I have.' I turned to the Bishop. 'If Henry were alive today, what would be his advice to me?'

'To get over rough ground as easily as possible with strategy and planning. Unfortunately my nephew would advise exactly the same.'

'I'm sure he would. And how do I plan against the unknown?'

After which there was not much more to say. Refusing offers of food, Beaufort and Plantagenet departed, Bishop Henry making the sign of the cross in blessing.

'May God keep you in His holy care and give you succour.'

'Amen. May He indeed. And open Hal's eyes to the iniquity of his actions!'

They bowed and made to leave, but not before a final blast of temper assailed them from the depths of my soul.

'Not one of you can propose any course of action to release me from this outrage. Do I have to call on my son of Brittany? My nephew of Valois? Do I have to beg them to come with force of arms to destroy the walls that curtail me? Not that they would, for neither can hold sway in this barbarous country against this atrocity of English law when a Queen can be shut away to rob her of her money. You are men of straw, all three of you. And you, Baron Thomas de Camoys, you persuaded me to stay here in England, to make my home in this nest of vipers.'

'My lady.' Bishop Henry's discomfort was a pleasure to see. 'Hold fast to your faith and to the strength that brought you here to your life with Henry. You have good friends.'

'But more enemies than I had realised. Leave me. You have done enough to destroy my confidence in the conscience of powerful men.'

Bishop and Duke bowed and departed, which left me momentarily, still trembling, with Thomas.

'Why are you still here?'

'I don't know what to say to you,' he said. 'So often in the past I have given you advice. Now I am at a loss.'

'If you were going to attempt to smooth my ruffled feathers with placatory words, don't even try. My feathers are un-smoothable.'

Thomas sighed a little. 'I'll come and see you.'

'When I am in a better mood? I doubt that I ever will achieve that state of grace. But you may come as you wish. I won't be going anywhere, will I?' How savage my response when he did not deserve it, as I knew in the depths of my heart. But he was the messenger and who else could I attack? 'I should be grateful, of course. I might have been facing death by fire. But somehow I cannot be grateful.' I turned my back on him. 'God damn you, Hal. Do you suppose he has any feeling of guilt over what he has done?'

'I would not wager your popinjay on it.'

'Unfortunately I no longer have a popinjay to wager.'

★

I was moved to Pevensey, Sir John's own property, with its bleak walls and vast towers. Then to Leeds Castle with its watery beauty, ironically my own dower. And always the fear accompanied me, that the next step would be the dread Tower where traitors were incarcerated. For there was no doubt that I was a prisoner. Despair set in, and with it anger throbbed in my mind so that my head ached with it. I had no kin to respond to my cry for help. No friends. All dead or estranged or powerless. Or disinterested.

So it must be. I made my decision. If this was to be my fate, then I would embrace it with cold bitterness. I would encumber no one with my plight. To do so made a woman vulnerable. I would live out my days in icy dignity, numb detachment. My world would be like a cold cloister, full of empty chanting and choking incense. Would I ever become inured to confinement? I did not think so, but I would be dependent on no one for company or entertainment. Even God, it seemed in my extremity, had forsaken me. I was abandoned.

Henry would not have left me so bereft. But Henry was dead. I could not think of Henry.

And Hal. The victorious King, hero of Agincourt, great soldier, loved, revered, the hope of England. What had he done? Destroyed me. Degraded me. Humiliated and betrayed me. He had not once visited me, to stand by his decision in my presence.

Cowardice to my mind, rank cowardice.

I was desolate but anger ruled me. I suspect that I was impossible to live with.

'You are to be provided with an allowance, my lady, and a clerk of the household, Master Thomas Lilbourne, to supervise it,' Sir John informed me.

'I have no household.'

'I will arrange for servants to be appointed for your comfort.'

'Now why would this be, Sir John? If I am thought guilty of the foulest of crimes against the King.'

'It is the wish of the Council, my lady.'

'A sop to their conscience, I presume.'

Which brought our conversation to a brisk end.

In a spirit of defiance, I began to compile a list for the long-suffering Master Lilbourne, a pale, resolute young clerk, purchasing all I needed for the life I must lead, and in its compilation I was driven by a vengeful delight. Master Lilbourne tried hard not to raise his brows at its extent.

'Are you certain, my lady?'

'Do you question my orders, sir?'

No, I was not pleasant to live with.

And no, I was not spending outside my means. It was after all an excellent bargain for the King. He had acquired ten thousand marks from me, paid into his treasury every year.

My allowance, worthy as it might seem, was a drop in the ocean to him. A bribe for my acquiescence. I would spend it.

When the result of my lists of commodities began to arrive, so too did Sir John, but in his inimitable fashion, made no comment, except to say:

'You may ride out using my horses which I will leave stabled here. You will of course be accompanied by one of my men.'

So prim. So contained, like honey running smooth over the back of a silver spoon. Abjuring all good manners, I turned my back on him and walked into my own property: that was no longer mine.

Sometimes loneliness had the sharp teeth of a rat.

★

Thomas returned at the beginning of April, a whole month after my arrival at Leeds, by which time I was ravenous for company but disinclined to admit it. My temper simmered, an endless bubble of it, like the surface of a winter pottage, but far less appetising. As he dismounted, still agile, still a man of action as well as supreme organisational skill despite his nearing his sixtieth year, issuing orders to the Captain of his escort who was to ride on to some prearranged meeting, all I felt was resentment. My welcome, if that is what it was, was unsmilingly chilling.

'Lord Thomas. So you have come at last.'

'Madam.' His heavy brows flattened for a moment. Then his eyes gleamed as he bowed. 'Can it be that you lack company? I would be flattered if I did not think that you might even welcome Sir John in the same fulsome manner.'

Which did not embarrass me one jot. 'Of course I lack company. And since you are now here, I hope you will give me some news. I feel as enclosed as a nun.'

'I thought you had been given permission to ride out.'

My temper leapt.

'With a tight escort. Of what value is that to me? If you can tell me nothing about my situation, at least we can talk about the weather and the poor quality of the salt fish. Lent can be very trying. My waiting women—do you know that I now have four English women to wait on me?—have no conversation at all. Although of course I should be grateful that I have the means to employ them.'

'No, I have nothing new to give you about your situation. But I promise I'll not talk to you about fish, or the weather.' He glanced at me as we began to climb the shallow steps into the entrance hall. 'You are favouring your right foot, I think. Have you suffered an injury?'

'No injury. Merely old bones,' I said, unaccommodatingly dismissive, stiffening my sinews so that I did not limp. 'Did you not know? I am graciously allowed to consult with Pedro de Alcobaca, Henry's physician of great renown.' I shook my head as I saw him preparing to question me as to my ailments. 'There is nothing wrong with me that freedom and justice would not cure.' I was not in a mood to be a martyr to my woes. I would not admit to them, even as they took my breath when I moved without care. 'While you, Lord Thomas, look to be in astonishing good health.'

Not waiting for a reply I led him to one of my favourite rooms, overlooking the river where water birds swam and squabbled and the scudding clouds made ever-changing patterns. Resentment swirled, much like the water. I was beyond courtesy. Inexcusable, but product of pain and sleeplessness, of formless grey fear and rampant injustice.

'What will I tell you that will keep you in touch with the world beyond your gates? And will sweeten your temper.'

It was typical of him to express it so matter-of-factly. And did nothing to remedy the problem, for I had been struck down by such pain, a swelling of tender joints, a tightening of skin so that every movement was an excruciation of agony, all exacerbated by cold and damp and, quite possibly, my own ill-humour. Any hopes to which I tried to cling fell around my suffering ankles, like feathers falling into a drift from a plucked capon, as I dragged myself from my bed to face yet another day of debilitating agonies. I could no longer stride along the wall walk. I did not even contemplate the saddling of Sir John's mare. Not only was I locked behind the walls of this castle but my spirit was entrapped within my failing body.

'My temper is beyond sweetening,' was all I said, voicing nothing of my compounded miseries. 'What have you been doing while I sew and read and petition the Blessed Virgin for mercy?'

'I'm sure the Lady will keep you in Her care.'

'Are you? I am finding it difficult to be so certain. Do sit.'

We sat in chilly silence as Agnes Thorley, Isabelle's equally colourless sister—for I had a busy quartet of English ladies to wait on me including a Margaret and a Katherine, as well as grooms and pages of the chamber—poured spiced wine, whereupon Thomas, blandly cooperative with my demands, proceeded to tell me of his travails to raise money to array and muster men for the French war.

'So you are busy,' I remarked when he had finished a tedious record, while I had sat in silence, refusing to drink. 'And what is the King doing?'

Thomas's stare was enigmatic. He knew what was in my mind. If the King returned to England, would he pursue the case against me? When he returned, would he dare to face me after all he had done?

The reply to my demand was flatly informative. 'He's busy as usual, building alliances, making his hold on France too strong to break. He's joined with your cousin of Burgundy to wage war against the Dauphin. An uneasy alliance since they were once strong enemies, but it will hold as long as the new Duke is furious with the Dauphin at the assassination of the Duke's father on the bridge at Montereau. At the same time Hal's in negotiation with the French Court. He is certain to marry the French princess if they can work out her value.'

'Katherine, I suppose, the youngest girl.'

'Yes.' Watching me, Thomas gave a grunt of a laugh. 'You'll appreciate this, Madam. The King has promised that she will have a dower, paid from the English Exchequer, of forty thousand crowns a year. He wants her, and he wants the French Crown. I doubt her father will be able to refuse such a windfall, even if it means he disinherits his own son.'

'I appreciate nothing about this ignominious position it has put me in.'

So much offered to buy this Valois girl. And with her came the promise of the Crown of France. It filled me with dread. My dower could never fill the purse that the King had offered for the French princess, thus making my future even more certain. I would never be released. I would never be restored to what was due to me. My son-by-marriage might even now take action to ensure that my dower always remained under his authority, exercising his right to bring me a trial.

I almost stretched to take up my cup, to drink, then hid the sad evidence of my hands, swollen-sore, beneath the luxuriant fur of my over-sleeves. I wanted no pity from Baron de Camoys. But then, perversely, defiantly, as if to prove that I did not care what my visitor thought, I retrieved the cup with something of a flourish, although I did not drink from it.

'At least I know where my money is to be spent,' I said.

'It's not confirmed yet, but it will be. Hal is determined on the marriage.'

'The King always was single-minded. Is that all you have to tell me? I fear it has been a long journey for you to make, no doubt out of your way, for so little.'

No, I was not courteous. I was angry, and afraid, and despairing.

Refusing to rise to my impolite bait, Thomas leaned back, his eyes holding a soft malice. 'I like your terminology, by the way.'

I raised my brows.

'Our King is no longer Hal in your thinking.'

'He is not. He deserves no name but that of his authority over me.' I would not acknowledge Thomas's apparent amusement at so spiteful a retribution, but the only one I could apply to my absent step-son.

I stood abruptly.

'Will you stay to dine with me?'

'I don't think I will, Madam.'

Which took me aback. 'Then you had better go,' I said.

But he did not stir. 'Do you not even wish to know why I will not? It was a very long journey for me to come here.'

I raised my chin. 'Then tell me. If you wish.'

Upon which he stood, took the neglected cup from me, placed it on the table beside the flagon and took my hands in his, saluting them with all the courtesy I had lacked.

'You cannot be angry all the time.'

'Oh, but I can!'

He squeezed my fingers so that I had to hide a hiss of pain. 'It's like conversing with a hedgehog.'

I inhaled sharply. 'I don't see...'

He interrupted, face and voice at one in gravity. 'You will drive away any visitor who might choose to come here. You will be even more lonely than you are now.'

'I am not lonely.' I prayed that he would not read the lie in my face. 'I am angry...'

'I know. But think. Your anger must be governed. Since when did you allow raw emotion to best your judgement? Your imprisonment at the King's pleasure could last for months. Years. Can you be angry for ever?' And as I opened my lips to say yes, he placed a finger there. 'I am here to give advice. Good advice. It will ruin your health and your beauty.' He rubbed lightly at the line that had obviously become evident on my forehead. 'And what good will it do? It will not change Hal's mind or the outcome. You have to be stalwart and courageous. You have to put all this aside and determine to live your life as lightly as you might, in a place that was once yours and that even now allows you some comfort.' He paused, as if waiting for me to object, but I was thinking hard. 'Laugh with me, Joanna. Smile. Welcome those who will come to see you and they will come more often. *I* will come more often. I tell you this as a friend who has always worked for your good. Henry—your Henry—would say the same.'

'Would he?'

'Think how he suffered. Yet he fought and mastered the pain until the bitter end. You are not near the bitter end. Fight, Madam. Live as the Queen you are, with all the regal dignity and beauty you have enjoyed all your life. Don't let this destroy you.' Gently now, Thomas released my hands and I sank back into my chair. 'Have I said too much?'

'I think you have. Or perhaps you have said what was needed.'

I studied my hands, willing them to relax in my lap, because clenching them was too painful, while, patiently, Thomas de Camoys waited for me. He had not seemed to notice their disfigurement, or was too compassionate to draw attention. Finally I looked up. To see such incomparable kindness in his eyes.

'I am ashamed,' I said.

'Understandable.'

'But unforgiveable. And you such a true friend.'

'True friends exist to give advice and support.'

'I am so sorry, Thomas.'

Retrieving my cup, he placed it back in my hand. 'Drink this. You are not well, are you?'

'I have been better.' I drank, and under his persistent questioning, because he would not let me be without his discovering, I told him a little, although not all. I would never tell any man of all my sufferings, for it was as if the tumult of my mind had transposed itself to my body, invading wrist and ankle and knuckle with searing pain and stiffened movements. As I told him, I felt my anger draining, in the relief at being able to acknowledge my growing sense of fragility.

'What right have I to complain?' I asked finally. 'If Henry could tolerate the agony inflicted on him, how can I not withstand a complaint that is more dependent on the incessant rain than anything else? I expect I have been impossible to live with,' I finished on a sigh.

'Which is the reason why your women look strained. As if they had been living with a feral cat. But now you are restored to your usual good sense.'

'I will try.' As I smiled for the first time for days, I found myself asking: 'And you will come again, if I am warm and welcoming?'

'Yes.'

'And will you dine with me now?'

'That's why I'm here.'

Relief, strong and sure, raced through me to remove my perennial headache. This was a friendship I had almost destroyed through my own wilfulness. I had been wrong. How could I have been so selfish not to see the consequences of my actions? I had deserved to be brought to account. My lessons with Henry on the vicious consequences of pride had not wholly been learnt. I stood again and stretched out a hand.

'We can offer you fish,' I said at an attempt at light-heartedness, so difficult after endless days of outrage.

'Salt fish?' Thomas chuckled.

'We can do better than that.'

We walked into the little chamber where a table had been laid for me with a white cloth. And sat, as one of my pages came with ewer and basin, pouring the fragrant water so that Thomas might cleanse his hands.

'Should I comment on this ostentation?' he asked, applying the napkin.

'If you wish to do so.'

But I was pleased that he had noticed. I was female enough to hope that he would enjoy these quiet moments after the turbulence. And when my page returned with a magnificent silver-gilt ewer to pour out cups of good Rhenish I felt a touch of mischief in my mind, newly born as if emerging from a grey sea-mist.

'I can offer you Gascon or Rochelle,' I offered innocently.

'A well-stocked cellar? I had no idea. I would have come earlier.' He drank. 'No, indeed. I am content with this. I see more than a touch of luxury.' He lifted a table knife of silver gilt, reaching to tap it against the carved stem of a candlestick of silver, skilfully engraved.

And I looked round the chamber, seeing it from Thomas's eyes. It had a comfort. And a wealth. My newly purchased popinjay sat in its decorative cage.

'For a prison, it has a touch of civilisation. And you too are looking very impressive, Madam.' He tilted his chin as he surveyed my gown of heavy satin, the sleeves and neck rich with grey squirrel fur. A girdle and rosary of gold. 'Fine feathers indeed.' And then as if it had struck him for the first time his eyes darkened with some emotion: 'You have decided to return to mourning.' He paused, knowing as well

as I that Henry had been dead for almost seven years. 'I'm
sorry if you must still mourn his passing so strongly.'

Touched beyond words, I closed my hand as well as I could
over his, regretful that he had misread my decision. Thomas
must think that I would mourn Henry for ever, allowing no
lightness into my soul or my spirit, for I was dressed from
head to toe in solemn and funereal black. Yes, I would always
mourn him, but not like this.

'This is not for Henry,' I explained. 'I lost Henry, wept
for that loss and I mourned him. I always will in my heart.'
I lifted the costly material of my sleeve. 'This outward sign
is for me, for my imprisonment. I have paid my respects to
the dead. This is in mourning for myself, who cannot obtain
justice. I will clothe myself in deepest black until the day I
die. Or am released.'

'You still look magnificent. You always did like beautiful
things.'

'And expensive ones. As parliament complained on more
than one occasion.' A little ripple of anger returned in spite
of my best intentions. 'Since the King sees fit to salve his
conscience by giving me an allowance, I see no reason why I
should not spend it to the hilt. It is a grain of wheat compared
with the full harvest that he has filched from me. There! I've
shocked you again. Spending on gowns and candlesticks,
while England is at war and in dire need of every coin you
can raise.'

'No. I am not shocked.' He pursed his lips. 'Or perhaps a
little. But as you say, the allowance is a sop to his conscience.'

'The King has no conscience! I have been thinking,
Thomas,' the anger abating under his honesty, to be followed

by cool logic. 'What if I bring my own case to Court? What if I petition the Council to bring the evidence against me, and prove that I am worthy of the accusation? Since there is no evidence against me, surely they will acknowledge it and be forced to release me...'

'No. You will not.'

'Why not? Is it not worth the risk?'

'No. This is the pain speaking. Let it lie, Madam. If you did indeed force the Council to put you on trial, you might, to your own disadvantage, discover the lack of evidence against you to be an irrelevance against the royal will. If you lose, if you are simply declared guilty, evidence or not, your situation could be dire. Even if they would not condemn you to death by burning, your imprisonment might become one of true duress and for the term of your life. Promise me that you will not.'

'I can't promise.'

Dropping my knife on the table, I covered my face with my hands, not to hide tears, which I would not shed, but to cover my fears.

'You must not do it, Joanna!'

He took my hand and wrapped my fingers around my cup. 'Drink.' And when I resisted: 'Drink, for God's sake, woman. You've less colour than a day-old cheese. You must promise me that you will not take issue with the Council.'

I frowned down into the cup. 'If I were guilty of necromancy, would I not be able to see my future in my looking glass? Or in a pool sprinkled with witches' herbs? But, in the name of the Virgin, I cannot.' And then in dismay, because of the personal hurt it had engendered: 'I am afraid, Thomas. I am afraid that the King will instruct the Council to complete the case against me. It is like a large bird hovering over me, its wings a constant shadow. At least if I petitioned for justice, it would be on my own terms.'

'Sadly, you have no terms at all, Madam.'

★

Then Thomas was making preparations to leave, as he must, so that I walked with him down to the courtyard, as I was allowed, where his horses and escort awaited him.

'I wish I could leave with you,' I said, without thinking.

He slid a glance. 'Shall I carry you off, in the tried and trusted manner of all knights errant, across my saddle bow?'

'I'm past the age of such exertions.'

'I may be as well.' He smiled as he kissed my fingers in farewell. I would not ask when he would return. But then, as he turned away to grasp his bridle and mount, I asked, because I could no longer hold my thoughts in check:

'Will it always be like this, Thomas? Trapped like a moth in a soft cloth? Leave-takings and loneliness? I will take your advice. I will not allow myself to sink into the morass of despondency, but in truth sometimes I can barely tolerate it. Books and music and the stitching of endless tapestries are all very well, but it is no life for a woman who has ruled a country.'

The bridle was tossed to his tactful squire who withdrew to a little distance. 'How can I offer you comfort? It will be like this. We both know it will.'

'Of course. I have to bear in good heart what cannot be changed.' I conjured a smile of sorts. 'I promise I'll not spoil your future visits by useless complaints and ill-mannered bleating.'

'You could never spoil my visits to you.'

'I tried hard enough.'

'And failed.' Now he mounted, but remained, looking down at me, his expression beyond my reading. 'Because I ride out through your gates does not mean that I no longer think of you, Joanna. Remember that.'

'And because you ride out does not mean that I forget you, Thomas.'

How easily we had slid into the intimate use of our names, almost without noticing it. Although perhaps we had.

'Look for me within the month.'

'If the raising of troops doesn't keep you from my door for the next twelvemonth,' but I said it with a genuine smile.

'And when I return we will not talk of salt fish.'

'Make good use of my money!' My final admonition.

He saluted and rode out.

And I? I buried my anger. By sheer force of will I determined to view my life with as much satisfaction as I could muster. For there really was no alternative unless I would wallow in misery and become a burden to myself and my twittering English household.

Chapter 19

I could not mistake the march of footsteps, from where I was taking the air with my women in the garden. Or the owner of the two well-laden sumpter horses, a wagon, a travelling litter and a tidy escort occupying the inner courtyard.

'I see you are journeying, Lord Thomas.' I was formal as the occasion demanded in so public a place. My cheeks were pink in the mild air. And then I stopped.

For out of the litter stepped a woman I knew.

'My lady, I am returned.'

I inhaled against the ridiculous surge of emotion, a very female emotion that almost drove me to my knees. When I could find no words, my visitor could.

'I have come to stay. God help me—it was a terrible journey from London, the roads a mess of mud with puddles deep enough to submerge us all. But I am here at last.'

'How? How were you able to come to me?'

It was all I could manage, but I was holding out my hands in welcome. Nor did I flinch when she took them.

'Lord Thomas said you needed me to play chess with you.'

'Among so many other things. Oh, I have missed you.'

It was Marie. Marie de Parency who I thought must have returned to Brittany, yet here she was, beaming with pleasure, her dark hair tucked into a coif, as solid and practical as I recalled. I did not ask how it had been arranged. All I knew was that Thomas had been instrumental in its organisation. My gratitude to him all but drowned me.

'I have no chessboard,' I admitted.

'How fortunate that I have brought one, my lady,' and Marie beckoned to one of my pages who staggered under the weight of a travelling coffer from the wagon. 'And much else besides,' she added as another figure, bent with years, eyes wet with emotion, was helped from the litter by one of Thomas's minions.

I took another ragged breath.

'Mistress Alicia. You have come home to me.'

'And about time too.' My ageing nurse, fragile but indomitable, was already looking round the courtyard, inspecting everything with a caustic gleam. 'There are things that need putting right here.' Removing an ancient travelling cloak, she was already chivvying my waiting women to set their veils, disturbed by the sharp April winds, to rights.

'All I know, my lady, is that you are innocent,' Marie stated, 'and it is not justice that you should remain here.'

While Mistress Alicia added: 'I know what went on in your household, my lady, from cellar to solar, and it was not witchcraft.'

'Any woman can be considered a witch in her own kitchen,' I observed.

'I don't recall you spending any time in a kitchen, my lady. And so I'll tell our fine King when he deigns to visit. Did I not plaster his face with tincture of Yarrow and dose him with Chamomile, the poor lad? No megrims of witchcraft then, was there?'

Perhaps not. I did not reply that a woman did not need to be conversant with the workings of a kitchen to be well acquainted with witches' herbs and their uses. That was not a subject to be discussed, now or at any future time.

What a pleasure it was to talk to these women I had known all my life, my heart even lighter after an investigation, there in the courtyard, of the contents of the coffer for, as well as the promised chessmen, I was reunited with my pen-case, my inkhorn, my much mourned tapestry.

I must thank Thomas, for the restoration of these much desired possessions was undoubtedly at his generous hand. And there he was, smiling at me, watching from beside the wagon. I made my way towards him, knowing that I was aglow with gratitude.

'Thank you. Thank you. And for your visit too.'

'I am not visiting, Madam.' Lord Thomas sketched a bow, face suddenly as expressionless as a knightly effigy on a gravestone, lifted my fingers to his lips in a brisk greeting.

'So you must leave immediately. Still I am thankful. And I have taken your advice to heart. I promise to be cheerful.'

'No,' he replied.

'No what?'

'Not a brief visit. In fact it is to be a very long one. I have come to stay.'

For a second time in that day, I could not speak. Shock, surprise, disbelief warred with each other. And a sly sneaking delight that I must not show.

'I thought you might be pleased.' He drew my hand through his arm as he led me towards the evidence of his intentions. 'Your gardener is keeping the grounds in good heart. So are the stables. At least Sir John has left you a decent animal or two for your use.' Thus allowing me the opportunity to recover with his inconsequential comment. How understanding he was. How thoughtful and compassionate, studying his escort unloading his belongings with a keen eye while I regained my composure. 'I'll need to know which chambers are fit for my use,' he said, summoning his Captain as if this was the easiest thing in the world to arrange.

But I knew the dangers, and my heart was thudding.

'You must not.'

'Why not?' Now the Captain was saluting, silencing me since I would not argue in public, and Thomas was taking matters into his own hands. 'Take my luggage inside, Hugh. Find the steward. Tell him that I want two rooms at least for my own use. With a view across the river or along the road to the north. Then make your own arrangements for yourself and my people.'

Hugh departing with a brisk salute, my response was equally brisk.

'You can't do this!'

The little interlude had been beneficial. Still extraordinarily disturbed from the prospect of his staying, of his ordering his accommodations with confident cheerfulness, ignoring my refusal, still I knew it to be impossible.

'Why not?' he repeated. He waved an arm in an expansive gesture. 'There was no one to stop me arriving.'

'But my guards…?'

'Your guards were open to persuasion.' He grinned. 'Or perhaps I should say that I gave them no opportunity to express an opinion. Here I am and here I stay.'

'But don't you see? Anyone who remains here might acquire the taint of witchcraft. Of treason. I can't allow you to do that.'

'And how will you prevent me?'

This man had an answer to every objection I presented. And I recalled a younger Thomas being just as adamant in the days of my wooing. But this was different. And in my mind I acknowledged that I could not bear for my hopes to be raised, only to be dashed when all Thomas's plans were foiled and he was ordered by the Council to go.

I pulled Thomas to a standstill before we reached the steps. 'What does Sir John say? Surely he would not agree?'

'Sir John does not know.' Thomas turned to face me. 'I doubt he'll complain. It's not my intent to help you escape. Simply to live here in confinement with you. Would anyone dare question my loyalty to the King? I think not.'

'But the King…'

I dredged up every possible reason for this being an impossible venture.

'The King knows the strength of my allegiance. If he could rely on me at Agincourt, he will not doubt my loyalty now. And he is in France. If he finds it in him to object when he returns to England, then he will tell me, and we will make other arrangements.' His fingers took and tightened around mine and his voice was no longer light, but full of command. 'Joanna…'

I was forced to return his gaze, and saw there such a melding of purpose and amusement. And there was something else. A care for me. There was no indecision.

'Are you not pleased to have me come to keep you good company?'

The question, so direct, compromised my breathing all over again.

'It is not fitting that you should be here.'

Oh, I wanted him to stay. I wanted him to overcome every problem I placed in his path. Which he did.

'Nonsense. I'll simply join your household. A Queen Dowager needs a steward, a chamberlain, even a temporary one. Who more fitting than I? I can organise all you require, my dear lady. I am adept at organisation. And I need to keep an eye on you, to stop you sending Sir John to ask the Council to put you on trial.'

I found that I was smiling, at the same time as tears rolled down my cheeks for I could no longer check them. In all that time since my arrest, I had not wept. But now I could not stop them, or the warmth in my belly.

'Don't you want me here?' Thomas was asking. 'There is only one argument that you could use to send me away. That you don't consider me of high enough birth to keep company with a Queen Dowager.'

'I think no such thing.'

'Good. So you want me to stay.'

'Oh, I do. You know I do.' I mopped my cheeks quickly with my sleeve when Thomas lifted his hand to do so. 'Drying my foolish tears is not within the role of my steward.'

'No, but it is within the role of Thomas de Camoys.' And when I shook my head. 'You know it is.'

'Why have you done this?'

'Because...' He lifted his head, as if suddenly aware of his surroundings, the coming and going as his luggage was carried past us. 'I'll tell you why I have done this when there are fewer ears to hear and tongues to flap. Enough to say, for now, that is because I cannot think of you being so lonely.'

'You have brought Marie. And Mistress Alicia.'

'So I have.'

'But, Thomas—how can you fulfil your duties and the demands of the Council?'

'Don't let that worry you. I can undertake all I need to do to deal with the rash of criminal behaviour hereabouts from Leeds Castle as well as I can from any of my manors in Sussex.'

'Have you taken pity on an ageing widow?'

'You know that is not how I think of you.'

All my doubts, my objections had been rolled away, as if Thomas was preparing a military campaign, eradicating all difficulties before the final attack. And in truth he had all the experience of doing just that.

'Any more objections?'

'None.'

'Don't cry again. Or not just here. My men are staring at us. Queens don't cry, not even Dowager Queens. We will go inside. I think I am in excellent time for dinner and you have a very fine Rhenish wine for me to sample.'

We walked slowly up the steps. If Thomas noted my halting progress, he made no comment. He would not, of course, merely altering his own gait to suit mine.

A softness, a sweetness enfolded me. I was almost happy.

★

What of our existence, this strange amalgam of two households in the days of my imprisonment? For me it was a true blessing as I was lured from that constant grinding fear, exacerbated by isolation, like a butterfly emerging from an ugly chrysalis. With no word further spoken of it, my despair slid into the background and with Thomas my loss of freedom became a thing I could tolerate rather than strive against. A blessing indeed. It was, I decided, strangely like living on an island separate from the rest of the world—which of course we were. Thomas came and went to fulfil his duties but always returned to me. Occasionally he visited his own estates, his children. But always he returned to me.

A steward? Not so, although Thomas took the burdens from me, like a caring husband might in a marriage of long standing. But we were simply friends. Good friends who had come to know each other so well over the years. That is all we could ever be. In those early days he never did tell me why he had decided to throw in his lot with an imprisoned Queen Dowager, and I did not ask.

Perhaps I was afraid to discover.

We read together. Enjoyed music. But we did not pray together, for Thomas did not own the all-powerful beliefs that Henry had. This was a different life, in which I made neither judgements nor comparisons. His hand at chess was superb, with more patience than Henry in capturing my King. We rode out together along the river with a discreet guard at our back. More than that I looked for him at the end of the day. He gave me my candle as I went to my bed. He gave me the space I needed.

We kept separate rooms.

Was it in our mind not to? No, it was not in mine. It was not in my heart to love again. Henry had been my utter delight, the measure of all my days. My love for him would never be snuffed out. It left me capable of strong liking, of deep affection, but nothing more.

'I am afraid,' I admitted to Thomas one day. 'I am afraid that I will forget Henry, however determined I am to hold him in my mind. Sometimes he is so distant from me, as if I met him in another life. I have to struggle to recall his exact features. I know the colour of his eyes, the contours of his face, I know his height and his stature. I know that I love him and will always love him, but some days I think I might forget. It terrifies me that I will lose the man who meant more to me than life itself.'

'You will not forget. I will talk to you about him,' Thomas said.

'I imagine you have better things to do with your time.'

'My lord Henry was a substantial part of my life. I will tell you what you don't know. It will take me back to my youth too. What more could an ageing knight enjoy?'

And so Thomas talked to me of the days of Henry's youth, before I knew him. Henry's character shone brightly again.

He lived again in my mind and heart. And so did Baron
Thomas de Camoys, soldier and diplomat. A semblance of
peace spread its wings over us. I repudiated happiness, but
lay claim to a contentment.

But not for ever. Of course it could not be forever. It had
to end, and we both knew what would shatter our idyll, at
least in my mind. And here it was, in the soft weather of June
when swallows flew low to feast on insects over the river, the
news arrived with Sir John visiting who, accepting Thomas's
part in my household without comment, discussed political
repercussions with much dry enjoyment and no thought for
my own discomfiture.

The King had wed my Valois niece, Katherine.

I could barely wait until, having drunk the obligatory cup
of ale, Sir John and his horse were beyond the gates.

'Will the King come home?' I stood before Thomas. 'To
bring his bride to be crowned?'

His regard remained steady on mine. 'I know what you
are thinking.'

'How can I not think it? Surely he will return to England
with her. But will he come here?'

His gesture was a denial. 'For what purpose? To explain?
To beg forgiveness? That's not the King we know.'

Upon which, anger erupted in an explosion of passion,
that ripped through my limbs with an anguish of pain. The
cup I had been holding fell. I looked at it with horror as
the pretty painted vessel spread across the tiles in shards of
ruined pottery.

'Joanna...?'

I turned away from him, hiding my hands in the folds

of my skirts. 'Sometimes my son-by-marriage's insensitivity is like a blow of a battleaxe to the head.' The joints of my fingers screamed with pain. 'Perhaps you should go until I am better company. Send Mistress Alicia to me if you will.'

'I'll not leave you now. Where do you keep your eau de vie?' He must have seen my glance. 'And don't deny you have it to hand. I know that you keep a store of it because sometimes the pain is too great for you to manage without help.'

So much for secrets. I had not kept them very well.

'Marie will show you. She knows.'

Thomas left me, to return with a small cup.

'Can you hold this?' And when I nodded, sniffing at the contents. 'Drink it.'

And I did, although I found it unpleasant and the fiery heat of the aqua vitae made me cough; until the heat of it spread through my belly, through my limbs, to give me some temporary comfort. I sipped again, acknowledging its power. Ashamed of that knowledge. My physician Pedro de Alcobaca had sent me the strong liquor for just such an occasion of extremity when no other remedy would disperse the pain.

'Do you pity me for needing this?' Thomas was watching me with sharp concern. 'I rarely need it.'

'Who am I to pity any woman who needs help to bear pain? Mistress Alicia is bringing you a draught of some noxious potion. Is it always as bad as this?'

'No. But today was difficult.'

He inspected my hands, the swollen knuckles, while I closed my eyes, reluctant to see the destruction of what had been beauty. And seeing it, he held me in his arms. Gently, so that I might step away if I wished.

I did not.

'I suppose I should resist and send you on your way,' I said. 'Your duty is to the King.'

'No, you should not send me anywhere.'

'I rarely break things. Forgive me.'

'For being angry at Hal? You are the most rational woman I know.' Drawing me with him we sat on the settle lately occupied by Sir John. 'This is what we will do. If the King returns to England with his bride, then we will wait. Until then there is nothing we can do. Don't let it disturb the quiet life we have made here for each other. Who can fathom the King's mind? You will be calm. You will eat and drink well. You will pray and shout at me occasionally and enjoy the warm weather that makes your health better. Why have you never told me the worst of it?'

I let my head rest on his shoulder because it seemed the right thing to do. 'I don't want pity.' Then relented. 'But sometimes the pain and the attack on my vanity lower my spirits into the grave. I know I should be stronger. I know I should be able to withstand this affliction, but sometimes knowledge and the reality of pain do not walk hand in hand.'

'I understand. As should you—you'll not get pity from me.'

'How did you know?'

'I asked Marie.'

'So you are in collusion against me.'

'So it seems. We both care very deeply for you.'

He kissed my lips. Then when I allowed him, he kissed me again, just as gently, making me forget a little. We sat in silence his arm around me, my suffering hands in his, the sun warm on our faces as it moved through the hour. I thought I might feel an embarrassment, but I did not.

'You never did tell me why you came to live here,' I said.

For I could not pretend that the love in Lord Thomas de Camoys's eyes did not exist. Had it not always been there? I thought it had, but it had been better for him if I drew no attention to it. He had honoured me, respected me, treated me with every dignity, and throughout every twist and turn of my life, and his, he had loved me.

'I did not think that I had to.'

'Oh, Thomas.' I turned my head to look at him with a level regard. 'I can promise you nothing.'

He lifted a shoulder in acceptance of something that could not be changed. 'I ask for nothing. You know me better than that. Simply that we might share the same space. Can we not be friends?' Humour glimmered through. 'I expect Henry would approve of that.' He took my hand and enclosed it within his own and spoke with his cheek against my veil. 'I came because I love you. I always have, although I knew it could never have been more than service and loyalty. You loved Henry and you were Queen of England. I was friend and servant to you both. And I think you are woman enough to have understood the strength of my feelings years ago, but were sensitive enough not to show compassion.' He moved a little so that he could look into my face. 'But now we are both alone, and why should you be living your life in so solitary a state here? So here I am. I ask nothing from you. Only that I can give you comradeship and friendship and company. Someone to argue with and berate and defeat at chess. Do you understand?'

'Yes.'

'I can give you more if you wish it. There is no need to tell me now. I am not going away. Tomorrow or next week or next year, if you are still kept here, I will live with you. Whenever you decide whether I be friend or lover, I will listen and be happy for you and for us. I love you, Joanna, but I will not persuade you into doing something in which your heart can not be complicit. Not that I think I could. And before you tell me, I know that your heart will always be Henry's. All I ask is to serve you and bring you some renewal of happiness.' I felt a light kiss against my hair. 'And now I will arrange for this to be swept up and send Marie to you.'

Leaving me sitting in the sun, blinking a little, he paused by the door, looking back.

'Don't hide your pain from me. I will be with you and nurture you.'

I know your sentiments towards me, Thomas, I could have said. But what are mine towards you? You deserve to know.

Instead I said nothing, unable to find words to explain my feelings or to be honest to so splendid a friend. I needed to make some admissions to myself.

★

A letter was delivered to me, one that had been opened by some busy-body on the Royal Council I presumed, and only when it was deemed to be of no real importance or danger, sent on to me. It was from my son, John, Duke of Brittany and a man full-grown now at thirty years. If I had ever been foolish enough to cling to hopes for succour from my distant family, this would have razed them to the ground.

I hear news of your difficult situation, maman. I have opened diplomatic channels with the Royal Council but they are peculiarly silent and uncooperative. I fear that I can do nothing for your rescue. You are in my prayers and thoughts. I know that you will remain strong against accusations that can have no grounds for truth.

Your loving son.

A kind letter in John's beautiful writing. A thoughtful letter. But one that, in its brief lines, displayed the helplessness that I experienced each day. All it did, had my son but known it, was increase the sense of my isolation. I refolded it with clumsy fingers and slid it between the pages of my missal. It changed nothing. I must not waste emotion on it, nor would I reply. I did not think that I could find the words, for I could not reassure my son that all was well.

★

The King had returned from France with his bride. Thomas was in London to petition for me. I was living in a state of high expectancy that Thomas would return any day, perhaps even bringing the King with him. Would he bring my niece Katherine? Would marriage make him a softer character, more open to reason? The weeks passed from a wet February into an equally wet March but still no sign of either. Of course the King would need time to take up the reins of government after his long absence, to show his new French wife to the people of England, perhaps even in a royal progress that might take in Leeds Castle.

I must be patient. I lived in a flurry of hope as early

blossom began to clothe the trees in white beauty. Thomas's advice clear in my mind, I refused to allow anger to flare and destroy. Even now Thomas might be persuading the King to come to Leeds and break my bonds. And indeed with the mild spring weather harnessed to my restored stability of mind, and the ministrations of Mistress Alicia with a tincture of precious colchicum mixed with honey, poison to some when drunk immoderately but healing when used wisely, my health improved, my joints were restored to something like normality. Vanity could once more allow me to admire the elegance of my fingers. My dexterity was restored to me. My stitches were even and my lute sang out with fervour. My habitual resilience had been reborn under Thomas's forthright handling.

Even if the King refused to see me, Thomas would come back to me. Thomas would not leave me in suspense longer than he must. Thus I watched the road from the wall walk, even when I promised myself I would not. How many times every day did I find a need to take the air from that vantage point, looking out towards the north and the road from London, my heart lifting as I did so?

Come home, Thomas. For I missed him. I wanted him here with me, for his company, for his erudition, for his rumbling laugh when something pleased him, his slow smile. For his embrace which reminded me that imprisonment could not rob me of affection. *Come home*, I urged, yearning to see the red and gold and white of his standard on the road.

Perhaps when he returned it would please me to allow our closeness to step beyond mere friendship. Perhaps it would be right to allow him to love me in more than thought; it occupied my mind.

And then the small entourage arrived when I was bathing in my chamber at the end of the day and least expected it.

'It's Sir John,' Marie remarked after taking a message from the page at the door. 'Arrived in a hurry and a cloud of dust too, which is not like him.'

'Fetch my gown,' I ordered, rising from the scented depths, pushing aside the curtains that shielded my modesty. For it was true. Sir John was always careful of his horses.

It took an age to clothe me to make a suitable entrance.

'It may be that the King has sent his decision by Sir John rather than by Lord Thomas,' Marie observed, buttoning my sleeves, knowing exactly the direction of my thoughts.

And so he might, the King being a stickler for protocol, and Sir John my official guardian. I fretted and fidgeted.

'I'll not allow you to hear of your release looking like a mad woman dragged from a ditch,' Marie said when I shook my head at the intricate caul and veil. 'Best to sit down and allow me to finish as I intend.'

I resigned myself.

Then I was down in the little audience chamber to meet with Sir John who had come straight from the stables and stood by the door with squire and page and an air of great weariness only offset by his irritation at my tardiness. I approached with eagerness, absorbing the scents of horse and sweat that clung to his clothes. The scents of freedom to me.

'What have you to say to me, Sir John?'

'My lady.'

He made a show of pulling off his gloves, then his jewelled

hat, handing them to his squire, before taking my arm and leading me away into a little space.

'Is it good news?'

Sir John's expression should have warned me.

'No, it is not. I don't know how to tell you this…'

I braced myself for the worst. 'So the King has refused to reconsider. I should have known that marriage would have done nothing to soften his emotions.' I smiled as well as I could through my disappointment. 'Don't worry, Sir John. I could not have expected it, could I? I have been building a fantasy for myself, where you presented me with a royal pardon for crimes I had never committed, before opening the gates and inviting me to ride through, a free woman at last.' I clasped his arm briefly. 'It couldn't be, could it? I must be a good hostess and offer you wine…'

'No, my lady.'

Sir John closed his hand over mine, something he had never done. 'I know nothing about the King and his decisions, my lady.'

'Is it my allowance?'

He shook his head, a dismissive little gesture. 'No, no.'

'Am I being moved again? At the will of the Royal Council?' I did not want to be moved. This prison was better than most. 'Where is it to be this…'

'My lady…' His hand gripped hard. 'It is the Baron de Camoys.'

'Oh. Is he not returning? Will he not come back to Leeds?' I realised why this might be, with the return of the King. 'Is it that the King wishes him to make another diplomatic marriage?' Of course that would be it. Thomas, a King's man through and through, was a valuable ally for any King, and a marriage would create another alliance to tie the nobility to the King's heels. I forced myself to reply with generosity even when my heart fell into a black void. 'His new wife would hardly want him living here with me, would she? Who is she? Do I know her? Will she make him a good wife, do you think?'

When Sir John did not reply, I realised that I had been less than appropriate. Perhaps he thought me insensitive to raise such a matter that was Camoys family business, and not a subject for gossip. Sir John was not one for gossip at the best of times.

'I expect Lord Thomas will come and tell me of his plans,' I said, but wishing that he had found the time to break the news personally. I wished he had not felt the need to send Sir John with a message that would have such personal repercussions for both of us. 'Has he gone to his estates in Sussex?' I asked.

It was only then that I realised the weight of Sir John's silence. The long drawn-out tension in his face and absence of explanation. The mark of emotion that I had never previously seen in Sir John. Perhaps it told me all I needed to know, before the words could be spoken. Before they could sink in and wound my heart.

'Tell me.'

'My dear…my dear lady. Lord Thomas is dead.'

It was a lightning strike. A fiercely unexpected slap of a hand against soft skin. A turn and twist of a knife. A bolt of unimaginable pain.

No.

'I am afraid it is so.' As if I had shrieked my denial of what could not be. I was aware of his hand once more on my arm, turning me, leading me back to the door. 'It is so. I came to tell you myself. It should not have been left to someone you did not know, who was not aware of the deep affection that existed between you.'

'How?' No more denial. I was aware of my nails digging into the palms of my hand. 'Where did he die?'

'In Sussex. On one of his manors. It was unexpected, and without pain as he took his ease at the end of the day.' Sir John shrugged. 'His heart just stopped beating, as I understand.'

'Was he alone?'

'Except for his servants who discovered him—yes.'

'Did he speak of me, at the end?' Selfish. How selfish! But how could he leave me so finally and not converse with me ever again? How could he be gone from this earth without sending me some remnant of his love and comfort?

'No,' Sir John was explaining. 'There was no intimation of ill-health. Lord Thomas did not even have a will. He was found in his chamber by his body servant.'

I found myself standing outside, the wind cool on my cheeks, the sweet perfume of apple-blossom touching my senses. From the stables I could hear the yapping of a new litter of hound pups. Around me the world continued on its habitual path. Only I was lost with undirected feet. And Thomas gone from it.

Marie had been summoned and was standing beside me as I fell into the mode of efficiency.

'Thank you for coming, Sir John. It was kind of you. I will arrange for Lord Thomas's possessions to be packed and returned to his family. To his grandson and heir. That is what he would have wanted. Will you arrange for the delivery for me? I think some of his swords are still here. They should belong to his grandson, of course.'

I should have been grieving rather than concerning myself with such details, but it seemed that my mind could do nothing but concentrate on the mundane.

Thomas de Camoys, my friend of so many years, was dead.

'I will, lady. I am so sorry.'

I walked away, muscles trembling. Never had I hated my imprisonment as much as at that moment. Unaware of climbing the stairs, of Marie following me at a distance, all I knew was the impossibility of taking it in. I had known death. With John in Brittany it had been unexpected but I had seen him fall. I had held his hand, tried to ease his breathing. I had been with Henry in those days of his terrible suffering when the final release had been a blessing. The experience had been real, the flesh cooling under my hands, the heartbeat dying until it was no more. With both John and Henry I had been free to arrange their burial, to mourn them as they deserved and as I needed.

But this? Unreal. Thomas could not be dead. He would come back to me. I would hear his footsteps…

At the turn of the stair I halted, looking back to Marie, seeing the grief in her eyes. Of course he would not come back.

'Leave me,' I said.

Beyond feeling, I simply sat in my room, in my chair, and looked out at the view of fields and low hills and water until night hid it.

Thinking. Imagining. One phrase.

You were fortunate to have his love.

Oh yes. And his admiration, his esteem, his friendship. It had been there in the recesses of my life since that day, now long distant, that Baron de Camoys had arrived in Brittany to petition me in the name of his King. I had not realised the depth of it.

I was blessed indeed. Such love, such friendship in my life. But what now? What did life hold for me now?

On impulse, when morning broke I retrieved the tapestry, once stitched with such frenzy, from my coffer, unfolding it, for I realised I had a mission to accomplish here. It was still incomplete. The falcon on the lover's wrist was perfect in its execution, but the pale flower in the lady's hand was far too insipid and did not tell the whole tale I wished it to announce to any future admirer. I sat and thought. Then I began.

I unpicked the stitches, beginning rapidly to re-stitch, as the day passed into evening. Then sat back to witness my achievement, with more than a modicum of satisfaction. The falcon was still adorning the lover's wrist, but now in his free hand he held out a miniature red heart in his fingers, offering it to his lady, for her to take if she had the desire. As for the pale flower in the lady's hand, it was quite gone, to be replaced by one of Henry's forget-me-not spangles, the symbol of everlasting love. It gleamed in the strengthening light, enhancing the whole with soft glamour. I was satisfied. It was truly a work of love.

'You will live in my heart for all time, Henry,' I said at last, my work complete, smoothing my hand over the even stitches. If there was evidence of tears falling, there was no one to see and it would soon be obliterated. 'What a glorious friend Thomas de Camoys has been. To both of us. His care and compassion have been beyond measure. I will mourn his passing.'

As I spoke, it seemed that I was alone no longer, even though the room was as empty as before. It was as if some spirit of Henry was with me, stepping from the tapestry, so strongly that I could sense the displacement of air. Not speaking, not moving, he was simply here, with all the familiar strength of his will and his power. It was as if he touched me with it. And so I sat and breathed, allowing my racing heart to still, allowing my thoughts to settle. My strength returned. My will that I would not be defeated. And although my sense of Henry gradually faded softly into the shadows, he had given me what I needed. I would wait out the term of imprisonment, however long it took, with serenity.

June 1422

'We are invaded, it seems.'

I was standing at the window. A hot June day, almost six months since Thomas had ridden out, not to return. The popinjay had died, probably from boredom, but I purchased another because my rooms were too silent without the occasional ear-splitting screeching. Irritation being more acceptable than silence, I decided. A kitten joined us from the stables, secreted into my domain by a sentimental Agnes. Tempted as I was to banish it, I could not. It took to curling in my lap, purring contentedly under my fingers. I ordered black clothing for my household. So did my stone-and-water-girt world continue without Thomas in it, when I was more alone than I had ever been.

It had continued without the King too, for within months of Thomas's death the King returned to France to pursue his military ambitions, with no thought of redemption for me. It proved to be a cold winter, an even colder spring, that did nothing for the spirits as the kitten grew into a cat and the new popinjay eyed it askance. I swear I had stitched enough altar cloths to furnish every church in England and Brittany.

Now the courtyard below was crowded with an escort and a magnificent palanquin which took my eye. Furnished with swags and garlands, all strangely foreshortened from my vantage point, its curtains vivid with newness, its four bay horses, impeccably matched and gleaming in the summer heat, it made a statement of grandeur. Now who would be visiting me with such ostentation? It was fit for a Queen, except that my niece Katherine had, Bishop Henry so informed me, gone to France, following her absent husband.

'It's Sir John,' I said, regretfully, noting his spare figure dismount, anticipating a half hour of clipped conversation. But Sir John was better than no visitor at all.

I stepped out, my women at my back, to where Sir John continued in some heavy discussion with my steward that seemed to involve much giving of orders. The gates were still open to the outside world, as if more visitors were expected. No one had yet emerged from the lavishly curtained marvel.

'Sir John...'

He spun round and bowed. If I had not known him better I would have said there was almost a bright excitement about his pale features, a burgeoning of emotion that tightened his mouth into what might have been a smile. If I had not known him for the dry stick that he was.

'Who have you brought for me?' I asked.

'No one, my lady.' And when I gestured at the palanquin, 'This is yours, my lady.'

I looked at it. I looked at him.

'But I have a loan of your horses if I wish to ride.'

Whereupon Sir John angled his chin towards the still-open gates.

'It is yours for your immediate use, should you wish it. As I imagine you do. You are free to go, my lady.'

'Go?' Even to my own ears I sounded foolish. 'Go where?'

'Wherever you choose. You are no longer under my juris-diction. The horses are yours, too, at the request of the King. They will take you wherever you desire.'

Slowly, while my eyes were blinded by the sun's rays, my mind assimilated this amalgam of words, drawing together the threads of an entirely new altar cloth. The King, Sir John had said. The King had released me. He had restored my freedom. I was free to go, and here was my means of travel. All announced with no more fanfare than the King sitting down to an intimate supper within his own household.

'Tell me that again!' I demanded.

Instead Sir John held out a letter. I did not take it. There was so much that had not been said, my freedom reinstated as if I were being offered no more than a new hunting hound. Uncertainty a slither of ice in my belly, I was not of a mind to believe it. Was this some new cunning punishment inflicted on me by my imaginative step-son? What was it he desired from me this time?

'What of the charges against me?' I asked.

'Removed. You are completely exonerated. This will explain.'

A strange weightlessness touched me, as if I had drunk too much wine, too fast. How could I believe this? After so long suddenly to be set free without warning, like my popinjay, released from its cage after years of captivity, only to flounder in the vast space of air and hostile birds, come to mob it.

It seemed that I had become inured to captivity, like my poor bird.

I took the letter, turning it as if I might discover the content through the outer cover. Seeing that the seal and superscription were Bishop Henry's own and the writing in his own hand. Surely he would not be complicit in any mischief taken against me? Opening it, proud that my hands were steady even though my heart beat loudly in my ears, I read it.

I read it again.

'How dare he. How dare he release me in this manner!'

'Madam?'

I crushed the fine parchment in my hands, turned my back on the means of escape and stalked back to my rooms where I had spent so many reluctant hours, like some wild beast taking refuge from the hunters in the only lair it knew.

'I do not need you.' My women, who had followed me, scurried out. 'Take that damnable bird with you.'

Hot fury was there, shaking me as I strode the length of my solar and back again.

'Do you know what it says?' I asked, sweeping my skirts behind me as I turned. Sir John had followed me.

'No, Madam. Only its direction.'

Flattening the creased folds, I read aloud from Bishop Henry's elegant script.

'This is what the King says: "…doubting that it should be a charge on our conscience, to occupy longer the Dowager in this manner, the charge against her will no longer be on our conscience…"'

Once more I creased the document.

'On his conscience! What is it that has prompted our noble King to such magnificent magnanimity towards me? Not my innocence. Not my despicable incarceration for a deed I had never committed. Nothing here about my state, only his fear of God's retribution for his sin against me. He would remove me from his conscience, and so achieve absolution and God's grace. My time of suffering is to end because the King wishes to put himself right with God.' I had to breathe more slowly as anger took its toll. 'Does he hope that I will understand and forgive him? I will not.'

Sir John's mouth thinned. 'The King is ill, my lady. He is struck down by dysentery, so I believe.'

I turned my back so he would not see the strength of the emotion that bruised the planes of my face.

'And you will make excuses for him in his brief moment of affliction, whereas I have been a prisoner at his behest for almost three years.' A thought struck me, a flash of light, like a reflection in a silver dish. 'And when he recovers from this dysentery. What then? Will our puissant King change his mind and rescind his humiliating pardon, because once more my wealth takes precedence over my reputation—which he has destroyed beyond all hope?' I turned on my erstwhile gaoler. 'Tell me, Sir John. Since there are no eavesdroppers here to embarrass you at a future date. Did you ever truly believe in my guilt?'

Would he reply? Sir John was pulling on his gloves as if he would like to make a prompt departure, working the leather over his fingers as if it were the most important task in the world.

'I will not press you for a reply, if you find yourself unable to make it,' I said with some venom.

'Yet I will make it.' Abandoning the gloves, he looked up, directly at me. 'It is a matter to which I have given much thought over the years of your sojourn under my care, Madam. And since there is no one to hear, I will admit that I always thought the evidence against you to be paltry. I have seen no signs of necromancy in your establishment. But then the decision was not mine to make. I am a servant of the King and of the Council, as I have always been.'

Well, at least that was some balm to my wounded soul. 'Thank you, Sir John.' But instead of being a source of comfort, it dug the old wounds deeper. My palpable innocence had held no sway whatsoever. My high reputation had not stood me in good stead. Perhaps no one in England had believed in my crime, but what good had that been to me? It had taken ill-health and a fit of guilt to stir the King's conscience into life.

'I could have done it, you know,' I found myself announcing as I tore Bishop Henry's letter into pieces, scattering them to the floor, like apple-blossom in a high gale.

I saw Sir John's slight frame stiffen.

'I have the knowledge. Did you not know? I have the plants and skill to bring any man to his knees, be he king, lord or commoner. If I had wished the King dead, he would be so, fast and sure, not lingering in France, wasting from some pernicious disease. It is true that my father, King of Navarre, was well versed in necromancy, as he was in the use of all manner of poisons. No one would deny it. Would his daughter be any less? I know well the witches' herbs and their uses.'

For the first time in our long acquaintance, I found Sir John Pelham lacking a response. I smiled thinly, enjoying my revenge.

'How do we know that the King is indeed suffering a malingering dysentery?'

Sir John cleared his throat and sidestepped the issue.

'Will you go, my lady? Whatever your guilt or otherwise, the King has granted you your freedom.'

And I laughed. 'So he has. And I will detain you no more, Sir John.'

I was free to go. And here was a decision for me to make. Strange after so long when I had made no decisions. Where would I go? This lovely home at Leeds had been my own dower and I had once loved it, but I could not stay. I would never come back again.

Within a half hour I was ensconced with cushions and soft linens in the equipage where, despite the summer heat, I ordered the curtains to be closed around me. I would not look back. Others would arrange for my women and household to follow me. For my possessions, the popinjay and the cat. I wanted nothing more than to leave Leeds and travel at my own volition.

But what did I take with me, into my much vaunted freedom as Henry's horses, so thoughtfully provided out of his callous generosity, carried me where I desired? Certainly a distrust of men, of their ambitions, of their selfish, clandestine plottings which could be used to hurt and wound. Overlying that was a sharp realisation, newly born, that I had no control over my destiny; my release had not been of my own making. My pride in my lineage, my authority, my influence on the circumstances of my life had been rudely shattered. Would I ever be confident again? Would I ever be compassionate and magnanimous in my forgiveness? I did not think so.

There was no contentment in me.

Epilogue

November 1422: Havering-atte-Bower

'I have no intention of pretending that I have any finer feelings for the late King,' I pronounced, sharp with resentment. 'I will not go.'

'It will be expected of you.' Bishop Henry was at his most stern, his exasperation filling my solar at Havering-atte-Bower where I had taken up temporary residence.

'By whom?'

'England.'

'Which I do not believe for an instant. You will have to use a stronger argument than that, your grace,' I replied, my brows expressing my scepticism of what England might think and want. 'England knows perfectly well how unjustly the late King treated me. England did not miss me when I was incarcerated in Leeds Castle. England would be amazed if I shed a thimbleful of tears for the late King. And if I were to do so, England would, and rightly, accuse me of blatant hypocrisy.'

The Bishop scowled.

'But I know you are strong enough to show public grief, whatever your private sentiments, Madam.' He too was excruciatingly formal today, even without the mitre. 'You are a woman of rare discernment. We both know what is due to a dead king.'

I flushed at the obscure compliment; even more at his overt criticism of my stand.

My son-by-marriage, the late King, was dead, brought low by what they said was dysentery. Still young, even younger than my Henry, the late King had been unable to fight the destructive power of the disease. The dysentery, or whatever dire form of it that had set its hand to him, had stopped his heart, stolen his breath, rotted his flesh. Now his body was returned to England to be laid to rest in Westminster Abbey with all the fervour England could muster for her heroic victor of Agincourt.

Witch. Sorcerer. Necromancer.

The words, words to strike terror, shimmered in my pleasant room, smoothing over the polished wood of the cushioned chair in which I was sitting, shivered over the tapestries. The fear never quite left me. I doubted it ever would, even though common sense reminded me that it was only the whisper of draughts through an ill-fitting window. I too shivered as I brought my mind back to the issue Bishop Henry was forcing me to confront. Was my heart untouched by compassion for my step-son's untimely death? That he had never laid eyes on his child, his heir? England's new king, another Henry, was a baby.

'Will you do it, Joanna?'

'No, I will not.'

I would not attend the funeral services planned at Westminster Abbey, fabricating an emotion I could not feel. My heart was cold and hard, my determination equally so. Like metal forged by a master smith.

'I think you should reconsider.' The Bishop was disinclined to retreat.

'Why should I?'

'Because Henry—*your* Henry—would want you to be there. It is his son's body they are bringing home. You have to be there. He would not understand your stiff-necked refusal.'

I flinched at the unexpected force of it.

'Damn you, Bishop Henry, for a conniving politician!'

'Hal could have made it far harder for you in your imprisonment, as you well know.'

Which statement undid all the Bishop's good work to persuade me.

'And that is the only argument you can discover to make me feel kinder towards him?' I had to work hard to hide a sneer of contempt. 'I will not be there. Now if you will forgive me, I have a journey to take.'

Bishop Henry bowed, while I set out in a spirit of defiance.

★

First to the little village of Trotton in Sussex, to the church of St George, built for the eternal resting place of the de Camoys family, of which Thomas had been so inordinately proud. Entering the little church, absorbing the quiet sanctity, I made myself walk to where I knew his tomb must be.

Of course he would have wished to be buried here. It was only right, with a fine memorial to preserve his glorious name for posterity. I studied the incised brass, for a moment taken aback, although I should have known what I would find. Here, superbly etched, Thomas, Baron de Camoys, and Elizabeth Mortimer were holding hands, her left slid intimately into his right.

Whereupon I felt punch of possessiveness below my heart.

'Once you held my hands,' I murmured.

He would hold them no longer, not even in friendship, since that was all I had been able to give him.

I studied the smooth lines, tracing the imitation of his face that some craftsman had so rapidly produced in the months since his death. So firm and stern, lacking all life, lacking all the humour and warmth of which I knew him to be capable. And the honour. But he was in his rightful place with his wife. I had no call on him and he had no duty to me. What a strange friendship it had been, that had deepened into unexpected affection, and perhaps even more. I would be grateful to Thomas de Camoys to the end of my days.

'Keep him company, Elizabeth,' I said, my voice muted in the empty church. 'You have the right to hold his hand. I return him to you, with good grace, and apologise if I took his loyalty from you. But I swear in your lifetime he never betrayed you. He was too fine a man for that.'

Elizabeth's features were as unresponsive as her husband's. Not a happy woman, I thought. She too had known death and tragedy, with Hotspur, her Percy husband, cut down in battle. Had Thomas given her any happiness? I hoped he had with the children he had given her. He could give happiness lightly and with great skill.

'Thank you, my dear friend.'

Once more, for the last time, I smoothed my fingers over the cold cheek of the engraved features, then walked from the dimness into the dappled sunlight.

★

Then to Canterbury. Where I braced myself before the tomb I had commissioned for Henry, where I had every right to be, to admire the image, created by a master stone mason from finest close-grained marble. I could not be anonymous here even though I might have wished it. I was escorted by some ecclesiastical dignitary who fluttered at my side, reluctant to be waved into the shadows.

I would have knelt, but the tomb was high and I needed to see Henry's face, and so I stood at his shoulder, taking a moment to admire the painted tester above him with its little carved angels. I knew that Henry would approve the heraldic flamboyance.

'I have not been here for a long time,' I explained, as if he would have been aware of my absence. As perhaps he had. 'I will not wallow in details. Perhaps you know them. There were times when I felt that you were with me.' How stilted my words sounded, how lacking in warmth. I felt as distant from him as I had when trust was an issue between us and insurrection dragged us apart. I did not want to talk about this, and yet I must. 'What I will say, Henry, is that it would be hard for you to forgive your son the late King, for what he has done.' No, there was no forgiveness in me, just as there was no emotion. 'Your eldest son did not have your strong principles of treating others with respect due to them. And now he is dead. Perhaps you knew that too. But I am here to tell you.'

I thought for a moment, and added:

'Perhaps you would forgive him, because you were inclined to err on the side of justice and forgive your family, even when they did not deserve it.'

In the ensuing silence, apart from a distant slide of feet and mutter of prayers from a gathering of pilgrims, I felt no closer to Henry. It was as if my experiences of the past years had excavated a void within me.

'There is a baby,' I said, groping for some semblance of joy, but failing. 'A grandson. With your name. Bishop Henry intends to make him into a great king, the greatest that you and England could envisage. You will not have taken Richard's throne in vain.'

I ran my fingers, as cold as my words, along the deeply chiselled edge of the tomb, then, reaching, along the marble curve of Henry's cheek, along the firm indentation of his lips.

'Forgive him.'

A voice in my mind that stilled my hand in mid-air. A strong clear command, which I did not question, merely resisted.

'I do not have it in my heart to forgive,' I replied aloud to the discomfort of the lurking cleric.

'Forgive him. He is my son.'

'Who imprisoned your wife for witchcraft!'

'Forgive him. There is no room in you for bitterness.'

But there was. Encompassing the whole of my heart, there remained a tight knot of resentment that Henry's son should have cared so little for me that he could condemn me to all those years of uncertainty, to a mindless dread.

'I do not even know that I will stay in England,' I announced, frowning at the priest who took himself off, perhaps fearing for the sanity of this Queen Dowager who held conversations with herself.

The flesh of Henry's arm might be unyielding stone beneath my hand, but to me he spoke as if he were alive, his body warm and strong with blood pulsing beneath the skin.

'Did I not make an Englishwoman of you? This is where you belong. I have a grandson. You might have an interest in his raising as a prince. What is there for you in Brittany or Navarre?'

I tried to construct a benign response, but Henry had not finished with me.

'Next you will threaten to go to your Valois cousins! I don't accept that. Here is where you should be, where you have a role. Since when were you willing to become a ghost at some foreign Court, where you have no influence?'

'He treated me despicably,' I answered, all the old bitterness rising with the incense around me. 'Your son diminished me, belittled me. He robbed me of all the certainties in my life. He cut my self-esteem to shreds. I doubt it will ever be mended.'

'My son had his reasons,' Henry stated as, in the choir behind me, the monkish chanting began the familiar cadences of the service of Compline to bring peace at the end of the day. *'Your self-worth is stronger than you know. Make your peace with him, Joanna.'*

'I will think about it.'

And so I thought, my hands covering the fine carving of Henry's beringed fingers as the rise and fall of the voices soothed my soul a little, while I sifted through all my familiar resentments, and Henry's uncomfortably honest observations.

'You left your sons to come to me. I gave you my sons in return. He is yours. You forgive your children, Joanna, no matter what their sins. Let God judge. You will find compassion for him.'

'It is too difficult, Henry. I have lived with such fear for three years.'

'Forgive him, Joanna.'

'You will not let up, will you?' On tiptoe, I stretched to kiss the curve of his cheek, as I had so often in life.

'You were not born to retire into bitter, ineffectual widowhood. Does pride still rule your generosity?'

Another deliberate blow to my self-esteem. Henry was in formidable mood.

I sighed.

'Do we both not know the power of money in the life of a king? It almost ruined us.'

Another smack of a blacksmith's hammer against the horseshoe of my intransigence.

Hearing footsteps behind me, I turned, expecting my persistent shadow to have returned. One day I would lie here with Henry, with my own effigy to complement his in magnificence. But not yet, not today. It seemed that there were things to do.

And there, waiting for me at a little distance, was Bishop Henry.

'I thought I would find you here,' he said. For Bishop

Henry, his episcopal glory replaced by riding clothes, was looking unusually wary beneath his habitual impatience.

'I hope I have kept you waiting.' I found that I was smiling. 'Are you going to batter me with arguments again?'

'I might. Have you decided, Joanna?'

I tilted my head, considering.

Forgive him, Joanna.

'Yes, I have.' I felt Henry with me still, a repeat of his final admonition no more than a breath in my thoughts. 'Yes, I have. You need berate me no longer. You can escort me back to Westminster. Your brother Henry would insist on it.'

Bishop Henry returned my smile and, sharp politician though he might be, it dispensed a healing that had been lacking in me for so long. My future swept the grey tiles before me, as bright as a late shaft of evening sunlight, as clear-cut as the shields carried by the angels above my head, as I took his arm to walk from the Trinity Chapel through into the Choir where Compline had ended and the pilgrims dispersed.

I looked back once. My grief was no less, nor my loss of the man whose mortal remains were at peace here, but perhaps my resentment had ebbed a little. I was calm and sure. My days of incarceration and terrified uncertainty were at an end. No, I would not become a bitter, ineffectual widow. I was Joanna again, once Duchess of Brittany, once Queen of England. Once a much loved, highly valued wife.

I had come here to England for my destiny. It was my destiny to live here to the end. I would take on this new role that was demanded of me, and fit it to my liking. And as I felt a sense of control slide once again through my blood, I said aloud, whatever my priestly escort might think of me:

'You have won, Henry; I will be there. I will engage myself in the wellbeing of the child.' Just a little pause. 'And I will forgive.'

I discovered that contentment was possible.

★ ★ ★ ★ ★

ACKNOWLEDGEMENTS

All my thanks to my agent Jane Judd who continues to adopt my medieval women and find as much satisfaction in their lives as I do. Her calm good sense and advice over the years have been invaluable.

My thanks to my editor Sally Williamson at MIRA who has enjoyed Joanna of Navarre as much as I have. I welcome her oversight from the distance that escapes me after living with Joanna for more than a year. And to all at MIRA who have helped Joanna step out of the shadows and onto the page.

All my thanks to Helen Bowden and her staff at Orphans Press who continue to rescue me from website problems, as well as turning my genealogy and maps into works of art. I am very grateful for their tolerance and friendship.

WHAT INSPIRED ME TO WRITE ABOUT JOANNA OF NAVARRE?

Joanna of Navarre was regal from her toes to her fingertips. Daughter of King Charles II (the Bad) of Navarre and Joan de Valois, who was a daughter of King John II (the Good) of France, Joanna was related to almost every important family in Europe through either blood or marriage. On the death of her first husband Duke John V of Brittany, Joanna, as Duchess of Brittany, became Regent in the name of her young son. Joanna was a woman of considerable presence, reputation and European status. She was also a woman of intellect, quite capable of ruling a medieval state.

King Henry IV of England, on the other hand, although of Plantagenet birth and royal blood as the only son of John of Gaunt, was a newly made King. What's more he was a usurper in the eyes of many established rulers of Europe, particularly France, because he had seized the crown from his cousin King Richard II, the rightful, God-Anointed King. Thus Henry was a dangerous entity. Few were willing to support such a precedent for the overthrow of a ruling monarch.

What was it that made Joanna, a renowned and highly capable ruler of thirty years of age, with a healthy family of seven children and an enviable reputation, give up everything - power, family, approval - to choose to come to England to wed the usurper Henry? Could it have been love? Was not Joanna past the age of frivolous emotion? Her duty surely lay with Brittany.

Furthermore it was to be no easy marriage for Henry and Joanna, with England torn apart in an ongoing civil war insti-gated by the powerful Percy family and Owain Glyn Dwr. Would Henry and Joanna weather the storms of political upheaval and open rebellion?

And then there was the terrifying accusation of necromancy against her.

The consequences for Joanna of the choices she made in her life were far reaching. They brought her enhanced status and much happiness but also condemned her to a life of great uncertainty.

This, I decided, was a story worth writing.

The Queen's Choice is the story of a Queen of England who has remained in the shadows. It is a story of betrayal and tragedy, but also one of great love and redemption. Joanna was a formidable character whose life epitomised the dangers inherent in the role of Queenship.

AND AFTERWARDS

Joanna's last years contain little of note, but she was free from any taint of suspicion, which is excellent proof of how lightly England regarded Henry V's accusations against her. There is no hint of any necromancy in her life.

After being released from her confinement in the weeks before the death of Henry V in 1421, Joanna continued to live in England. The possessions confiscated from her were gradually restored, although not all her dower lands and she was still trying to recoup some of her problematic Breton arrears in 1428.

In her later years, Joanna lived in a semi-retired state on a reduced but still comfortable income, first at Langley and then returning to Havering-atte-Bower, where, typically, she continued to be frustrated by the poor management of the estate. She seems to have had an interest in the promotion of scholars at Oxford and Cambridge but she was not a notable patron.

As for her family, Joanna remained in contact with her son Duke John until the end of her life and also with the young King Henry VI of England. She played no active part in Court life but clearly King Henry had an affection for her and treated her with courtesy, giving her a gift of jewellery at New Year in 1437.

Joanna died at Havering-atte-Bower in early July 1437 at the age of sixty nine years and was buried beside Henry in Canterbury Cathedral where her own marble image was added to the tomb.

It has to be said that Joanna left no important legacy to England from her days as Queen, except for her signature of '*Royne Jahanne*' the first of any English queen to be on record.

The coffin of Henry and Joanna at Canterbury was opened in 1832 when it was recorded that Henry's face was seen in a complete state of preservation with a russet beard until it disintegrated in the air. There was no evidence of leprosy on Henry's skin. Joanna's remains were left unexamined.

IN THE FOOTSTEPS
OF JOANNA OF NAVARRE

For those of us who like to travel and enjoy the palaces and castles that Joanna would have known, or even if we browse the web or the pages of a travel guide on a cold winter's day, here is some inspiration for you:

Falmouth: where Joanna landed, blown in on a storm. No sign of her footprints in the holiday resort in Cornwall, but it's possible to imagine a cold wet January day when she had given up everything and Henry was not there to meet her...

Winchester Cathedral: the scene of Joanna and Henry's marriage on 7th February, 1403. A 'must visit' on your itinerary. Also find time to admire the superb tomb of Bishop Henry Beaufort, a most gifted and ambitious politician.

Westminster Abbey: on everyone's list who enjoys royal occasions and tombs. Joanna was crowned Queen of England here on 26th February 1403.

Eltham Palace: Henry's favourite palace, and so the home of choice where he and his family spent most Christmas and New Year celebrations. Much rebuilding has been done to create the Art Deco jewel it is today, but the Great Hall is much as Joanna and Henry would have known it.

The Shrine of Our Lady of Walsingham in Norfolk: where Henry prayed for a miracle of healing. The Roman Catholic shrine was destroyed at the Dissolution of the Monasteries. The modern shrine is Anglican, restored in 1934, allowing pilgrims once more to visit the holy site.

Leeds Castle, Sussex: one of Joanna's dower properties and where she spent most of her captivity for necromancy in

1420–21, even if it was a cushioned one. A beautiful setting, but not if you are forbidden to leave.

Pevensey Castle, Sussex: the property of Sir John Pelham, another place of confinement for Joanna in 1419. The walls and towers of the impressive ruins have plenty of atmosphere.

Rotherhythe: very little remains of this royal manor on the south bank of the Thames where Joanna began her captivity. It was a favourite haunt of Edward III and Henry IV. Now there is little more than sporadic stonework.

Canterbury Cathedral: an essential visit. Here is the tomb of Henry and Joanna, commissioned by Joanna, showing their figures in high quality marble carving. Henry chose to be buried here, perhaps because of the nearby tomb of his uncle Edward, the Black Prince.

The Church of St George, Trotton, Sussex: the church dedicated to the de Camoys family. Here is the tomb of Baron Thomas de Camoys and his second wife Elizabeth Mortimer in beautifully inscribed brass.

In **Brittany** there is little to see that is contemporary with Joanna in her days as Duchess and Regent. The chateaux of the Dukes of Brittany in **Nantes** and **Vannes** were rebuilt almost totally after Joanna's day so although the site is correct, the buildings are more recent. The tomb of John de Montfort, Duke of Brittany, paid for and created by Joanna in the cathedral at Nantes, was destroyed in the French Revolution.

QUESTIONS FOR
READING GROUPS

1. Joanna was presented with a very difficult choice: power, family and European status or marriage to Henry IV, with unpredictable results. Could you have made the same choice that Joanna made?

2. Which do you consider to be Joanna's strongest emotions when she made her choice?

3. How difficult was it for a woman to follow her own desires in the early fifteenth century when morality and duty had such a strong influence? Is it easier for us today?

4. In your experience, how difficult is it for a man to accept advice from a woman?

5. Do you consider that a deep platonic friendship, such as the one between Joanna and Thomas de Camoys, is possible between a man and a woman?

6. How would you respond to a 'wooing by proxy'?

7. Joanna could not have anticipated the repercussions of the choices she made in her life. Have you experienced similar difficult, unpredictable consequences from any choices you have made?

8. Can we justify to any degree Henry V's treatment of Joanna?

9. What is your opinion of Henry's role in the death of Richard II? Can we justify his role in this event?

10. What does *The Queen's Choice* tell us about the state of medical practice in medieval times?

11. Which aspect of Joanna's character do you most admire?

Visit Anne online at:
www.anneobrien.co.uk

You can also find Anne on Facebook, Twitter and Pinterest
www.facebook.com/anneobrienbooks
@anne_obrien
www.pinterest.com/thisisanneobrie

Anne blogs at:
www.anneobrien.co.uk/blog

ANNE O'BRIEN

'Anne O'Brien has joined the exclusive club of
excellent historical novelists'
—*Sunday Express*

O'BRIEN_COLL_NEW

Loved this book?

Visit Anne O'Brien's fantastic website
at **www.anneobrien.co.uk** for
information about Anne, her latest books,
news, interviews, offers, competitions,
reading group extras and much more...

Follow Anne on Twitter **@anne_obrien**

www.anneobrien.co.uk

OBRIEN_WEB